Descent Into Madness

The Chronicles of Bree

Catherine Woods-Field

Willow Press
Illinois MMXIV

ISBN: 0692249893
ISBN-13: 978-0692249895

Bob Boblett

1929-2003

Forever Remembered

"The blood is the life!"

- Bram Stoker , *Dracula*

CONTENTS

PROLOGUE
1

ONE
2

TWO
8

THREE
16

FOUR
22

FIVE
31

SIX
41

SEVEN
57

EIGHT
67

NINE
85

TEN
101

ELEVEN
118

TWELVE
130

THIRTEEN
147

FOURTEEN
158

FIFTEEN
168

SIXTEEN
176

SEVENTEEN
182

EIGHTEEN
192

NINETEEN
197

TWENTY
205

TWENTY-ONE
216

TWENTY-TWO
223

TWENTY-THREE
230

TWENTY-FOUR
239

TWENTY-FIVE
250

TWENTY-SIX
260

TWENTY-SEVEN
271

TWENTY-EIGHT
281

TWENTY-NINE
292

THIRTY
302

THIRTY-ONE
311

THIRTY-TWO
319

THIRTY-THREE
324

THIRTY-FOUR
327

THIRTY-FIVE
336

THIRTY-SIX
344

THIRTY-SEVEN
351

THIRTY-EIGHT
363

THIRTY-NINE
371

Descent Into Madness

The Chronicles of Bree

PROLOGUE

October 21, 2012

There are moments that define us. Moments that shape our thoughts and actions, even shape our entire purpose for being. These moments - so catastrophic, so intense - rip our souls and split our hearts. They force us to choose which path we will walk in life's terrifying journey into the dark, unknown abyss. They are moments of sheer survival – when our hearts whisper their last breaths, and we have a chance for redemption. These moments erase our pasts and define our futures. Nay, they are our futures.

What follows was a moment for me; a mere moment that flickered quickly yet burns in my eyes still with the intensity of a scintillating flame against a black sky. It was a night I will never forget.

What follows that in these pages are moments – so many moments – some frightening and some indescribable, but that define *me*. They have cumulated here in the penning of this account of my... descent into madness

ONE

M y story begins on a night too much like tonight – stormy, with lightning christening the sky. The moon - overcast, blanketed in a thick haze of gloomy clouds echoing heaven's thunderous chorus. A night that was so beautiful when it first began that had I known what lurked in the distance, what watched me from the shadows, I would have prayed my Hail Mary's before retiring. Now, after all these years, I know that even God could not have saved me from him.

The lightning painted the sky cobalt as I withdrew the covers and climbed atop the straw mat. Stray blades of dry hay poked through the rough, cotton sheet scratching my legs. For a brief moment while pulling the white sheet away from my pillow, I thought I had seen an outline of a man in the bushes just outside the window. It had been a shadow, I told myself, nothing more, and I climbed beneath the sheet; my worn limbs greedily slipping between the fabrics.

Then out of the corner of my eye, as the lightning danced upon the glass, I saw it again. The figure stood near the bush line, skirting the moonlight just enough that I could make out its visage looming dangerously near. Its cloaked head was buried, revealing only a nightmare that has come to taunt my peace of mind.

As I peered out my cell window, my eyelids growing heavier while the fog rolled in off the moor. I watched the figure stand motionless in its pursuit, until my eyes finally closed and I heard a whisper arise from the far corner of my cell. It was a subtle hiss, a low, almost guttural growl, alerting me of his presence. Although the shadows concealed his body from my eyes, his presence in my cell was certain.

I had lain there in my bed, quiet and fixed; my breathing labored by fearful constraint. I trembled, struggling not to scream as my nightmare became reality. I laid there quietly clutching the sheet, staring into the waiting darkness. The air surrounding me grew stale; gone was the subtle scent of lily wafting in from the garden, and in its place a stagnant scent of musty, old earth.

"Who is there?" I remember whispering. Yet only the cold silence of the stale night replied. My limbs trembled; my mouth quaked. Tears pooled beneath my fluttering lids. The presence bore down, projecting a familiarity from the surrounding gloom. I knew this person now. I knew him.

"Be calm, dear sister," spoke the man. He had come for me, to take me from the only home I had known these past five years. He came to steal me from the peace, the joy, and the love of the only family I thought I had left in the world. He came to claim me that night, and, as I would find out, I was powerless to fight him.

"Wesley, how is this possible?" My knuckles were white, the bed sheet wrinkling in my grip.

"What do you want, my brother?"

My eyelids fell and I trembled, hoping his presence was a nightmare from which I could wake.

Yet, then I sensed him moving to the foot of my bed, the specter now looming over me. My trembling ceased, and my body stiffened against the straw pallet. My eyelids widened as his cold eyes stared into mine. He stood above me, a living being, but I could not comprehend how that was so. Again, I asked, "What do you want?"

His raspy voice replied, "You."

Freeing my stiffening bones from the sheets, I rose and rushed into the corner nearest the window. It was then, in the dim of the moonlight, that I first beheld his face. His features had become refined and pronounced, and his demeanor deliberate; the man was no mere specter come to haunt me, and he appeared far more noble than I had remembered him being.

Black buboes had covered his body. Blood was oozing from the festering wounds, and as I left him, the acrid odor of death misted his body in its grey veil. Our parents had already perished from the horrible plague, and I left for the convent before I could witness Wesley leaving this world.

Now, his once dark hair was as black as the clearest midnight sky. It was long and moved with such ease, each strand independent from the other. His eyes were translucent; when glanced into, it was like peering into an endless crystal orb. Even his voice was deeper.

My own voice cracked as I stared into his familiar eyes. "Me?" I questioned, cowering in the corner. Trapped.

I was transfixed as he moved closer, sliding his fingers through my hair. There in his crystalline eyes were love and hate, mingling and living as one emotion. These emotions threatened me as he stared into my eyes. Still, even as I trembled, I was entranced, unable to steer my eyes from the menacing creature before me. The images he projected into my mind – the two of us living together again, traveling together – were both haunting and beautiful. For a moment I forgot myself; the fact that I was a pure, untainted nun, betrothed to my maker no longer mattered. In that single moment, I wanted the life he showed me.

All I wanted was to be sixteen and to be with my

older brother. To run, frolicking in the lavender fields until the sun set on our weary faces and tell ghost stories by the fire. To eat roasted quail until our bellies burst and watch the minstrels perform at court. To dance again.

I fell into his arms, embracing the monster before me.

Yet in that embrace, he robbed me of my innocence. My life. My everything. He held me forcefully; I could feel his lips upon my neck as he whispered into my ear. There was an unnatural coldness to his words. They sent ripples of reality coursing through my body, until I realized what he meant to do. But by then, it was too late.

"I have come for you, Bree. I'm delivering you forever from the day and bringing you into my world, the world of endless night," he whispered, his raspy breath trickling trails of icy air down my back. "I have missed you, sister."

Before I could question him - before I could plead - he roughly embraced me. In a brief moment, I felt the sharp sting of his teeth ripping into my jugular. I struggled. My nails scratched at his ashen skin. Tears welled in my eyes, but his grip was unyielding. As my life passed into him, ounce by precious ounce, I succumbed, no longer frantically thrashing beneath his arms; the strength drained from my body and with it, my will to live.

He tossed me onto the bed. With each breath I took, a searing pain washed over my chest. My head spun in dizzying circles. My throat closed. I could see the crucifix hanging on the wall and I rallied to pray for my soul, but I had not the strength. I was dying.

"The pain will soon stop," he said while leaning over me. "When the darkness comes, do not fear it. Embrace it. Take it in; make it a part of yourself! Or you will die, Bree."

I remember the waves of vertigo bathing me in sweat, one after another; violently they crashed inside my skull – a million violent hurricanes. My stomach churned, that night's supper erupting from my body.

"I am… not… afraid… of death."

"Heed my warning!" he commanded.

Then the night descended with an obsidian sky that somehow grew darker. My mind became clouded in a vague gloom. My thoughts swam in a sea of vertigo; my hands struggled to grasp onto reality in the void. I could hear nothing. See nothing. Taste nothing. I was powerless.

That is when I resigned myself to death. Seeking to find an eternal sleep and escape from this painful torment.

"Embrace the darkness, Bree. Do not fight it!" he yelled from the corner.

I surrendered, I let it draw me into the bleak eternity it promised. I allowed myself to become one with the cold, ethereal essence enveloping me, instead of fearing it. Instead of it suffocating me, it helped me to breathe again.

Once I came to, I saw the world anew. I opened my newborn eyes and there were billions of crystals floating weightless in the air, suspended along numerous currents in an atmospheric stream. My hands reached out to grab whatever existed in the surrounding mist. Yet the crystals slipped through my zealous fingers. Beads of sweat poured down my burning cheeks. Then the void returned and I started falling, weightless in a perpetual tunnel of nausea and vertigo.

Finally, the beating began - the last pumping of my human heart. Its cadence slowing until I feared it would cease forever, then, quick as lightening, it returned. It shattered in my chest.

My eyes closed. Sweat moistened my palms. My fingers twitched in agony. As I felt the last beatings of my human heart rip through my chest, each beat a pain sharper than the last, I screamed to my Maker. I pleaded with Him! Why was he forsaking me now? What could I have done?

Thump.

"Oh Lord," I panted.

Thump.

"Please take away this pain!" I howled.

THUMP.

"Please!" I screamed into the shadows.

Then like a vice tightening its grip, my heart squeezed from it the last of its human life. The last precious crimson droplet fell away, invaded by this new, frigid vampiric eternity.

TWO

Somewhere – between the night descending and the searing pain coursing through my body – I realized life was no more. My eyes had closed. My breathing stopped. Then my eyes reopened and Heaven denied to me.

I felt hollow and cold.

Alone.

That night haunts me still.

Why had this happened?

I knew my life in the hallowed convent grounds was no more. Instinct invaded me, urged me forward.

That life of sanctity and peace is a past I often find as a place of reclusion. Its images, odors, the names of my fellow sisters, flood my mind at least once in a century. No matter how far I travel, or the years that distance me from them, they are there. When the memories come, I am lost. The feelings, the smells, the love, suck me in, and pull me down and add to the gaping, murky chasm that replaced my beating heart.

That existence - with its future – with its finality - was shattered the night he took me from them. And I now long for my lost innocence.

He had taken my body, spent from the transformation, to the moonlit sky and secured us from the day's sunlight. While the sisters searched the surrounding hillsides, I slept in an abandoned castle's ruins that overlooked the ivy-covered convent walls. We slumbered, safe from the golden rays, in the castle's dank cellar, in dusty alcoves. I awoke the next night unaware of my true form, unaware of the monstrosity I had become.

The world had changed when I found him sitting near a piece of wall, its brick slowly eroding into the earth. He had been anxiously gazing into the night, avoiding me.

"How is it that I can see the candles so sharply, Wesley?" I asked, walking to his side. "It's over a ten minute walk to the convent from here." He did not answer. "I can see through the shadows, even," I whispered. "The shadows, Wesley, are misty and no longer dense. I no longer fear them. What have I become?"

The flame light brilliantly wavered in the convent's windows, the red and orange flames weaving shadows on the brick. Their brightness was clear and crisp, as if I were standing close enough to touch them. I could almost feel their heat against my cold skin.

He merely stared into the distance, ignoring me.

I turned away from him and watched the amber flames licking at the tiny candlewicks. I averted my eyes heavenward where the stars were diamonds – delicate, sparkling jewels in an ebony pool.

Near the bank of the river Avon, moonlight reflected off the yellow Monkey flowers – wee buds twinkling like crystal. The world was renewed, a magical playground of sight and sound and color.

"You have the gift now, Bree," he finally said. "Just accept it."

"What gift?"

"Bree," he began, "you are a vampire."

Vampire. My heart sank, along with my knees as I dropped to the riverbank, my reflection in the water betraying my angst.

This was not the first time I had heard this word.

Orphaned female children found safety behind the convent doors during the darkest days of the plague. They were malnourished and lost, in need of salvation and love. They whispered that word – vampire – in stories and through feverish, nightmare-riddled sleeps.

The creatures haunting their dreams were dead but walking amongst us, spreading a putrid curse. These tales began when a German child came into the convent's care shortly before her mother passed. She told the children horrific stories of a creature named "Neuntöter", a plague-spreading, vampire-like fiend that haunted villages. Each child, it seemed, had their own versions of the vampire myth to share, and their own names for the horrific monster that fed off the living.

"Pamgri", "mullo", "upir", the names for the wicked beasts were plentiful, but the one I remember most came from a quiet and comely child. "My father traveled the country," she had said, "and he spoke often of the vampires. He would say, 'always carry your wild rose and wear your crucifix, for you never know when the vampire may strike with cunning force in the night.'"

Her mother had succumbed to the sickness, so had her sister. Her father, a tradesman eager to leave before he met the same fate, abandoned the child at our gates. He left her prepared, though, tucking a sprig of wild rose and a worn silver crucifix into her satchel. A few sisters began carrying the same with them, but I thought it superstitious and childish.

How could it be so that I was now this myth - a monster haunting the dreams of innocent children!

"I am an undead fiend?" Those words slipped through my lips, and I shuddered with the reality they contained.

"You make it sound so… terrible."

"It cannot be true," I whimpered.

"It is," Wesley replied, "but it's not so bad, in the end."

"You took the only thing, the only pure thing left in your life, Wesley, and tainted it with... with this curse. Why? Why could you not have let me be?"

"I was lonely," he stood. His lanky legs began trotting toward the crumbling castle.

"Lonely?" I called out. "Lonely!"

"You will understand in time," he mumbled. "You will crave companionship as the centuries wear on. You will need humanity, to be like them again. This need will make you take desperate measures, as I have done by making you."

"Wesley, you should have left me alone. That life – my life! – it was peaceful. It had purpose. Where will my soul go now?" Unable to sustain my tears, I allowed one to roll gingerly down my cheek.

"Your soul," he began, "that is between you and your god."

Silence fell as we stood atop the hill looking over the convent below. My soul wept for my former life. It had been naïve of me to think I was impervious to harm behind those hallowed walls. Since the first moment I stepped through the enclosure gates, I felt safe. The wild heather invited me in with its pleasing scent, and the sun - safely warming my cheek - welcomed me home.

Now, I knew I had never been safe. Not from the evil this world bred in its dark underbelly, and especially not from him.

"In time you will forgive me, Bree," he said, the silence breaking between us.

"Perhaps in time, but for now I cannot imagine that time coming."

He gazed out, eyeing the convent. "I remember you once asking for forgiveness and it was freely given."

"Wesley, that was different. I was a child." My shoulder touched his arms as we stood side by side. He grabbed my arm, calming my wavering body. Dizziness jellied my legs and blurred my eyes.

"Slow your pace," he said. "You're faster now. Your steps are effortless."

"It sickens me," I whispered, "this uneasiness; the unceasing buzz in my head."

"It will ease after you've fed." My nature – the monster within – understood his words, yet I did not.

My hand clutched his, its iciness now lessened by my own unnatural coldness. "I was sick then, too. I was dying."

"I don't enjoy thinking of that day," he said. His fingers intertwined with mine.

"I know," I admitted, my eyes meeting his. "But you forgave me. I didn't think you would."

"Bree, I watched your body wretch upon the bed with that fever. Your brow was covered in sweat and your eyes were blood shot." He released my hand and wrapped his arm around my shoulder, pulling me into him. "I would have traveled to Hades and back to heal you."

"But I should never have asked you to abandon Rosslyn.

"It was my decision," he said, releasing me. "I chose to stay, to break off the engagement." He stood and walked to the ledge's edge. "Leaving you for dead," he began, "Bree, I could have never forgiven myself."

"But you stayed," I said, my words a knife stabbing my back, "and then I left you for dead."

"And I forgave you," he said. "After all, I was the one who commanded you to leave."

"If I had not asked you to stay, you would not be the monster before me, Wesley."

"We cannot erase what has been done," he said. "Speculating on past events is a futile exercise." He sat, letting his gangly legs dangle over the ledge. "You have forever ahead of you and I do not suggest you put yourself through that anguish."

With this, I left him. My feet descended the hill and followed the winding path that led to the convent. Candlelight still graced the spacious rooms. The closer I approached, the more I began seeing and hearing comfortingly familiar shapes and sounds.

The sisters gathered in the main chapel for evening prayer, singing "Agnus Dei." There was Mother Abbess at the lectern, her shrill voice as high as her upturned chin. There was Mary Elizabeth sitting in my usual spot in the front pew. She tightly clasped a handkerchief and rosary in her gnarled, aged hands. Everyone had a handkerchief and bloodshot eyes as I glanced about the room.

Sister Veronica, my closest companion, was not there. An unquenchable misery filled her heart when she learned of my absence. She knew what the others did not. She understood I would not return; that whatever lulled me away was more powerful than what they offered.

She was the one person I thought I could never live without, and now I had to. Her vacant spot – fourth row toward the back – reminded me, again, of what this curse had already cost me. We had been friends since childhood, entering the convent when the Black Death annihilated our families.

Some girls our age sought solace and education within the convents hallowed walls. They waited for the plague's end, for the return of wealthy men willing. We knew this future no longer belonged to us.

Veronica was in her chambers, her head sunk into the straw mattress. She had long since succumbed to the deep sleep that comes with grief. So I watched in silence as the others said the Rosary. I wanted to speak, to call out — to scream — but found my voice mute.

"I watched you do that last night," he said approaching from behind. "You sat with them, singing, praying. I thought I was seeing a ghost before me."

"I wish I could say good-bye to them. Look how distraught they are. I cannot even imagine where they think I have gone to, Wesley."

"Your Mother Abbess," he said, pointing to her, "she thinks you escaped in the middle of the night, afraid to take your solemn profession. And that one," he pointed to Mary Sr. Anne, a portly postulant newly come to the convent from a prominent French family, "she thinks you have run off with a secret lover."

"Stop, please," I demanded. "I do not know how you are doing this, but I do not want to hear anymore. It is bringing me nothing but pain."

"Listen to them, Bree," he said.

I could hear their rhythmic and melodic chanting filling my ears, but nothing else.

"Focus on one of them, try to single out what that person is saying, then stop listening to their words."

I focused on Mary Katherine, a thin woman, mid-twenties. The sight before my eyes was a shame to see. She had been of noble family, but she came to the convent when her betrothed perished of plague. On that night, her weak frame crumbled in the pew. She squirmed on the cherry-wood bench, and her pew mates struggled to calm her. Mary Katherine bit at her nails and sobbed heavily all through her prayers.

As I watched her, I heard her. Not just her voice

whispering "amen," but her thoughts were cascading waves of emotion crashing into my mind. *Lord, please just bring Mary Clare back. Please, God, please! I will give my life for her safety. This is torture, Lord. TORTURE! Lord, please, bring her back safely. Lord, hear my prayer!*

Hearing that name – my sacred name – pained me. I wanted to flee from my brother's side, to run back to the convent and embrace my sisters. Alas, though, I could not. The hollow space Wesley's curse created now ached. This was the first time I felt different. I realized, standing there watching her – listening to her thoughts – that I was no longer *like* her. Like *them*. Warm. Untouched. Mortal.

They would never find out what happened to me – it had to be.

I grew hungry watching them file from the chapel, heading to the dining hall. Bowls of barley soup and fresh baked bread sat before them on the stone tables. I could smell the spices, the pungent aroma of chicken stock emanating from the wooden bowls. None of it tempted the knot forming in my stomach.

Uneasiness strangled my throat, as the knot grew tighter.

"It hurts," I told him. My hands clenched my stomach and I crouched to the cool earth.

"You need to feed. Those first hunger pains are the worst, Bree. I promise," he told me. He knelt down and placed a hand on my shoulder.

"It gets easier. Come, I will show you how to feed." With this, he motioned for me to follow. I glimpsed the convent once more as I walked back up the cliff. Just once. Then I turned away and never looked back.

THREE

Feeding. The biting into living flesh, savoring the warm, metallic essence tickling his tongue – this was a sport for him. I detested the idea of partaking in such a vile practice. There had to be another way, I insisted. I had hoped. I could be a parasitic mosquito leaching Wesley's leftovers, participating, but never fully playing his game. This could satisfy me. This could help maintain my innocence, or some pathetic mirage of what my innocence had been and would never again be.

However, this would not do. Wesley said the hunger would consume me. The animalistic need to succumb and devour would taunt me, bringing me to the brink of sanity, until I was helpless to submit. I would wander in bloodlust, and then having given in to temptation, having fed, would lose everything of my former self.

The scenario he painted slowly became reality. The hunger ate at my mind, ate away at my soul, leaving an abysmal craving that threatened to erase everything I had been and so dearly struggled to retain. I resigned to the temptation in an effort to avoid becoming a slave to my bloodlust, and to survive.

Had I known how the blood would make me feel, how the need for it would consume me, I would have fought the cravings with more earnest. Yet, I willingly bent to the vampiric will of this curse. I allowed it to pull me in, to call to me from the shadows, to lure me with its promise of nourishment.

One sip was all it took. One tiny, metallic drop falling gently onto my tongue and the animal inside, the animal growing from this curse, purred with delight.

With every drop, a hypnotic song played brightly in my ears. He had promised this ecstasy. He had known I would eventually be powerless to resist it. Just as he knew that once I tasted the blood, it would own me as it owned him.

I remember standing there watching the man I would later dispatch from this life. The craving distanced me from the act, and I saw this turning point as if watching a play unfolding before me. Locked inside, deep but still there, was my former self. She struggled with this. She argued. Yet, the blood controlled the body – the will.

As we stood there watching my prey, Wesley reassured me of what was to come. "You will become accustomed to it, I promise," he said. "And soon the drops will be ecstatic beads of joy sliding down your parched throat." It was the bluntness of his words, how they stung with a truth the curse living inside identified, that widened the distance between my conscious and my hunger.

Caving to the bloodlust is what I feared. This animalist appetite for blood could drown the last remaining shards of humanity left, and I could not allow that to happen.

The man, a baker from the neighboring village, had supplied the convent with wheat the years our crop had poor yields. I knew him, his family, his daughters Rebecca and Hannah. He was an elegant man despite the time spent toiling in the field and the dirt caked beneath his thickened nails.

We watched as he read by the candlelight, and the memories I had of him bringing wheat to the convent, of his daughter's gifts of bread for the orphans faded away. All I could hear was the rhythmic pounding of his heart. The smell of his blood – oh, the rich, buttery aroma – was a siren's call.

It led me to his door, which opened effortlessly. Entering, I found him slumped in the chair, the book lying in his lap. His throat throbbed, the veins bulging and pulsating, singing to me.

"I cannot do this," I told Wesley.

"You must," he said. Wesley placed his hands on the man's head and angled the neck for my access. The man's plump artery quivered beneath his tanned flesh.

Disgust mingled with lust as I watched the artery pulsate. I could hear the blood rushing, a raging river waiting eagerly for me to drink.

"This first drink will be the hardest thing you will ever do," he whispered, "but you must do it."

He was wrong. There were harder things in my future. But without this blood, without this act of defilement, I would have no future. I had no choice.

Acting as his executioner, I pierced the man's tender flesh with my newly formed fangs. The metallic blood gushed into my mouth - a warm fount of everlasting life. I savored every drop until his heart stopped, licking the last bits from my lips.

His blood was more than satisfying. The drops – each of them – shared with me his history, his feelings, his life. I realized, after having drained him of his essence, that we vampires needed this almost more than we needed the blood. The blood fed more than our bodies; it fed our loneliness.

Once it was finished, I looked about for Wesley. He came to stand near me and signaled for me to watch him. Carefully, he bit the tip of his index finger until it bled. With this, he smeared the liquid onto the bite marks, effectively erasing them. We left the man slumped as we had found him. Asleep... just now that sleep was eternal.

Wesley and I were together for four years. We hunted nightly, even though he no longer required it, and I learned from him everything I could. In that short span of time, really an insignificant hiccup to us, we traveled the vastness of Europe.

We held a residence in London, a rented estate near the Jewel Tower. Later, in Dublin, I would frequent Christ Church Cathedral in the hour right before dawn. My presence in the shadows fueled a rumor, a rumor that the angel of death haunted the chapel, waiting to collect sinful practitioners coming for morning vespers.

It was our year in Paris, though, that Wesley cherished. Near dawn, he would sit on the banks of the Seine and imagine how the water looked bathed in the nearing sunlight.

Being young in the blood, I still remembered the golden sky, afire with deep oranges and radiant reds. My favorite time of day, though, had been that moment just before the sun finally set in the evening sky. The crimson ribbons swirled with vanilla clouds, and plum and pink stripes weaved a symphony in the sky – a melody sung to a child at bedtime. This time of day seemed more magical to me than even the twinkling stars that replaced it.

There had been St. Petersburg, Berlin, Moscow, Madrid, and even a brief week in Rome. Each city was a new adventure. I was living a completely new life with him, with new eyes with which to view the world. We had the finest attire, made new in each city. Jewels from St. Petersburg, perfume from Paris, dresses from only the most delicate imported fabrics.

With time, I grew more accepting of my fate. As the vampiric powers seduced me, I further suppressed my former nature. I delighted in posing as an English duchess and he, a gallant duke; we made fools of entire cities. It was effortless to weave our spell over their innocent minds. This became a game, something to distract me from this horrid curse.

Eventually, the journey ended just as everything must end. Even eternity must have a final destination. I admit that I can no longer envision what this looks like.

Making me, Wesley had craved loved; he only found companionship. He desired more than a best friend or sister could provide. Year after year, I saw this in his eyes. He would watch women, talk with them, and then walk away. With time, he did this more often. He repressed the need to be with a lover, not a sister.

In Paris, there was a countess he spent nights with. He always came back just near dawn only to return to her night after night. The court grew suspicious of their activity and rumors grew. Once her father demanded a marriage proposal, we left Paris. Months passed after that before he was anywhere near his former, jubilant self, and I wondered why. I had no concept of love, or of loss. Having lived in the convent, I knew not of passion, of love, of being loved in return.

That was the first time I knew he needed more than I could give. He refused, though, to turn them. One after another, he would fall in love and then, in anguish, abandon his women.

It was the night before I left him when he finally told me why he always resisted.

After receiving the blood, Wesley had traveled only to find himself back in the city where we had grown up. Most of the people we had known perished with the plague. The city, he said, was a changed entity. Commerce struggled, no longer flourishing as it once did, and many of the plague's survivors were relocating to the larger cities.

The night before he left, he heard a familiar voice singing near the lake. It was there that he came upon Lady Abigail, his betrothed. She recognized him in the moonlight, called to him, and he took her as he had taken me. A week later, still in shock and unable to live with what she had become, Abigail lit her childhood home ablaze and threw herself into the fire. He vowed never to repeat that mistake.

The next night, I left him. Not out of hatred, for I have never held anything but the deepest love for my brother – despite the curse he has placed on me. No, this time *I* needed more. And although he denied himself of it, he did too.

With a note left on his writing desk and my belongings in bags and trunks on their way to a new country, I left as he hunted. I took with me the valuable lessons he had taught.

Surviving on little sips was acceptable. It was not necessary to kill your victim. And to keep my sanity, I lived by this. Change your name, your residence, and anything identifiable at the first hint of rumors. Holding too tightly to a place or a person can bring your destruction. And the one he most stressed, love from a distance.

Of all the things he taught me – to hunt, to survive – I would quickly forget the most important one.

FOUR

For that which has come, there is Urd
For that which is here, there is Verdandi
For that which will come, there is Skuld

Memories remained after the change. They were faded whispers, with images softened yet real. Memories invaded my mind when I least expected them to, when I began feeling more like the monster I now was.

The night I left, such memories slipped into my thoughts and veiled my eyes. My father, reclining on his favorite chair; his hand scratching over three-day whiskers; his eyes drifting, glazing over, lost and reminiscent.

Always in December, when the snow fell on the pines, and there was nothing to see for miles but the white blanketed countryside, my father would bundle us in furs, plant us gently near the fire in the Great Room, and relay age-old tales of the Norns.

The Norns, he would say, were supernatural women – masters of the seidr. Eagerly, and with great care, they tended the world tree Yggdrasil, spinning the Web of Wyrd. The fate of every mortal is revealed within their mystical patterns and woven strands. Even the skaldic poets heralded their influence over death and battle.

When a Norse child was born, the legend says, one of three Norns blessed the babe with its fate.

Urd, the Keeper of the Past, my father said, was an old hag— her straggly, silver strands hanging past her shoulders, her mouth grimaced in a snarl, her eyes encircled in the lines of time, and wrinkles scarring her haggard face.

Skuld, the Keeper of the Future, merely stands, her finger erect, pointing into the unknown. Her face stoically hides secrets of the future of which she will never tell.

In the middle of the three stands the fairest, Verdandi. She is the Keeper of the Present. My father's eyes twinkled and his voice faded when he spoke of her. Verdandi was breathtakingly beautiful, her golden hair drizzling down her back, its strands an endless ocean of rippling butter cream; her eyes, my father would say with a forlorn echo lacing his tongue, were warmly hypnotic.

To some, though, the Norn's presence was a curse. They were seen as witches and scorned. That was how my mother saw them. My father's folklore was heresy to her Catholic ears, and his poisoning of my soul with false idolatry was a constant source of strife between the two.

My father had wished to name me Verdandi, but my mother objected. Verdandi, after all, was not a proper Christian name. She felt a proper name would ensure me a prosperous marriage – and salvation. My father, though, was forever lost in the fairy tales of his mother's homeland.

His affection for Norse mythology extended to the mother country – to Norway. His mother had been a Norwegian Countess before marrying into English royalty. She had once taken him to her homeland when he was but a boy, and he always reflected fondly on those short months. Frolicking with anglers and playing with village children - those were adventures my grandfather would never have allowed him to have in England.

My mother had been Italian, a Duchess, of equal standing in society as my father. He married her for her title and a wealthy purse, and they had never learned to love one another. Their marriage was one of acquiring property and amassing wealth, of bridging royal bloodlines and creating alliances.

She came, of course, with the trappings of aristocracy: a palatial summer estate on the coast, a traveling staff, and a cache of jewels. Her jewels – what was left of my mother once she fell to the Black Death - came to me, and I deposited them with the family banker when I entered the convent. Through means, I wish never to know and only to assume, Wesley reacquired them for me after his transformation.

When I left for Norway, I arranged to procure those jewels. I took with me my grandmother's diamonds; her sapphire and ruby tiara are all home where they were crafted.

The journey there was arduous, for I took great care in transferring my belongings to my new home. I sailed most of the way, only traveling by land when it was of the utmost necessity. I was still in my infancy and not in full command of my vampiric powers. I greatly coveted Wesley's ability to raise me into the sky. When the clouds tickled my cheek, the misty vapors moistened my skin; it was bittersweet. He had always assured me that my powers would eventually come, but each time he displayed a power I did not have, my frustration grew.

Once, when I was unable to fly onto a tall tree branch, I rushed over to a tombstone, pulverizing it with a flick of my toe against the marble. The rubble scattered, leaving a marble stump stuck in the hard earth. I had fallen onto the ground and begged for forgiveness at the sacrilege I had committed; Wesley openly mocked me from far above. His laugh echoed in the silent cemetery, shaking the surrounding stone monuments and skittering the loose soil beneath my knees.

But I had fled to Norway to separate myself from Wesley, to leave the blood-sucking monster that was leaching my humanity, my purity and my sanity, behind. I needed humanity, to reconnect to a world I had lost when he took me from the convent.

I had a cabin built on one of the Lofoten Islands without Wesley knowing. It was nestled safely in a fjord, surrounded by rugged coastline and a nearly impermeable mountain range. I took every precaution I knew. It was far enough from the villages, yet not too far. It was a barren plot, but still habitable.

The anglers found the choice odd, but not suspicious. That I was a lone female drew more speculation than where I settled an estate. I only wanted to live beyond suspicion, beyond fear of discovery and to exist – to make peace with what I had become.

The men who built my humble cabin and painstakingly dug my cellar through the frozen earth, were disposed of. I fed off them, one by one, and allowed their bodies to slip into the frigid waters. Their lives flashed in Technicolor glimpses before my eyes; their inner thoughts whispering to me as I drank from them. Their souls plead as I leached the life from their hearts.

I had pity for them, I truly did. But I had to secure my survival. I made concessions with the corpses, slipping their bodies into the icy waters. The moon was my sole confessor; its silvery haze falling on the tide absolved me.

I stood at the shore and watched the moonlight fall on the tide. Those rippling Norse waters caught the moonlight; much like the small convent pond near the statue of St. Anne once did, where the willow trees swayed in the sticky summer breeze. It was between the apple orchard and the vegetable garden, the water adopting a mystical haze whenever the grey light graced it.

Sister Veronica and I had been sitting on the bank the last time those waters mesmerized me. Our feet dangled in the cool water, our naïve minds blissfully calm. We were alone during a time of quiet, religious reflection, and while we were supposed to be silent, we were not being faithful in this task.

Sister Veronica and I had grown up in the same inner circle, when she was but Elizabeth, a duke's eldest daughter, and I was simple Bree. Her father had hunted with my father, our mother's took tea together, and that was how one socialized then, within the confines of society. When her mother began showing signs of the Black Death, her father sent her to the convent and her brothers to France.

She complemented me nicely as a friend. When we were children, our friendship seemed easy. We laughed, we talked, we made merriment. It was effortless, and our friendship was invaluable in that convent.

Behind those hallowed walls, days stretched into eternity. I struggled with contemplation, with silence, with obedience. Days passed where I tightly shut my eyes and envisioned my arms were wings, outstretched eagles wings, and I would see myself soaring high above the convent wall only to see an unfamiliar world beckoning below.

Then there were days, other days that would linger for weeks, and often times months, where I felt comfortable and at home in my surroundings, in my decision.

But that night, I was consumed with boredom as I stared at the reflection the moon cast on the water. Its silvery hue shone atop the waters vibrating ringlets, my foot dipping below the surface, its toes twirling in the tepid water. I was wondering about the outside world; how life carried on since the last remnants of the plague swept through the area; since I had locked myself away behind the enclosure gate and stone walls five years ago.

That evening, I sat along the water's edge, staring at the moon, wishing it were my eyes so that I could see the world for one brief moment.

"There is something bothering you, Sr. Clare," she whispered.

Sr. Marie St. John and Sr. Mary Catherine sauntered past, their habits swishing against the garden walls. I pressed my finger to my lips as they glanced our way. Laundry duty had been our punishment, for a month without reprieve, the last time our talking during contemplative hour was discovered. The laundry water blistered my hands; unsightly large, red, itchy splotches that peeled, and that stung as I dipped them into the lye bucket.

"Do not worry about me," I said, once they were out of sight.

"You have that look in your eye, Bree."

"Do you want to get us into trouble?" I whispered, glancing among the shadows. "Someone may hear you call me that!" She knew using my birth name was forbidden; I dared not imagine the punishment that would ensue.

"No one's out here now. Calm yourself. Why are you so paranoid tonight?"

"I am not sure," I explained. "I feel on edge. I have been so since the sun went down. It almost feels as if I am being watched."

"You are troubling yourself for nothing, my friend. Nothing and no one is watching you." She moved closer to comfort me and placed her arm around my shoulder.

"I know!" I replied. "Elizabeth, I have this... urge to open the front gate and run out; to leave! It has never been this strong before."

"Do not be foolish. Mother Abbess has the key."

"I have even thought of going into her office and getting it. I know where it is. I have seen it myself!"

She placed both hands upon my shoulders and looked into my eyes. I remember the look in her eyes; the frightened look of a friend terrified of losing someone they loved.

"Listen to me, Bree. Don't do it. Do not leave here. Please?"

We sat like that, in that embrace for several minutes. Her eyes moistened with tears as she waited for my answer. In the distance, we could hear the shuffling of feet in the cloister, and soon followed the hollow ringing of the dinner bell.

"What will it be, Bree? Are you staying here with us or flying away?"

"I could never leave you, Elizabeth. You are my best friend in the whole world and this place, with God - this is all I know now. I do not know what has come over me. I do not! Perhaps I am just unwell."

As we embraced, our tears mingled and blended, dancing and shimmering upon each other's cheeks, before we erased the evidence of friendship and made our way to the evening meal. Shortly after prayer, an inexplicable pain seized my head. Thunder crashed against my skull while my stomach twitched and twisted. Once excused, I returned to my cell, saying good night to no one.

Wesley came for me that night. Whenever I remember that evening, my agony returns. I seldom regret promises I could not keep, because I've made them with little intent on keeping them. However, I greatly regret making that promise to Sister Veronica. I never sought to cause her anguish, and especially not pain. Not my dear friend, who sat by the pond with me, basking in the moonlight before the dinner bell rang, reminiscing about a long-gone life we once lived together outside the convent walls.

The Norse breeze wasn't as warm as it had been on the night Wesley took me from the convent. It blew icy on the island as I stood watching the bodies float out to sea, my thoughts slipping from the past.

I finished preparing my house while the moon still held its fixture in the sky. I prepared my bed in the earthen cellar, dug deep under the house and secured with a mechanism I had acquired from a learned man in Italy. It required three keys with which to secure it, and all from my side of the cellar door. No one could enter from the outside when locked, and I had a separate key, a single one, on the outside, that locked the room when it was not in use.

An ordinary root cellar – that is how my sleeping chambers appeared to visitors. To me, it was a return to the bed: a staple for mortals, but often not for vampire kind. Tradition, folklore, call it what you wish, but the stories are true. Vampires take respite in the dreariest of places: coffins, sarcophagi, crates, caves. The darker and heavier, the better.

Wesley had felt that cumbersome marble sarcophagi assured our safety. He had taught that marble was impenetrable to mere mortals, but posed no hindrance to our kind. Our strength, he would say, was stronger than ten men were. Even in my first hours as a vampire, my strength had surpassed that of three mortal men.

I had missed the luxury of sleeping in a bed, though. It was comforting, feeling the gold satin slipping against my skin as I climbed into the bed right before dawn. I used silk fabric, cobalt, and even crimson velvets, to adorn the cushions beneath my head. I had carried them with me from England to remind me from where I had come.

I was in exile on that island – the island of my father's fairy tales. I was with the rune casters of old – the witches – as my mother once taught. But to my father, I was home.

FIVE

Ten years I ventured only into the surrounding villages, feeding at night. Back then, I still kept to the small drink, leaving my victim alive. I could go three, maybe four months like this, taking just enough to survive. Humanity was still precious and unspoiled, and I took no pleasure in sacrificing the occasional fattened lamb.

Murder was never pleasant. I never grew accustomed to it as Wesley promised. I never liked it, either.

There were times, though – times when my survival demanded that I kill. Even then, the vile act of taking someone's life turned my stomach. Their blood left a sour taste on my tongue, and I would sometimes feel as if my gut would wrench its contents onto the floor. The thought of killing is unnatural to me, even to this day. Even though I am a monster, I cannot revel in stopping a man's heart and listening to the soul whisper its last mercy plea. I am not God.

It was during these ten years in Norway that I discovered I could take to the skies in flight as Wesley had. Vampires are faster than humans, and we must be conscious of this. We must always slow our movements to a mortal pace, blending in amongst the masquerade of mortals pretending to be what they are not. It was atop a peak, overlooking a barren valley; my speed was limitless that evening, when I learned of my flight ability. Crystal flecked stars lit the sky, their luminescent carpet unrolling, as I looked skyward.

A seemingly endless meadow of dulled green grass stretched before me, tickling my toes as I ran into the unknown, not releasing my eyes off the stars' shimmering presence on the blackened carpet overhead. My feet quickened until the stars blurred in my view. The wind caught my hair, twirling and twisting it, blowing it into my face. Then I looked about me— the tree line was below me, my feet were no longer on the ground. My body soared within a cloud, its puffiness enveloping me, the nighttime birds and brisk air current were my companions.

It took a few nights to harness this power - to master the art of flying. Once I did, though, the world became an endless conquest of places to visit.

I ventured first to Bergen, for this was the first time since coming to Norway that I had not needed the ferry to travel to the mainland. What would normally have taken a few hours now took minutes. The newly found ease of travel allowed me to stay there longer, and so I acquired an apartment in the heart of the city.

I cherished those evenings lingering on my wrought-iron balcony, savoring the rain as a mist accumulated on my cheeks. The hustle of city life moved below in sharp contrast to my peaceful solitude on the island. It was comforting, at times, to be amongst humanity, to hear the sound of a hundred hearts beating simultaneously. I felt less alone in the universe, and slightly more human.

When one watches society evolve around them, babies born, growing, and later dying, trends spawning and fading, one looks at themselves – an unchanging fixture in the world – and realizes they are different than the masses they have watched over. They become isolated, drawn to the familiarity of the past. As much as they crave humanity, the more they are amongst that which breathes and ages and dies, they realize how far removed from it they are. Because of this, eternity can be extremely lonely.

Isolation on my island home often drew me to Bergen. However, one month when my gloom refused to abate, I ventured further until I discovered the hidden gem that is Trondheim. From the clouds, I spotted a looming gothic cathedral. Its spires tugged my memories with vivid flashes of my First Communion in such a church. I descended onto the stone steps of Nidaros Cathedral, its doors closed.

I pulled at the heavy doors. The aroma of incense bombarded me with memories. The smells, while familiar and comforting, caused me quiet unease. The last time I had smelled such a pungent aroma, I had been human. Now, it was different to me. The aroma of incense, of myrrh and altar wine was stronger now, and sour. A sickening acridness stung my tongue when I tasted the air. I missed the wine's delicate bouquet, and the nuttiness of myrrh.

I stood on the steps, frozen with the gentle flood of emotion, admiring the untainted images adorning the West Front. The sculptures of Adam and Eve, of the prophets Daniel, Zachariah, and next to them the patriarch Jacob; there was King David and even King Olav, the founder of Trondheim; and in the center fixed for eternity in stone – the Crucifixion group, Jesus surrounded by Mary Magdalene and John the Baptist.

The cathedral candles burned, casting mystical shadows on the cobblestone, beckoning me to enter. I attempted to resist, but the ghost of my former self urged me onward, calling me home. She urged me to enter, to sit in the pew, to sit through evening prayers. She urged me to remember my past, to take solace in it, and to find comfort in a religion I had once adored.

I took to a pew in the back and watched as the priest began his ascent to the altar. His chanting became rhythmic; the candlelight flickered in the corner of my eye and ignited a lost memory of nights spent in contemplation and reflection in a pew much like the one in which I now sat. The priest, his thick accent muttering the delicate Latin, "Te Deum laudamus: Te Dominum confitemur."

There I was in the convent, clothed in the protective habit, hidden from the world. I was safe then; the world was safe from the creature I was to become, and I was oblivious to what lurked for me in the night.

They were next to me – Sr. Catherine with her knotted cane, Sr. Angelica Marie, and Sr. Veronica knelt beside me in the pew, their eyes closed in solemn reflection.

For a moment, I inhaled the burning incense, wondering if it were possible that the reality I had been existing in these years had been nothing but a nightmare. For a second, I pondered the possibility that I was truly there in the convent with my sisters. Time had not passed me by; I had never taken a life; Wesley had never come to me that night.

All of this seemed possible as I beheld their faces - their serene, ethereal faces. They appeared before me as mirages in a desert; wavering and fading yet so real that I could almost reach out, grasp onto their thick habits, and pull them to me into an embrace.

Yet then a hand touched my shoulder and the figments from my past, their faces once so vivid before me, became like sand in a windstorm, blowing again to the recesses of my mind. Old blood had risen into my throat when I realized this reality, this vicious, damning nightmare, was my reality.

"If you have come for confession," an older feminine voice spoke to me from behind, "they are hearing them now."

"Thank you," I replied.

She made expert use of a cheaply made spruce cane as she hobbled by, favoring her left hip. Her grey kirtle - with its white sleeves, skirted the floor, the hem already soiled from excessive wear; her head covered in a white cloth, grey hair peeking through. Her face reflected years spent under the harsh Norwegian sun, toiling in a garden. Her nose was bulbous; her cheeks rough and thickened with patches; her chin sporting hairs and a single black wart on its right outer curvature.

Her kirtle - patched here and there with brown fabric - shown extensive wear, as did her stained fingertips, tinted a purplish hue. My kirtle was sage green with an elaborate pattern made from imported fabric from England. Dying and embroidery was reserved for the wealthy.

The old hag hobbled down a row of pews and slipped into a confessional. I waited until she emerged a few minutes later, and then watched as she slipped away from the church.

I traced her footsteps toward the confessional, unsure of what compelled me to that box and to the man behind that curtain. I had not given confession since three days before Wesley took me from the convent; my largest transgressions back then had been falling asleep during vespers and talking when not allowed.

Since then, I had murdered and been forced from my God. I had committed unspeakable crimes against man, against the promises I had made to God, and could not face myself, let alone him. The fact that I could not be absolved through mere confession and "go and sin no more" stung me like a poisonous whip lashing at me by a hidden tormentor.

I entered the confessional, the thick burgundy curtain swaying around me as I pushed past it into the darkened box. The smell of lanolin and cod permeated from the other side, and I could make out the faint outline of the priest sitting vigilantly behind the screen.

"Good Evening, Father," I said as I sat down on the small bench.

"It is customary to begin with 'Bless me, Father, for I have sinned,'" he said, politely correcting me.

"Yes," I replied, remembering the numerous confessions of my youth and the many confessions I gave in the convent. "I know, and I have sinned but you cannot possibly bless me, for I will sin again."

"Why will you sin again? If you are aware of your transgressions, can you not change?"

"No, sadly I cannot," I said, remorsefully.

"What is the nature of your sins, my child?"

"I have murdered, Father; murdered to survive, and though I do not wish to, there will be a time when I must kill again. I will hate myself for doing so; I detest what I have become. But I will kill again. For my survival, I will take a life before God determines its time on earth is done; I will be forced to sin. For this, I will never be forgiven. Not by you, not by myself, and I do not believe even by our maker."

I could sense his pause on the other side of the screen. He breathed in and exhaled, heavily and with much conviction before he spoke.

"What you or I cannot forgive our Holy Father can forgive, my child. You must come to Him and ask for his forgiveness, and then commit yourself to sin no more. If you speak the truth and your intent just, the Lord shall be forgiving. God forgives even those who slaughter on the battlefield if they are penitent. Even St. Olav was forgiven for all those he killed in the battle of Stiklestad."

"That is true, Father," I replied. "But I am not in battle."

"Perhaps, my child," he whispered as I stood, "you are."

I reached for the heavy curtain, opened it and left. When it came to religion, I knew not where I belonged. If God accepted the vile acts this curse forced upon me for survival, then perhaps one day he would absolve me. But from that moment, I no longer felt that a man sitting in a booth had the power to bestow upon me absolution. And for the first time, I felt God had deserted me.

Yet, there were nights when I would still find myself at the cathedral, sitting in St. John's chapel. I would go to admire the stained glass and the aroma of incense, staying hidden away in the shadows like a ghost.

It was from these shadows in Trondheim I broke from my lonely cocoon. I emerged from the Cathedral one balmy summer evening and decided to spend the remaining hours of moonlight lying on the beach, my toes dipping in the tide.

Even with my eyes to the stars, to the constellations, that clear night, I could see him approaching. His feet dragged along the sand, making a grating scuffle as they shuffled toward me. The moonlight bounced off his hard frame, but it was not until he was closer that I could see his features— his wavy, luscious locks, his legs of chiseled marble, and his chin - prominent and proud.

I sat up as he approached, my palms sinking into the cool sand. He was a Greek god in the moonlight; Apollo himself descended from the heavens to make me his Daphne. Despite my immense power, the capability to crush his fragile humanity with one pierce from my fang, his presence left me weak and speechless.

I arose and brushed the sand from my kirtle. He introduced himself as Aksel Hansen, a local boat maker. We talked of the weather – it had been surprisingly brisk for this time of year, he had remarked. We talked of his boat making— an asinine trade he had made for himself. The conversation continued throughout the evening at a mild and temperate tempo, until I felt dawn creeping from the recesses of the night's silky void. Yet when I went to leave, he urged me to wait.

"I walk this coastline every night; my house is right there off the shore." He pointed to the east toward a quaint cabin nestled a few meters from the water. "I have watched you from my window."

"You have watched me?" I asked. It was not often that a mortal noticed me before I noticed them.

"Yes," he shamefully replied. "Will you be coming tomorrow night?"

"I do not yet know..."

"I urge you; come. I will find you."

With this, he walked toward his cabin. I watched as he went through the door and was out of sight. When I was safely out of view, I took to the skies, landing safely in front of my Lofoten cabin.

There was something about this Aksel... his image haunted my mind.

The next evening came and went. Three more followed and I did not return to Trondheim as he had requested. On the fourth night, I began to feel the pains of loneliness pulling me toward the city. I struggled against it, but after another week, I craved for interaction. No longer could I stand to be alone with nothing but the stars and my thoughts for company.

Perhaps it had been loneliness, perhaps curiosity, perhaps self-preservation, but I had to return to the man by the shore.

The rain was relentless that night, forcing my feet to slop their way toward Aksel's door. The storm was violent, with its dagger-sharp drops piercing my face. Lightning lit the sky in brief bursts of pale violets and shocking whites, its brilliance illuminating the Heavens. The wind howled and smacked the waves onto the shore, thrashing them into the rocks.

His house was inland— far enough to be safe from the rising tide. Light flickered from within one of the rooms; a haunting glow played on his walls from a fireplace, a raging fire swelling within it. I could see him inside, standing near the flames, stirring a pot that hung over the embers while the red flames licked eagerly at its bottom.

He moved to the table, grasped a knife, and started dicing root vegetables: a rutabaga and a carrot. He carried them to the pot, tossed them in, and stirred it once more. I watched as he hung the spoon on a rusty hook near the fireplace, and then settled down hearthside, rubbing his worn hands over the fire. His legs stretched in front of him, a reprieve from the day's labor. The slender, shoeless legs were but gangly tree roots emerging from the rustic floor.

He intrigued me the way he appeared, so effortless, so relaxed. I should have left him alone to linger in his reflections, but my hand moved to meet the oak door and gently tapped upon its roughly carved surface.

I should have let him be, left him to linger, to age, but I could not. I was lonely – just as Wesley had been the night he came for me.

SIX

Aksel bolted from the chair, the sound of my knocking startling him. He hurried to the hearth and slipped on his shoes. They had been resting on the slab, drying from his labors at the docks. That morning he had launched his newest boat, and as he held a tentative breath, it was determined that the vessel was sea worthy.

The wooden masterpiece, with its intricately carved relief of Aegir, God of the Sea, had been a labor in progress for months. With it finished, Aksel could relax before beginning his next project – two small passenger boats for a monastery in the south. They wanted the saints depicted in a carved relief along the outer edge and for it to be adorned with a crucifix at the stern. This was not the monastery's first commission and the monks were easy to please if you fulfilled their wishes.

His shadow engulfed the door as he moved closer, opening it slowly, and peeking out into the dark. He had retrieved a candle from the door-side holder and held it out and up to my face.

"I am surprised to see you here," he said. "Will you come in?"

He offered me a tart wine, imported from Italy, said he carried it from there himself; but I politely refused, then settled near the fire as he stirred the odorous stew of root vegetable and lamb broth. His cottage was quaint, decorated in rich browns – rough, tweed braids and animal hides - and accents of green and burnt reds. His furniture was sparse – two chairs near the fire, a larger one I was seated in and a smaller one for his feet to rest; a bed adorned the far right wall with furs covering it in piles, and a table sat off to the left sectioning off what served as the kitchen. The fireplace served as both a source of warmth and a stove. And the light it cast created shadows that taunted my imagination.

As I sat, watching him stir his stew, the fire flickered and shadows wavered, making the furs on the bed dance with life. With each flame came a new flicker, and a new chance for a shadow to pop into existence in one of the cabin's darkened corners. The bright embers licking the far corners, struggling to stay lit as they flew into the night, looked like eyes; eyes staring back at me. Eyes, that's what I saw in those cabin corners; staring into my soul, those eyes were.

As the night ebbed, and our conversation deepened, I wondered how Aksel could live in this cottage, haunted by these ghastly shadows and flickering flames. The secrets they must contain.

"Does the lack of lighting bother you?" I asked. "The shadows?"

My hand gestured toward the furs covering Aksel's bed. There was a bear fur lying on the top, its hide glistening, appearing to respire. The beast could have been hibernating on the straw mat, its rib cage moving in rhythm with its slumbering breath.

"The shadows?"

"Can you not see what I see?" I inquired. I motioned toward the fireplace; the embers were dying and he rose to stoke them. Tiny sparks of red and orange licked the air as they danced, fading the higher they sailed. "The firelight in your cabin is playing tricks with my eyesight. I think I am seeing things in the shadows."

"The darkness is comforting," he explained. "I spend most of my day in sunlight working. At night, the last thing I wish to do is recreate the dawn with a splendor of candles adorning my windowsills and tabletops. It's true that most homes are alight at this time of evening, but I prefer a quiet solitude in front of the glow of my fire with just enough candlelight to get by."

He sat back and stretched his limbs in the small chair as I had watched him do earlier that night. He spread his hands into the air, joining them in a clasp before returning them gently to rest behind his head.

"In the darkness there is little to distract me from the beautiful sound the waves make as they crash against the rocks, or the gentle purr of the tide as it rolls in."

"Then how did you ever see me as I walked the shores. If it is dark in this cabin, then its pitch black out there with nothing but the stars to light my way; how did you ever see me?"

"I happened upon you one night, purely by accident. You were just lying there in the sand, your feet in the water letting the tide crash into them. Had you seen me before I slipped away, I am not sure what I would have said to you," he admitted.

"I sensed you near," I replied, caught unguarded and exposed.

"You never turned around."

"I was reflecting on the stars that night; lost in a memory from my youth."

"Was it a troublesome memory?"

"No, it was a lovely memory," I said. "I knew someone was near. They left, though, before I could get up and turn around."

"I saw you again a few nights later. You walked past my window," he motioned toward the side window near his bed. "I was preparing for bed and had the candle near the window when I saw you walk past and sit on the rocks outside. I watched for a while. Why do you walk alone at night?"

"I enjoy the night," I answered.

"You came again two nights later; did the same thing, then walked out into the water 'till it reached your waist. You lingered there for a long while, and then disappeared in the swelling waves. I waited for you to reemerge but you never did. In a panic, I ran into the icy water in search of you." Aksel rose from the chair, moved to the window, and peered out onto the now calm waters.

"A storm brewed that night. I should have warned you, but I did not. I let you enter the water. Then you were gone! And I thought the tide had swept you under, but there you were, to my amazement, three days later walking along the shore. I would think you a figment of my imagination had you not spoken to me that night, and then returned this evening."

"I swam out a ways and then down the coast. It was dark; you could not have seen me. The waves were choppy. I emerged down near where the rocks brake by the cove."

His head cocked my way; his brows flinched.

"The water was icy. I shivered and could not stop, even after I came in and shed my clothes, wrapped myself in fur, and lumped myself directly in front of the fire. How were you able to stand in the water that long, so still and calm, let alone swim to the cove?" he asked. His inquisitive stare bearing into me.

"I have conditioned my body to withstand the icy, Northern waters," I responded, standing, a thread of unease coursing through me. I moved cautiously toward the window and stood by his side, placing my hand on his.

"I have a man who works for me; he swims in the cold waters as well," he said as he looked into my eyes.

"But at night, it is risky. It is far too cold."

My hand slid up his arm, groping at his bicep. My fingers, a pearly medusa, slithered until my hand reached his cheek. I rubbed his chin, relishing the roughness of his facial hair. Beneath my touch, the red bristles emerged from their hidden homes in his skin; and when I reached his mouth, it stood open to me. I took my fingers, stroking them over his lips. They were soft, but marred like worn Italian leather, scattered with rough patches from the harsh sun.

His arms gripped my waist and pulled me closer, tighter to him. Gently, I leaned in and caressed his lips, feeling the weight of his body surge next to me. With an unknown passion, he held me in an embrace and moved his lips down my neck; his hot breath was fire against my skin.

In rapture, I grasped for the tuft of strawberry hair at the nape, and swiftly angled his neck. His jugular popped; its blueness a shadow against his tanned skin. With my left hand, I scratched it, licking my finger. My lips grazed his neck, striking it with the tip of my tongue. He moaned, biting my shoulder, his arm tightly seizing against my body. His will, in that moment, was mine.

My tongue felt at my teeth, where the evidence of my horrific fate grew, threatening to protrude and sink into his tender, innocent neck.

His heart raced, straining to break from his sternum. Its siren call was deafening; its rhythm reverberated in my ears, tempting me. I smelled the richly aroma of his blood; I could taste it through his salty skin.

My lips met his neck once more, as my vampiric teeth nudged the top of my tongue.

A tiny drink, my intention was for nothing more than to satisfy my carnal need for blood – to appease this unrelenting thirst. Yet, his mind was strong; his thoughts, his wants and desires assaulted me. And the shred of humanity that heard this yearning betrayed the monster within me. It listened, it yearned for the same basic wants and desires, as well. I could not drink from him.

I withdrew from his neck and stepped away. He stared at me, his flat eyes reflecting my weakness. I edged closer to the door, close enough to feel the wood frame beneath my fingertips; the grainy texture a sharp contrast to his downy skin, the coursing flow of blood beneath a rhythmic symphonic tapping of a tympani drum.

"Do not leave," he spoke, as he lunged forward to stop me.

"I must."

"Stay!"

"I must go," I reached for the latch, pulling it forcefully. The door opened revealing the serene blackness of night awaiting me. "Do not follow. I will return. I promise"

A week later, I upheld my word.

Aksel had been in town one evening; I hunted the crowd for his thoughts, and upon hearing them, was near him in a blink of time.

Drummers kept beat next to the raging fire light, while others gathered and took turns rolling a flaming wheel down a hill. The drummers, the fires, the wheel rollers – all would welcome the dawn. They would stay to greet Sunna, the sun goddess, and mark the Summer Solstice.

By the fire is where I found him. He was dancing with a local girl when he spied me working my way through the crowd. She was a portly thing, the girl, and fourteen and covered in red splotches that she scratched incessantly. For two years now, her father had been unsuccessfully trying to marry her off; tonight was no exception. With her dowry once again increased, the man, a wealthy butcher, traversed the crowd.

Patiently, I watched the pair twirl as I waited for the next dance. Yet, while his hands remained fixed on the girl, and his feet never missing a step, Aksel's eyes fixed their gaze upon me. Three men tried engaging me, but I politely refused. My dance was his and his alone.

When it was our turn, we coupled with the other dancers, taking our turns as the citizens watched.

Five months, that is how long it took. From that dance, that night, and each night thereafter, we remained inseparable. He did not question why I only came at night. He did not question my shyness, my paleness. He never questioned the need for our clandestine meetings.

Storm clouds were oblivious to us as we twirled under the stars that night, and each subsequent night. In time, my influence over him decreased in effectiveness, though. Tight embraces loosened. Kisses turned sour. Love turned into rejection. A dark storm rolled in.

It was during those lulls in our relationship when I feared losing my connection to humanity more; and it gnawed at my sanity like an ulcer.

But dark days came later. Much later.

Shortly after that first dance, I told him where my apartment was in Bergen. The apartment served as an occasional living space, nothing more; I only stayed there on stormy nights; after all, those were the only nights worth staying in Bergen. When the weather was temperate, I flew back to my Lofoten Island cabin, to my moonlit solitude.

How was I to know the night would come when Aksel would fail to be waiting. The storm swelling the sea, eating at the beach, my feet drenched and mud soaked as I landed on the coastline. His heartbeat was long gone from this spot, and his hearth as cold as a mid-winters night. I had lost him.

Then I found him, in my apartment, in Bergen. He was waiting for me.

Through the curtains, I saw the outline of his splenetic figure poised in my ash-white chair. His fingernails snarled the fabric as he raked them with impatience. I never used that chair and kept it pushed away in the corner. It collected dust and was now an antique, a relic out of time, and displaced, like myself.

That chair. It was from the convent. It was my confessor, my consolation when madness crept by, taunting me with its vicious poison. When I left Wesley, I sought, with every means possible, to find it. The white chair, the place I would spend daydreaming of life outside the convent walls. Where Sister Veronica and I would sneak private chats and imagine our lives at court once again.

He was sitting in my chair now, though. He appeared out of place and I felt violated. That chair was a sacred relic from my past and Aksel was a fixture from the present. It was unnatural for the two to fuse.

"What are you?" he asked, for a moment his words rendering me speechless. I entered the room slowly, lighting the candles on the dresser and the chandelier with a blink, simultaneously. He vaulted from the chair, gasping as the wicks quivered with fiery life. In that moment, the tides had turned - there was no return to blissful ignorance.

"It will terrify you to find out what I am, Aksel." I sat down in the chair next to him.

He edged closer, his torso bending toward me, but I cautioned him – my hand poised in the air, stiff and unyielding. The odor of his blood was intoxicating. I had not fed that evening and his blood was too tempting. Its scent permeated the surrounding air with a fragrant perfume, reminiscent of Chardonnay and bitter chocolate. My craving for his blood – to devour him – made my fangs peek.

"Bree, I have the ancient gods on my side, not yours." He reached for me, but I thrust my hand in the air again. "Nothing can frighten me, especially the rumors."

"You must not believe them."

"And why not?" he asked, attempting to edge closer. As his feet stepped nearer, I inched further away. "If you are truly favored by the gods, then why not believe it?"

"Aksel, you know not of what you speak," I spat.

"Your old gods, they have nothing to do with this."

"The couple you rent this room from, they say you have the strength of ten men. The men in the tavern," he pointed, he extended his slender finger toward the window, "say your beauty is of the gods."

"Aksel," I began, but he stopped me.

"Then yesterday, I went to the tavern for a meal and the lady who lives above the tavern," he said, his voice dimming with disbelief, "She said she saw you coming to your apartment here. Bree, at first none believed her. But then her tale captured every ear around the hearth."

"Stop," I begged.

"She said you flew through the air, your golden locks catching the wind. You were the vision of Verdandi herself, she said. Then you landed on this balcony." He gestured to the balcony as a breeze caught the linen curtains. A storm was sweeping in and droplets began falling on the balcony's floor.

"I did not believe her – none of us did – and we told her so. Now I have seen it for myself, though. And the trick with the candles!"

Tears assaulted my eyes, but I resisted them. They were blood tears, crimson droplets that would have terrified him.

"Stop, Aksel. Leave this place, leave me," I urged.

"I do not think you're Verdandi come to the realm of man," he said. "The men below, many of them, have long abandoned our gods. They believed her story a fanciful tale."

"Aksel, I offer you mercy," I told him. "Do not make me regret doing so."

I left the chair and moved to the window, turning my back on him. A symphony of rain fell over Bergen as the city dimmed; candles everywhere extinguished, people retired to their beds, and even the yowling alley cats gave their voices a rest. The city was soon to be fast asleep, but inside my apartment, I was already mourning a relationship. This could only end one way, I thought. And it would leave me heartbroken.

"Odin has returned to his people," he said as he kneeled. "And I am ashamed that I did not recognize his maiden when she first appeared on my shore."

"Stand fool," I whispered. "Æsir's cupbearers died with their religion." I walked to him and, as he stood, took his hand. I placed it on my chest. "Valkyries may be Odin's maiden's Aksel, but they have a heartbeat." The air grew quiet and stale, not even the rain could be heard.

He dropped his hand. His body tensed, his carotid artery pulsed and swelled and my bloodlust quickened. "Gjengangar!"

This term was popular among the hunters of Trondheim, where I had first heard it while feeding in a tavern. A mythical werewolf-vampire hybrid, the gjengangar stalked the forests of Norway.

He darted for the opposite side of the room, and cowered into a corner.

I eased toward him, my steps cautious, as if approaching a startled doe. "Aksel, I am not a Gjengangar," I whispered, reaching him. My hand rested near his temple, and my fingers slinked slowly down his cheek.

"Do not worry, my love, I would never dream of harming you. You are why I wake to greet the moon, why I hunt to maintain my strength. It is all for another night spent with you; so I can hold you, look into your eyes." I leant in, close enough to caress his cheek, but he pulled away from me.

He pointed to my teeth, his finger touching one on the elongated canines. His lips quivered. "Gronnskjegg," he whispered in a raspy, shaken voice. The Gronnskjegg were vampire-like creatures of Norwegian folklore. The name means "ghoul."

His finger retreated, its parent hand quaking as it fell.

"Yes," I resigned. "But I am no monster."

"You are!" He pulled his knees to his chest. "You murder; you feed off living flesh. You are dammed – a monster!"

"Aksel! I can do many things, but you should not fear me. You are not prey, my love. You never were my prey... and you never will be."

"You spoke of mercy, please let me leave," he begged.

"I feel just as you feel; I love just as deeply, just as passionately, if not more than you do," I said. "You must not fear me."

"But I do," he said to me. "Show mercy now, please. If you do love me, let me leave."

I tried to reach out for him, but he hid his head between trembling knees and covered his neck. I walked out onto the balcony and peered into the night sky. The same constellations graced the ebony blanket as did the night I was turned. The irony— it now marked the anniversary of both my turning and the first time I revealed my true nature to a mortal.

"Aksel," I told him, "I am going away now. It is best this way."

"Will you ever return for me?"

"You are safe," I said, glancing back. "Your old gods must still be with you after all."

I retreated, as a wounded soldier retreats from the battlefield, to lick their wounds and heal from the battle of their lives. In a brief moment, I had descended into the clouds and could sense his jumbled thoughts. He feared me, but my face haunted his heart. He was simply bewitched, and though, in time, this may overpower his fear for me, I would eventually kill him. I knew what I had to do to keep him safe - stay away.

For six weeks I remained a hermit in my Lofoten cabin with only the puffins and sea lions my companions. This was after the time of the polar night and the region was drenched in a forgiving blanket of darkness during the day. I could ascend to a mountain peak and sit where the snow-capped rock met the wisps of clouds and admire the Aurora Borealis, and recall the nights I lingered on the beaches below with Aksel.

My belongings from Bergen were to be shipped discretely, so I would not have to reenter the city. I thought I had planned carefully; concealed my traces well, but I had been wrong.

Sometime after my belongings found me, I found him standing at my door; just standing there, as if I had been expecting him. His audacity bewildered and intrigued me. It had been six weeks since I had left him in Bergen startled by the revelation that I was a vampire, and now he stood before me tempting his fate.

How had he found me? I had been cautious in extracting my belongings from Bergen. The parcels passed through several carriers along the way, and the names to whom they were addressed, even, changed three times. I had been meticulous in my instruction. I had not returned to Bergen, or even Trondheim, since that dreadful night. Yet he found me here on this isolated portion of the island - at what had become my self-imposed prison of a cabin under the majestic twilight canvas.

My feet froze at the shoreline, where I had landed. When I saw him standing near the door it was all I could do not to rise back into the clouds, but I no longer had anywhere else to run. His being here could have been out of hatred, anger; his mind swam still, confused and hurt, drowning in a sea of pain. He stood there, though, apathetically, waiting for me to come to him. He knew what I was, what I could do to him.

"Aksel," I shouted, "Why are you here?"

"I fear you," he shouted, "and I know you are evil," he began walking toward me. "And I have tried forgetting you. It is no use."

"I am a monster, Aksel. I am a monster who has bewitched you," I hollered. "I will kill you! Even I see that now."

"I tried, Bree," he said, panting as he walked. "I tried so hard to convince myself that you were gone - gone forever, I told myself - but I just could not live with that. Even if you are a gronnskjegg, I could not lose you."

"You would die to be with me?" I asked. "Die for me, Aksel? Could you *die* to live with me?"

Reaching me, I could see the pain - the agony, the longing, the misery – in his eyes. The conflict seized within him, and for a brief second I feared I would lose him again. Reaching out, I grabbed his hands. I clutched them so tightly he flinched.

"Could you, Aksel? Would you become a monster like me? Because that's what it takes to be with me." I asked him, fearing the answer either way. "Would you give up the morning, the golden sunlight, and the pleasure of its tender rays on your face? For eternity? All you will ever know is the darkness of night. The nighttime, Aksel; it *never* ends."

"A lifetime of sunshine could never compare to an eternity spent in midnight with you," he replied. A tear rolled down my cheek, the moonlight masking its ruby color. He lifted his finger to wipe it from my face.

"When you weep, I will be there to wipe away the tears, now and for eternity. Nothing else matters. You are all I want and need, and if I cannot have you, then I want nothing, not even this life. And you are free to take it, one way or another – my life is yours." He knelt down and caressed my quivering lips.

"You will watch friends, loved ones, empires fade into history, and you will remain unchanged," I whispered. "It is not easy."

"I will have you by my side, my love. Together, we can weather the storm."

"I have bewitched you, my love; your mind is not your own," I said, turning my face from his.

"If you have bewitched me, then I do not want to wake from the spell," he said as he pulled at my chin.

"Then we will be together for eternity. I will not lie to you, Aksel, there is going to be pain – pains like you have never felt in your life," I explained to him. "It will be temporary. I can promise you that. But when it is over, you will never feel earthly pain again."

He let me embrace him, his arms wrapping tightly around my waist. I slid my finger down his neck and pierced the tender flesh. His blood - the long-held object of my desire, finally touched my tongue and erupted in a fountain of pleasure. It seared my tongue and tickled my throat, warming my chest. Its cosmic magic snaked through my dormant veins and rushed into my dead heart.

I pulled away as his heartbeat dulled. His eyelids fluttered and his face paled – the life drained from his cheeks. I bit the tip of my tongue and covered his open mouth with my own. My lips twisted around his as I thrust my tongue deeper. He gasped for breath as my blood trickled down his throat.

"It hurts." He pulled his mouth away as his head rolled back.

"The pain will end soon," I whispered. "I promise."

"Help me," he said through half-closed eyes.

I brought his head to mine and caressed his lips. They parted, allowing the blood to flow into his hungry mouth. Once his body began trembling, I took to the air and waited for the howling to cease.

The transference process had weakened me and left me vulnerable.

Our life together was more interesting than his brief mortal death. It was tantamount to a path of thorns sprinkled with rose petals. When it was good, it was great. When it was bad, it was horrible. Eternity affects everyone differently, and it affected Aksel in a most peculiar way.

SEVEN

Sixty-one years we lived together, co-existing in a turbulent love affair.

Months would pass in silence, his words slipping through cold lips only out of necessity. Then out of nowhere, he would blast through the doors, erupting with endless chatter or scathing demands and poisonous condemnations. We would argue over the most trivial of things— the way the servants spread rumors (which they never did), or how he wanted to feed alone and I wanted to feed together (a demand I had never made).

Not every one of those 22,265 days we co-habited was miserable, though.

There were silver-lined clouds in our storm. Days filled with laughter that could turn into weeks and months, and, rarely, years. Sometimes he would become genteel, softening his hardened nature. The old Aksel – the Aksel I remembered, the human- would show in brief sparkling glimmers. When this happened, we were happy. We existed then in an ethereal bubble that floated high above reality, and not even the outside world with its growth, its prosperity, its ever-evolving nature, could permeate it.

It is hard to say when I truly lost *my* Aksel. I know it all began in 1458 – a common year—starting on a quiet Sunday.

For centuries, we had a peaceful relationship with the Norwegian anglers. We kept to ourselves and traveled in shadow. Yet slowly rumors surfaced from Europe of vampires – hideous, ashen-skinned creatures with fangs and blood dribbling from their mouths, robbing gentle virgins of life and stealing their eternal souls. Images of vile monsters stalking the night, feeding on tender babes, spread like the plague that had once wiped out whole villages.

Other accounts claimed these creatures were stunning visions of femininity that prowled the streets luring unsuspecting fools with magical kisses, ending their lives with deadly embraces.

How correct some of their assumptions had been, but when they began eyeing Aksel and I suspiciously, I feared for our safety.

Desperately, I wanted to leave Norway; Aksel was vehemently against it. "I will never leave my people," he screamed and took to the sky. He was gone for a week and I thought this time he would stay away for good.

He returned, though, carrying a charred scrap of door; what remained of our estate in Trondheim. It was fall, 1458. We packed our belongings and fled the land that constantly enveloped me in its magical allure. Survival left us no choice. Yet Aksel remained resentful, blaming me. And by turning him, I knew it *was* my fault.

Aksel believed his love for me was stronger than his love for his country. At least he tried, so diligently, to convince himself of this. However, I feared his love – faced with the insurmountable pressures of immortality - would be fleeting. His love, as true as his intentions had been, did fade. And when it did, what remained were two estranged beings and a gaping maw of guilt that became my cilice.

For twelve years, we traveled together; as we traversed Europe, his mind began its subtle decline. I absorbed myself in the culture - the art, the architecture, and literature of Paris, of Madrid, of Berlin, of Moscow. I relished in the nightlife, in the festivals, and the balls. At times life seemed bearable for Aksel; then he would slip into a fit of hysterics or sulk into a room surrounded by darkness, and sit this way the entire night. Leaving him alone was the only thing one could do. He became irrational and sentimental, and spoke of nothing but the "old country," as if his lamenting would erase time. His sanity was slipping with the years, and I was powerless to help him.

Aksel spoke often of returning to his mother country – as if it would be a simple feat for me.

"And do you think you would find tolerance there, Aksel?" I would ask him each time. "Acceptance?"

He never answered me.

"Wesley forced me from the convent; you chose this." I explained to him as gently as if I were speaking to a child.

"The loss you feel for those you knew and loved, for your home land, it will never go away. You must now accept change, Aksel. Change will happen at a rapid pace now that you are immortal. You have to witness this for yourself! Time is nothing anymore. A century is but a decade and a year is but a moment. Life, my love, is nothing but a flash. Can you not see this?"

"The ones you loved when you were human, they have all passed this world. The ones you know now will be gone in the blink of an eye. It goes by that quickly with us, and we must treasure every second of it. Hold yourself not to one place, not to one moment, but be open to the change. It is going to happen, with or without you."

However, he would not heed my advice, and resentment swelled within him. It ate at him like a cancer. He became a mirror for pain and despair, reflecting blackness; and I had no cure for his ills.

It was winter, 1470, and we were now in Buda, traveling along the Carpathian Mountains. Buda was the capitol of Hungary until the Ottoman Empire captured it in 1541; it later merged with the town's Óbuda and Pest to form Budapest in 1873.

Everything stunk of paprika in Budapest; it lingered on its peoples clothing, in their hair, and even in their blood cells, which we greedily drank. We slept in caves, abandoned mines, and fed off fattened villagers. I still left my prey dazed but alive, but occasionally Aksel would drain his, knowing too well that this would cause unwanted attention from a superstition people.

Buda, Hungary…

There was a cabin in which a couple resided on the outskirts of a tiny village, and we found ourselves there one night, about to feed. We had watched them prepare their meal, and observed the violent aroma of paprika and garlic wafting from the cabin.

Our senses, more acute than before the transformation, revolted against these pungent aromas. They stung at our membranes, burned our eyes. Merely odorous nuisances, they did not work as apotropaics deterring our entrance.

Yet as I approached the house, I turned my head to see Aksel still in the bushes a few yards back, carefully concealed in the shadows. He turned and walked a few feet before vanishing into the dreary night. I let him feed alone that evening, a night that became one night after another until they all blurred into one.

On that particular evening, a night where the mist was a warm glove clinging to your skin and only worsened by the stifling lack of wind, I had fed from the fattening couple in their sweltering cabin. Drenched in sweat and smelling of burnt pig, I wandered into the village expecting to find Aksel along the roadside, sulking on the outskirts of town. Having not found him, I entered the only tavern this miniscule village kept and decided to wait for him there. In a village this size, I had surmised, it could not take him long to find me.

A broad stone fireplace graced the farthest corner, warming the tavern with its raging golden flames. A long bench, wooden and worn with knots and cracks sat in front of it, and I removed the hood of my fur-lined, emerald-green cloak before sitting down between two burly, stinking men.

Both reeked of sweat, and the second one, the nastier of the two, with filth; his hands, saturated with fresh dirt, his fingernails splintered and jagged, and his hair —wild, and flaring at the temples in winged patches of blackish-grey tufts, tipped in debris.

Both men were past their prime, wilting examples of the men, they once were. Their thoughts revealed that they had been hunters, prosperous before the gout ate at the first ones toe and before the wild cat attacked the second. They were now legends with a fading story, the kind that dies slowly over time.

Silently, I fed from these men and left them slumped together - peacefully asleep on the bench.

It was nearing dawn when I left the tavern. The sky was growing ashier as the sun threatened to erupt from its horizon-bed, and birds in their tree top slumbers were beginning to wake and make their morning calls to the god of sunshine. Knowing I had not long to get to our hiding spot in the cave not far from the village, I flew into the sky only to look down and see him in the distance.

He was not a few miles from where the tavern sat, sitting near a brook. He had pulled his cloak over his shoulders, the hood covering his head, but I knew it was Aksel. The amber hide of his leather cloak was creased and rippled from wear, and all I could see slither out from beneath the massive piece of fabric was a red leg and black shoe pointed at the edge of the brook.

Even though my landing had been faint, I knew he would hear me. Still, he did not move to acknowledge my presence.

"Your sullenness of late is troublesome, my love. Let us talk of this, please, and be done with it!"

"Perhaps," he replied remaining fixed on the flowing waters of the brook that flowed effortlessly in front of him.

"We will talk tomorrow then, dawn is approaching. We will deal with your hurt, your pain, your anger, Aksel; and then we will never speak of this madness again."

I left him and walked to the cave. He followed behind shortly after and took to his slumber without a single word spoken to me. The tears, the blood tears, which he had hastily wiped from his face before he returned, spoke louder than words ever could. I could not ignore his pain, his sadness, any longer. Nor could I do anything to relieve it.

When I awoke the next evening, he remained asleep on the uneven earthen floor; a vision of a man I once knew who had walked along the beach on moonlit nights and captivated me with his wit. He had dug a ditch and concealed himself behind a pile of rubble. I had done somewhat the same, and was now dusty and filthy and needed the brook to cleanse me; to make me appear the unblemished phantom survival required me to be.

I then soared into the clear night that was ablaze with the twinkling of a billion stars and sought refuge on a high tree branch. The admiration of the universe, its magnificent brilliance alive in that moment surrounding me - existing eternally with me - was all I had the energy to acknowledge. I wished not to fight with Aksel; to argue, to be in eternal discourse over pointless matters, always dancing around what really mattered but never grasping it, never pulling it to us and tackling it down.

Buda was not the beginning of our parting, though. The moments awaiting me that night were long in the making. That night, the air clung to me – a wet blanket reminiscent of a time and place, not too far back in our history, when a chasm began to grow between us. The stale sky had shown the same dulled constellations that night, too.

The first time Aksel had left me, he had been away nearly a week before returning. That was shortly after we left Norway while in Paris.

I had been standing on the Le Pont Saint-Michel overlooking the Seine, watching a wedding procession advance down the river beneath me. Their barges of merriment were aglow with bulbous torches and shimmering silks, emanating an erotic aura of rippling waves that trickled out from the inanimate objects and even from the people. Perfumed sachets adorned the pillows that the women clung to their bosoms as men, ripe with cheap wine, threatened their decency; and the women, who were drunk from spirits and intoxicated with lust, gave in to their lovers' desires. Barge after barge, the same one after the other, floated beneath me until the final barge passed before my eyes of the bride and his groom; a couplet swathed in a tent of silks and shimmering satins, lying atop a bed of virginal white. They appeared asleep, enveloped in each other's arms, lost to where one began and the other ended.

"A festive party," a voice behind me remarked.

"I have been to this bridge before and watched processions like this one," I remarked.

"And wedding processions will continue for ages to come," he replied. "They will sail under this arc, blissful and ignorant."

"Perhaps it is best to be ignorant," I said. "The world's evils cannot touch you if you do not know of them."

"Gaze upon their faces, Bree," he remarked, pointing to their sleeping, drunken forms. "The women believe love and bravery will conquer all, while the men see only a rich purse. Absurdity."

I watched the lovers float past. Their candlelit faces were smug with merriment and wine. "Where have you been all week?" I spat while fixing my eyes on the barges below.

"Soul searching," he replied. He moved next to me putting his arms along the edge of the wooden railing, peering down into the water.

"Did you find what you were looking for?"

"I believe I have."

"Are you going to…" but I could not finish the sentence. I could not ask him if he was going to leave. I was terrified of the answer. "I have already fed. Do you need to feed?"

I quietly rejoiced that he did not question me, that he did not prod me. We had left the city three nights later for Italy.

He kept secrets now, since leaving Paris; and left for weeks at a time. But even if Aksel was intent on changing, I could always rely on the sky to be an unchanging force in my life. The moon and the stars always remained steady in the sky, the same as they were that night as I sat on the tree branch in Buda waiting for him to awaken. Yet, I did not know what it was I was waiting for. Would he remain with me, travel with me, continue to be my companion; or would we part as friends? Or as two who had been lovers but are no more?

If he left, would I ever again behold his face? Did I have time to memorize every line, every imperfection? A week without him, I could endure. But eternity… I was not so sure.

Then a whisper came forth from the mouth of the cave and it startled me from my silent musing. "Bree?" he whispered into the night air. I was apprehensive, hesitating on my branch. "Bree!" he called louder. I slowly glided down from the branch, landing softly in front of him. He stood not two feet in front of me, yet his mind was miles away.

"Let us talk." He took my hand and guided me toward a rock slab, but I refused to sit with him.

"What is it, Aksel?" I asked, snatching my hand from his grasp and stepping away from him. I turned to glance out over the brook, not wanting to see his face.

"I...I am returning to Norway."

"Without me?"

"With or without you; I am going home." He slumped forward; his elbows pressed firmly against his knees and his heels digging furiously into the dirt. "I am done with this life: city-to-city, living a farce! I cannot do it anymore."

"Then you will be going without me."

"Is there no way I can convince you to come with me?" he asked as he rose from the slab and walked toward me.

"No." I turned to him. "Is there no way I can convince you to stay?" I struggled to form the words, to shout, "Nothing but danger greets you there. Nothing but death!"

I wanted to tell him that if he left my heart would break into a million pieces and would never mend, but I knew this was not true. I knew it was in our nature, a natural progression that forever did not exist with our kind.

Mortal marriage has its natural expiration and so did ours. With time, we gravitate away from each other, both having morphed into completely different creatures than which we were when we were human. With Aksel, he had changed completely from when I turned him. He was full of melancholy - prone to fits, and would go off on his own. Just not the man I had known sixty-one years ago.

"Bree, if I do not go now, I will only grow to resent you more." His voice pulled me out of the fog of my own thoughts.

"Then you do resent me?" Facing him, I could see the turmoil in his blood-shot eyes.

"I resent leaving… not you," he stammered.

"But it was my decision to leave, Aksel! You followed. Have you held it against me all these years?"

He tried embracing me, but I pushed him away. He tried to grab my arm, but I jerked back.

"You do resent me, admit it. At least be a man and admit it!" He turned and began walking away.

"Do not walk away from me, Aksel!" I shouted, but he continued to walk and then he looked back at me and took to the air in flight. In a panic, I followed him.

The higher he flew, the higher I flew. The faster he flew, the faster I pushed through the clouds. I followed him until he realized I would not relent in my pursuit; then he landed in a meadow. He had his back to me when we landed, but I quickly seized upon him.

"I will ask you one more time, Aksel; one more time. Do you resent *me*?"

He faced me and, for the first time in our sixty-one years together, he looked terrified of me. His eyes searched mine before answering in a whisper, "Yes. Yes, I do."

My hands reached up and secured his vest in my fisted palms. He remained fixed on my eyes and did not struggle against my strength as I picked him up into the air, flinging him into a nearby tree. He smacked into it, the impact ratting the top branches. Birds flew into the darkness, their wings beating noisily against the wind.

"Go," I said to him, as he lay there at the foot of the tree unfazed. "I am done with you." I walked away, not glancing over my shoulder to see if he wept for me.

.

EIGHT

Buda became my home, my solace, for the next thirty years. Rumors of vampires and werewolf-like creatures were spreading, and I found I could not escape them. It did not matter where I was— these tales, these folklores existed. I learned to conceal myself behind people's ignorance. From these fictitious legends, I had nothing to fear, for not even one was true. Yet they gave nations a false confidence, while I strolled merrily among them.

Through the tradesman, I heard the folklore of many lands. The people of Moravia claimed a vampire could only attack while naked. Bavarian vampires slept with one eye open and thumbs crossed. I wondered how these legends took shape and grew roots.

Then I heard of the atrocities these people were committing against their own dead in fear that they had become vampires. They defiled newly buried graves, staking corpses or removing the newly deceased's hands and feet. Other cultures removed the head, or they would remove the heart and burn it to ash, making the supposed victims drink of a concoction containing the ashes to break the "vampire's curse."

These rumors followed me everywhere, but no one ever suspected that I was a *vampir*. That is what they called my kind in Buda – vampir. I first heard the term from a man during a Gypsy celebration held in the summer season. Hearing it for the first time sent had chills down my neck.

"It appears that Miklos Tomas was a victim of a vampir," he had whispered to me, as he twirled me around the bonfire. "Stay inside and bolt your door tonight, for a group of us strong men will be slaying the demon at midnight." His pálinka-laden breath was warm against my cheek. The liquor's sweet scent – from Hungarian fruit – wafted violently past my nose.

"Why midnight," I asked as his grubby hands gripped my waist. Against

"That's before the creature rises from its grave. We need to strike between midnight and the witching hour to send it to the nether world, my beauty." He leaned toward my cheek, desperately pressing his filth covered lips against me as I pulled away.

Miklos Tomas had not been a victim of a vampir, though. Men from the village and church had exhumed the poor man's corpse as I watched. The corpse displayed the usual signs of decomposition - the long grown fingernails, hair growth, peeling skin, bloated body, the presence of blood at one corner of his mouth. And the men were convinced these natural signs were evidence of a vampiric curse.

They had burned his remains and scattered the ashes. How could his soul find rest now? It would have taken considerable restraint not to leave a scrap of evidence when I descended on the huddle of soot-covered men. It would have been easy to conceal the fang marks in their fattened necks after I ripped into their jugulars – the smug looks of self-importance wiped clean from their faces. But the marks were there, though, for those with a head intact. Some corpses I left with their heads lying next to the feet, or with a stake jammed snuggly into their lifeless heart.

In that moment of anger, I had broken my vow not to kill.

I fled the villages; their nescience showed me the depths that humanity can sink. Instead, I enjoyed my time among the elite of Buda, disguised as a widowed Countess.

My marital status and lack of familial connection in Hungary was often a topic of courtly gossip. There was much speculation as to why I had not remarried- when I would marry and to whom I should be married. Suitors played the game nightly, making my hand – and the supposed purse it contained – a prize to be won.

I fed off these men, each one. I stole their essence while luring them in with the promise of riches and the ability continue their lineage. How short and insignificant their lives really were. They wanted nothing more than for someone to be theirs, to have something to possess, to devour completely. It was such a shame, a real pity that I could not return their devotion.

But my heart hardened after Aksel. I was resolved not to fall in love. Nor would I ever again plague those I loved with this curse.

I spent years fending off suitors, attending balls, and enjoying what I could of a solitary, restful life in Buda. Existence carried on smoothly without Aksel, and I was at peace with myself. I came and went as I wished, kept a modest house, and answered to no one. I was not missing his sulking for a minute.

A majority of my time while alone, though, was not spent in fancy balls. Elaborate gowns – Italian silks, French ribbons and Persian lace - I laid aside for simple cotton garments, while biding my time in the Royal Library of Buda's Royal Palace. My candle and I submerged in the stacks, lost in the library's vast literary treasures until the birds began to wake.

I devoured the codices - of which there must have been over 2000 – and savored the incunabula they kept there, safe and preserved. Histories, plays, literature, I perused them all. I experienced the words - absorbing each syllable in my mind, holding them there as one holds their breath, until my head ached with abundance. My candles would burn out, forcing me to light another. Dawn would threaten to approach, forcing my retreat, only to return the next night and the night after, and the night after that.

Those were the merriest times I spent in Hungary, there in that library, amongst ratty tomes of forgotten lore and newly, blocked volumes. The smell of the ink, the crispness of the paper, the smooth feel of the leather binding between my fingers… it was all very intoxicating.

Change comes with all things in life, seasons, people… relationships. Eventually, it happened with Buda, once more spoiling the city.

My fondness for the city, and even the country of Hungary, had grown over time. I walked its streets during the age of early absolutism, as the Renaissance King, Mathias Corvinus, ruled. His reign experienced great expansion, both southward and northwesterly. King Corvinus was a ruler of the people, and the common folk adored him immensely.

His legacy, the Bibliotheca Corviniana, was like none other. The Bibliotheca was an expansive collection of historical chronicles, scientific and philosophic works - Europe's premiere collection. The Vatican's own collection was the only one that could hold a candle to it, but those were mostly religious volumes.

By then, though, I had seen all the Royal Library had to show me – the Bibliotheca Corviniana included. I was ready to bid adieu to the paprika-laden peoples of Buda in order to create new beginnings – to reinvent myself, as my kind must always do. Always running, and never staying still for long.

Wanderlust had pierced my disinterested heart with its visions of splendid new places and exotic locales. So one night, after my belongings were packed and my preparations made, I once more ventured into the city, to the blind beggar, whom I had used as a host.

I slipped into his hand enough coin to buy clothing, an estate, land, and perchance a title, if the King willed it. My directions were clear. The names of my court contacts, the location of my residence and its deed – now left to him. He fell prostrate thanking me, but I had moved on.

I bid farewell to the crowd at Heedstead Tavern, and bought a round for the mass of patrons - most of whom I had fed from over the years. I slipped into the Royal Library and walked amongst the volumes in their primitive bindings. Dust collected on my fingertips, a grey veil that had a stagnantly clean odor – an essence of history - that I savored, before rubbing it away with my thumb.

A single candle glowed in the drawing room when I returned to my estate. A messenger waited for me on his steed near the door and, upon seeing me, quickly disembarked. The letter, which I read once inside, had Aksel's seal.

The fire licked to life as I entered the drawing room, boxes littering the corners, furniture already dressed for preservation. I tossed the letter on a writing desk, deciding not to open it. Then the envelope's sleek crispness teased me, curiosity finally winning. Beyond the crimson seal, an aura of white with hastily scrawled writing unfolded before me. He was coming tonight, the third night of the New Year, with urgent news – dire, he claimed.

I searched a nearby box of dusty miscellaneous items: small trinkets from desk drawers, candlesticks and silver pieces tossed in to ruminate until they reached their new home. Just as I had selected a palm-sized stack of paper, sat down at the desk, quill in hand, I sensed a presence behind me. Then I felt his hand rest on my shoulder. He was standing there as I turned around: as a figure in a gray suit and dust colored coat. His ruggedness, the features that had once defined him, had strangely softened.

"Who do you have with you, Aksel?" I demanded.

I could sense her, a young one, lingering near the porch, just within earshot. Her feet gnashed the grass and clacked loudly as she stepped on the cobblestone walkway. Her mind was a cyclonic whirlwind of pointless images that she assaulted me with, thrusting them at me as I pushed them away. She willed those thoughts through the door, through the thick, burnt-sienna wall. The agony she felt was a cumulonimbus, but the pain was self-contained.

This young one had felt her heart bleed, break in two, and die, and all this before he had turned her. She had seen things, incomprehensible images of torture, of unspeakable horrors; harmed and scarred and now existing eternally to live the nightmare within her mind as if it were a constant record – stuck in a loop. Now it wept, yet her visage was serene.

"You act surprised," I said as I moved to a linen-covered chair, sitting down without removing the cover. "You must teach her to guard her thoughts; if you expect her to survive around others, that is."

He asked if she could come in. After I had given my permission, Aksel sat down on the chartreuse sofa, glanced toward the candelabra nearest to him – silver with gilded gold leafing and ornate twisted leaves aspersed on its arms, an item considered antique even then- and lit the candles in its cups. Twelve golden flames fluttered to life across the room as she entered.

Her face was simplistic, child-like in quality, but she was no child. Her round emerald eyes glimmered against the starkness of the rigid ebony bangs clinging to her forehead. She cowered near the door, afraid to enter further. She was nearly five feet in height and appeared waifish standing alone on the outskirt of the room, shrouded in darkness, buttoned to the neck in her floor length wool coat.

"Come and sit with us," I said, taking pity on the poor creature.

"Why have you come here, Aksel?" The female sat next to him, glancing at him coyly. He quickly jerked his head from her glance to meet mine. "What is so urgent?"

"I need your aide," he admitted nervously.

"Thirty years have passed," I said, glancing at the female. "And now you come to me under mysterious pretenses, under urgent conditions? You have sought help! Does this pertain to Evelyn?"

"She knows my name!" the female screeched. "Aksel, she knows my name! I have not even told her!"

"You need to teach her to guard her thoughts, Aksel," I said. "I heard you outside, walking up my front steps, munching your feet in the grass; your thoughts were a jumbled river and you need to learn to control them. Control them before someone controls you with them."

"Can they do that, Aksel?" she gasped.

"Yes." He glared at me from his side of the couch as she drew her legs up and sat on her half.

"I need a favor from an old friend, Bree."

"I have not seen you in thirty years, and under the circumstances of our parting," I glared, "do we honestly hold each other in friendship?"

"Bree, I have nowhere else to go," he sighed as his fledgling threw up her arms.

"I told you this would not work!" she stammered. He glared at her. Evelyn's lips twisted as she rose from the couch and left the house, slamming the door as she did.

"What would not work?" I asked him. "I want the truth. Now, before I remove you from this house."

"The story is long," he began, "long and unforgivable."

"I am not your confessor, Aksel; I cannot absolve your sins. Explain yourself, please."

He rose from the couch and walked to the window, pulling back the drapes. His fingernail scratched at a square of unwashed glass, the grime collecting at his cuticle. He struggled through the layers of filth to peer into the darkness. He scratched some more, ignoring me, until he managed to remove enough muck to let a few meager twinkles of twilight shine through.

"I am not seeking absolution," he stated, finally. "I just need pity, and assistance."

"You do not deserve either," I snapped. "Get on with it, then. Dawn is soon upon us and my patience is teetering."

"You were once a woman of great patience, Bree," he said, turning toward me, his hand covered in the filth from the window. He brushed it against his pant leg, marring the elaborate gray fabric, as he once again sat upon the couch.

"I was once a woman of many things, but you will find me now much changed. And I pray that you tell me what is going on before I hurl you from my premises," I demanded. "How old is she, Aksel?"

"Fifteen," he stated flatly, gingerly shifting to the left corner of the couch.

"Fifteen! Aksel, how could you make one so young?" I relaxed in the chair and listened for her footsteps on the cobblestone. "What insanity possessed you to do such a careless thing?"

"I had no choice," he began. "She was going to die if I did not intervene."

"Then you should have let her die... or assisted, killed her; given her a merciful end clouded in a painless fantasy. But, this life, it is no place for one so young!"

"It is complicated, Bree," he groaned. "I was walking along the road that leads into Oslo from the north. You must remember that road – we used to hunt there – it was there that I found her. She had been abandoned and was lying alongside the road, bleeding, curled up into a tight ball like a wounded kitten. Her pain was agonizing."

"You should have ended it for her, given her some peace. You are weak."

"Your words are monstrous," he howled. "I tried to, Bree! I meant to! But, when I reached down and glanced into her face," his voice softened as he spoke, his eyes glistening with remembrance, "She resembled someone I once knew. When the light caught her face and she opened her eyes, I *remembered* those eyes. I could not place them, or her. I took pity on her and took her with me. I don't know why, I just did. I know I shouldn't have, but I could not leave her to die, nor could I kill her. I entrusted my housekeeper with her daily care and oversaw to her every need at night until she was nursed back to health."

He sighed heavily, continuing, "It took over a week, but eventually rosy life bled into her cheeks. Her eyes glistened. Then one evening she demanded to speak with me. She had been throwing things at the housekeeper and refusing to eat." His voice trailed off.

"Then what happened? What did the young Evelyn wish to know?" My question brought him back to the present, back from the dream world his mind wandered in; he rose, slowly pacing the room.

"My nightmares came true, that is what happened." Aksel stopped in front of the fireplace and leaned against the proud mantle, staring into the empty hearth as if a wild fire consumed the darkened space.

"She knew who I was – even what I was."

"How could she have known that?"

He moved to the window and resumed scratching at the grime, his fingernails screeching at the glass. I ignored the noise. The clear glass beneath glimmered as each spec of dirt trickled to the floor.

"I killed her mother," he finally answered.

"When was this exactly? You found the girl near the roadside, half-dead."

"It was the night before," he said, looking directly into my eyes. "I was hunting... nowhere near the city. I was hunting on *that* road." His voice softened and he returned to the couch. The velvet crinkled as he sat, even beneath the cotton dust covering.

"I was walking through the woods, as I do on most nights, and in the distance I heard a carriage of drunken men singing on their way toward the city," he paused.

"It is my fashion to haunt this particular pathway. There is even a legend about me. On that night, I caught a scent lofting from this carriage. It was not the smell of rum or the atrocious odor of tobacco originating from the two putrid drivers. No. It was the smell of women's perfume, the sweet aroma of sugarplums and crushed violets. The scent reminded me of you," he looked up, a smile gracing his worried face. When I did not respond to his flattery, he continued.

"I flew into a nearby tree, and within a matter of moments I was upon their group. The two men were effortless. But, as I was finishing with the second one, a gorgeous woman emerged from the carriage. She began cursing me, holding up a crucifix. I grabbed hold of her, as you had done to me, and I threw her. She slumped to the ground and died. I heard a large grouping coming up the path and I fled to my rest," he lowered his head and sighed.

"When I returned the next evening I found Evelyn."

"Was there any sign of the carriage?" I asked. "Of the mother…"

"No," he replied. "They had taken it; taken it after finding Evelyn inside and raping her. Then they left her, concealed in some brush near the road for the vultures to feast on."

"Was there any sign of the other travelers?"

"No, her mother and the two drivers' bodies were nowhere to be found," he replied. "They just left Evelyn, a defenseless child, Bree, for dead."

"Humanity can be a cruel and destructive people, Aksel. They are often senseless and quick in their actions."

"Then you no longer consider yourself human?" he asked as he moved back to the fireplace and blinked the dead embers to life. The hearth became a growing belly of orange heat with tongues of red, licking against the burn-stained brick hearth. A warming glow permeated the room, reached into every corner, enveloped every object, every air molecule, and suspended itself as if it were holding me in a loving embrace.

"No, I have not for centuries," I replied, the syllables catching the crackling embers and fading as they fluttered into the air. "But, ask yourself, are you any less cruel or destructive, any less of a senseless monster?"

Aksel remained at the mantel, his left arm perched on the polished wood, staring into the raging flames. "No, I am not. We *are* no longer the people we once were. We can be cruel, selfish beings; perhaps we have always been that way."

"No, it comes with the blood and with time – the passing of time, and experience. But, that is inevitable," I replied.

"We don't intend to be monsters, though. It's in our nature to be heartless and solitary."

"For some," I noted.

"Will we ever mend the rift between us?" he asked. "Or, are we destined to," the words trailed, his chin quivering.

"Aksel, why did you turn Evelyn?"

"She was frightened and fought me, but soon she softened and became like a daughter. Then sickness swelled in her belly, and she burned with an intense fever. She slept, would not take food, and the doctor said she hung precariously to life. Then one evening she howled in pain and bled, and clutched her belly." Tears stung his eyes.

"She was pregnant, Bree."

"Where is the child now?"

"Dead," he said, his eyes closed, tears at the creases. "Born still and malformed. The midwife removed the babe before Evelyn could look upon it."

He continued, "The bleeding wouldn't stop and she was dying. The life drained from her and I could not let her go, Bree." He sat down on the couch and leaned back, sinking into the weight of the heavy cushions. "It was her choice. She had begged me to save her, Bree. She begged me with her dying breath, and she knew the monster I was. She knew the monster she would become; she knew this curse, and she wanted it! Out of selfishness, because I was not strong enough to live knowing I had allowed her to die, I did this to her. I created another us."

"We all have our demons, Aksel, and we must live with them. She is yours."

"I cannot live with her any longer, and she cannot care for herself," he said, his words rushed.

"You should have thought about that before you created her, Aksel. She is your fledgling and your responsibility."

"She is capable, but society only sees a fifteen year-old child, Bree. She has become too masculine, too influenced by me. She needs a feminine influence." He smiled shyly at me, reaching for my hand, but I refused the offer of companionship.

"I will not care for your offspring, Aksel."

"She needs a mother, Bree. She needs to learn womanly ways, to hunt as a woman hunts. Please, I beg of you, take her," he pled.

"Aksel, I am nobody's mother and I do not wish to become one now," I answered firmly. "I could tell from her thoughts that she misses her mother; cries for the woman who smelled of sugarplums and crushed violet, but I cannot replace this person. No one ever will."

"Then what am I to do, Bree?" His hands fidgeted in his pockets, his voice cracking. "Of all the times I have needed you, this is the most grave of times, and you deny me. Bury our past, please! This is not about us, but her. She is innocent, Bree. Innocent! Do not let her pay the price for our sins."

"What are you not telling me, Aksel?" I demanded.

"I can tell you what he will not," a voice whispered from behind the library door as it opened. Aksel stood, moving to the fireplace, warming his shaky hands over the orange aura.

"It was my idea to come here and to seek refuge with you. Let me apologize for this, and please, do not harbor any ill will toward Aksel. He is merely playing along with my farce."

"Why are you seeking refuge?" I asked, curious now.

"One night I was hunting when I came upon a small camp of miscreants. There were only three there and I thought I could take them alone. The first man was simple. He had been sitting near a fire and I had snuck up behind him. It was an effortless kill. Then I created a noise diversion to lure the others out of the tent.," she said.

She continued, "When they emerged, we all recognized each other. In panicked and flew off. Eventually, we took care of them together, but they had reached Oslo and spread word first that I had slaughtered their companion. I was cursed as a demon in Oslo, and we realized the problem was unfixable."

"And so you have come here seeking asylum?"

"It is the only way," Aksel interjected. "I must keep her safe."

"And what would you do if I granted Evelyn this; if I take her in and care for her?"

"I will return to Norway, of course," he replied. "They have renderings of Evelyn's face circulating around the country, but they do not suspect me. I can go to a different city and start over."

"That is what I was expecting you to say," I said as I walked over to the fireplace, facing him. "Aksel, I cannot do this for you. I will not take her with me, nor will I stay here with her."

"How can you refuse her?" he asked, his words still shook with fear. He collapsed onto the couch, a plume of dust escaping the fabric as his body met the cushion. "Can you seriously not grant me this one wish, Bree?"

"You are still blind, Aksel, blind and unwilling to see the truth. She is fleeing Norway for the same reasons I fled, and yet you do not flee with her. Why do you hang onto that place? It is just a place! Yet, you cling to it as if it were the only thing in this world providing sustenance! You forsake those who you love," I glanced at Evelyn, "and loved you, for a people that would burn you without a second thought."

"Relinquish humanity before it destroys you. Let go of your past and move on before it ruins your future." He remained motionless as I spoke, my words assaulting the human in him.

"What is to become of me?" Evelyn asked, her voice a hot knife slicing through our conversation.

The gravity of her situation made me pause – made me flash a peak at her naïve, haunted eyes.

"You can stay here, Evelyn."

"I could not!" Her voice quaking. She clenched her fists and stammered into the room. "I cannot live on my own - look at me!"

Tears trickled down her cheeks. Her petite hands brushed eagerly to clear them away; but, unable to fight them, she turned her back to us in shame. Aksel walked to the window and hid his face.

"You will not be alone," I assured her.

I walked to Aksel and placed my hand on his shoulder, gripping it. When he faced me, there was solitary tear gliding toward the cusp of his upper lip. He stopped it with the swipe of a knuckle.

"Aksel will stay here until you find a suitable mate, Evelyn," I called out. "You owe her that much," I whispered to him.

"We will start right away, I promise," she assured him through her veil of tears. "Just, please, do not leave me."

Evelyn was the object of innocence and purity, just as I had been when first turned. Time and blood: these would corrupt her. That is our kind's natural cycle. For, from the moment we are first bitten, we enter an eternal battle, a war with no end. Century upon century this war rages, battling our sanity, until we hunger for innocence... for our wasted humanity. The cycle of time, the ceaseless battle of ages, hardens our hearts. It strips from our minds, from our realities, all that are innocent and pure. Evelyn's heart and mind would one day harden. Not out of fear or hatred, but out of necessity and self-preservation.

She could not understand my reasoning for leaving – or Aksel's unwillingness to stay, though. She was naïve and still in need of guidance. So was Aksel.

"He is in no hurry, my dear. Once you find one, he can return to his beloved Norway until they run him into the ground," I growled.

He stood motionless until I released my grip on his shoulder. Despite his pleas of change, he still feared me. He would not go against my demand.

He walked away, a queer look in his eyes as he glanced in my direction. He now understood that I would not forgive him. Evelyn rushed to his side and embraced him. He softened there, as he tenderly held her. He appeared fatherly, and it fit him.

"I am going to leave then, tonight. I will send for my belongings," I told them.

"Do not go!" she urged. "I want to know you. I have heard so much about you and I would love to spend just one evening in your company, please?"

Aksel interceded, "She has to leave. It is her nature." He faced me, a remorseful glimmer reflecting in his eye with the firelight. "She is a bird, Evelyn, a bird that must stretch her wings and fly. You cannot cage her, for then her wings would break, and her voice would be stifled. No, every once in a while, Bree must shake the dust of the centuries from her wings, and then fly off to somewhere new."

"Like a Phoenix – be reborn," Evelyn said, a tinge of reverence in her voice.

"Like a Phoenix," I replied.

"A Phoenix who flies alone," he whispered.

"Only because no one will fly with her, and she refuses to sit still and die."

He reached for my hand, but I pulled it away.

"I thought I hated you, Bree; hated you for spoiling my homeland. But I learned that it was not you I hated; I was angry at myself."

"Why?"

"I was frustrated because I could not surrender my humanity, at least not enough to be with you. And because of this, I lost you."

"It was just a matter of time, Aksel. Our kind, we do not do forever because forever is too long."

"Can you stay here and we try again?"

His eyes smiled and wept, lost in emotion. The painful memory of thirty years ago further soured an already unpleasant evening.

"No, no we cannot. There is no restarting. As you said, Aksel, it is time for me to fly. And, you need to be here with Evelyn. Do not seek me out again. It is best that we part now, for there is nothing left between us but animosity."

I left the house and took to the sky, flying toward a new adventure. I started the next chapter of my existence just as he said I would – a Phoenix reborn from the ashes of her past.

NINE

My past is filled with ghosts. They fly about, cruising on the cusp of the wind. History, secrets: they bring nothing but sadness and pain. Guilt and remembrance of time wasted.

Now, I was the phoenix – reborn, anew. This could be my chance to silence the ghosts. For how long, I did not know. But perhaps, for a little while, they would leave me be. I felt unsafe in my own skin, awkward. Restless and unsure, I roamed, tugged in directions by an invisible force I called Fate.

I searched the people around me, searched in their faces for clues as to who I should become. I was a bringer of destruction, of pain, of misery… the marker of death, my purposes clear as a full moon.

I had developed into nothing more than a monster. Even after I had struggled to retain my humanity, I had evolved into the creature that plagued children's dreams. Not long ago, I had sat on a hardened pew, rubbed to a shine with linseed oil that glistened in the softened candlelight, and sung my Benedictions with the rest of the choir. Not long ago, I was clothed in the black veil of piety, the brown scapula that grounded me to the earth… dust to dust.

That veil would cover me, my face, my eyes, my shoulders; envelop me in a radiating blanket of warmth. Before Wesley revealed the truths behind life's mysteries, that veil was my comfort. I was prepared to spend my days peacefully cocooned inside its ignorance.

Peace - that is what I had then. I believe. Now, though, I am not sure if I have ever known peace. I know I will never have it again. The blood robs you of peace... among other things.

I long for naivety, to return to a time when I was not intimate with the true evils lurking in this world. When I was not this vile creature watching eternity unravel before my eyes.

I long for that veil to slip over my eyes in a splendid blanket of warmth. I long to retreat into ignorance and pretend there is still some mystery in life. This is a foolish fantasy, though; one that I know can never be. I ache for that mystery, though. I ache because I remember feeling that peace, having had it, having held it in my hands and embracing it securely to me.

In a desperate search for what I had lost, I traveled.

Initially, I was unsure of my destination. I packed a bag and left behind everything else in the house for Aksel and Evelyn. With only a small satchel of clothing and jewelry, I took to the stars and let my heart guide me.

I clenched my eyes tightly and tuned my ears in to the cadence of humanity. Only then did I notice the smooth scratching of a painter's brush stroking against plaster. In the distance, I could hear the painter sigh, pausing to curse the night air in his rich Italian tongue. Michelangelo's work on the Sistine Chapel had just begun; his artistry barely conceptualized. He was finishing his nightly work, applying the wash to newly dried plaster.

Right next to him was a fresh plot of plaster drying, awaiting the master's brush in the morning.

He was finishing work on the Creation panel; the iconic image of God and Adam, their naked forms stretched on downy clouds, their fingertips nearly touching. The words from long forgotten sermons played in my mind as I beheld Michelangelo's God, his outstretched fingertip. "Let us make man in our own image... God blessed them."

Bathed in incandescent candlelight, Michelangelo's images – on the walls, the ceilings - danced with life. They howled, "Remember us? Remember your oath?" I did not want to listen to the angelic beauties wavering overhead and beside me, swathing me in splendor.

Despite the brilliant wash of color, these surreal forms cast shadows that encircled me in an almost comforting nightmare; sadness grew in the pit of my stomach. Cherubs, heavenly scenes - this represented a life lost to me forever – a life stolen. Gazing at those painted scenes, at half-finished sections with visible stroke marks from the maestro's brush, I wept.

Then I heard a voice trail in the distance, and the pungency of frankincense fluttering on the stale breeze. I left the master to his work and drifted toward the lingering wisps, the tendrils snaking through the marbled halls to seek solace in the cool Mediterranean air. The phantom vines wrapped about me, luring me from building to building under a splendid canopy of fading starlight. The moon, full in the sky, an ever-present orb – an unchanging brilliance – lit my way.

I saw him then, Pope Julius II, knelt at an altar of golden opulence, his head bowed. I remained near the archway, watching him. He wore an undyed cassock, the rough browns matching his blemished stockings. His nightcap slipped with the breeze, allowing a patch of straggling white hair to escape. They matched his beard, stained red from dinner wine.

My eyes beheld the aged man clutching a rosary, reciting Latin. Oh, what would I have not given to be in this situation in my former life? Now, though, I was taking chances I should not. And drudging up feelings – and memories – that are better left buried.

Prayers. Incantations. They were of no benefit to me, so I turned my back to him. I slipped between two buildings – outside of the candlelight's reach – and slumped against the smooth brick. My feet emerged first, then my head, as I looked back at the altar. He remained, his knees creaking as he stood. He turned as I began to ascend, my body moving higher. I was above the altar before the summoned guards arrived.

The three men stared into the sky, shouting vehemently, and rapidly diminished as I rose.

I could have let them catch me – for a second, I had pondered the thought. What if I had let them end the pain and anguish, the isolation. Yet, instinct prevailed. Instinct was not ready for eternity to end.

From a distance, I watched them scurry in a panic, my vampiric existence hanging as a heavy shroud around my body. Leaving Rome was a priority.

I spent twenty years in Italy, but not once did I again venture near St. Peter's city.

The Renaissance, the rebirth of thought and art, of life and discovery: this was the moment to be in Italy! Artistry saturated Florentine society, and became the hub of Renaissance life. Nightly, I flocked to the city, as did anyone else who desired beauty.

Painters sprinkled their magnificence on the city's landscape, dripping magnetic lapis blue and earthy ochre with every brush stroke. Soon after, a sea of color consumed Italy. The Renaissance had spread and the country could not contain the beauty within an artist's soul, or the deepness of the philosopher's mind. The masters left trails of paint drops, like breadcrumbs, weaving throughout the country. While their bodies now wither to dust, their works live eternal in a country of stone and paint.

Titian's *Assumption of the Virgin*. Botticelli *The Birth of Venus*. Leonardo da Vinci immortal *Mona Lisa*.

These mortal men with celestial talents left their imprints on Italy.

On the world.

On time.

My eyes witnessed sculptors working by candlelight, painters scrutinizing masterpieces, wealthy patrons squelching creativity. These artists were men I spoke and danced with at court, and befriended. Their works – hanging now in pretentious museums, guarded by laser grids and rental cops – are snapshots and reminders.

History is rich with the blood of great men and women, many of whom I have known. Napoleon, Beethoven, and Mozart - their genius blood swims in my veins. Their thoughts, feelings, love - these I carry with me, for eternity. The price for this gift is unforgivable. The weight alone is so cumbersome that a mere mortal would turn to dust from its weight.

Twenty years to a mortal may feel like a lifetime, but it was a blip to me. And even though I adored Italian discovery, it was necessary to keep moving. I had exhausted Italy's libraries, not a volume or scroll left unread. Its scholars and philosophers, I had befriended. I could learn no more.

More brilliant minds and elaborate works would come. After all, this was only the beginning. What began in the Renaissance – the innovations, the art— has never slowed. Science, literature, man's quest for immortality, has evolved on a miraculous and splendid path. As a witness, I have been here for the journey. Each century has been a movie playing live before my eyes, in a wash of crimson-tinted Technicolor.

I enjoyed the movie that played in live motion before my eyes.

I left the temperate Mediterranean villas for the frozen north of Russia. Fate lured me as it had attracted me to Italy twenty years before. In Russia, there was a sense of peace, of home. This was a nearly foreign feeling, as it had been ages since I truly felt I belonged – even in Budapest.

I was a vagabond at first, roaming for three years. I hopped cities searching for permanency, but finding no comfort. Then, in 1528, I found Tver.

The city, itself, was of no particular importance— its buildings were superb, and its people fair. However, what captivated me was the resonance of a solitary heartbeat. It was strong and pure. It was righteous, yet not prideful. It reverberated off the buildings during my nightly walks through the city.

It called to me. Those heartbeats lead me to its source, just as those smoky vines led me to the Pope in Rome.

My first sights of him were glimpses: wisps of his jet-black hair swinging past his dancing partner, or the glistening of the garnets from an ornate dragon clip that held a chunk of fine hair in a bundle, tightly bound behind his head. His smile appeared playful behind a noble and stately chin, squarely set against his jaw. But, one could tell, nevertheless, that his words – when spoken, were gentle and yielding as they slipped perfectly into their mistresses' waiting ears. I watched, half the evening, from the outskirts of the ballroom, as I circulated through the crowd.

It was a Grand Ball in honor of the Prince's birthday.

I do not know what enticed me, what possessed my eyes to stalk his every move no matter where he danced or walked. I was under a spell and had no choice but to watch.

Then the hunter became prey as his ebony eyes met mine from across the crowded hall. As he bowed his head, a curious smile crept on lips. My feet were fixed to the floor, my arms frozen to my side, until he walked from my sight.

His heartbeat pulsed within my skull, pushing aside the suffocating conversations and music. The room dizzied as it grew louder, faces blurred, lights dimmed. I lowered my head and turned to leave, trying to conceal myself in the crowd. Bodies pushed against me as the music swelled and the mead flowed, the smell of human sweat and blood surrounding me.

I had not gotten far when a black boot stepped into my path. That black boot belonged to an ash gray, satin pant; and that satin pant belonged to a dusky uniform dress coat with rich Russian embroidery gracing the lapel. That lapel, that richly Russian, embroidered lapel of such noble distinction, belonged to him and his smoky eyes. The heartbeat was in front of me now, not three inches away; and for the first time in centuries, someone had managed to surprise *me*.

"May I introduce myself?" he said, bowing.

"I already know who are, sir" I curtsied in reverence. "You are Prince Viktor Vladislous, and today is the celebration of your birth."

"You are correct, and you are, my Lady?"

"I, your Highness, am Bree of Trondheim," I replied, the hum of heartbeat distracting me.

"Bree of Trondheim, I was told of your coming to Tver. You have traveled far from home, and not everyone at court is eager to host your presence tonight."

"I hold no diplomatic functionalities, Prince Vladislous. I am merely a traveler, an explorer."

"You are a woman!" he jested. "A woman cannot explore."

"Yes, my prince, she can."

"Can she dance too, then?" he asked.

"I beg your pardon, your highness?"

"Will you dance with me?" he asked. "It is my birthday. And, after all," he winked, grabbing my hand, "if you say no, I can have you thrown in the dungeon."

He led me onto the dance floor. As the violins began their crescendo, he embraced me, taking me tightly into him. The tempo swelled and I closed my eyes; and as the violins sautilléd, we danced.

Somehow, he had bewitched me. His captivating eyes teased me; his heartbeat, pulsating against my skin, rendered me useless. The dance was a momentary reprieve from my melancholy.

We had danced together the rest of the evening, with me feeling the jealous eyes of every eligible woman in the ballroom glaring at us. Yet as the hours passed, the night grew older and the morning threatened to approach. Attendance waned, but the musicians played on. I slipped away while Viktor fetched a servant to prepare me bedchambers.

Leaving him was out of necessity. For if I could have, I would have stayed to greet the dawn, hand in hand. He would have needed to force me from his side, I feared; and this concerned me. His influence over me concerned me.

Once he had faded from view, I left the ballroom, slipping into the main hall. Down the main steps I flew. Past the waiting carriages, come to collect their wealthy patrons. Past the torch lit path lining the main steps. There was a forested path in the distance, and I quickened my steps heading for it when I heard footsteps behind me.

He was panting by the time I turned and stopped.

"You were just going to leave, then?" he asked.

"I am sorry, but I have to go."

"Where – into the woods? Come, let me fetch you a carriage if you will not accept my invitation of hospitality."

"Really, you must not bother. There is somewhere urgent I must be," I explained.

"Will you return to court?" he asked.

"Perhaps," I said, walking in the direction of the carriages. He followed.

Viktor took my hand and drew me into an embrace. His hearts tympanic rhythm tapped steadily in my head as the moonlight caught his ebony eyes. They shimmered down at me as girls gathered on the steps to snicker. "Perhaps, I should find you?" he whispered.

"You will see me again at court," I rushed. "I promise."

I wiggled from his embrace and ran toward the hovel of carriages. The drunk and exhausted littered the congested carriage lines as the ball wore down, the morning hour creeping upon us. I slipped into an open carriage, escaping him and the waiting sun, watching as he held witness to my departure.

Three nights passed before I returned. Those were three nights of agony, spent pacing urine-caked streets. Each shadowy passage, noisy tavern, child's boisterous laugh, echoed his heartbeat. There was not a safe place in Tver for me to escape its thunderclap song. It was constant and maddening and beautiful.

Nothing, not even the hustle of the night market could drown out its assuredness. So, I found myself seeking solace in familiarity, in custom.

The hay-strewn pews did little to warm the chilled, splintered wood. And I could hear the scuttle of vermin on the mud-laden stone floors. The dimly lit altar, with its gilded idols, hid the filth keeping warm on the chapel's floor.

There was a haunting stillness in between creaturely movements – an unsettling quiet. I sat transfixed on the images of Russian saints, martyrs in a war I no longer fought. Their anguished faces, lined in melted gold and crushed jewels, shimmered in the candlelight. A subtleness of linseed and lavender clung to the air, kissing my skin as I sat there.

Distracting as they were, I could still hear that gentle thud calling to me. So on the third night, I resigned to its siren song.

The overcast moon struggled behind a delicate sprinkling of eager rain. The drops trickled from rooftops, rolling into the gutters, onto the streets, their hypnotic pitter-patter luring me forward. The buildings sparkled with what little starlight managed to peak through the clouds.

The city appeared more alive that night, even though most of its people were safely inside their homes;

hidden from the raindrops, hidden from the violent storm that would soon follow.

His *heart* spoke to me. The *blood* spoke to me. They drew me to him, to the palace.

His balcony was grand and furnished, but unused that night. Instead, the doors were opened and the ruby curtains closed. They were all that separated me now from him, from his heartbeat. From his blood. Its palatable aroma of succulent, metallic sweetness seduced my mind.

If I was to begin again, though, to fall in love, to be loved, I could not make the same mistakes. I had to reveal to Viktor my true nature. Something about his heartbeat, the way it lured me to him, told me it had to be so.

I drew back the curtain and spied him fireside, lounging. Its unending war-like flames raged their undying evil that he dutifully stoked. And he was completely unaware of my presence; so innocently naive to a world that encroached upon him, threatening his very life. But, I knew it was time to shatter his serenity.

I could have flown away – left Russia that evening. I should have done so. Then, he would have just died with the rest history, a meager player in his own timeline. Would he have known love in his lifetime? Perhaps. But then, if I had never spoken his name whilst out on his balcony, I would have missed out on his endless, passionate affection. And the twins.

And I did speak his name, but softly. It was almost a whisper, for I was terrified that he would hear me and be frightened.

"Prince Vladislous?" I had whispered into the quiet room. He turned, startled, and when he saw me, he jumped back and froze.

"I am not here to hurt you, Viktor."

"How... how did you get in here?" his voice quivered as he spoke. "Guards!" he called.

There was an immediate rustle in the stairwell, followed by a skirmish of metal outside Viktor's door. The guards smacked their leathered fists against the door, shouting for their lord's attention.

"I can do many things," I said as I inched into the room, slowly advancing toward him. "I've barred the door."

I looked toward the fire and with my thoughts, it extinguished. Smoldering ash remained where there was once flickering flames; and nothing was left in the fireplace as evidence of the great fire that once consumed it except for it and a few grayed logs. The display of power made him back into the wall as he tried to retreat from me, to hide.

"I told you, Viktor, I can do many things. Now, call off your guards."

"Sorceress!" he shouted as he stumbled on the corner of a rug.

Regaining his footing, he dodged toward the bed, trying to hide himself behind the crimson velvet and vanilla damask curtains. He kept his glare on me as I lingered near the fireplace.

"Viktor there is no escaping me. I can be on top of you before you can bat an eye, or shout for those blessed guards. If I wanted to hurt you, I would have already done so."

"Then, pray thee, mistress, why have you come if not to kill me? For, I do not know what wicked treachery this is but to me drive mad with fear."

"I promised that I would return. I always keep my promises," I explained.

"Now, before I change my mind and leave this place, call off your guards. And, pray, if you must, that I not give you reason to fear me. For, dear sir, it is not my intent."

"It is a false alarm, all is well," he told the guards through a cracked door. "Return to your posts."

"Come here and sit with me by the fire." Waving my hand over the fireplace, a vibrant array of orange flames licked to life, touching the stones and crackling the near-ash wood. "Come," I said, patting the spot next to me.

"I do not believe you," he replied, as he remained, fixed behind the curtain. "I...I do not even know you."

"We danced, Viktor. You know me well enough," I whispered.

"I fear, somehow, you are better acquainted with myself. This puts me at a grave disadvantage."

"And yet, you feel the connection, do you not?" I turned. He still clung to the fabric, his face now paled with moonlight's glimmer.

"Even as I struggle you now, I cannot deny I'm pulled to you," he replied; his words catching a wind and trailing off the balcony, softening as the sentence lingered between us.

"Then you should not fear me, nor fear your feelings for me."

"But I do fear your sorcery, duchess."

As promised, before he could blink, I was on top of him. I threw his body upon the bed and lay against it, his heart now beating furiously. His eyes stared into mine wildly. His breath was fire upon my face as I hovered over him. His dressing gown opened; his chiseled chest was nothing but a spot for me to rest my palm against as I pressed bore down to restrain him. My strength was far greater than his was, and when he realized this, he conceded. His mind was plagued with thoughts of death, thoughts of escape, thoughts so jumbled that I blocked them from my own.

"I could kill you this minute, Viktor. I could have killed you when I came here without you even knowing it was me," I confessed. "But I do not wish you death, Viktor; so rid those images, those thoughts from your mind this instant. We will have no more of that, do you understand? No more unrest and unhappiness. Loneliness."

With him still quivering beneath me, I bent my head and caressed his naked chest. His heart pulsated, its cadence quickening as my caresses advanced their march up his neck, then to his chin.

When I reached his ear lobe, he whispered, "You are not going to kill me?"

"No," I replied, softly. I glided him from the bed; his legs jelly twigs and his arms mere globs of putty in my own. "I promise, Viktor; I will not, ever, take your life."

"Why?" he asked; but I was not sure how to answer.

In that moment – as his blood intoxicated me – his blood that I could taste on the tip of my tongue; that bled in his sweat; that mingled on my lips with each delicate kiss, I too wondered why I spared his life.

"Why do you not just kill me? I know what you are now."

"No, you do not."

I released him, and let him watch me as I sauntered over to the chair and sat down nearest to the fire. The flames, the orange and red beacons calling to me, they felt inviting as if I could jump right in, right then, and end this facade; this joke of an eternity. But, in the end, not even that would have killed me. In time, I would have healed; and I would become jaded by the pain.

"Then what are you if not a sorceress, who can appear on a man's balcony in the dead of night?" he asked. "You are not a ghost; not a figment of my imagination either. I know you are real. I have felt you – with these two hands; with these lips."

"You would not understand," I explained. "You would be afraid of the truth."

"I am already afraid of you, how much harm can the truth do?" he replied. "Why did you come here tonight if you are someone, or something so frightening that you cannot reveal your nature?"

"I am lonely," I told him, and then he rose from the bed but stayed near it, holding onto the bedpost.

"Everyone gets lonely, Bree, but not everyone can scale a tower wall and breathe fire to life with the wave of her hand." He clutched the bed curtain, tightly, winding it in his fist. "Nor, can they press a man twice their size – at least – down with impressive force, rendering him immobile."

He loosened his grip on the bed curtain as he took rest on the edge of the bed.

"And, while your frighten me, and I realize my guards are within an ear shot, awaiting my command – you surprise me. You intrigue me."

"I did not scale your tower wall, Viktor," I commented.

"Excuse me?" came his reply, as if he half heard me.

"I flew."

"You flew?" he asked, glaring now, directly at me. "From the ground to my balcony, you flew? Like a bird?"

"Yes, Viktor," I replied, watching the glaze of bewilderment creep across his face.

"Then you *are* a sorceress," he remarked; his words tinged with sadness and awe. And laced heavily with a brewing undercurrent of terror.

"No," I assured him. "I am no such thing. No such thing exist, I can assure you that."

"Then, before I call my guards," he demanded, "What are you?"

But, before he could blink; before he could close his eyes; before he could turn around, I was in front of him.

Before he could protest; before he could cry; before he could fight, I had a hold of him. Before he could grasp onto something; before he could dig his heels into the rug; before he could claw at me in retaliation, I had him in mid-air. Before he could blink... before he could breathe... before he could say a prayer... his blood was in me.

TEN

His body lay upon the bed; my lips, stained with his blood, had more life in them than his body. He lay motionless, gently cushioned by a pillow, as I untied the bed curtains and watched as they fell softly around the bed, concealing my sins.

Not once did I take my eyes from the slumped hulk of man as I inched to the fireplace, reclaiming my spot on the worn chair. Heavily, my body sunk into the dust trap, and I licked the remnants of his sweet blood from my lower lip. There had been just one drop, one small and insignificant drop from when I withdrew, that escaped my wanting mouth.

I sat watching him sleep, watching his body walk a thin tightrope between life and death. I had brought him to the brink, just a few more sips and his precious heart would have stopped.

That wondrous chorus of throbbing heart that had first attracted me now struggled to sing under the strain of its weakened blood supply; and slowly faded to a gentle tapping beneath his clammy skin. It was this slowing that made me stop. His luscious nectar still clung to my lips, though, and now all I could do was stare at him lying helpless. He had come close to death that night, and I had come close to taking him there.

I had come dangerously close to breaking my promise.

His flesh glistened in the candlelight. This was not the first time I had brought a body close to its end. It would surely not be my last time, either.

I sat for hours in that chair next to the fire, with his blood swimming in my body, warming me, as he slept. I was fixed to that spot, and my eyes to his face, watching for any manifestations of movement, but none came. His forehead, bathed in a moist covering of dew, and lips were pale, but I could still hear his heart beating. Even if it was but a faint whisper, it was something to embrace.

Morning threatened its approach, forcing me to leave his side. I caressed his ashen lips and left the room the same way I had come.

For two weeks, I wandered the streets of Tver, carefully avoiding the castle. News of the Prince's strange illness spread, but with the passing days, he rebounded and gained his strength.

I knew it best to avoid the prince, avoid the castle grounds. I made plans to leave the city, but when time came, I was unable to leave. As he regained strength, his heartbeat sang to me, beckoning me through the dingy alleyways, and past crowded taverns. It begged me to be near, to love it. To care for it.

The busy streets, I used for concealment. I hid in the loud noises, the constant onslaught of a hundred thoughts channeling into my mind as I resigned, allowing them to wash over me in a tidal wave of reality.

These noises did nothing to drown out that unceasing vibration, though. It haunted me, terrorized me.

His blood, lying stagnant in my preternatural veins, drew me to him as a flame attracts the moth.

It was at the wedding of his sixteen-year-old sister Natalia where I would return to him. The prince, himself, was pushing a scandalous thirty-five years of age and unmarried. It was on the eve of his betrothal – at the age of nineteen – when his fiancé perished in a carriage accident while traveling to him. After that, Viktor refused marriage contracts from local and foreign courts.

Unless Viktor married and bore a son, the principality's future fell on Natalia's shoulders. And it was a burden he eagerly relinquished that night as he surveyed the crowd.

Russian dignitaries swarmed Natalia's wedding feast. Viktor sat to the right of his mother, a proud woman who was long in her years. In three months, she would die of pneumonia. Her gray hair pulled back, a crown of pearls and ruby jewels adorning the silver circlet resting atop her head. The candlelight kissed jewels accentuated the woman's piercing cobalt eyes. Their brilliance had not dulled through the years of childbirth and worry. Her wrinkled hands had seen seventy winters and two children buried in the frozen Russian soil, yet they persevered to hold a delicate wine goblet that evening.

Her daughter, Viktor's younger sister, was a delicate chalice of femininity reflecting in her mother's eyes. Natalia's lengthy, silk charcoal locks hung freely in the back, while tiny strands of crystal beads interlaced with two thin braids extending from her temples, kissing each other in a tight bundle at the back of her head. They were bound— eternally, it seemed— with a diamond clasp.

Viktor's father had died five years before during a hunt, but he would have been proud of his daughter's beauty in that moment as her dress shimmered, and her hair sparkled in the candlelight.

As I scanned the room watching, the drama unfolded before me: humanity rejoicing the bonding of two, not out of love though, but necessity. And, I sensed a slight shimmer to the air that was not reflecting from Natalia's hair.

Again, almost as soon the shimmer cleared, it began again. The room wavered before me. Someone, or something, projected this mirage into my mind, making its vaporous glow rapidly disappear. Then it came again: a subtle glittering suspending itself in mid-air, gingerly dissipating the more I concentrated on it. I followed this allusion with my eyes trying to find its source, but was unable to; that is when I caught the lingering of a familiar musty scent, so subtle that I almost overlooked it.

From across the room, near a curtain leading onto a balcony, my eyes spied him leaning against the wall. At first, I thought I was mistaken; but when he smiled, I knew it was he.

He nodded toward the curtain and then slipped behind it and out of my view. Unsure whether Viktor had noticed me, I remained close to the wall, concealed in the wedding crowd. Approaching the balcony, I drew the curtain back, and could no longer conceal the rush of feelings breaking through my calm. I ran to him, grabbing him about the shoulders, pulling him close.

"I was beginning to wonder if I would ever see you again," I whispered.

"And I you," he replied. "I have missed you."

"I have missed you," I told him, leaning away and releasing him. "I could have used you around when I have managed to make a mess of things. You always came in handy for that."

"Oh, I held you back; you needed to find your own way."

"That I have, Wesley," I replied. "That I have. But how did you ever find me?"

"It is a long story; too private for this balcony," he explained. "I have been looking for you for a long time. It was in a nearby town, not a week ago, that I heard about Prince Vladislous' illness."

"You knew it was me?" I asked.

"The symptoms sounded familiar. My maker made the same mistake with me before returning the next night and delivering me over," he continued. "So... I went to this Prince. As he slept, or so I thought - he was in a feverish stupor. I ascended and crept in from the balcony. As the moonlight flooded the room, he sat up in the bed and called out for you. I stood there watching him, not believing his words. Then I watched as he recovered. I knew that it was only a matter of time before you would return for him."

"I almost did not," I confessed. "I almost could not."

"What are you doing with him, this mortal?"

"I honestly do not know, Wesley," I admitted, more to myself than to him. "I drank from him, nearly to the point of death, when I had promised myself I would not. Yet, his blood has invaded my body, my mind; like a plague, it has consumed me and now he is an obsession."

"Does he know what you are?" he asked.

"I am not sure how much he remembers," I answered. "I have stayed away since that night."

"Perhaps, you are afraid to see him," he noted. "I think you are afraid he will not fear you; that he will love you, that he may even want to be turned." Wesley grabbed at my turned-up face, but I moved away.

"Living as long as we have has its disadvantages, Wesley," I explained. "You get tired -tired of being alone, tired of watching time race by in this toxic rainbow of color that if you touch it, just briefly, it may just burn you."

"It is so vivid, that... But, you also get tired of losing the ones you love, seeing them waste away and slip into shadow – to where you will never be able to reach them. Everything around you – buildings, people – they erode, turn to dust, while you, you remain a constant force, indestructible, like the Heavens. And, you say that I may be afraid to love someone? Cannot you see why? This is no existence to bring anyone else into."

"What Hell are you existing in, dear sister?" he implored. "What have you seen, done, since we parted for you to feel this way? You still cannot see the beauty in eternity, Bree," he replied.

"What beauty lies there in death, Wesley?" I asked as I left him, moved the curtain, and re-entered the ballroom.

The wedding party was still seated and feasting, and their guests were still partaking in the festivities as I casually tried to escape along one of the sidewalls. There was little room to maneuver given my cumbersome bustle and the elaborate table arrangements to accommodate the plentitude of wedding guests in attendance. Wesley followed closely behind, and, catching up with my quickened steps as I neared the main doorway, he clutched my hand.

"Even death is beautiful, Bree," he replied. "When you embrace your nature, you can see the magnificence in both life and death. You should give yourself a chance to feel something other than the bitter cold of loneliness."

"I have become accustomed to this feeling, to being alone. There is no need to embrace anything or anyone. I am surviving just as I am," I told him as I pulled away, slipping through the crowded doorway.

He continued to follow me through the Great Hall and down the steps, and still out into the courtyard where only the horse-drawn carriages and the stars were witness to our conversation.

"Eternity, Bree, you should not spend it denying yourself the comforts of love, or the solace of knowing who you really are. You are bound to go mad."

He came toward me as only a brother would, gently and securely, and embraced me. He sensed my pain, my turmoil. He had been there for me since I twisted my ankle running through our neighbor's field - I had been but a wee child then- to when they took our father's plague stricken body from the house. His advice never came without love and sincerity.

"Give him a chance to share this with you," he urged.

"Wesley, I shared eternity once before, and I lost the man I loved in the process," I explained, "I could never do that again."

Wesley paused and held me closer. "And what will become of him then, of this prince of yours?" he asked.

"I will leave him, leave Russia. It is best that he forgets me."

"Do I not get a choice, then?" A familiar voice snuck through the darkness behind me. I turned to face Viktor, eye-to-eye. "I see you have taken another lover; my wooing was for naught."

"This man is not my lover."

"My Lady, I am not blind." He locked his eyes upon my own, yet I sensed he was fully aware of Wesley's movements. His pursed lips and tense arms, affixed to his side as a toy soldier paused in mid march, conveyed the man's inner turmoil.

"Perhaps my illness, or your sorcery, has weakened my eyesight, but from my dining table I saw you emerge from the balcony and he pursue you. It took me some time, yet I did manage to worm my way through the crowd only to find the two of you in an embrace!"

"Viktor," I tried to explain.

"And after the night we had, my mistress, even if you are a heathen." He shook his head and began walking away. I started to yell after him – to ask him to stop – but I could not. I needed to ask him what he remembered about that evening, but when my lips parted, I found my voice mute. Then Wesley glanced at his feet, whispering, "He remembers…everything."

Everything, I thought. That night once again washed over me as I watched Viktor walk away: the bed curtains concealing his face, his ashen lips and clammy skin. These images now haunt the hidden recesses of my psyche. He remembered my coming to him that night, embracing him, forcing his blood into me. He remembered how it felt when his life was draining from him; how it felt when his heart struggled to pump, and his mind spoke with angels.

And he was walking away, this man who knew too much.

I was allowing him to go, as this was for the best.

Then, from out of the corner of my eye, I saw my brother, who always knew when to intervene on my behalf, jog up to Viktor.

"I'm not her lover, Your Highness," he said to the prince.

Viktor stopped, glancing back my way.

"He is not, Viktor," I called out to him. "He is my brother."

"Your brother?" he asked. His eyes wandered between Wesley and me. I gently advanced toward them terrified Viktor would turn the other way in disbelief. Yet, the moment I was sure I had lost him, his solemn lips morphed into a quaint smile.

"My apologies, I have been foolish," Viktor bashfully sighed into the night as he bowed. Wesley gentlemanly returned the gesture.

"No apologies necessary," my brother politely explained. "Now I will take my leave and enjoy what is left of this gorgeous evening."

With this, Wesley set off for town. His footsteps were rough as they ground into the walk's loose pebbles; but when he had submerged into the shadow, only I could detect the faint sound of his ascent.

"What are you?" Viktor bluntly asked.

"You should not ask questions you do not want the answers to, Viktor."

"The other night, in my room, something happened. I felt pain, and death, and... my heart," he struggled to explain as he clutched at his chest, reassuring himself that his heart beat stayed strong and steady.

"You almost died," I told him. His cheeks took on a sudden ghastly shadow as the blood drained from them.

"What?"

"I almost killed you."

"How?"

"The vampire's kiss."

His body stiffened; his heart raced.

"You have heard the tales, the myths. The vampire will come in the night. It will drink your blood; steal your soul."

"But the vampire is a demon, Bree, and legend" he said, still guarded - still uneasy. "And you look nothing like either."

"No, you are right, I'm not a demon, nor am I a legend" I told him. "I am a nightmare. I haunt and stalk, and destroy. And nothing I touch is ever the same again."

"I do not believe any of this," he said. "You are telling a farce, I am sure of it!"

"If it helps you to believe that, then believe what you must. But, for your safety and for my sanity, please just stay away. I cannot go down this path again."

With that, I left him in the courtyard. I walked to my carriage, entered, and rode off without looking back. The hollow pit inside where my heart should have been still felt an ache, a dull sickness where his blood had been. I could still hear his heart beating, feel his eyes watching the carriage, but I pressed on. The song his heart sang to me – its intoxicating melody – would have to still itself, or I would leave Russia.

The next evening, I shut myself in out of desperation. I struggled to remove the rhythmic sound of his heartbeat from my mind. I immersed myself in Anselm of Canterbury's philosophies, but even that was not enough to distract my thoughts for long.

Staring into the fire, watching the flames lick at the bricks, and listening to the wood crackle, was driving me mad.

I found no solace in the garden either; only the moonlight casting its dusty glow over the sleeping plants as they kept me company, my haunting obsession taunting my clouded mind. I never get to experience its vibrant beauty, the arrays of color, touched by sunlight; and I have forgotten what flowers look like in the daytime – stretched out, ready to bathe in the sun's glow, ready to grow, to live. Now I only watch them sleep; forever cursed to watch them sleep, forever cursed to view life beneath the pale fog of moonlight as my guide, and casually forget the sun-kissed glories that I am missing. I fear the day I can no longer remember the warm glow of sunlight.

However, the moonlight is passionate, and the night air calm and the waters still flowed into the marble fountain at the center of the garden; and, being drawn to it, I went over and sat at its base. My fingers playfully tickled at the surface as droplets from the tier above fell onto my hand. The water was cool and dark with a silver tinge from the moonlight. That is when I heard footsteps sneaking onto the garden gravel.

"The stars are hidden tonight," he remarked.

"But the moon is full," I replied.

"It is always there shining on us, is it not?" I stood, finding him at the edge of the garden in a cobalt suit, his hair impeccable, as always. I motioned toward a wrought-iron bench near the fountain. A patch of ivy had coiled itself around the structure's arms and legs, binding it to the plant, concealing the bench.

"I have much to share, Bree," Wesley said, taking my hand. "So much I must tell you, but, to be honest, that I fear sharing."

"Wesley, what is it? Why have you sought me out after all this time apart?"

"After you left, I made another. I needed a companion," he began. "Her name had been Bethany. She was a servant in Paris. Remember Paris?"

"Yes," I replied. We spent an entire winter in Paris during our youth because our mother wanted us to experience France while we learned French.

"The man who owned her, he was cruel, Bree. He did not just beat her; he raped her. He raped all of female servants, and cruelly beat both the men and women. He was so vile, such a putrid excuse of humanity. I would watch her at night- watch her serve him, bathe him, but it did not stop there. She was his best servant, never made a mistake, yet he just beat her senseless."

"One evening," he continued, "I found myself at his estate and he bragged to everyone at the event about how he treated her, how he tied her up... And, I watched her filling his goblet - the sadness in her eyes, that level of dejection, it was more than I can handle, Bree. I could not allow it to continue."

"Why did you not just kill him?" I asked.

"I did," he replied. "Later that night, once the party had dispersed, I returned and killed him."

"Why did you not leave it at that?"

"She saw me. That always complicates matters," he half-chuckled. "I made her that night, but she could not handle the reality of what she had become. She went mad and lasted almost a year before going into the sun. I found her ashes next to an opened window in our house, no note. At least you left a note before you left." He smiled. "But, you know, it was for the best. Some just cannot handle it. Some were not meant to be turned."

"I completely understand you," I replied.

"That is when I began searching for you," he said. "But..."

"Wesley?"

"I did not know where you had gone, Bree," he began.

He pulled his hand away and stood from the bench. His feet scratched at the pebbles as he walked to the fountain, his fingers skimming the water. He stared into the water as if he were searching it for something, then he turned to me.

"You were harder to search for than a grain of rice in a pail of sand!"

"Wesley, where did you go?" I asked.

"I... I went to the convent."

"You should have never gone there!" I declared. "What did you do to them?"

"Nothing, I promise." He insisted. "When I arrived there was such a cloud of death over the place, so heavy that it called to me. I searched the minds, but I did not find you, not even a thought. Then I got to one, one whose heart was failing. She was calling out to you from her death bed, calling out for help passing over."

"Calling to me?"

"She kept screaming 'I want Bree. Get me Bree. She has flown into the world... get me my angel, Bree,'" he replied. "I was shocked to hear your name, so clear after all those years. Of course, no one knew who Bree was. They thought she was seeing angels, beginning to cross over. Someone was constantly with her, right up until she died. So, I could not safely visit her, question her."

"Who was she?" I asked, already knowing the answer.

"They called her Sr. Veronica..." but I interrupted him.

"Her name was Elizabeth," I stated. "How did her life end?"

"It was serene, quiet.. in the end."

"In the end?"

He shut his eyes.

"You do not need to know this. It is not going to bring her back."

"Either tell me or go away right now, because you have already told me too much for it to hurt," I said, tears misting my eyes.

"Her death was preceded by violent attacks," he reluctantly began. "It began with seizures. Then her eyes failed. She stabilized, and stayed this way for months, but then she suffered from convulsions. A priest sent for, to bless her room, but this did not help. As her convulsions increased, her health grew weaker." He paused and his voice grew softer.

"But the night I came, the night she passed, that night was peaceful. There were no convulsion, no seizures. Her ears heard perfectly, but she was calling for you. She was reaching into the dark void trying to find you."

"She died," I said aloud, making it real.

"Yes, she died calling for you, my sweet sister."

"What did she say?" I asked. "I... I need to know. Tell me what she said."

"She told the women gathered at her bedside that they needed seek you out, but they did not know who you were. One of them suggested you were an angel, another said you were a deceased friend or relative. That is when," he paused. "That is when she said you were not there."

"What do you mean I was not there?" I asked.

"Bree, you do not need to know this. There is only pain in these words!" he urged, but I could not listen to his warning.

"She said her angels were there for her, all over the room, faces she knew, faces she loved, but that you were not there. And she knew you should have been there..." He would have continued but I cut him off.

"Just stop. Please."

I left the bench and walked through the garden, opened the doors to the main room and entered. My plush, cranberry armchair sat in front of the fire with the volume of Anselm of Canterbury's philosophies lingering on the seat. I snatched up the dusty tome and tossed it onto the floor where it made a moist thud on the oak boards.

"You do not remember her, do you?" I said to him through my tears.

He had followed me and stood behind at the door. The fire was raging, its crimson claws grasping at the orange sparks escaping the consuming warmth of the fireplace.

"Should I?"

"We all grew up together," I said. "As children, we would spend our summers together. You knew her brother Phillip."

"Phillip. The child who ate bugs?" he asked.

"That would be him."

"Whatever happened to him?"

"The plague. They sent Elizabeth to the convent as father had sent me. She ended up dying in the end anyway, just like everything else in this world. It all eventually dies, does it not?"

He sighed. "Yes."

"Except us," I replied. "We are doomed to stand back and watch them all fade into nothingness until we forget they even existed."

"Humans die, Bree. We survive; it is what we do. Call it a curse, call it a gift, call it whatever you wish, but you have to move on," he told me. "You must move on; so do they."

I could not move on, though. I let the fire slowly die out until it was nothing more than smoldering embers, and when the first rays of dawn threatened to approach, then finally did I take to my room. Wesley was still in the house somewhere, long since retired. I took comfort knowing he was there as I slipped away from reality.

The nights stretched on into a seeming blur of eternal nothingness, a black void eating into my mind, and all I could focus on was her face and all the faces of those I had lost through the years; the faces time had robbed from me. Their heartbeats were drums echoing in my ears, tiny saccadic glimpses of ghosts from a past, from several pasts, that I could no longer visit.

They were all lost to me, and I wept for them, for her. I had become a creature of habit, a creature of force. I had shed so much of my humanity that I had forgotten the most fragile thing about mortals: They are mortal and they die. Just as the seasons change, as the wind grows colder in autumn and the leaves turn brown and fall from the trees, they die. Still, her death shook me. Her death changed me.

If it had not been for Wesley, I would have walked into the sun, ending it all. What had I become but a monster? Did she even know as she laid there dying, did she know what she called out to? She thought me an angel, but I was far from it. And I did not even know what I was or where I belonged. I was an abomination that should not exist, but I could not do it. He would not allow me. He held me back. He saved me.

For months, I hid from the world. I watched the flames dance before me in the fireplace and shadows creep along the walls, night after endless night. I detested my nature, the way I had to feed to live and I then refused to feed. Wesley eventually brought me victims when I got so weak I could not hunt, but I still lived without killing. I vowed to never take a human life. They were too precious, I told him.

Viktor came to me three times and Wesley sent him away. At first, I was too distraught to see him. The blood tears stained my face nightly. Then the second time he came, I barely had the energy to sit up from lack of feeding. The third time he came, I told Wesley to tell him I was dead, but he refused. Instead, he told him I had found another lover.

I may not have had the energy to feed on my own, but I could read Viktor's thoughts. He knew I had not found another love. He had been watching my home. He knew I had not left during the day or during the night. No one had seen me in months. He was worried his sorceress, his vampire, had left him.

And I had.

ELEVEN

There she was, Sister Veronica, in her solemn black and white, her veil loosely slipping from that tender spot just above her brow. She pinned it to her wimple every morning, but by noon, it would begin to slip. She would struggle with it, but to no avail. Her feet or her hands would catch on the fabric and pull it askew.

The habit hung on her, as did her scapula, the fabric becoming an obsidian tent cocooning her frail features within. And that is how everyone but I saw her – Sister Veronica, a clumsy little girl who did not fit in her clothing; a mere child struggling to become a woman. I recalled those summers, those endless warm walks tiptoeing in dewy grasses, reading forbidden poetry, counting the stars, and believing we were impervious to harm.

The more I thought of her, the more real she seemed. There were moments I could reach her, touch her, and even smell her next to me. But, those moments were but fragments from my past.

Those bright sparks shooting from the fireplace, those were her soul escaping this earth. The shadows, as they crept about the house, were her slipping from me. Little reminders of her were everywhere.

The crucifix I had worn in the convent, that I was still wearing the night Wesley came for me, rested in a drawer wrapped in layers of protective cloth all these years.

I kept it there, hidden, so that it would not remind me of her, of them, of that life I once lived. Now I held it in my hands, admiring how it glinted in the fire's light. Its smooth edges worn from time, yet it was resilient and still alluring to me.

The cross was in my lap. That face was staring back at me. I could sense the agony in its eyes, and the rage that consumed the fire before me. The amber glow cast haunting shadows on the figure lying in my lap; it was hypnotic. I snatched the crucifix and held it tightly to my bosom. That life was gone now. And she with it.

"Can you imagine dying?" She had asked one day. We had been sitting on the bank of our pond, avoiding the others and their righteous glares. You get that treatment when you are the youngest, and when you cannot stop laughing when Sr. Claire falls asleep during morning prayers. The day had been hot and lingered on endlessly like so many Augusts before it. But, this had been our last August together.

"I try not to," I replied. "Neither should you."

"I cannot help it."

"What do think it will be like then, dying?" I asked her.

"Oh, it will be peaceful. Nothing like that cursed plague."

She tossed a pebbled into the pond rippling the still waters' surface.

"I hope mine will be peaceful, too," I said.

"You are going to live beyond this place, beyond death," she told me.

"What makes you say that?"

"I have seen it," she said, turning to me, "in a vision."

"You don't have visions."

"I had this one," she said. "You are going to live beyond me, beyond the people here. I cannot even explain it, Bree, but you do. You are timeless."

"No one lives forever," I had whispered, half hoping it was true, that we could live forever.

"No, I guess they do not," she agreed. "It was just a dream after all. But it was such a pleasant dream – living forever."

"Was I still young, or had I grown all old and wrinkly like Sr. Margaret?" We both laughed.

"You were not a day older."

Three weeks later, Wesley came for me. Perhaps she knew all along, in her heart of hearts, that in some magical way, I had found a way to live forever.

If I had known she was calling for me, I would have gone to her. I would have delivered her from all that pain and all that suffering. That is what stung at me now, ate at me like a festering wound refusing to heal - that if I had known, I could have done something for my old friend. Maybe then, I could have found peace.

The touch of his hand lured me back. I would have been lost in the past, tumbling down that endless rabbit hole of memories with her face affixed to the sides, smiling at me, for an eternity had he not awoken me from myself. I would have lingered in nothingness, lost in a vat of turmoil, if it had not been for him pulling me out of the void.

"It has been four months, my sister. That is plenty self-wallowing for one lifetime," he said as he led me from the house one evening and into the moonlit streets of Tver. It was December, and snowing, and I could scarcely believe time had passed so quickly while I hid away from myself in a fog of thoughts and memories.

"December?"

"Yes," he replied to me as he kicked at the gathering snow on the stones below. "And much is changing. Viktor is taking a bride this week."

"What!" The falling snow... his words... they were making my mind ache.

"He is taking a bride, Bree," Wesley explained. "For the crown or for love, I have not ascertained. But he is to wed on the next full moon."

"Why?"

"He is mortal," Wesley chuckled. "That is what mortal men do."

"Wesley, do not belittle me!" I snapped. "Why *now*?"

"Perhaps it is because he thinks you have abandoned him, my sister?" Wesley replied as he turned his gaze toward the east, toward the direction of the castle.

A solitary window on the third floor remained lit. Those were Viktor's private chambers. I would have known that window from any window in Tver for it had haunted my mind for four months.

"Every night, Bree, those fires burn; his candles are not extinguished until dawn. He still has hopes that you will return to him."

"Then I must," I replied.

"And do what?" Wesley asked. "He is to be wed to an Austrian princess. This is a prosperous match for him, and for the royal line. What do you offer? Nothing. Let the world of mortals be. Let this one go. Come with me and let us leave this place."

"I can offer him myself, and that is all anyone can offer another person; mortal or immortal, Wesley. That is going to have to be enough! If you wish to leave, so be it. Farewell. But I cannot leave him."

I left Wesley standing in that darkened street, the crystalline snow glistening on his shoulders. Snow piled on the cobblestones, and people, huddled under layers of clothing, moved about in the slush from one building to the next in the cold night, oblivious to my presence.

I found myself underneath that familiar balcony once again. I could hear the fire crackling and his quill scratching at parchment. His thoughts were mundane and ordinary, so tiresome. There were documents to sign, papers for the upcoming wedding, none of which he wanted to concern himself with. He did not love her. He did not even know her.

It was my face swimming in his thoughts. When he slept, he dreamt of me. This pained him, though – sleeping and seeing my face. The more he dreamed, the more he hoped. And the more he hoped, the more his heart ached.

For nearly an hour, I stood at the base of the castle, concealed in darkness. Perhaps Wesley was right; I should leave the mortal world to itself. In time, he would forget me. In time, my power over him would diminish and he would fall in love with his Austrian bride. And in time, I would forget him, as well.

Then I heard his footsteps on the balcony above me and his voice whisper out into the night, "Bree? Are you out there? Come back to me." That is when his heartbeat began to thunder in my ears again, when I knew he had pulled me in.

I listened as he walked from the balcony, sat down at the desk, and began writing. I ascended to the snow-littered stones, my feet now covering his fresh footprints. Moving the cumbersome curtains aside, I spied him sitting at the maple desk, just inside near the fire. I watched as he worked, quill in hand, his fingers smeared with ink. His heart serenaded me, building into a crescendo as I watched. It needed me. I needed it.

"I am here, Viktor."

He dropped the quill and swiveled in his seat. He looked at me as if seeing a ghost, and then he smiled. He stood, pushing the chair aside, rushing to embrace me.

"Where have you been?" He asked as he held me tightly to him.

"Lost," I told him.

"Lost where?"

"Inside myself," I replied and then caressed his lips. They were hot against my own, hot and soft.

I tried not to crush him as we held each other. His fingers grabbed at my hair, and then skimmed my cheek, his fingernails gently scratching at my skin as he moved to hold my neck in his palm.

"Do your thoughts still trouble you?" he asked, looking into my eyes as he pulled away.

"No, I have made peace with my demons."

I told him of Elizabeth, of how she died. I told him of how I was not there, and how I should have been. I told him of my past, of the convent, of my former life that I sometimes long for. I told him many things, many sacred things, and still when dawn was soon due, and I had to bid him farewell, I did not want to leave. Not even for one night.

"Promise me you will come back," he demanded.

He refused to release my arm; and even though I could have broken free, I did not resist. I let him hold me there, hold me to him in that room, in that moment.

"Tomorrow night," I told him, "and the next night, and the next, and the night after that, I will always return to you. I promise."

"I will hold you to that promise," he whispered into my ear as I kissed his cheek.

His blood smelled familiar with its comforting sweetness, but I fought the temptation. If I ever drank from him again, I would surely kill him. I withdrew from his embrace slightly intoxicated by the rhythmic symphony his heartbeat played.

"I will need you to," I whispered to myself as I slipped away.

Wesley had yet to retire when I returned home. He sat comfortably in front of the fire, book in hand, waiting for me. The candles were nearly all down to their wicks in the spacious sitting room, all except the one nearest to him. The rest of my house was dark.

"How did it go with your prince, sweet sister?"

"I do not think I will ever leave Russia now."

"Ever?"

"Not until he does," I told him as I left the room, extinguishing the candle as I went by, bathing the room in darkness.

He followed behind as we crept up the stairs, not saying a word to each other. We both retired to our rooms. And this is how it went for centuries, him residing with me in Russia.

The next night, as promised, I returned to Viktor. He sat next to the fire, his feet drawn up. His mind was pensive, waiting to see my face. His ebony locks graced the edge of the chair. His eyelids were heavy. But, when he heard me draw back the velvet curtain, the bulky fabric rubbing at the stone floor, he turned in his chair; his eyes wide and alert, a broad smile gracing his eager face.

"You returned to me."

"I promised I would."

I walked over to him as he stood up from his chair.

"I am to be married," he said as I put my arms around his shoulders. My lips caressed the smooth crease of his jaw, and then his stubbly cheek. His breath, warm and thick, caused tingly vibrations cascading down my neck.

"But you do not love her," I whispered as my fingers tousled his hair. The intoxicating aroma of his blood threatened to suffocate me and I struggled to resist it.

"No," he replied, pulling me away. "I believe I love you."

"Then marrying her will not change that," I explained to him. "Do what you must for the crown, for your family," I told him. "And I will be here for you."

His hand slid around the small of my back, and with a gentle tug, my cloak, the titian silk gathered in his grip, tumbled to the ground.

"There is no need to do that," I told him, and he stopped. "I feel no pleasure... in that way."

"Then how can we?" he asked but I interrupted him, placing my finger on his lips.

"The difference between you and me is that heartbeat," I told him.

"Then make it stop," he begged. "Make me what you are. We can be together forever. Then our hearts, they will be the same."

"No," I told him. I kissed the skin above his heart feeling the pulsation in my lips. "I can love you like this, but never like that."

"You say never, but never is a long time, Bree."

"You have no idea how long it is," I said. "I see time differently than you do. This moment, this one moment as we stand here face-to-face, embracing one another, it is so important to you. But this moment is just another moment to me, like so many moments from so many lifetimes that I have lived before and will live again once you are gone."

"Then why did you return to me?" he asked. "Why are you with me now if you cannot love me as I love you?"

"Because I need you," I told him. "I need to love you the way I love. It is different from how a human loves... deeper. In time, you will learn that. But, I need you. I have been so dead inside. So alone. So afraid of myself. But you, you make me feel alive."

"Alive?"

"You make me remember what it is like to be a human, and I... need that," I said as I kissed him. "I never want to forget what it means to be human again."

"Then I will not let you."

I spent that night in his arms, our bodies intertwined and pressed together. The moonlight and the stars fused us, by the vanilla and musk perfumes, by the raging firelight and the shadows that played on the walls. We laid our heads on feather pillows and fine satins, covered in fur. And from that night on, neither of us were lonely again.

Days passed like this, until the time came for his marriage to Mavra, Grand Duchess of Austria, and the nightmare grew into focus. She was but a child, a mere waif of sixteen. She was nothing more than a transaction, an exchange of property between two houses. Her father had sold her to the Russian Royal Court for amnesty. And she knew it. Behind her beauty, those pursed lips and genteel blue eyes, behind that smooth, fair skin, and lusciously combed hair the color of amber and gold fire with a spark of life all its own, was a mind so corrupt in jealousy and scandal that it spoiled what she could have been – a true goddess among men. At first, even Viktor fell under her spell.

"Be wary of her," I had told him on their wedding night. "Her mind is clouded and dark."

They had bedded, producing no heir. I never told him, but she had been relieved.

That is when her veil dropped— after that night, after she had met her marital obligation. That is when she allowed her true colors to shine. Her lies were plenty and a vile poison infecting Tver. She visited the men of the city, various men, and made no secret about it. She did not discriminate with her lovers, and once used, she discarded them as if they were bits of meaningless scrap.

To her, people were to be used, not loved.

Five years passed and the hatred between them grew to be a gaping chasm. In public, they were civil. In private, they were silent enemies.

The men she slept with talked, and people watched her. And the more they talked about her, the more they talked about Viktor. They talked of his weakness, of his inability to control her, but there was no controlling her insanity.

Then one night I came to him, as I did every night, but this night changed everything.

I found him sitting at the edge of the bed, his head resting in his hands. His mind was foggy, clouded and jumbled.

Terrible thoughts invaded my mind. I pushed them away. I had never seen him so consumed with darkness. The room was black, the fire dying. I entered and sat next to him on the bed, placing my arm around him, drawing him closer to me.

The moonlight filtered in from the balcony. His curtains were pulled back, the heavy oak doors to the outside world still open to the inviting July air. The warm staleness of the night clung to him, to his hair, making it stick to his brow; clung to his shirt - the fabric resembling thin, wet plaster against his chest.

"She is with child." His mouth quivered and the corners of his lips turned south as he spoke.

"Congratulations," I told him as I soothingly ran my fingers through his hair. "She will produce for you an heir."

"It is not mine."

"Does it matter?"

"Of course it matters!" he stammered. He stood from the bed, and began to pace about the room, his hands gripping his waist. "This child is not mine! Everyone knows it, Bree. She has made no secret of that fact."

"But it is already done, Viktor, you cannot undo it. You will just have to make the best of this." I went to his side and reached for him, but he shuffled away. He looked distant, vacant, too far to comfort.

"Who is the father?"

"My uncle, the tsar," he replied.

"She is a powerful seductress, Viktor," I said, putting an arm around him, and then leading him to a chair near the fire. "He stood no chance with her. No man does."

A heavy sigh escaped as he eased into the chair. The brown high back swallowed him and he leaned his face into the side trying to ease his worries. The fire had gone out, the room was nearly bathed in darkness save for a torch in the far side of the room by the door. I glanced at the fireplace, filling its dying hearth with a brilliant, caramel rainbow of color. A warm glow permeated the room and yet he did not even flinch.

"I am being punished," he whispered, looking away from me.

"For what?" I asked.

"For loving you," he said, his eyes not turning from the firelight. They held their haunting glare at those amber flames, those burning embers brightly licking at the stones in the fireplace. His voice was eerily calm.

"You will never be punished for loving me," I assured him. "Not now, not ever."

"What do I do about this child?" he asked, looking at me.

"What do I do?" he shouted.

I knelt down at his feet and took his hands in mine. His hands, his mortal hands with their ability to age and change – they were a miracle. I kissed those hands, each one, and held them to my cheek. Time could have paused in that moment and I would have been happy, truly happy. However, it did not. It continued on, as it had to.

"You let her have the baby," I told him. "You accept it as your own. And I will deal with the rumors."

TWELVE

On a Sunday evening, while the heavens poured forth a horrendous rainstorm of tears, Mavra delivered the child.

From birth, the male babe was destined to live an uncomfortable life. His left arm grew shorter than his right, and one eye deadened to the world. There were episodes of sickness, and the child had to be quarantined, unable to experience and grow as a normal child would. It knew little of sunlight or of its mother's touch.

After a brief life of suffering, the Russian dampness finally delivered him to peace. He lingered those last months in bed with pneumonia. The seriousness of his illness finally drew Mavra to visit her son. She had only seen him twice in the two years he had graced the planet.

She was cold-hearted and cruel - even refusing to caress the child as he lay dying. The unrelenting fever shook his body with chills as his lungs filled with fluid. The air slowly choked from his tender body. And all she managed was a "good-bye, Stefan" as she walked from the room. That was the last she saw him alive, and somehow, her soul found peace with this.

Viktor had shed a tear for the child and nothing more. He wept for the insignificant trivialities that escaped everyone else. Viktor wept for the mischief the boy would never make at court, for the girls the child would never kiss, and for the hearts he would never have the chance to break.

All this while Viktor's uncle donned mourning clothes and refused sustenance for three nights before fainting on the palace steps. He and Mavra had continued their affair during the child's illness, visiting in secret. However, after Stefan's death, the two spoke not more than three words to each other. The tsar refused to look at her. She, in turn, barely acknowledged his presence. Not a single person at court failed to take notice of the peculiar behavior.

Through it all, I remained at Viktor's side. I came at night, each night, and slipped away before dawn approached.

I was a rumor around the castle: a shadow that played against the walls. Sometimes the servants would spy me lingering, slipping in and out of the darkness. Yet when they came looking for me, I would have already disappeared.

There were whispered conspiracies; Mavra's ramped up attempts to strike Viktor down, ending the charade that was their marriage. Nightly, I concealed myself, creeping in and out of dusty, forgotten corridors to listen, as Viktor could not. Mavra was devious and promiscuous, but predictable. She always arranged her liaison's in the same fashion: sending a coin to the Master of the Horse, who then sends an able bodied – and pleasing – servant to her chambers. Discretely, of course.

Her assassination attempts, likewise, were just as predictable. Constantly, Mavra fetched a skilled man – well worth their weight in gold, she thought. These attacks, though, were distant, and never coming to fruition. They blundered— killing the wrong man, or missing completely – their arrows catching the wind as they ran.

Then on a humid night a few months after Stefan's death, as the stink of sweat permeated the castle, I heard a malicious murmur: Mavra's siren song seducing its way into another assassination attempt.

Following the acidic sound, I found her in a passageway leading to the dungeon. Dust clung to the stone and thick Belgium tapestries, and one's footprints, if not careful, were traceable. She was there, leaning against a heavy gold and cranberry tapestry. Knights dueled in front of a forest of muted ivory trees – muted by centuries of dust. A thick smudge of thick grey remained on her ebony gown as she edged closer to the cloaked figure at her side.

The person's identity concealed, their face cleverly shrouded by a grey cloak; and what they did not conceal in this fashion they skillfully hid with the surrounding shadows. I watched as the stout and twisted being reached into its cloak and handed her a round, sapphire bottle, which she held to the candle light in her hand and then, quickly tuck it away in her cloak pocket. She left in one direction, and the figure in the other.

I followed her toward the kitchen, where she instructed the cook add the contents of the bottle to Viktor's stew. She then slipped out, casually and carelessly.

From the shadows, I emerged, startling the somber cook from her mid-day lull in duties and retrieved the bottle from her hand.

"What is in there?" she snorted.

Her attentions remained on the stew, as she quickened her pace stirring the ingredients in the pot. The brew of fresh meats and vegetables bubbled in the heated cast iron, the flames reaching the pots lip.

"A tonic to cure the prince's insomnia," I answered her.

"Blessed be," she sighed. She reached around me and gathered a pile of root vegetables from the counter, tossing them into the steaming brew. "Talk says he has not slept well since the lad sailed on to Heaven, my Lady. But, pray forgive me; it's not my place to speak of such things."

"Sleep is only refreshing if you wake up," I whispered to myself.

I flung the bottle into my cloak and exited through the staff entrance, the odor of onions and garlic pursuing me like an eager bloodhound.

This would not be the last attempt on Viktor's life. What had started after Stefan's birth only increased with the child's death. Mavra now hired spies to catch us at night, to murder us while we were together. However, these spies, quiet as they attempted to be, never made it past the stone staircase to his chambers. I would come upon them, drain them into confusion, then discard the bodies in the courtyard. They would awake the next morning with a crashing headache, wandering aimlessly in a dazed wonderland.

This left Mavra befuddled. How could her cream of the crop, richly paid group of assassin fail so miserably in their attempts? Her contempt grew, and with it her despair to be rid of Viktor. To be rid of me, as well.

Over the next two years, most of which coursed on in an endless blur of monotony and assassination attempts, Mavra became pregnant twice. The first breathed nothing more than her first breath before turning a grim shade of blue and shaking violently. Mercifully, its soul flew northward. The body, Mavra rushed away, entombed before anyone could see it. Excuses were made.

Viktor had not been the father. This honor went to a young soldier whose regiment was re-stationed three months prior to the birth.

The second child was more fortunate than her sister had been. She survived six days and was a beautiful dewy pink. She cooed when you stroked her cheek, wiggled her toes when you tickled her feet, and opened her eyelids and gazed at you with bold, hazel eyes. But, she was a girl and could not inherit the crown. Therefore, as the babe slept in the cold, crisp dawn-light, when life was waking to face a new day, Mavra smothered her. As angelic as the girl had been, she, too, had not been Viktor's.

It was August when this second child perished. The balmy August air wreaked a foul, poisonous odor that lingered from the sewers and rose up through the streets and into the homes, reaching into the highest tower. That stench permeated the highest rooms, the most perfumed halls; and percolated as it brewed in the city's underbelly. No one could escape it. That child – that gorgeous infantile angel – had been cursed to live to breathe such air. Perhaps it would have been better if she had been born blue.

I had gone to him the night she passed.

It was near the end of August; the smells were almost unbearable and he kept the balcony door closed. When I opened the doors, he was lying on the bed covered in a thick blanket of sweat. His bed covering were neat beneath him and the drapes tied back at their posts. He laid there, defeated, his legs bent and his feet resting along the edge in their stockings; his hands fixed behind his head. His eyes were closed, relaxed, but a seething cauldron of turmoil bubbled beneath his chiseled face. The sweat dripped down his weary cheeks soiling his white collar, soiling the lush bedding underneath.

"I heard Yalena died," I said, approaching the bed. "I came as soon as I fed."

I cradled his pallid head in my hands; his sweat was salty and tasted of blood on my lips as I kissed his wrinkled brow. He was aging right before me. His forehead wore the brunt of his worries; lines grew from his eyes; and his hair was streaking with grey. While time was being unkind to him, worry and grief was a burden his body could not hide.

"Did she kill her?" It was more of a demand than a question. I tried to quiet him, but he insisted. "I know you can hear her thoughts. Tell me."

"Do you really want to know?" I asked him. "The truth may be hard to live with, knowing your wife is a murder." He nodded. "Yes, Viktor, she killed Yalena. And right now, she is planning your demise, my love. Her vile thoughts were so loud I heard four blocks away."

I ran my fingers through his thinning hair. He sat up and stared wildly.

"She is downstairs in her room mixing arsenic into your wine. She is going to bring it to you herself this time because she will no longer stand for failures, Viktor. She is insistent that this time, you will die."

"She is planning to do it herself?" His eyes were vacant orbs staring into the fire behind me. His hands quaked as they reached for mine. "I am going to kill her first, Bree."

"You will do no such thing," I scowled. He glared at me, his eyes piercing with his hatred for her. "Let me handle her."

I watched as the man I loved, a defeated and terrified hulk of flesh, traversed the room and fell with the full weight of his being into a chair. He was broken. She had broken him.

His mind and body were weary from constantly being on guard. Everything had to be checked – his food, his clothing, even his bath. There was not a single moment, not a scrap of precious time, when Viktor was not susceptible to her assassination attempts. Despite what had transpired between them, his uncle refused to throw Mavra in the tower. Worse, even, convict her to death.

I stayed with Viktor every night, watching him sleep. The nightmares plagued him: the fits tangled his legs and the sweat clung to his weathered brow. Before dawn, when I had to leave, I would wake him with kisses and reassurances that I would see him at nightfall and that he had again survived.

But, that hell in which he lived would cease tonight, I told myself as I waited for her. He had had his last nightmare.

I could hear her footsteps in the hallway. Viktor concealed himself on a corner settee. Her scent wafted heavily now; she was not far. I urged him to remain absolutely quiet and hidden. Then she was there, just on the other side, and I could hear her heartbeat pulsating through the wood and nails as she knocked upon the oak.

"Enter," I said.

Several seconds passed before the door creaked to life, a ruby slipper poking itself from around the corner. Her petite face peeked in afterwards and curiously peered around as she hugged the door, slightly ajar now, to her chest.

"Come in, Mavra," I demanded.

"Where is Viktor?" she asked as she entered. She remained close to the door.

"You just missed him."

"I will return later, then." She fingered a gold goblet in her right hand and turned toward the door, preparing to leave hastily.

"Drink it," I demanded.

"Excuse me?" She turned toward me, startled.

"The goblet, drink it."

"This was not intended for me," she stammered. "It was for Viktor."

"He will not mind if you take a sip, Mavra."

"Oh, I could never do that," she replied. She shuffled awkwardly, shrinking closer to the door. "It is for my beloved."

"Drink it!"

"No," she said. "You cannot make me, harlot! I will have you thrown from this castle."

Quickly, and without warning, I glided to her side and grasped the hand that held the goblet tightly in my own. My other hand encircled her throat. At first, she struggled against me. She attempted to jerk her hand away, or drop the goblet, but I held a crushing grasp on both. When she tried to retaliate, I dug a sharp nail into her neck.

"What are you?" she whispered.

"Keep fighting me and I will show you." I released her and she nearly spilled the wine onto her velvet bodice. I caught her arm as she steadied herself.

"Now drink it!" I commanded.

My hand steadied her lifeless arm and lifted the goblet to her quivering lips. Tears formed in the corners of her eyes and began to fall the closer the liquid traveled north. Yet, she did not resist.

She closed her eyes, but when the cool metal hit her lips, a hurricane of tears poured forth and she refused to open her mouth. Instead, she dropped to her knees, my hand still grasping her own with the goblet attached.

"Please," she begged. "It is poisoned; do not make me drink from it! Please, show me mercy."

"Why should I have mercy on you, Mavra?"

"Please," she begged.

"You have disgraced yourself. You have disgraced Viktor. You have disgraced your position. Do you deny these accusations?"

"No," she sobbed. I took the poisonous goblet from her grasp as her arm slumped to the floor. She remained on her knees, her eyes consumed with tears.

"You have tried poisoning Viktor, having him murdered and even maimed. Do you deny this?"

"No," she whispered.

"I should kill you as you would have him be slain." I told her. She looked up at me, her dewy eyes red and glassy. "Will you cease this senselessness, Mavra? Do you see now that it is pointless?"

"Yes," she answered. "He is safe from me. Just, please, spare my life."

"I will spare your life if you promise to do one thing for me," I told her.

"What?" interjected Viktor, emerging from the shadow.

Mavra bounced to her feet, glancing between the two of us. I reached out with an open palm and she remained near the door, quickly wiping the tears from her eyes.

"Mavra, Viktor needs an heir."

"Give me the poison," she said as she stared at him. "I would rather end my life."

"I would rather kill her than bed with her!" He yelled as he approached us.

"Viktor, you will do as I say," I told him. "Mavra, you do this or I will kill you. We both know you lack the courage to take your own life. You did not possess the strength to do so when you were raped at twelve."

"How did you know?" She inched closer to the door; her eyes suspiciously fixed on me.

"She can see everything, Mavra," he told her, his hand gracing her shoulder, steadying her. "She can see inside yourself, to your soul."

"You want power, Mavra. Revenge. Your craving for them has consumed you; blinded you from the ability to love, to feel." I reached for her. "But wait, there is a glimmer of hope, in your mind, I can sense it. It is reaching for me from within the darkness that eats it. It is singing to me, asking me to feed it, to free it. Can you feel it there?"

"There is no such thing, I can assure you," she whispered. A tear rolled from the corner of her eye, and I watched as it slowly descended from its watery birthplace to its death as it slivered its way onto her lip, where she licked it away. "Not anymore."

"Just kill her, Bree. The sight of her is making me ill," he said as he walked to the bed and sat dejectedly on the edge.

"I provided my liege the required marital duties already this month, if you must know! And that is only because his mother demands it," she spat. "Until next month, he will not touch me. I would rather kill myself than have his hands near my body!"

"Just kill her!" His fist struck a bedside table, knocking a vase over. "Be done with it, Bree. I cannot stand her harpy shrill."

"The glimmer," I whispered. Swiftly, I glided to her side and clutched her to me. She gasped, her eyes filling with dread as they stared back into mine.

"You will not remember this," I told her, and then, gently flexing her head back so I could see the veins in her neck popping in the dim candlelight, I bent forward sinking my teeth into her moist flesh.

Her blood was thick on my tongue; thick and hot and haunted by nightmarish images. Images of beatings as a child, royal prostitution to guarantee her mother's position; the foolish purchase of pardons, incest; everything foul that could haunt the mind and corrupt a person had happened to her. Then I found the glimmer I had seen, and realized why Mavra could not see it for herself.

"She is pregnant," I told him as I withdrew carrying her body to the bed.

"Is she dead?"

"No, just asleep, but pregnant, Viktor."

"Pregnant?" he asked. "Is it mine?"

"Yes, they are yours. Two glorious miracles struggling to shine through a soul drenched in torment and hatred."

"Twins," he remarked as he sat and moved next to her on the bed, placing his hand over her thriving womb. "And I would have killed them."

"Because that is what humans do; they fight hatred with hatred, murder with murder. For once, try forgiveness. She is the mother of your children. They are yet to be born, but they will be spectacular. I can feel it. That light... it is blinding. It called to me as your heartbeat called to me, Viktor. It is that strong."

"I could never forgive her. The hatred she has bred, the death, deceit. I just cannot."

"Some have not lived splendid lives, Viktor. Some do not enjoy pleasant and joyous childhoods, as you have been fortunate to have. Not even in royal circles. She was raped, Viktor. Can you not see? Our pasts, they determine who we are more than we care to believe. Her own mother..."

"Her past," he stated as he withdrew his hand, "is of no consequence to me."

The next morning Viktor moved Mavra into the tower, despite his uncle's orders. Her every move and morsel was carefully guarded. She was allowed no visitors except for Viktor and me, and soon her name became but a whisper at court.

Rumors spread of insanity, of her "madness," and the need for her removal for her own safety. No one beside the tsar questioned this. Slowly, as the months crawled past and Mavra's stomach grew with life, the people of Tver forgot about the mysterious but strikingly beautiful princess and replaced her with tales of a frightening, shell of a woman haunting the tower. Rumors were she was with child, and people were already mourning for the babe. They knew all too well her checkered past.

For nine months, the gentle sparks grew in the darkness of her womb. For nine months, she struggled against them. Starvation only met with forced feedings. Suicide attempts resulted in her spending days and nights locked in dank dungeon cells. In the beginning, she fought relentlessly until one night the fighting ceased, her spirit broken.

I went to her then. She remembered nothing of when I tasted her blood, but I remembered every vivid image. They softened me toward her. Viktor saw her only to reassure himself that she was alive and that her stomach grew with the passing weeks. But, I went to visit, to comfort, to know the mother of Viktor's children.

"What will happen to me once they are born," she asked me one night.

"If you cooperate with us," I told her, "I will let you live."

"By 'live' do you mean in this tower, locked away from the world?" She tossed a leg of mutton onto the plate in front of her and pushed the dish away. "Because that is not living."

"You will be allowed to return to the main palace if he feels you are no threat to the children."

"He will always consider me a threat, you know that to be true," she said, as she stood, moving to the slit window.

The rain pelted the stone walls, muffling her voice. It had been pouring for days with only sporadic breaks and the fields were flooding. Farmers cried that the crops were ruined, famine would ensue, but Viktor cared for nothing but the children growing in Mavra's womb.

"I have tried, Mavra, but he doesn't care what you've gone through. He does not care to understand."

"And because of this, I will never be safe. He will always be suspicious of me. In my sleep, he will come – or in the day – you know he will. Even you cannot watch him all of the time."

"Would you rather remain here in the tower? I can keep you guarded, safe from him."

"No," she said turning toward me.

"Mavra, your options are limited."

"I have no future, Bree. None. These children are the only things sustaining me. After they are born, I will do it."

"Mavra." I rose to her side taking her hand in mine. "Taking your own life is not the answer."

"There is no other way. This existence – any existence under his control and his suspicion, is not worth living. My own guilt constantly gnaws at me. It has created a pit," she said placing my hand above her heart, "an ebon void in my heart, in my soul. I can never make amends for my travesties. It would take another lifetime to even begin to."

She never had the chance to take her own life, though. Her destiny lay dormant in her womb, waiting patiently. On Christmas morning, 1543, two daughters were born to the house of Vladislov. Two flawless daughters, born from the darkness lay snuggled, wrapped tightly in furs, their father holding them as the fire warmed their newborn skin.

They were angelic as the moonlight trickled in from the balcony and the firelight danced off the ruby and gold highlights in the fur wrappings. They both had heads full of striking red hair, and Mavra's delicate features. That is how I first beheld them. That was so long ago.

"She is dying," I said as I walked in from the balcony.

"Yes."

"I can hear her heart slowing. She is in pain," I told him. He was focused on the sleeping twins. "She is alone; I should go to her."

"Leave her. It is what she deserves," he remarked, his eyes were ice as he stared at me.

"That is heartless, Viktor," I told him as I walked through the room. "Heartless and cruel." I opened the door to leave and glanced back at him. He had returned his focus to the twins as I went through the door.

Her heartbeat was faint as it sung to me through the stone corridors. I ran to it. It struggled and skipped, her thoughts becoming cloudy, but I willed her to remain. She was lying there on the bed, her saffron gown soiled with sweat as I burst through the door. The priest knelt beside her, praying. She whimpered as he finished, anointing her forehead with oil. "She is in God's hands now," he whispered as he left. The nurse hung near the corner wringing out bloodstained sheets and I dismissed her from the room.

"Mavra," I whispered as I sat on the edge of the bed. "Can you hear me?"

"Please, help me," she cried softly. What little color remaining in her cheeks faded as she coughed. "Please," she begged.

"Mavra," I wiped the sweat from her brow and cupped her face; "I am going to take the pain away, take it away forever." Her heart beat, what little was left, surged beneath my touch. She could sense the end coming and the pain was unbearable.

"Do not be afraid. Close your eyes and sleep."

I could feel the tears falling down my cheeks and could see their vivid crimsonness as they fell on her ivory shirt. Startled, she reached her feeble hand to my face and wiped away a tear. "An angel?" she hissed, the words barely escaping through labored breath.

I embraced her frail body, a mere shell of the powerful woman she had once been, and brought her to me. Her breath was warm against my skin, her own skin clammy. Gingerly, I moved away the hair that clung to her neck. My teeth remembered her skin, remembered its softness. My mind remembered her fevered blood, metallic but sweet. And, I remembered her memories. With each drop, her heartbeat slowed and I resisted the urge to stop. My desire to end her agony went against my promise not end another life – ever. Had my connection to humanity become too intimate?

With each drop of her precious blood, each slowing rhythmic pulse of her heartbeat, I wondered if I was becoming too close to *them*. Then she made the decision for me. "Farewell," she whispered before her heart failed.   Farewell.

Her body slumped from my arms and I sat, gawking. Lifeless, it laid there. Her eyes pressed back at me from the void; her skin was as ashen as my own. What had I done?

Suddenly, the smell of death revolted me and I fled the room. Viktor was reading and the twins slept peacefully near the fire as I entered his chambers.

"It is done," I told him.

"Bree?" he asked, dropping the book and walking toward me. I brushed him away.

"Are the girls well?"

"Yes, I've named them Aleksandra and Anastasia. They are wonderful."

"Tell them, Viktor, tell them of their mother. Tell them of how she gave her life to bring them into the world."

"We will tell them together, Bree." He reached for me and I moved away from him.

"No. I must leave you now," I told him as I moved toward the balcony. "I have... stayed too long."

"Bree?" He moved toward me. "Do not do this."

"Viktor, I just murdered her!"

"She was already dying. You merely helped her, ended her suffering."

"Why should it matter that she was already dying? I am not God. I should not have that power; It's unnatural!" I screamed.

"I've stayed too long amongst humanity. Way too long and now I've gone too far. I am a monster. A monster! Not God."

One of the twins began to cry, and as his attention diverted to the whimpering babe, I slipped into the cold night.

It was Christmas night, 1543, and two children were born: their destinies yet to be seen. Their mother had joined the stars twinkling in the frigid, Russian sky, and I could no longer bear it.

THIRTEEN

Wesley was in the garden as I approached the property. His muted brown clothing blended with the moonlight; he appeared to be part of the garden, a fixture weathering with time. Then he moved in my direction, breaking the spell the dancing moonlight weaved.

"You're home," he remarked as his footsteps closed the distance between us.

"I'm not staying," I whispered as I walked toward the house, the only light emanating coming from the sitting room fireplace. The house staff had long since retired but the fire raged on, awaiting my return.

"You've been crying," he remarked as I strolled past, my feet maintaining a slow, almost human pace.

"Bree, what troubles you?" He followed me now, but I declined to answer him.

As we entered the sitting room, the fire cast a warming orange glow and he walked past me, sitting down in his usual chair. Its cracking mahogany leather crunched as his body melted into it while the firelight warmed his profile. I glanced at him and then my fingers found the hidden box, the one covered in a thick layer of dust in my desk drawer.

"Talk to me, Bree." His gangly legs stretched out from the chair, reaching towards the warm flames. My silence frustrated him, but I could not form the words that matched the thoughts swimming in my head. How could I explain what I had done that night? How could I explain that I had to flee from the nightmare in which I had found myself?

My fingertips glided over the box's contents: the jewels were cold beneath my touch, but somehow still living with the memories they held in their hard, sparkling forms. I pulled the emerald and diamond necklace from its home and held it to the dim light. The firelight reflected off the diamonds and made the emeralds shimmer.

"You have not touched those in years," he commented, watching me.

From my cape, I pulled a velvet pouch and gently placed the necklace into it. He watched carefully now, eyeing me suspiciously. I found the rings, gold and silver with ornate carvings. They were as old as I was, and fragile. They, too, went into the pouch clanging sweetly against the necklace. Then, as I fingered the locket lying at the bottom of the box, the tears returned, cascading down my left cheek. The locket's hinges had broken centuries ago, but the painted picture remained – faded with age but intact. Too many memories invaded my mind as I looked at the image. That was a lifetime ago – not mine, but someone else's.

After wiping away my tears, I placed it in the pouch, as well.

"I am leaving," I told him, breaking the silence engulfing us.

"Where are you going?" he asked, moving to my side.

"I am not sure, but I have to go. I can no longer be here."

"What happened tonight?"

My eyes roamed the room, centering on the fireplace. The flames fondled the stone and I gravitated toward their effulgent orange and red fingers – their fiery tendrils hypnotizing me. An aura surrounded the elaborate marble mantel and extended to the sitting area, casting shadows on my chair's clawed feet.

The nights I had spent in front of those flames, comforted and tempted by the warmth, played before me. I remembered the times I had wanted, more than anything, to enter the hearth, to set myself ablaze, to end this existence. But, in the end, the courage to do so escaped me and dawn would approach, and Wesley would secure the room from the coming sun. And I would be safe. The perfect older brother, he was a constant at my side.

"Wesley, I think it is a season for change." My fingers grazed the marble mantel, the thought of change, of leaving this place, turned my stomach.

"Why?" he asked. He came to me, resting his hand on my shoulder. My stare remained fixed on the flames averting his questioning glare. "Why now?"

"I have gone to the edge and fallen off, Wesley. I can no longer be around these humans with their mortality, and their rich blood tempting me, and… their love." My eyes met his, tears forming in the creases. "We are monsters parading around as if we are as they are! We use make-up to look mortal, clothing to appear complete! But, we are not so. We are not human. How can we pretend to be and not lose our minds doing so?"

"We do not have a choice. You know this. We are not monsters, Bree, we are just… creatures of habit."

"Monsters lurk in the dark, Wesley. Monsters haunt the dreams of little children. Monsters kill. My brother, we *are* monsters."

"Where is this coming from?" He tried to embrace me but I yanked away. Dejectedly, he moved to the chair, the leather creaking as he sat down. "What has happened to you?"

"She is dead, Wesley," I told him. "I murdered her."

I walked to my chair that angled his. Its velvet felt soft as my hands firmly grasped the arms. Viktor was right; she was already dying. Still, I should have left the moment her heartbeat beckoned me. I should have flown away until the beating stopped, but I had not. I interfered.

Wesley's eyes met my own and he reached for my hand, taking it into his. My hands quivered as I recalled how I ended Mavra's life. When I was finished, he embraced me and let my tears stain his tan shirt.

"If you must leave, then I will go with you." He ran his fingers through my hair, reassuringly and protective. "You are my sister and my responsibility."

"No. I need to be alone," I told him. "Stay here and wait for me."

"Are you sure I cannot go with you?" He asked as I stood and moved toward the French doors; a heavy gray cloak hung on a hook near the door and I grabbed it. "If I must wait then, I will."

"Stay here so I have somewhere to return to," I whispered toward him as I walked into the darkness. There was no sound of following footsteps as I took to the sky. Only the dotted darkness followed me now. I was alone. Inside, I was lost and that frightened me.

I stopped first in Moscow and there I remained for several months. This was years since the city was liberated from Tartar control, and centuries before the city had replaced my beloved Tver as Russia's political hub. My nights were plagued with wandering – roaming the streets, listening to the thoughts of the city's inhabitants, and slipping further and further into despair.

These people, this place, it was too familiar. Russia was too familiar. These people, their blood, reminded me of Mavra. Her blood haunted me.

I eventually left, and I did not dream I would ever go back. In twenty-eight years, the Crimean Tartars would assault Moscow. They would sack the city and watch it burn. When the embers lay dying, only the Kremlin would be left standing. I am relieved I was not there to witness such needless destruction.

I have lived long enough to see war and pillage repeat itself. I have seen humankind unwilling or unable to learn from their ancestor's mistakes. However, to see destruction and greed erase history – buildings, peoples, gone forever— this is almost insufferable. It serves to remind me just how removed I am from the living, from time itself.

I spent my last night in Moscow near the waterside, watching the ships come to port. The Moskva River was abuzz that evening with traffic. Candlelight from the ships reflected softly on the water, the moonlight casting a silver aura on the ships, on the people, on the bustling city that surrounded me. I watched as one of the ships came to port and waited while the passengers disembarked.

I followed one of them, a gauntly fellow with sunken eyes and a cough that echoed as he walked through an alley. The bloodstained handkerchief clung to his mouth. The darkness disoriented him, and I watched as he stopped halfway through the long alleyway and took a map from his pocket. I approached him, offering directions in his native German. Feeding from him was effortless and I left him sleeping on the floor, the map scrunched in his aging palm.

I should have shown him mercy and relieved his suffering, as I had done for Mavra. But I couldn't. I abhorred murder, even though it was in my nature. Something in this man's blood had whispered to me, though. It had been faint, a warning perhaps, but I heeded its call. I gathered my belongings and took off for Germany not sure what awaited me.

The air was still that night – a comforting blanket surrounding me as I traveled. Just before dawn, I could see the Mainz Cathedral with its Romanesque triple nave. The cathedral's muted titian and gold sandstone facade, most of which is now covered with bland plaster, was inviting in the pre-dawn moonlight. The stones shimmered and danced with vigor, welcoming pilgrims, beckoning them in. The inside had to wait, the sun had begun to creep over the horizon and my body required rest.

The next evening after dusk, before the city slept, I crept into the bustling streets. Traffic weaved along. Merchants packed up their wares, taverns grew with chatter, and children ran home for their supper. The night was mine, as it had been for centuries; and yet the dullness of reality could not shake me from the newness of that place.

It offered fresh discoveries and adventure. Alone, I was left to do as I pleased – to go wherever and whenever my mind took me. And, that night, the cathedral weaved a welcoming spell into my heart. The sandstone drank the moonlight and spilled the excess onto the streets, and the Benedictine chants, a welcome specter, beckoned my feet to enter.

Two chancels were built into the church, one for ceremonial processions and the other for bishops and pontiffs. Priests and a bishop had gathered in the second chancel and I discreetly wandered to the other side of the cathedral.

There was a sense of solitude in the abandoned chancel. I spied a wooden pew, worn with centuries of use, and I rested there, staring at the altar. A parishioner joined me, but remained near the back of the nave. Her thoughts were troubled and she came for guidance. The stones, though, offered her no solace, and she left as quickly as she had come.

The candelabras, ablaze with their minute fires all along the stretched nave, cast somber shadows on the plastered walls. Their light had a limited reach leaving the pews darkened, remaining in the shadow. My feet grew weary of sitting, so I ventured through the cathedral.

I could scarcely see the ceiling, its ribbed vaulting concealed by the night. I ached to see the square quadripartite vaults in the daylight, and the sun filtering through the cathedral's expansive stained glass windows. The vaulted ceiling allowed for more windows, windows that depicted ancient stories, and for the angels and saints who visited to intercede in parishioners' prayers. And, I was cursed to see this splendor in drab candlelight, concealing the cathedral's true beauty.

The spectacular cathedral with its antiquated pews and marble statues would never be the same as when my eyes explored its niches in the pale moonlight, though. The year 1792 would see the advancement of French troops, which led to its misuse and ruin. Large portions were destroyed in 1803, the war erasing history. The holy place was robbed of many artifacts while serving as a bunker for troops.

Yet, by 1831, restorations were nearly complete. The history was lost, though, as it always is.

Three years after I arrived, I left Mainz for Rottweil. Under the control of the Swiss Confederation, but originally a prominent Roman settlement, I found a city in transition. It struggled to hold onto the fragments from its past while Swiss progress urged it forward.

The ancient Rottweil Roman baths are just now being unearthed, discovered buried in a cemetery, along with the dead who time has forgotten. I was not there for the Roman baths or for cemeteries, though. There was a newly constructed triple nave basilica in the parish church of St. Cross, and I wanted eagerly to witness its splendor first hand.

The architecture dwarfed me as I hung, like a vapor, in the shadows. Something was different here; I could taste it in the air.

I hid from it.

There was a niche not far from me, a statue of the Madonna, flanked in candlelight. The flickering light flitted off her indigo veil, her eyes concealed in darkness yet still bearing down at me; judging me, guiding me. Sliding toward the statue, I lit a candle and offered a silent prayer, not knowing whether God could still hear me, or even wanted to. My prayer for solace, I thought, would surely fall on deafened ears.

As I was exiting the church, I heard the faint whispering of thoughts. They pressed me; they rushed me. They crashed into my skull.

I heard his name. A name I had heard before – in Mainz. The priests and the bishop had been whispering it in their corner. Wanting to hide within, I shut out their thoughts. Now, however, these thoughts were too loud to ignore. Martin Luther, the man's mind screamed, is dying.

Please Lord, the man prayed, *forgive him, he knows not the gravity of what he believes.*

"Who is dying?" I asked, boldly, walking from the shadows to sit at the man's side. Startled, he attempted to shuffle further down the pew but my hand, clamping on his shoulder, stopped him. "Tell me, please."

"Martin Luther," he whispered, eyeing the priest before glancing my way.

"What consequence is that of yours... of a Catholic?"

He tensed at my words. His shoulders squared as he sucked in a breath, his hawkish eyes widening. A rich chanting filled the back of the nave, coming from a separate part of the church. A woman, young but burdened by pregnancy, sauntered in and sat two pews ahead of us.

"His wife is my cousin," he replied, his voice hushed. "I do not agree with him, with his preaching, but I do pray for his soul."

I confronted him. "His preaching? Which ones? I beg of you, divulge."

"I beg your pardon?" he replied, bewildered by my questioning.

"Do you oppose the assertion that one cannot be absolved through his purse? Or, do you oppose his recent madness, that the Jews should have their homes destroyed; that we should burn their synagogues, or that we should confiscate their moneys, their properties?"

"I oppose it all," he answered. His chin, firm and proud, jutted from his neck as he edged his upper body closer to me. "Every last word that man speaks is a lie."

"And yet you sit here praying for him?"

"It is not too late for him," the man said, easing back into the pew, observing the priest as he knelt at the altar. "It is not too late for you either." The man's eyes met mine. "You, too, can repent."

"I have nothing to repent for." His voice was sharp, cutting the air. The woman sitting ahead of us turned and glanced our way, her finger to her mouth – her eyes piercing with intent.

"Repent for your intolerance," I told him as I stood. "Repent for your own wickedness. You, surely, are not blameless. Why then do you judge your fellow man? For we shall all stand before the judgment seat of God." The words, long since implanted on my psyche from days spent in study, effortlessly rolled off my tongue.

"Who are you to quote scripture to me? You do not sound Catholic, so who are you to judge me?" He grabbed the back of the pew in front of him clutching the hardwood until his knuckles whitened. His eyes, beady slits, peered at me.

"I am not Catholic," I told him, my voice trailing into the past. "I am… nothing."

I left him, the reality of my own words violently assaulting me; I quickly paced down the aisle, clicking my heels softly on the stone.

I reached Mansfeld Castle as the sky morphed into pre-dawn, the purples easing from the horizon, reaching for golden daylight. The whispering traveled high in the wee hours as Eisleben awoke. My eyes grew heavy with the coming light, and as I found shelter from the coming heat, I heard the news: Luther was no more.

When the evening returned, his soul had already begun its march into eternity. I listened to the city speak of him, of his controversy, of his life. Then I ventured on. There was no longer anything left for me in Eisleben. That is, if there had ever been anything there for me at all.

Germany still held precious treasures for me to

explore, the wine country of Esslingen and the Merseburg bible, and the city's now famous Domburg. But, the Domburg's Romanesque triple nave held nothing new for me, either. Its stain glass windows of saints made grotesquely distorted images on the slate floor when the moonlight hit them. They reminded me of Norway, but I was unsure as to why.

The Merseburg bible, held in the Domburg's library with other dusty tomes telling the history of these proud people, was just another decrepit volume. It was not even that old when I first saw it, only a spot over three-hundred years. It was wildly unnaturally that I was older. It was wrong.

Time passed swiftly for me as I traveled about. Almost four years flew by since I left Russia and I had found no happiness, no peace. My attempts to detract from humanity were futile; in every city, in every landmark, people surrounded me. Their thoughts inundated my mind, corrupting my solitude. Their blood intoxicated the air, making me long to unite, forever, with something other than myself. I was lonely, lonelier than I had been when I left. I had to return. The running had to cease.

FOURTEEN

W hy do you keep that picture?" Wesley asked. "That girl; she is lost now. You will never get her back."

Three nights had passed since I returned to Russia. Not once did he question me about my absence. Not once did he pry into where I had been, whom I had seen, or why I had now returned. Nor did I question what he had done in my absence.

"And who is responsible for that?" I asked.

I snapped the locket shut, its aging hinges creaking, and tossed it back into the velvet bag hanging from my waist.

"Being here with him, with them, it will kill you, Bree. You should not have returned."

The fire lit his eyes; the black orbs looked sunken by the dark, gloomy room. Time had forgotten both of us. But sometimes, in the light of the fire, or in the way he scrunched his brow and wrinkled his nose – time caught up with Wesley. It made me fear what we had become.

"It cannot kill me, my brother; I am already dead."

I gathered the rest of the jewels, the ones resting on the mantle – my precious links to a past I could scarcely remember – and crammed them into the pouch. "I have to go to him."

"You will regret this. So much has changed."

"It is only been four years, Wesley."

"Four years for mortals is longer than you realize. Be careful, my sister, you may be dead, but your heart can still be broken."

The shadows frolicked against the walls; the plaster images – peacocks and flowered vines – shimmered and danced. The flames were the only things alive in the room, and their warmth reminded me of my utter coldness, my lifeless existence in a world inhabited with mortals. Their blood constantly coursed through their bodies, taunting me. Their heartbeats, haunting my ears with vibrant rhythms, seduced me back. And there I was, a specter, a monster, tainting their perfect world – lusting to be with it, among it, yet consuming it.

"Perhaps I will. However, I will also regret not going back. How do I choose which future will haunt me?"

The fire was dying, its glow fading. It was time.

"What will you do when he dies?" Wesley asked, taking my hand. "And you will remain the same. His hair will gray, he will get sick, and he will be no more! Yet your hair will never gray, you will never get sick, you will never die."

"How will you explain to the children your unchanging form?" he continued. "A child's keen eye can see through a disguise, Bree."

He grabbed my chin and turned my face to his.

"What will you say when those girls ask you how their mother died?"

"I will tell them everything, Wesley. There will be no secrets. Not anymore."

The fire had died, bathing us in a darkness that matched the silent recesses of my heart. His doubt now poisoned the air.

"You are a fool," he said, dropping my hand.

"Maybe," I replied. I walked to the door, twisting the knob, and peered into the night, its luminous canopy of stars beckoning me. "Perhaps I am, yes."

I slipped into the night, its ebony cape shrouding me from the living. He was behind me, not too far, but there. That night, I found Tver changed, and still somehow the same. The mellifluous rhythm of Viktor's heart euphorically called me home. I could not ignore its siren cry.

Tracks of rainfall collected on the cobblestone streets and glistened in the starlight. Wesley had landed behind me, his hand now on my shoulder.

"Go to him," he whispered, "Nothing I could say is going to stop this, so be off with you, then."

I embraced him, feeling his hard coldness against me. I needed human warmth, human comfort, not his frosty tightness.

"Just remember why you left and do not get lost in the humanity's dream world, in his dream world, again. Remember that you are a vampire and not even he can change that."

Wesley's words swam circles in my mind as I descended. The castle was still except for the candlelight shining in Viktor's quarters. His curtain was open to embrace the brisk night air.

That is how it always was on nights like this. His curtain would be open, the fire raging; and he would be on the bed, sprawled out, reading a book. His eyelids half open and half closed as he turned the pages. By now the candelabras would be near to the quick, the wax pooling and spilling into colored icicles, gently cascading down the silver bases.

"Miss me?" I whispered as my feet landed on the cold slate floor.

I could have snuck up on him, tapping his shoulder as he read, but I did not. Instead, I stood just inside from the balcony, preparing for his response.

"I must be dreaming," he remarked, rising from the bed.

"No dream, Viktor."

"No dream?"

His fingers fondled my hair; his eyes glanced about my face, dancing with excitement under his heavy eyelids. My smile reassured him of reality, and his arms wrapped about me, embracing me with their warmth."

"I thought you'd gotten lost. That you had forgotten your way back to me."

"I am back now, that's all that matters," I told him as he held me. "That is all that will ever matter, Viktor. I am never leaving you again."

His hair had grayed more that I thought it would in four years. Heavy creases graced the corners of his eyes, and his face showed the weariness of time in each wrinkle.

"Where has the time gone, Viktor?" My fingers traced over them, slowly, wondering about each wrinkles history. "I am getting older and you have stayed the same, just as you said you would," he said, kissing my cheek.

"This will end, even though you have come back to me, one day this will end, will it not?"

"One day, you will die. That is the only way you will get rid of me," I told him as I smoothed his graying hair. Four years before, there had been more black peppered in, but now the black had nearly faded.

"Turn me, make me what you are. Then this will never end," he urged.

"No. I cannot. This life, living forever, you eventually get tired of constantly watching everything you know, everything you love, fade to dust. Everything ends, Viktor. Even I will eventually cease being."

"For four years I have longed to see your face again, to feel your lips on mine, Bree," he said.

"For four years I knew that if you ever came back, I would make sure we were never again parted."

"I will never turn you, Viktor."

"But can you not see how beautiful you are to me, my eternal love?" he urged, pressing his palm to my cold throat. "How unchanged and mysterious you are?"

I laid my head upon his shoulder, wrapping my arms around him. His warmth struggled to permeate my hard coldness.

"If you love me, you will stop asking for this. You pain me with your pleas, and I will flee again. Flee forever."

"You will not hear my voice utter those words again, then." His voice softened with defeat.

"You will ask me again, just one more time," I told him.

"When? Have I not just promised such?"

"When you are dying," I told him. My grip tightened around his torso.

He was silent, his hot breath whispering across my neck. His chest swelled with a deep breath, which he hung onto as tightly as I hung onto him. I heard his soul mourning; crying over its utter mortality, the eventual journey to a place I could not venture to. I nearly succumbed to my weakness, my teeth almost sinking into his tender flesh, when he released his breath and his soul was at peace with my decision.

Aleksandra had grown into a delicate child, her features a perfect blend of her parents. However, Anastasia could not hear. She lived in isolated quarters, communicating in grunts and crude hand gestures, a wet nurse her only companion. Violent seizures gripped the child and wracked her frail limbs with uncontrollable spasms. The sound she made, a guttural yowl, as servants struggled to hold her down during these episodes made even me shudder.

A little over a year before I returned, Viktor had the girls separated because Anastasia's fits frightened her sister. Anastasia would bite Aleksandra, drawing blood. She could not function with other children, and so she could not be trusted around those her age. Viktor went to Anastasia often, but she could not hear his words, and he felt powerless – unable to communicate and connect with his darling girl. Even he, on a hidden level – one Viktor was not proud of – was afraid of the child.

When the girls turned seven, I convinced him to send Aleksandra to an English boarding school. Her Russian tutor stunted her intellectual growth. She tired easily with the mundane and had a seemingly limitless thirst for knowledge. She would become a noble queen, I had told Viktor; she just needed room now to blossom.

Viktor was torn, but even he could not fail to see the connection been Anastasia's disabilities and how it affected Aleksandra – restraining Aleksandra's growth. Aleksandra pitied the weakened mirror image that was her twin. Pity was not enough to foster love.

My attempts with the child, who was always exquisitely dressed, having the most gentle and skilled nursemaids available to the Crown's richly purse, were futile. She was kept comfortable, but we were powerless to do anything more for her.

When the girls were ten, I convinced Viktor to send Anastasia to a school in Paris ran by one Abbe Charles Michael de L'Épée, a prominent teacher of signs for those who could not hear. The school, using a theory that deaf people could learn to communicate through hand gestures, was a dawning concept, but one I found hope in. Her struggles, her fits, I reassured Viktor, were because she could not hear us; she could not communicate. Others in the castle and beyond its walls however, felt they derived from evil; much like her mother.

In 1558, six years after we sent her to Paris, a letter arrived from a man, a doctor who treated the students at Anastasia's school. He begged for her hand in marriage. *I can care for her better than any other man can. I love her. She loves me,* he wrote, his nervous scribble scrawled on the parchment in a series of smudged, disorganized pen-marks.

As the weeks passed, I encouraged Viktor to accept this match for his daughter. Even with her royal title, the disability left little to no chance of any marital match, and this one would prove beneficial to Anastasia.

The pair returned to Russia and were wed in a simple ceremony in a Tver church that has long since burned and been forgotten. The groom, a meek man of thirty wearing wire-rimmed glasses, gladly accepted the dowry Viktor offered. The purse made him a rich man, yet the couple returned to Paris and invested the funds in the same school where their love dawned. Their life was comfortable and pleasant for several years.

Anastasia had matured into a charming woman. She wore her hair curlier than Aleksandra, and had a small scar on her chin. Their hair was the same blazing red – a fiery color, bold and brazen. Their features were delicate and regal, and their emerald eyes sparkled in the candlelight. Anastasia was a bit thinner than her sister was, but made a stunning bride regardless.

Having been in an English boarding school of my choosing, Aleksandra returned to Russia to stand with her sister.

Unlike her sister Anastasia, Aleksandra resisted the notion of marriage. Several prominent men had pursued her hand, but all without success. Her quest for knowledge, for answering life's unanswered questions, left no room for attentions of men. Her books were her companions.

Yet her compassion extended from the page to the cities poor. She welcomed the needy with open arms – and a bottomless heart – as she fed, washed, and clothed them in droves. While her exterior was calm, her patience was short for the ignorant of mind; those who never questioned, never wondered, never showed concern.

After the wedding, Aleksandra took residence with Wesley and me. Her father allowed it without question. Viktor and I would spend most nights together while Wesley entertained Aleksandra, educated her. I did not speak of England, the memories of my life there were too painful; but Wesley filled her head with exotic images and tales, of lands and times long forgotten. She begged me to take her back. She wanted to explore, to travel beyond the borders bordering the school's village. Wesley would argue with me, offer to go himself, but still I refused.

Her studies in philosophy and religion, her readings of Aquinas, Heraclitus and Ephesus, even of Diotoma of Mantinea were no match for Wesley. Their debates, in those earlier days, were something to watch and rival. For hours, the two would toss words, truth fueling their passionate exchanges. In the end, regardless the winner, they would come together as friends, embracing each other with warm smiles.

Then Wesley left, as we all eventually do. He was running – hiding, but from what I could never have guessed.

My eyes were blind in those days. All I could see was Viktor, once a noble, youthful man with ebony hair and piercing eyes. Now all that remained, time having waged its war and won, was a frail, ill and fading remnant of the man I loved.

I had seen people die; I had caused them to fall. I had seen kings and noble families succumb to sickness; and witnessed indescribable tragedy. Time has blurred past my eyes in strokes of brilliant color, yet I have failed to feel it. In the year 1560, at the end of February, a light in my soul – if I still had a soul – extinguished and became an angel circling above me.

He rallied until nightfall, waiting to die in my arms.

I gently slid my fingers over his face, over the wrinkles. They were the same wrinkles I had touched years before, yet they felt different. His eyes glazed over in death's shade, mere grayed orbs in sunken sockets, but he could still hear me as I sung him to his sleep. His breathing became shallower as his heartbeat dimmed.

The hours stretched before me, one agonizing moment after another, as I held him, as I talked to him of the past. When I thought the end was imminent, when I nearly succumbed and brought him into my world, his mind spoke.

"You will never be without me, Bree."

My tears marked his face as I leaned over it, kissing his forehead, his eyes, his cheek.

"I will never forget you, Viktor. Never," I whispered to him. "I love you, and I always will. Dying will not change that." As his hand found strength, he reached for my face and stroked my cheek. Then with one last raspy breath, an unforgettable sound now eternally trapped in my ear, he fell limp in my arms.

That night I vowed I would never love anyone else the way I had loved him.

FIFTEEN

You must carry on," Sr. Veronica whispered in my ear. She was resplendent, the sun vibrating off her black veil. Her gown crumpled slightly in the summer breeze. The sun was beginning to set as we carried water from the well. We were naïve, sealed off from the world, promised to a higher power. We believed that evil's villainous grasp could not touch us. Our minds were lost and jumbled in theological theory, in absolution via confession, in being good and proper. We had no concept of true evil. Or what it could do.

The second to last load of water weighed a ton on our shoulders as the sweat cascaded down our foreheads, stinging our eyes with each glistening bead. We could speak freely out here next to the well, far from the prying ears preparing the evening meal.

"Is this our punishment for being the youngest?" I asked her with a chuckle.

"I believe Sister Margaret wishes this to be our penance for having once lived in luxury."

"Well," I told her, "that life is long gone, is it not?" Sr. Veronica nodded. "And we will never see it again."

"Oh, yes we will," she replied, her face aglow in the fading golden sunset, "When we get to Heaven."

The forlorn reality stung into my pale flesh as night dawned, awaking me from the memory of her, of those innocent days. She had reached her Heaven, I only assumed, while I lived in my Hell night after endless night.

Wesley had been right. Again. I should have listened to him and never returned to Russia. The visage of the man I cherished, the mortal I had allowed to love me, would have remained that of my handsome hero. Now when I thought of him, when I gazed onto Aleksandra's face, I saw his frail body slumped in my grasp. I saw the man who struggled for life, who struggled for clarity behind Deaths shadowed veil.

This memory left an acrid aura in the air and a bitter taste in my mouth, a taste that blood could not relieve.

I had been naïve believing I could handle loving a mortal and witnessing his body – the aged lump of bones and skin and blood now tainted by the finality of death – release its soul into the waiting afterlife. What existed beyond now cradled the man I adored. His body, his memories, his words, perished and relinquished to the family mausoleum.

He existed only now in oil paintings and the memories of others. And sometimes, to the outside world at least, it was as if he had never existed. They mourned him and did something I struggled with, they let him go.

It was 1561; Aleksandra was but forethought in the minds of Tver's people. Her own bloodline ceasing to exist with the swift upheaval Viktor's death caused. His bloodline, without an heir, seceded to a far off cousin.

We packed Wesley's possessions when we moved to Paris and they remained that way, sealed off in a cold and lifeless room.

That room was a void, a time capsule collecting dust, waiting to open, to reveal its secrets. The atmosphere was grayer without him. This reflected in Aleksandra's brilliant eyes, which dulled some when he left and continued to dim, her light fading as she waited for his return.

It was then that I should have seen the future. Yet I was ignorant, still lost in grief. Marriage proposal after marriage proposal, Aleksandra refused them all. Dukes and princes, none could secure her hand.

She buried herself in books, in dramas, in scientific texts. Her room filled with gadgets and potions, and odorous ingredients that caused my sensitive nose to twitch on more than one occasion. It was uncommon for a woman to behave this way, and rumors circulated. Yet one after another, they fell on her deaf ears. She was distracting herself with knowledge, book after book, and experiment after experiment. I should have realized why.

It was 1562 when he returned. It was as if sunlight returned to our shadowed world. At least how I remember sunlight feeling as it trickled in through the convent windows, warming me to the soul. It returned to Aleksandra as soon as she beheld him walking through the gardens, approaching the house, the moonlight softly reflecting off his face. He came for her, not me; and she had been waiting for him. The world existed for them; for how long I did not know, and I was just now seeing it.

She was a tender, innocent nineteen. He had centuries ahead of her. Yet they both saw a commonality, a shared passion. I realized this as I watched him gaze into her eyes as Viktor had often gazed into my own. The smile graced her face in return, her quickened heartbeat granted her a livelihood that had been sorely missing; and it pushed the shadows away. Between them, love blossomed, and I wondered how I could have been so blind as not to see this happening.

"You are sad," she told me the night after Wesley returned to us, to her. "What has made you that way?"

"The sunlight," I remarked.

Her hand gently came to rest on my shoulder, and she patted me as one would pat a sickly child. "What is there to miss about the sunlight? There are days – hot days, scorching hot days, when I wish the sun would hide forever."

"Never wish for such a thing, Aleksandra," I answered her. Rain droplets were beginning to fall, gently at first and then in a torrent beating and bouncing off the terracotta fountain in the garden, and slamming violently into the windows.

"Oh, but I could live as you live… by candlelight. It is a romantic view of the world, mother. Moonlight and candlelight." Her eyes locked onto the cloudy sky, void of starlight on this dreary night. There was a haunting spark in her eyes, as if the world was hers but only now, only at night, only when it rained.

"With Wesley?"

"Yes," she answered, her sight remaining fixed on the evening sky. "I love him."

"He is an uncle to you, Aleksandra." I remarked in disbelief, yet I knew this revelation was eventually coming.

"He has never been like an uncle to me," she said, turning to me, "you have just failed to notice."

"Does he love you?" I asked, again knowing the answer. Perhaps I needed to *hear* it. Our eyes, after all, can deceive us.

"You ask questions you already know the answers to." She turned to me. "You already know what this means, too. You do not want to accept it, and you will try to talk me out of it, but you know your words will be pointless. I have not entered into this in haste. I never enter into anything in haste."

"I need time with this, Aleksandra. Please, can you do that for me?"

"What is time but mere moments combined to span the centuries, mother? We will soon have a million moments and yet you ask me to delay this wish of mine?" She asked, turning away. "That, I cannot do."

"Time? What do you know of time?" I demanded. She paused in her step, her left foot catching at the toe, her heel finally finding rest as her body pivoted toward me.

"Time is an endless blur once you are immortal. Eternity, Aleksandra, it's a wave of color bleeding into itself, yet with distinct edges, distinct frames that pause – shortly – allowing oneself to reflect on the multitude of such instance; until one night, you'll discover you've lost yourself – bit by bit, leaving little pieces scattered throughout the centuries. Lost, my child; that is how one eventually feels after having witnessed ages pass. Lost. Alone. Tired."

"Would you change one second of this eternity Wesley has provided you?" Aleksandra asked. "Would you erase Aksel?" Her eyes grew misty and her lip, the bottom one with the freckle that swam in its center, quivered. "Would you erase my father?"

"I loved them, Aleksandra. Their fates, both of them, haunt me." I stepped closer and laid my hand on her shoulder. Her eyes moved downward, averting my glance. She was but an innocent, a child, so pure. Nineteen could have been ten, but she surpassed the ages. "And there has not been a night where I have not longed for the peace a natural death would have afforded me."

"To grow old?" she asked, her voice subdued by our closeness.

"Aleksandra, peace comes with age."

"You are old now, older than you could have ever been being a mortal!"

"Yes, then why am I not at peace?"

I had left her that evening standing at the window, glancing up at the stars. My words gave her pause, but not long enough. She came to me three nights later. "This is what I want," she stated. I did not deny her.

At first when my teeth pierced her tender flesh, the pulsating blood a siren's call, and she struggled. Then it rushed into my mouth, the crimson river, lulling me deeper with each rhythmic gush into the shadowy veil now covering my eyes. The tunnel stretched before me, the vague and familiar place I had been too many times before. Her thoughts inundated the darkness, ricocheted, screamed; but I pushed them far beyond my reach. I could not know these things, these precious jewels in her mind, in her heart. Then Viktor's face flew at me in the darkness, faster than a shooting star, and hung on my tongue. I drew away, the image of him filling the tears now dripping down my ashen cheeks.

"Am I dying?" Her breath was hot on my palm as I cradled her head.

"No, but you will wish you were." I drew my head to her neck once more, the vein now placid against her ivory skin. "Aleksandra," I whispered, "this is going to be the worst pain you have ever felt. Are you sure you want this?"

"The light... it is fading," she struggled, her rasping voice dimming in the moments before death. "Help me, mother."

Then my teeth sank deeper and drained the last vital drop of life from her body. As the body died, as the heart stopped beating, and the air squeezed from her lungs, I slumped against the wall, releasing her. My body now lay burdened with the weight of her; burdened by her blood collecting in my immortal veins, which now invaded my cursed cells. Her gasping faded with the candlelight. My vision faded with it.

Her blood intoxicated me; lured me into hidden pathways where my haunted memories reside. As my vision dimmed, her forbidden essence swimming inside me, those memories were unrelenting. They demanded my presence. And the years I spent resisting them mattered less and less with each drop of her blood. The gate was open.

The crisp autumn air wafted through the halls, and the stones felt cool beneath my bare feet. The wool brush scratched its way through the soapy layer, scrubbing away the collected dirt and grime. The sun, slipping through the cloister windows, burned through my black habit as my hands shriveled from the dirty water.

"We will be in the scriptorium tonight," Sr. Veronica remarked, walking past me.

I whispered as she walked by. "You will have us both in Mother's office if you are not quiet."

The morning was long, scrubbing and mopping, but it was similar to the previous morning. And, the morning before that. Life would continue on this way until we died. The predictability of it, the mundane, drove me silently mad. I would push this feeling back, hiding it.

That night, though, was longer. I had been quiet while we sat copying by candlelight. She noticed this as she noticed everything about me, all the time. The candlelight flickered and dimmed as the hours passed. The morning would be creeping over the clouds soon and my eyes grew weary, blurring the colored ink spread across the vellum.

"We should retire," she told me, jarring me from my dozing.

"Does it seem to you that the night has secrets?" I asked her.

"Secrets?" She was putting scrolls of vellum on a shelf, extinguishing candles near the window, and straightening the inks.

"There seems to be something missing that is all. As if the night held a secret, something we cannot see. It is there, you know. Just hidden… hidden and watching."

"You are delirious with exhaustion," she whispered, leading me out through the scriptorium door. She quietly latched it, her left arm still firmly braced on my shoulder.

"We could both benefit from a good rest."

She has achieved her rest, I thought as I returned, the Parisian night beckoning me home. Aleksandra was moaning, lying on the floor, gripping at the pain seizing her body. Her life was almost over. Watching her, I remembered that agony. It was the last pain I felt as a human, and I realized I could benefit from a good rest now. Sr. Veronica had gotten hers, after all.

SIXTEEN

In the woodlands of Wiltshire stands Lacock Abbey – a stone fortress, a testament to the everlasting British country society. A lifetime ago, I ate fresh blueberries and picked roses from its quaint gardens. The lilac bushes grew wild then, the fragrance calming the rushing imagination of youth.

The sun warmed me as I worked in the lawn, toiling fresh fruit from the garden. The musky scent of earth reminded me of my fleeting mortality.

Before the dissolution of the monasteries in 1536, Lacock Abbey had been a convent. My convent.

There I had known blissful innocence.

It was not so in 1562, when the once tender and pure Russian princess Aleksandra Vladislov had become a timeless fixture for her people through the vampiric gift. She was now, unlike her mother country, unchangeable – a living time capsule.

Our time in Paris was short lived. Three nights after Aleksandra received the dark gift, we left for my beloved England.

Lacock Abbey now stood resplendent against the moonlit sky. The stars glistened against freshly fallen dew collecting on the rose bushes. The centuries changed nothing of the grounds. Time stood motionless as my eyes misted with memories of Sr. Veronica and me wasting the hot nights before bed, dipping our toes in the fishpond, or picking lilacs to sell in the village. Lacock Abbey was persistent in its resistance to the natural evolution of time.

A faint light shone from Sharington's Tower that night. Henry VIII sold the abbey to Sir William Sharington, who demolished the church, destroying my sacred history, turning the abbey into a home. Sir William stored wondrous treasures in the tower he had built, and that night he stood amongst the glimmering jewels, surveying his legacy.

I snuck into the warming room. During my time there, the warming room was the only place in the nunnery in which we kept a fire. No fire raged that night, though. A lone torch hung on the wall but remained unlit.

Sr. Veronica's voice whispered from the corner. "If we allow the fire to dim, we will be frozen by morning."

I swung around, yet she was not there. Her voice was but a fading fingerprint, a ghost still trapped between time and the limestone walls.

"I failed you," I whispered into the nothingness surrounding me. "I failed all of you." No one remained to comfort me. Even the familiar stone walls, holding their memories and their ghosts, were foreign and removed. I no longer belonged there. My presence seemed perverse and I left as silently as I had come.

England, every bit of it – the sound of the Clydesdale hooves on the cobblestones, the aroma of mince pie, the laughter from the pubs – was all wrong. This was no longer my England.

I stayed in the West Country. The eerie calm of Savernake Forest in the darkness of midnight was dreamlike, but the absence of the golden sun left the forest's spectacular fauna and flora to the realms of imagination and memory. As a child, there was an old oak tree the locals called Big Belly Oak. Legend says dancing around the tree naked will summon the Devil himself. We never tempted the myth. Now, I wondered if the Devil would be more afraid of me than I would be of him.

I was in West Country but a month before venturing to London. Winter was in full throw, snow collecting on the cobblestones: blanketing the rooftops, and obscuring the shop signs. Fire raged in packed pubs and shoeless children froze, begging for pence in the streets.

The scene – straight from a Dickens' tale – dripped with despair. I walked to one child, shoeless, clothed in rags that stank of pig dung and were too small for the frail boy's frame, and dropped a hand full of coins and then another of precious stones. The boy's eyes, after beholding his new bounty, glistened up at me as if I were Father Christmas. He scurried off, calling to the other beggars and disappeared into a darkened, fog-filled alley. The lost children of London, I thought, would at least eat well that night.

I went first to the Tower of London: a fortress of imprisonment and elaborate display of royal power. It stood before me, a goliath of brick and mortar. My first evening there I spent lingering on the Tower Green where, eight years prior, Queen Mary Tudor ordered the execution of one Lady Jane Grey. The "Nine Days Queen" roamed the Queen's Garden at will, enjoying the warm sun on her face; and sleeping contentedly in her state apartment, a comfortable purse at her disposal. The naïve queen, Lady Jane, now resides in the Chapel Royal of St. Vincent ad Vincula, alongside the bodies of Catherine Howard and Anne Boleyn.

Not two years prior had Catherine Howard, in 1552, lost her life on the Green; and prior to that, Anne Boleyn in the summer of 1536. One-year prior to Anne Boleyn's death, Sir Thomas Moore faced the executioner for committing high treason, for refusing to sign the Act of Succession. The blood of England's past saturated and stained the Green's soil with bureaucratic corruption. And, I found great relief that I had not been there to witness it.

The muted blanket of moonlight dulled the Tower Green and masked the Queen's Gardens splendor, so I traveled instead to Westminster Abbey. The Early English Gothic architecture, with its pointed arches and ribbed vaulting, reminded me of the things I adore and sorely missed about my mother country. These walls would be testimony to a rich history; the stained glass windows reflections of a religion once embraced by all whom hailed from England, including me.

I spent an entire evening in front of the shrine of Edward the Confessor. Mary had pieced it together as best she could after its dismantlement during the Reformation. Gone were the elaborate Cosmati swirls that once graced its stone base, the monks' thoughts revealed. Gone was the golden feretory covering Edward's coffin.

A week's worth of evenings were exhausted combing through the books in Merton College's library, torchlight in hand. Oxford's academic jewel is one of the oldest libraries in England. The tomes I held then, the vellum and parchment smooth beneath my fingers; they are now either lost or tucked safely away in locked, glass cases, or hidden in Vatican vaults. But I will never forgot the smell of leather and vellum, of ink, or how the shadows moved against the whitewashed candlelit walls, shifting between the bookshelves and tables. It has been said that if you put an idea in print, it becomes immortal. That is what I witnessed in the library – immortality.

During those nights, I fell in love with histories and stories from times I had actually lived. I had read of people who were once real to me, but who were now only a sentence in a history book. Names brought into mind images, feelings, experiences, and I realized in the dim candlelight, tucked away beneath of stack of leather bound pamphlets, that history lived within me.

Aleksandra and Wesley accompanied me to Christ Church one evening, after I had left the books and memories on their shelves. Christ Church was not just a college but also the diocese of Oxford. The Norman pillars and the vaulting choir captivated Aleksandra, who spent an evening sketching their intricacies. The newly reburied remains of Katherine Martyr, the wife of Peter Martyr Vermigili (Regius Chair of Divinity, and Protestant reformer as appointed by Edward VI) and those of St. Fridewside (foundress of a nunnery where the college was formed after the dissolution of the monasteries) now found peace. When the college fell again under Catholic rule, the new dean had been ordered to exhume Katherine's body, leaving it to rot in a dung-heap.

We parted at Christ's Church. For Aleksandra, her new eyes were first beholding the beauty of my mother country. But, for Wesley and me, this was a homecoming – a surreal homecoming where the familiar was saturated in change.

SEVENTEEN

I've lived long enough to realize how lost one can become when fixated on the minutes of each day.

Confronted by your past, life stops in a breath-sucking moment of terror. Where had those moments – all the cherished, fleeting seconds that seemed random and insignificant, gone? Had years really flown by as I stood, an unchanging sentinel, guarding memories, fixating on the mundane particulars of an uncertain future, only for the epiphany to arrive too late to matter?

I struggled to reattach myself to a past that I knew was gone to me. Forever. Time stole those moments, those years, from me, and ruined my connection to this place.

We existed in England, nevertheless. Wesley took ownership of an estate outside Winchester. It was rather spacious, a sprawling monument to forest conservation and stout British architecture. A far grander place than we needed, but Wesley never downplayed what he felt was our natural place in society and history.

The house itself was elegant and modern for its time. Two parlors – evening and morning (the latter unused), a modest ballroom adorned in ivory and marble and hard, darkly stained woods, and three grand libraries. The main dining room's windows filtered sunlight through its stained glass that played on the white tablecloth, and made music with the crystal goblets. Or, so we were told.

At night, the candlelight reflected the colors bouncing off the gilded mirrors weaving a rainbow-aura, and this was sufficient for us.

It had to be, after all. We seek sustenance in candlelight. In all its golden glow touches, reflects off, bleeds through. Candlelight is our sun.

A dense forest encircled the property with a modest pond only a short walk from the house. Eventually Wesley had a pebbled lane installed; yellow and white imported Italian stone, which led a path to the main gate, circled around to the back patio and ended in the fountain garden to the east of the house. He called this his chemin de soleil – sun path – and lined it with nerium oleander and lilac. The fountains – the trickling aqua over marble, gently gushing sprays of water sprouting from cherubim mouths – mingled amongst rose bushes and stone benches. Walking this path on warm, summer evenings, or sitting in the fountain garden – the scents could be intoxicating.

For ten years, we lived a stolen life.

Near the end, when all talk turned to the New World, to exploration and new beginnings, Aleksandra and Wesley's wanderlust set in. Stationary and stagnant are not the traits of my kind. We are a nomadic people.

I had no urge to travel, though, keeping to my own country.

It was 1572 and Wesley and Aleksandra ventured toward Paris and then on to Rome. They settled for a few years in Dublin to observe, as Wesley often wrote, "the Calvinistic tendencies running rampant." However, they never really *settled* in any one place for long.

Occasionally, they would return. A month here and a month there, but never long. Until the winter of 1612,when they returned for three years.

I once spent seven months, during our years apart, in the city of Exeter, in the county Devon. It was Isca when the Romans settled this fine, rugged land. They had invaded southwestern England in 50 AD. Since then, Exeter has survived a seventh century German invasion, an 8th century Danish raid, and stood no chance against a Norman siege in 1068. Even Henry VIII's religious civil war against parliament could not shake the town's second century Roman wall.

Neither could it tumble Exeter Cathedral. The first stone was set in 1112, twin Norman towers were built, flanking an expansive Gothic vault, and provided Saint Boniface a place of solitude. There he converted northern Germany to Christianity. There, history happened.

My travels to York were also plentiful with Aleksandra and Wesley gone. In my former life, before the Dissolution of the Monasteries, before Wesley turned me, York served as a monastic retreat. Many religious houses and hospitals existed within the city's walls. After Henry VIII dissolved the monasteries, though, the religious landscape was in turmoil. On November 5, 1605, Guy Fawkes, a Roman Catholic restorationist, was caught and arrested while guarding hidden explosives under the House of Lords. An assassination attempt was thwarted, saving King James I and Protestant officials.

When I visited, the city seemed lost, in transition. Much like myself.

I spent countless nights sitting on the bank of the Ouse River watching ships sail through the calm waters. When the Romans settled the city, they named it Eboracum. It had been a stronghold until 400 AD, when the fighting in Gaul placed a strain on Roman resources. The Roman Legions were withdrawn, sending the town into a spiral of change. Anglo Saxon tribes filtered the area, seized control, and Christianity spread. With the Viking invasions, the city became a crucial port in the Norse trade routes. Eventually, William the Conqueror took possession of the city.

With time, York became the capitol of northern England. Its growth was halted in the 1400's with the War of the Roses, but, as everything will do in time, the city rose like a phoenix from the ashes of its past.

My phoenix came to me in Bath, though. It was my ninth trip to the city and one I thought would go as uneventful as the previous eight had.

Standing amidst the rubble of Bath Abbey – the crumbling stone, the broken glass parables – a reminder of Henry VIII's treason against his country, a feeling tickled my throat. A subtle, familiar scent wafted from the desiccated tombstones, hidden in overgrowth and forgotten. I sensed movement in the shadows, an unnatural movement – slow, deliberate, stalking me.

It stopped near the chapel wall.

I called to it. "Come out from the shadow."

Shards of glass crunched under its footsteps.

"Is that you?" It asked.

"Who is there?" I questioned as I leaned into the blackness. "Come out."

"You will never change," it spoke as the figure moved from the darkness. The light caught on its chin until the image before me morphed into a man.

"Aksel?"

His hand reached for my hair and I let his fingers slip through the strands. His fingers caressed my cheeks and traced my lips, before I caught them, holding them in my own.

"What are you doing in Bath?"

"I have searched for you. You are difficult to find."

"Why?"

He moved from me, sitting on the edge of the crumbling chapel wall. His hair was tousled and messy. His tattered clothing pulled at the seams from wear.

"Where is Evelyn?" I asked.

"She grew up," he said, resting his face in the palm of his hands. "She no longer needed me." He stood looking up into the starlit sky. "She fell in love, Bree. Evelyn and her lover – once joined in the blood, they quickly began making more. Now they have a little coven in Paris. There must be thirty by now, if not more. Can you imagine?"

"That sounds dreadful; why would I want to imagine such a thing?"

"It is." His eyes met mine. "I want to be with you, Bree."

"Askel, stop, don't speak those words."

"No. I do! Please." He moved closer and forced his hand into mine. "I've searched for you. Twenty years, Bree, for twenty years I've wandered this globe looking for any sign of you. Any mention of your name, of our kind. Bree, please, do not turn me away! We must come together, for our sanity and companionship. Bree, eternity, it drags on so, does it not?"

"I just cannot, Aksel. I cannot. I will not."

"Please, Bree." His fingers stopped the tear sliding down my cheek.

"You cannot stop them all, Aksel."

"I can try," he said.

"I cannot love you again," I told him. "I will never, ever, love again. And I will not pretend to. Not even to pass the centuries in peace with you. There'll be nothing but strife, growing yet another chasm between us. Just give it time, Aksel. It will happen again. And this time," I said, turning my cheek from his view, "this time our love will not be there binding us to the other. Loneliness is not enough."

"He must have been someone extremely special." He spoke with knowledge and understanding. "Bree," Aksel's fingers gingerly crept against my chin as he turned my face toward his, "I am not trying to replace him. It is apparent that no one will ever replace him."

I spent the rest of the evening telling Aksel about Viktor. It had been too long since I smiled with the mention of his name. Far too long had I buried his memory inside my heart.

"I can still feel him in here." I pointed to my breast. "I may have no heart beat, but that doesn't mean I do not have a heart."

Centuries passed and Aksel traveled with me. My faithful companion, my friend.

In the winter of 1612, when Wesley and Aleksandra returned, we all left the fog stricken land of England for the Mediterranean.

We spent an entire summer in Athens, weaving our way through ruined temples. Aksel adored the Library of Hadrian on the north side of the Acropolis. The architecture amused him, the materials used to create the structure, the artisanship. He knew its history as well as his own. There was special significance to the Western Wall because, unlike the other three walls, which were limestone, the Western Wall is Pentelic marble, and decorated with an elaborate row of Corinthian columns. He told us that Pentelic marble came from the quarries of Mount Pentelikon in Attica. We found his facts amusing, but I could not share his passion for stone.

I enjoyed walking through the Kerameikos instead of taking part in his Greek architecture lessons. In 431 BC, Pericles had given his famous funeral oration there. As a child, I learned its call for democracy and freedom. Aksel never understood my desire to linger there in the wee hours before dawn. Morbid. That is what he called my fascination with the place.

Before we knew it, a year of Mediterranean midnights had passed as we traveled throughout Greece. Mykonos. The Pan-Hellenic sanctuaries. The birthplace of Apollo and Artemis, as Poseidon revealed it – the island of Delos. The legend of how Delos grew from the sea is one of jealousy, of betrayal, of human nature. When Leto, the goddess of motherhood, became pregnant with Zeus's child, Hera, Zeus's wife and queen of the god's, raged with jealousy. She exiled the pregnant Leto, forbidding her to give birth on Earth. As labor neared, Zeus, besot and desperate, appealed to Poseidon for intervention. Poseidon then parted the sea, revealing the island of Delos, and Leto gave birth to the twin god's Artemis and Apollo.

The Venice of Greece, Mykonos, a sparsely vegetated island surrounded in deep, sapphire seas, with cresting pearlescent waves stands as the legendary battleground for Hercules and the giants. The monolithic rocks scattered through the island were believed to be petrified remnants of the giant corpses, having fallen in battle and cursed to serve as eternal reminders of Hercules's power.

While breathtaking under a star drenched sky, I felt no connection to the place and quickly left it for Crete.

Even on the darkest of nights, the sweet aroma of olive trees and orange groves, of cedar forests and sunshine followed us on Crete. The Aegean Sea stretched before us, vineyards grew at our feet, and cedar and palm forests wildly inhabited my nightly walks.

I recall now a spot near the edge of an olive grove, the grass grew knotted, and sand blew in from the coast. The waves crashing at night could be deafening, drowning out the world, drowning out the past and all future cares. There existed a few hours each night, right before dawn as tomorrow edged into today, when we would all separate, going our own ways before surrendering to sleep. Aleksandra read. Wesley explored. Aksel wandered about. And I would always sit at the spot near the edge of the olive grove, gazing into the Aegean's azure waters.

Three nights before we left Greece, Wesley came to me there. I had known this talk would happen since he found me wandering through the Kerakeimos, ruby tears falling against my milky skin. He knew better to question me then.

Now, as even he sensed the parting ways that would soon come, his need to speak with me became urgent.

"What if tomorrow never comes?"

His voice snuck into cadence with the cicada's song, into the drumbeat that played on the waves.

"Then it does not come," I replied, brushing away the tears.

"Is that how you truly feel?" His hand rested on my shoulder as he sat down next to me on the olive branch.

"How should I feel, Wesley?" His silence deepened the insidious emptiness existing in my bones. "I would give all of my days to know where I belong." I fingered an olive leaf. It felt like smooth satin between my fingertips.

"To have him back," I whispered. "My innocence. My peace."

"You cannot trade tomorrow for yesterday, my sister." He turned my face toward his and wiped at my tears with his own thumb. "We have to look to the future."

I stood and faced him. "The future scares me. I have no faith in it."

"Listen." He rose, grabbing my hand, pressing it into his own. "The end is merely a beginning. You will love again. You will find peace again!"

"My heart is far too broken for that."

"He would have wanted you to love again." Her voice sliced through the shadowy night.

"Aleksandra," I began before she cut me off.

"He had faith in you. More than I think you have in yourself," she said. "He would want you to have hope that his love would not be the last you will experience in this lifetime, mother."

"Not all is lost, Bree." Aksel's voice crept from behind, cutting through the crashing waves. "I think it is time you start living as if tomorrow *will* never come."

"What is that supposed to mean?" My arms rose in exasperation!

"Stop dying inside," Aleksandra said. "Live!"

Wesley came to my side, gently caressing my back. "The future will not kill you, Bree. Living in the past, holding onto Viktor or to the convent, that is only going to fill you with regret and pain. It will slowly drive you mad."

I gazed at them and realized how blurry time had become – an irrelevant stream of endless phases and movement. We become caught in the years and months, in the centuries, in the moments that make up each night, that sometimes we feel as if we are getting lost, but I *was* lost.

EIGHTEEN

On our last night in Greece, I returned to that spot on the edge of the olive grove. The moon clung to the sky as a lost child reunited with its mother. Had that conversation really happened?

I watched them in the distance, preparing to leave. We were to meet back at the mansion in England. We were to resume our old lives, as if time had stood still.

However, I did not return.

Trading olive trees and warm sea breezes, I descended onto a cloudy snow-covered mountain peak. There was isolation here and a chance for reflection, a place to rediscover my purpose.

I watched as a group of women, clad in colorful peasant dresses, backlit by several small bonfires, paced around the Qinghai Lake. They were clearing their sins; washing them away with ritual. Each woman paced seven times until they stopped, seating themselves around the bonfires. Some of the women cupped the water, droplets spilling from their wanton fingers, and spread it across their parched cheeks. They cried out as the saltwater stung their skin.

It was cold here. Bitterly cold.

I took to the skies until I saw a scarcely populated area of nomads, their tents alit with the warm glow of oil lamps. There was a central fire pit and surrounding it was a group of men. They wore double-layered flowing robes – their heads naked to the elements. Sheep and cattle mingled nearby while children slept inside the tented compound.

Not far from there, I came upon a city. Tucked into the southwestern Chinese frontier in the nomadic Tibetan countryside was Lhasa.

It was Losar, the Tibetan New Year, and people of all ages danced about wearing brightly colored dresses, the married women sporting ornately patterned aprons and the men in simple robes. Strings of metal coins hung jingling, loosely woven into the partygoers' garments. They made a magical sound as they tinkled and chimed through the streets, the darkened corners, around the raging bonfires.

It was autumn then, and the apricot trees were blooming. The scent of fallen blossoms permeated the blackness. It was the time for the festival of ritualistically burning incense to appease local spirits.

Before Buddhism, the Tibetan people practiced Bon. It was an animistic religion rife with contradicting rituals and customs. Scholars now argue that Bon was nothing more than pre-Buddhism, with Buddhism becoming a syncretistic hodge-podge of the two traditions.

It was in the Lhokha Yarla Shampo region where legend claims the festival was born, during the reign of Pude Gungyal, the ninth king, or karály. It replaced what was then referred to as the farmer's festival, a time to mark the harvest. After the advent of rudimentary astrology, the festival changed to mark the day of lunar New Year.

Celebrations, feasts, dances, they would be conducted for fifteen or more days and nights. Now, after the Chinese invasion into Tibet, celebrations are a short three days in duration.

This was the fourth night of Losar, though, and at small areas near the central fire people gathered, bowls in hand, to find their fortune in guthuk dumplings. Simmering in a spicy meat stew, guthuk dumplings lay in wait to reveal their hidden treasures. Nine chances existed for the diner to get a sugar cube, a small nip of wood, folded paper, wool string, a raw bean, pebble, a cotton ball, or a hot chili pepper, with each symbolizing, in a comedic jest, the receiver's character. Good luck would come to those whose treasures are white, while coal means the receiver has a heart of black.

I stayed in the shadow, removed from the crowd, and watched as two children explored doughy dumplings while sipping the steaming broth from their bowls. There is a transcendent innocence when children laugh. It freezes time, blurring the lines of reality.

I watched as the first child uncovered a chunk of coal, his eyes widened as his friend pointed and laughed. He tossed it into a nearby fire. The second boy, his friend now urging him, reached into the bowl and pulled out a moist dumpling. His pudgy fingers fumbled as the glob of dough slipped around, falling out of the bowl and landing on his lap. He smashed it with his hand, revealing a wisp of cotton thread. The first boy now grimaced and playfully shoved the second child.

"Remember when we were their age?"

I closed my eyes. The smell of linseed oil hung in the air. I breathed it in slowly, clinging to it as the tears formed.

"I remember many things," I replied. The Tibetan countryside faded, replaced with candlelight and stone. The pew was hard beneath me. I could feel it. I could smell the linseed oil.

I could see her. Sister Veronica.

"We had forever in front of us," she said, her face obstructed by the heavy black veil. She clung to the marble crucifix attached to her prayer cord. Her hands were as real as my own, down to the tiny hairs on her knuckles, and the scar on her thumb from that mirror she broke the summer of her eighth birthday.

"Do you remember when you broke that mirror?" I asked her, pointing to the scar. "You bled so much that we both cried."

"You do not cry over blood anymore, do you?" She clutched the crucifix harder now. Her head dipped to an almost impossible low; her voice stifling tears.

"No," I whispered. "No, I do not."

A sniffle escaped her veil. Her head lifted, turning toward me, her eyes piercing through the years that separated us. Creases lined her eyes from worry. Her cheeks ashen and sunken away, her lips pursed as if to speak. Then a solitary tear – a real tear – glistening as it fell, rolled down her cheek.

"I can change all that," I told her.

"It is not your time, Bree." She touched her hand to mine. It was warm and firm. My unnatural coldness did not scare her. I closed my eyes, let the flood of pain and guilt, of loss and longing, wash over me.

The delicate touch of her lips brushed against my cheek. Then I heard the laughing and singing. I heard the children playing nearby.

She was gone when I opened my eyes, the candlelight and stone transformed into cool grass and a festival of lights and sound.

"Who were you talking to?" he asked.

"I knew you would follow me," I told him. He sat down beside me, placing a concerned arm around my shoulder. "Why did you do it?"

"Because I knew you would need someone." He leaned in, playfully resting his head on my shoulder. "I knew you would need me."

"No," I told him, "That night in the convent. Why did you come for me?"

"I have told you this already. I was lonely," Wesley replied.

"I want the truth," I demanded. "You ruined... no, you stole my life. And I want to know why you felt you had that right."

"Why did you make Aksel?"

"I had no one," I replied. He removed his arm from my shoulder. "I left you and then I had no one."

Wesley let the air grow stagnate with our silence. He lowered himself onto the cool grass, stretching his long legs. I watched the crowd below disperse, the people going home to their mortal beds. To age. To change. To die.

Finally, the words escaped in a whisper. "I was lonely."

"And why did you let Viktor die?"

"Because I was lonely," I replied. "And I knew that was no reason to rob him of peace."

"Then you have learned from my mistake, have you not?" he said. "Now, my sister, let your ghosts rest." He stood. "All of them."

He left after that.

Our kind, we are lonely and small, and weak. We are lost and falling, uncertain where we will land. We are needy and breakable.

We need companions, friends. We need to exist. We need breathed in, savored, and loved.

We have all lost who we once were. And we all need to be found.

NINETEEN

When the English elms went dormant and even the waters slept on the convent grounds, we all slumbered in spirit. The world paused around us when the winter snow fell. The hearth fire warmed the center of a room while the rest of the convent grew drearily cold.

I remember the frigid hardness of those convent stones on my bare feet each morning. I remember the agonizing walk to the central hearth. Even my soul felt bathed in ice.

How I had been wrong then.

This, this immortality, was far colder than any English winter night. And no fire existed that could warm me now.

It was 1618 when I finally returned to them. I had roamed the Chinese countryside. I thought about Russia, but could not find the strength to return. And despite my sincerity, the whole experience blurred into a rolling fog of lost time.

None of it mattered.

The others, though, had been busy while I aimlessly and futilely roamed.

Aleksandra had bestowed a substantial portion of wealth to a local society, which in turn built a boarding school. They knew nothing of her identity, of course. She never visited, and instead merely insisted on quarterly reports to a mysterious A. Vladislov. To this day, she still acts as a beneficiary through a fictitious trust in her memory.

Wesley established a hospital. He was never a doctor or one for medicine, really. But money? He had plenty of that. What began as one local clinic, merged into a giant conglomerate. He works, from behind the smoke screen of anonymity, to further medicine. Later, in the modern centuries, after the move to America, Aleksandra took up the cause of genetic medicine.

I, for one, was as lost as I had been when I departed Crete.

I came back to progress, to my kin living, existing. But, I was but a shell of what they had become.

While I was gone, Aleksandra had come across a painting of her father selling at auction. There was an unnamed woman in the painting, her hair long, her dress flowing. She lingered in the back of the scene, watching Viktor from behind a curtain. Viktor, regal and stoic, was dining on a winter's feast, talking merrily with the then princess, Mavra.

The scowl on Mavra's face was unforgivable. The artist, unknown as the painting was unsigned, captured the turmoil in the princess's eyes. She had one eye fixed on Viktor and one eye fixed on the mysterious woman behind the curtain. And I could still feel her icy glare boring into me, haunting me, chasing me through time.

"Who was she?" Aleksandra asked me the night I found it hanging in the gallery. She had placed it there, near a corner, uncertain if she should keep it. She recognized the half-veiled figure. She recognized her father. She did not recognize the woman with the icy glare.

"Mavra Vladislov," I whispered, "your mother."

She ran her fingertips over the painted face, over the white cheeks, the ashen hair.

"You remind me of her sometimes."

"We never talk about her," Aleksandra said.

"It was complicated for your father, Aleksandra," I tried to explain.

"When was this painted?"

"I am not sure," I told her. "Before you were born, I assume."

We sat down on a corner couch, in the darkness. I told her everything. How Viktor married Mavra, but loved me. How Mavra was vindictive and cunning, and loved Aleksandra and Anastasia. Loved them but never knew them. I shared fond memories from the time before their birth when Mavra had changed. How what happened to her had been a tragedy. How Viktor could not see how different Mavra had become.

I then told her how I had killed her mother. The description of it, so clinical, distant, that I almost believed it happened to someone else.

How those moments, the last breathes and thoughts of a complex woman, still haunted me. How it formed a chasm separating me from humanity, even more so than I already was. And how because of it, I had to let her father die.

How letting Viktor die ate at me until it formed an enormous void which no other love could ever hope to fill.

"He loved you, though," she said as I wept.

"And I loved him," I whispered. "I have not seen his face since I left Russia, Aleksandra."

"Me neither," she said. "Sometimes, I forget what he looked like."

I reached up; my fingers met her cheek and slowly made their way across her ashen skin. Her eyes revealed the secrets her face held away, unseen. Her age. Her wisdom. Her history.

"I can never forget because I see him every time I behold your face, see your smile."

She hugged my shoulders, and then strolled to the painting. "I never knew her," she said as she traced Mavra's emerald gown with her fingertip. "I will never know her."

"She was your mother," I told her. "A piece of her will always live within you, whether you knew her or not."

"No," she said turning toward me. "You are my mother. She just gave birth to me."

The next night, when I went to see the painting, it was gone. Aleksandra had it removed and reframed.

A month later, I found it hanging in my room one night after I had been feeding. Over the fireplace, framed in gilded gold, was an image of me, peeking out from behind a curtain and Viktor, sitting at the meal, alone. She had Mavra removed, erased.

Every night I would stare up into his eyes until the emptiness gnawed at me. I would remember how it felt to be in his arms, to feel him around me, breathing, his heart beating – the smell of his sweat, the taste of his lips on my own.

Then it became impossible to look at it without wanting to depart from this existence.

I had it removed. I had it hidden. I tried to forget once again.

By the mid-1680's, I had suppressed Viktor's ghost. It was difficult, because a large part of me did not want to lock him away into the past again. A large part of me wanted nothing more than to be lost in that past forever. That part of me had to succumb, once again, for his spirit to go with it.

Then in 1719, the painting resurfaced. Wesley and Aleksandra had left for France. They had been gone for seven months. Then Aksel left for Russia but I could not go with him.

Alone, I went wandering through the attic. There was enough history tucked into dusty trunks, placed in shadow, to fill a dozen museums. Centuries of trinkets and art, of stories waiting to be told.

I spent my nights romancing memories.

I found the fur blanket Viktor wrapped the twins in the night they were born. I found a bag of my mother's jewels and a painting of my great-great-grandfather that had been in my father's library. Wesley had gone back for it and taken it, days after he became a vampire.

There were trunks of books covered in dust, many falling into the void, their moth eaten pages disintegrating as I touched them. The leather binding cracked with age, and the odor was history weathering away with each passing moment.

Then the painting slipped from the shadows, from that place I carved into my psyche to bury it in forever. I sat in that dreary land of memories and stared at that painting, at his face, the whole evening. I kissed the image and shook from the pain his memory caused.

Those eyes. Those dark, brooding eyes. The first time he looked at me with those eyes, I melted into nothingness. All my supernatural being became his.

That dark hair was now but a memory in a painting. How it had grayed, thinning at the temples, moistened with sweat on his last night with me. How I had run my fingers through each silver strand, smoothing the peppered locks, kissing his forehead as the fever seized his weakened body. Those eyes and hair, haunting, untouchable immortal specters, and the figure behind the curtain, she remained unchangeable. And she always will.

I ripped the painting from the frame and, rushing to the parlor, tossed it in the fire. The raging orange tongues devoured the fabric, melting his image, my image, as it burned.

Captivated, I watched until nothing but ash remained. I reached into the fire, touching the spot where it had burned, and brought the ashes to my lips. Once again, I kissed Viktor goodbye.

I stayed away from the attic for several months, but eventually I returned to those boxes and memories. Loneliness and a need to feel, to know those times again, those people and ages locked away in the trunks, it was powerful. Resisting the past was impossible for me.

Five more months slipped on as I sifted through those boxes, and still no one came home. They had forgotten me as I had forgotten the memories hidden before me.

I finally came across a small maple box, an ornate filigree graced its edge, faint gilding wearing away, tucked secretly away in an unobtrusive trunk. The clasp had been broken and now rusted from its hinges. When I opened it, an ivory crucifix stared back at me. Its whiteness drowned in the heavy red velvet lining, but still managed to call to me. It had once been attached to my prayer cord.

This has been mine. From the convent. From *that* life.

My tears slid down onto the white crucifix. They slid past and down the side of the small, maple box. They fell into the void of the trunk below and then landed on blackness.

I reached into the trunk and pulled out the black fabric, unraveled it, and trembled.

"Do you remember the first time we wore those?" Sister Veronica said. Her voice did not startle me as it had in Tibet. The aroma of linseed oil married lavender and was gentle in the air, the way I always remember her smelling.

"Yes," I told her without looking up. "The fabric always scratched you. Remember that rash you got on your back?" I began to laugh. "Nothing healed it and you had to start wearing an undershirt beneath your habit. You still itched incessantly during mass. The looks on Father Patrick's face as you flinched…"

"You kept those clothes." Her words were flat.

"I forgot about them," I admitted.

"He never forgot them," she said.

"Who?" I asked. "Wesley?"

"He broke the lock," she said.

I took the box and tucked it back into the fabric, burying both in the trunk.

"He holds it, feels it, lets the heaviness wear down on him."

"Why?"

"Because he refuses to forget what he has done to you," she told me.

I watched as the hem of her habit circled in front of me, moved down to a red trunk I had yet to explore.

"He is not the only one choosing not to forget, Bree," she said.

"What do you mean?" I asked her, she but faded from me as my eyes moved up, into the path of the red trunk staring at me from down across the attic.

The red trunk was unlocked and I opened it. Lying on top of a crimson gown was the snippet of a woman in emerald. Mavra's vindictive glare teased me.

The painting scrap was rough beneath my fingers. I let it fall into the trunk and I shut it away.

The air no longer smelled of linseed oil and lavender. The house was still barren. I was still alone.

TWENTY

A fortnight passed when I received word that Wesley and Aleksandra would be returning. Aksel followed them by three days.

The house was off-kilter with their return. The once silent halls bustled with life again. The air, no longer stagnant, and the rooms alight, received a reprieve from the blackness. Spring was around the corner, not a week off, and everything and everyone was thawing from the long winter's frost. All except for me, that is.

Time was a mirage passing before my eyes, wavering and fading as I moved through it. I clung to my ghosts, to a melted image in a painting, to a worn robe hidden in a cedar chest. Life shifted about me, while I hid in shadow. I watched them – Aleksandra and Wesley, the city – from behind misery's lonely veil.

Wesley recognized what I could not, and told me it was time: time to sleep.

I resisted.

A year passed while I wallowed in my melancholy. We tried returning to Greece, Aksel and I. The magic was gone, though— the olive trees were no longer aromatic. There was a tint of sadness in the rolling tides of the Aegean, and an unsettling feeling followed me along the shore.

Another year in Paris transpired as I dipped my toes in the Seine night after endless night. The magic of

Paris, that indescribable essence that flitters throughout the city enhancing the rich culture, was a vague, muted blur of colors and people and sounds. Nothing made me smile there. Nothing made my ears perk with enjoyment. It became pointless – dipping my toes in the waters, walking the Parisian streets at night. No matter how desperately I tried capturing the innocence of this place, I failed miserably.

The night before we left, eager to return to my familiar rooms in England, I ventured toward the Notre-Dame Cathedral. Commoners filtered eagerly in, climbing the 387 steps for evening mass. I stayed below, sitting on the steps, watching the herd of people file past. They were penitent, they were guilty, and some of them were lost souls.

I was downcast, staring at the cracks in the aged stone step, when mass bell rang. The heavy doors closed with a bang. I stayed this way until the familiar scent of linseed oil and lavender bled through the air.

"Why are you so lost?" Sr. Veronica's innocent voice asked.

"I do not know," I admitted. My eyes reached the hem of her black habit, and followed to meet her glare. We were in the abbey, alone, in our corner beneath the third station of the cross. This is where we met in secret, night after night, after everyone had gone to bed.

"You need sleep, Bree."

Sleep. Her words echoed in the silent air that followed. My head bowed to hide my emerging tears. She took my hand in hers. Her skin was soft and warm and her touch gentle.

"That is what Wesley said, that I should sleep. I do not even know what that means! Not anymore."

"He knows; you should listen to him," she whispered. "Close your eyes and sleep a long uninterrupted sleep."

"I cannot," I told her, rebelling against the idea of finding the peace I so desperately needed.

"You must," she said, "and you will."

"How?"

She melted into the surrounding shadows as I glanced up. I reached for her habit, but it turned to mist – my greedy fingers slipping through the shimmering vapors. Stragglers still climbed the cathedral's steps as the mist cleared my eyes.

Returning to England, we found the house deserted, the staff relieved of duty, and a solid layer of dust blanketing the furniture. Aksel busied himself with rehiring staff and dressing the rooms, even the ones we rarely used. Wesley and Aleksandra's whereabouts were unknown, but it was common, after all, for our kind to wander.

Months passed, and they had yet to return when the indwelling blackness swelled. The stars, bright in their sky, constant and unyielding in their presence, burned my eyes. The cicada's song, once a lullaby, now pierced my ears until they bled. The genteel summer rains that once tinkled at the windows, captivating my thoughts, now stung at me incessantly until I rallied against them -- standing beneath their showers, cursing their existence. How dare their refreshing droplets cleanse the night, but not cleanse me?

It was that musky soil – the smell of England's earth after the rain. It would greet me when I awoke. The moist peat filled my nostrils and triggered memories I wished to keep buried – forever. The reminders of purity and promise lay within each village. Each young woman appeared as I once did. Their lives blessed in a gilded fantasy. There was no threat of death looming over their pristine futures.

That is how the madness consumed me – watching their pleasure.

Raged seethed beneath my calm exterior, and anger and sadness bled together, molding me into that which I feared: a monster. A truly haunting, terrifying, horrid creature, of which I had read of in books and swore I would never become.

The countryside became a playing field as I mercilessly slaughtered cattle, tossing them into trees with my thoughts, flipping them, drowning them. The drunken men exiting the tavern in the bleak hours before dawn were of no match for me, either. I hoisted their fattened bodies, slowly dying in their alcoholic graves, into the balmy summer air and fed from them, tossing their dazed remains into the sewers. Wallowing in filth, they sobered only to face another night of my wrath. No one was safe.

There were nights I witnessed the destruction I brought; I felt my victim's pain as I drank from them, but I was powerless to stop. I was but a soulless vessel, void of empathy, void of compassion. My humanity – that iota of it remaining from my former life, the ounce I clasped tightly to throughout the centuries – leeched away as the fullness of this dark curse invaded me.

For months, I was this monster, laying siege to nearby towns. People began to fear, began to suspect, and began to question.

Then it all stopped as quickly as it began.

"I burned it down," I told Aksel, returning home on that last night of that life. "It is nothing but ash now."

"You burned what down?" He had been reading by the fire. My words punctured his innocent ignorance.

"The village." I stared into the burning flames, but I could not feel the warmth they produced. "It is gone now – all of it." My hand waved over the fire, the flames stretching to kiss my fingertips.

"The village?" he asked. "You burned it down?"

I sat next to him, rubbed at my knees as I drew my legs up into the chair. I ran my fingers through my hair, releasing the ash that collected there as it fell like dust onto my dress. Ruby tears fell unhindered and rolled down my ash-smeared cheeks.

"Bree," he whispered, "What did you do?"

"She called me a monster," I told him, staring into the fire – dazed by its radiance.

"Who?"

"The child. The innocent little babe." Her cheeky face, plump and young, emblazoned itself on my mind, imprinting itself there for eternity.

"Bree," he said, clutching my hand into his own. "What did you do?" he demanded.

"I did not kill her, I swear!" I broke from his grasp and fled the chair, hiding in the corner, sitting on the cold floor as a naughty child would. "I'm not a monster!" I spat, the chandelier rattling in the darkened room.

The village flames were visible from the French windows and I watched him turn toward them, surveying the madness. Forever slipped away as he watch the landscape beyond burn before he turned to me, walked over, and grabbed my shoulders, hoisting me off the ground.

"What have you done?" he demanded.

"I was hunting and she saw me," my haunted voice quivered. "When I found her watching me feed from her father, I told her she was having a nightmare. She screamed." Releasing me, he turned again to watch the fire burn.

"I do not know what happened, Aksel, but I was possessed with a burning rage, and then desperate panic. It ate at me so, that rage; I have never experienced a feeling so consuming and exotic," my eyes closed with the recollection.

"I picked the child up and threw her, far, and into the river. Villagers scrambled to the shore. Oh, I heard them coming, even as I watched her splash into the murky water. She was alive but her body sank to the bottom. People emerged from their homes, from the taverns, and started searching for me. I watched them with their torches, combing the countryside, the city streets, the alleyways."

"I hid in a house by the shore. It stood empty," I recounted with vagueness in my voice, "I went to an oil lamp sitting on the mantel, picked it up, and threw it onto the bed. Then, as I watched the thatch mattress catch aflame, I turned toward the dying embers in the fireplace, renewing their golden swords to fight in my war, Aksel. Then, I caused those flames to twirl and twist and reach high until they spilled out of the fireplace; I commanded them to destroy everything."

"Bree," he said turning toward me. "Please tell me this is not true."

"It is," I continued. "Then I fled and watched as villagers scrambled to extinguish the burning cottage. I spread those flames until the village burned. I watched as women and children fled, as the men desperately tried to squelch the flames. I watched as boats sailed into the waters, moving south to the next port, carrying people and belongings. I watched as people fled into the countryside, blending in with the shadows."

"Bree, you should not have done this," he began.

"Why?" I asked. "They are humans, Aksel – mortals! Mortals! Have you forgotten how powerful you are, how beautiful? We masquerade and exist in shadow, while they relish the sun and pretend to be omnipotent. But, they are *not* omnipotent, Aksel, we are! We are gods."

"We are dust if we do not leave now," he told me. He grabbed at my dress but I moved away. "Now," he urged. "They are whispering your name, Bree. Someone saw you leave the village. They are coming for you."

We both heard a band of villagers marching from the distance that night – their torches bleeding into the darkness as they marched toward our estate.

Aksel called for the servants; told them we were leaving and to tell the villagers we had not been home that evening. Then he held on to me, led me through the French windows onto the cool English grass, and told me to close my eyes. And I did.

Before our feet left ground, though, a voice broke through the far off screams.

"What has happened?" it asked. "Mother, what did you do?"

My eyes opened to see Aleksandra. Wesley was descending, his eyes concentrating on mine; his jaw set and his lips pursed.

"She burned the village," Aksel told them. "I am taking her away from here before it is too late."

"Mother!" her voice quaked.

"Let us go," Wesley said. "Now, we must hurry. They are close."

Together we fled into the stars, my eyes concealed in Aksel's chest, oblivious to our destination.

There was a familiar aroma when we landed—clean ocean waves and earthy peat. The air was cold, just as I remembered it being. We had returned to Norway.

The entrance to my Lofoten Island home was in the distance, its door still barred as Aksel and I had left it. Overgrown trees and shrubbery obscured it from normal view, but it still stood – a prison awaiting me.

"Why are we here?" I asked them.

"You need to sleep now," Wesley told me. "You have no choice."

"I do not know how!" Rocks scuttled off the overhead cliff face with my reply. "You talk of sleep, of finding peace – she talked of this too, but I do not know how! I do not seek what cannot be found, foolish brother."

"Who talked of this, mother?" asked Aleksandra.

"Sister Veronica. She speaks to me, Wesley." I turned toward him and watched his mouth twist when I spoke of her. "She haunts me, brother; she is my sweet agony."

"You need to sleep, my sister," he said holding me, hugging me.

"You have gone mad, Bree," Aksel whispered. "I thought I would never see the day happen – to any of us, but especially you."

"How did it happen, then?" I spat. "Why me, if I am so strong?"

"It is my fault," Wesley said as he released me, "All my fault. I should never have made you."

"But you did, brother. You made me!" Waves rushed the shoreline, which harmonized well with the falling rocks each time my voice swelled. "I was spotless and then you scarred me, Wesley. You blackened me, marked me. And look, my brother, look what I have become!"

Aleksandra clutched Aksel. She hid her tear stained face from me, but her pain stung me regardless. Wesley watched on as I sobbed uncontrollably, his eyes not once leaving my face. Aksel turned away, the sight of my agony a sight too burdensome for him to behold.

"You need to sleep, to heal yourself from this madness that is seizing you, Bree" Wesley spat. "Hopefully, when you wake you will no longer be troubled."

"And if I still am, will you shut me back up?" I demanded. He led me toward the cliff-side home, toward the buried door.

"Wesley!" I shouted, but silence followed. The overgrowth parted as we approached. I looked back and saw her face through the weakly parted branches and vine. Cloaked in misery's veil, Aleksandra sat on her knees, clutching Aksel's pant legs. She whispered good-bye as our eyes met.

"Please, do not do this," I demanded, but understanding now it needed to be done.

Wesley opened the door. Inside, dust saturated the cabin; cobwebs surged through the house, mapping the years with their silken strands. He cut through them with his hand, leading us on to the sleeping chambers intricate doors.

"Wesley, stop, please just stop!" I hollered. Aleksandra wept in the distance as Aksel struggled to calm her. "Please, my brother, do not do this!"

He reached for the locks. Each turned and unlocked as the door opened. We entered the chamber, its darkness ebbing away as his breath lit the candles surrounding the circular chamber. There rested my bed, with its silk covering and moth-eaten pillows, cobwebs and dust littering the old fabric.

He urged me onto it. I glared at him; and I trembled. "What have I become?" I asked him. "What have I become, Wesley, if not a god?"

"My Bree," he replied as he eased me onto the bed, stroking my forehead as he had done when I was a child. "You have become lost."

"But I do not want to be lost," I cried. "Please, do not leave me here. I do not want to be alone."

"It will be different when you wake, you will see," he assured me. His voice was gentle as he forced my eyes closed. "The world will be different, and you with it."

"What if I don't wake up?" I asked. "What if I cannot wake up?"

"You will," he said. "I promise." He pulled the covers aside and covered me. He placed beneath my head a pillow. "This was mother's pillow, do you remember?" I murmured in recognition.

"Here," he said pressing something smooth into my palm, "this will protect you."

I felt the defined edges of my old crucifix, the one that hung on my prayer cord.

"I don't believe this works anymore," I told him.

"It does not have to work, Bree," she said, "but it can be a reminder while you lay here."

"A reminder of what?"

"That you are *not* a god."

I felt the bed ease as he stood. His footsteps dimmed as they moved toward the door. And the smell of extinguished candles was already polluting the air when I heard the locks click. I was alone. I was frightened.

I laid there uneasy, unable to rest, unable to sleep. How long would they keep me here? How long would it take to heal my troubled mind?

"Please," I yelled knowing no one could hear me. "Let me out!"

Then the room overflowed with the scents of linseed and lavender and I sensed her near me. Then she stroked my hand.

"I will sing you to sleep," Sr. Veronica whispered.

"I am frightened," I admitted. She reached for my hair and I felt her fingers slide through the loose strands. She reached for the hand holding the crucifix. She removed it from my palm until the crucifix lost its cool smoothness; and then she pressed it to my breast. Her lips grazed my cheek, as she bent her face down – her habit brushing against my forehead. The rough fabric scratched my skin.

"Sleep now, I am here. I will not leave you," she cooed.

Her song lulled me into a deep slumber and I slept a peaceful sleep.

TWENTY-ONE

I could feel her hand clasping mine and could hear her voice as I slipped into a tranquil cadence with the universe. Her voice allayed the emptiness, softening the blackness around me. The words melted into each other as her singing dimmed.

Surrounding me was the sound of chanting and the smell of linseed oil and lavender. My eyes beheld the melting candles weeping on their stands, foretelling the universal truth: everything ends. Sisters flanked the scriptorium benches, meticulously copying scripture, their fingers stained with ink and their eyelids fading as the moon rose high outside the gilded windows.

There is one thing that binds the world of man and the world of vampires together. It always has and it always will. We all dream.

That is what I did as I slept. I dreamt, in glimpses and vivid colors of my past and of the present progressing outside.

"Why are we here?" I asked her. Sr. Veronica was to my left, holding my hand, her finger pressed urgently to her lips. "Can they hear me?" I asked her, yet she did not answer.

Sr. Margaret stood, her arms reaching into the sky as she stretched. Her head bent toward her chest, her body went limp and she slammed onto the stone floor. The other nuns fled from the benches, flew to her side, shaking the body, screaming her name. She was motionless, her lips upturned in a serene smile, her eyes now closed forever.

Sr. Veronica turned to me, her eyes speaking words her mouth could never utter. The sadness, the joy, the mingling of emotions I could not share. Their images melted into the darkness as I felt her grip tighten. Everything washed past me as I stood there, helpless and frightened.

"Where are we going?" I asked. Again, she remained silent.

The darkness lit with the sparkle of a million stars and the rain fell gently, yet I stayed dry. Sr. Mary Anne sat near the garden fountain, her tears melding with the rain.

"Why is she crying?"

Sr. Veronica pointed to the woman, her habit heavily soiled. Her veil lay in the mud before her, her cropped red ringlets now soaked. She clutched a crucifix as she knelt praying. She spoke perfect Latin, screaming her words to the Heavens. Several sisters came, took her frail body in their arms and carried her inside. She lay on the stone floor, gasping for breath.

We watched in silence – part of the universe but not part of this time – as she succumbed to pneumonia.

"Please," I begged, "stop this. I can no longer bear it."

Sr. Veronica led me down the garden path, past the roses and oleander, past the herbs and root vegetables, and as I looked back, the world melted away into the starlit sky. Reaching my hand toward it, the colors slipped through my wanting fingers. I could not hold on to this time. I could not go back.

Forward we went, color blurring into a surrounding mist. Wind rushed through my hair, knotting the curls. My dress flapped; my necklace struggled to remain on its chain.

Slowly, the world came into focus once again. A fire consumed a tiny fireplace, the one in my room. Aleksandra stood in the fire and candle light; her hair pulled back, a tear staining her cheek. She removed clothing from my wardrobe, packing them away in my sating-lined trunk. She cautiously removed my jewelry from their maple case, putting everything in a velvet bag that she tucked into the trunk with my favorite gowns.

Wesley entered, hugged her, and added a bundle of framed art to the trunk. He said something to her, something so faint I could not hear it. She scowled at him. She yelled. She threw a paper into the fire, the flames instantly consuming it. He grabbed the trunk, slamming its heavy lid shut, and toted it from the room as she fell to her knees sobbing, clutching onto my ruby necklace. The one her father had given me.

"Is this happening now?" I asked. "Where are they going?"

Sr. Veronica looked to her left and I watched as Aksel gathered Aleksandra and the rest of my belongings. They left the estate, their shoes clicking on the yellow stoned pathway.

A carriage was loaded; they embarked, and as the horses took off down the path the world around me melted with them.

Silence followed.

Sr. Veronica and I were all that existed, swimming in a vague nothingness. The frigid air stung at my cheeks, the wind twisted and gnarled my hair, and her eyes burned with the ferocity of a white star as she glared at me.

Time was hollow and magnificent. Nothing mattered, and it felt as if nothing would ever matter again.

Then the whiz of gunfire awoke my eyes to a smoke-filled lawn, men in grey clutching bleeding wounds. Soldiers cried out in agony. Men in red coats, riding great horses, rifles clutched to their sides, passed through surveying the carnage.

We walked through the dead and dying, my feet treading over foreign soil. This land and its people were unfamiliar. She directed me toward a huddle of white tents perched at the top of a large hill. Soldiers busied themselves, rearming and recharging weapons for tomorrows skirmish. The painful screams of the injured men pierced through the chaotic hum.

Women in dresses with bloodstained aprons tended to the maimed. They bandaged and cleaned wounds; they administered medicines and fed the hungry. They knelt and prayed by cots as men died before their innocent eyes.

Amongst the men and gun smoke clouds, Aleksandra sat tending to the wounded. Her angelic face pierced through the muddled mess of humanity, clawing its way to the top. She glanced in my direction and I thought she recognized me there, in the middle of the lantern-lit battlefield – the blood stained earth beneath me feet.

I later learned this was Yorktown, Virginia, and the British, our people, would soon surrender to the American troops. Soon a treaty would follow and the new land would get its sovereignty. But, in that moment as we stood surveying the violence, it was just war. Man pitted against man: a tale older than me.

As I turned toward Sr. Veronica, the tall grass below bled into a blur of greens and browns, grays, and reds. The breeze picked up and the white tents clouded my view. Aleksandra's face faded into the consuming grey shadow.

"Why are you doing this to me?" I asked Sr. Veronica. "Have I not suffered enough?" Still, she did not answer. "What are these places you are showing me?"

Finally, as we flew through the darkness, she replied in a whisper, "These are thing you must see."

"Why?" I begged. "I do not understand any of this!"

"You will understand. Soon," she replied as the blackness gave way to a building and an approaching roar.

The large beast raged along a metal path, smoke billowing from its head. Its circular feet moved with great swiftness as the hulk of it drilled past us. The sound it made deafened my ears.

"That is a train," she told me.

"It is a beast!" I exclaimed.

"No," she explained, "it is a machine."

As I watched the train ease into the countryside, its tail slipping into the valley below and out of my view, I felt myself tugged backwards. Once again, the world went dark and quiet.

Suddenly, the void edged into a lit room, music wafted from a piano, people danced on the ballroom floor. Glowing orbs of glass, that Sr. Veronica called electric light bulbs, replaced candlelight. The Turkey Trot, the Grizzly Bear, intimate one-on-one dances had replaced the elegantly refined country waltzes. Industrialization had changed not only the landscape, but also the minds of the people who worked and lived amongst the giant machine-driven factories.

"The world has changed so much," I whispered, watching the men and women pair off, twirling on the dance floor.

"Has it really?" she asked, surprised. "This is not the first time you have witnessed progress."

"But it has always been slow," I told her. "Not like this. Not so much in so little time."

Then the dance hall swirled as the people faded from sight. Darkness replaced the electric light bulbs, and silence invaded the energetic piano notes. The wind tossed my hair, the loose strands stinging my eyes as they whipped freely about. Sr. Veronica held out her hand to me, and I took it. She smiled.

"You have not seen anything yet, my friend!"

We traveled in and out of the void, in and out of reality. She showed me Swing music and automobiles, buildings rising into the sky, television, and the telephone. She showed me Internet Cafés, and grand public universities, and women, robed in the religious cloth, preaching as men would in our time.

Then she showed the room I was in and I saw my body lying on the bed. I saw the dust of time blanketing me. The candles had long gone out and I was alone. I was sleeping and peaceful.

"This is where I leave you," she said, as we stood by the door.

"I cannot be alone," I told her. "You promised you would not leave me."

"But I must, Bree," she said. "It is time for you to wake. They will be here soon."

"Who?" I asked.

"Wesley and Aleksandra," she told me.

"And Aksel?" I asked, but she faced me, sadness swimming in her eyes.

"Good-bye, Bree," she whispered and faded into the darkness.

"Veronica!" I reached for her, but she was nearly gone.

The peaceful calm that comes with solitude again descended, and then I felt his hand on my shoulder. His cologne was pungent and musky, his fingers soft. His voice, though, was the same.

"Wake up, Bree," Wesley said. "Wake up."

As my eyes opened, I saw him and Aleksandra standing beside the bed.

"You were there, in the war," I told her. "You were helping the Americans."

"How did you know?" she asked.

"Hush, sister." He helped me to sit up.

"What year is it?"

"2005," Aleksandra whispered as she drew the covers back.

"You will need to feed right away," Wesley remarked, clearing the cobwebs from my hair.

"2005?" I said in disbelief. "How could I sleep through so much?"

"You needed rest, mother." Aleksandra said as she helped ease me from the bed. My stiff limbs ached.

"How did you know to wake me?" I asked.

"We just knew," Wesley told me. He flashed his eyes at Aleksandra, who quickly returned his glance before helping me to the door.

"Where is Aksel," I asked. My eyes strained in the candlelight, but I could not see him. "Wesley? Where is Aksel?"

Aleksandra hesitated at the door. "Let us go, mother," she said, then pushed me forward. "We have a long way to travel."

TWENTY-TWO

Aksel once told me he would go wherever I went. He would never leave me. So where was he now? The television gave me endless mornings, its backdrop a burning, golden sun. The telephone gave me access to global communication, but I had no desire to talk. The computer, the internet, showed me a world now vastly connected, yet I still felt desperately alone. Without Aksel here, without my family whole, I was still lost.

When I was in my darkest of days, he had promised to guide me through.

Oddly, in a way, he had. He had forced me to take refuge in the Lofotens. He had forced me to sleep. The last image of him, though, still breaks my heart. Tears dripped from his downcast eyes onto Aleksandra's fiery locks as he held her from me. He realized then, as he watched Wesley walk me to the door that he could not go there with me. His promise would be broken.

As I cautiously discovered the changed world, I felt removed from it. I was but a museum exhibit walking amongst the living. Gone were the elegant gowns and customary manners. Gone were the candlelit nights, mellowed by the mirage of time passing slowly. Electric lights brightened a room with the light of midday. Buildings stretched to the clouds, lit with colored lights all night, bringing fire to a darkened sky.

Madness consumed the world. People ran through the streets, eager to get to places they had no desire to be. Cars roared down dirty highways. Buses honked and jerked behind them. People were plugged in and logged on; tapping into the twenty-four hour culture stream, obsessed with celebrity babies, haute couture, the 2012 apocalypse, and living through other people's lives. The whole of humanity had gone mad.

This society bustled about under the illusion of control, as if they had a choice in anything. While I sat on my Chicago balcony overlooking the chaos of State Street, watching them scurry like rats in a rainstorm. They were oblivious as to just how little they did control in their puny lives.

Sleep had concentrated the madness percolating beneath the layers of age and time that made up who I was. Waking in an age that encouraged madness was nothing short of dangerous, but they had not known this. Any peace my past had afforded me was gone now, and Aksel carried a piece of any remaining sanity wherever he had gone.

"When did he leave?" I asked Aleksandra one night. We were watching the eleven o'clock news, a piece on Middle Eastern violence played to my deaf ears. War was war. It never ends.

"Five years after," Aleksandra remarked as she flipped the channels to a travel show. Vivid images of a Hawaiian beach, placid crystal blue seas and white sands stretched before us on the screen. All bathed in the youthful glow of sunlight.

"Have you heard from him?"

"Every ten years. He writes wanting to know if you're awake," she said, flipping the television off and tossing the remote onto the side table. The firelight and a small tabletop lamp now lit the room in a soft glow, and I felt more comfortable with this. "And no matter where we are," she continued, "he finds us."

"Have you found him?"

"No such luck." She stood, walked to the corner desk, unlocked a drawer and pulled out a stack of letters. These were the most recent. She handed them to me. "Look through them yourself, if you wish. You know him better than we do."

"Why did you wake me up now?" I asked her. "After all this time?"

"He has stopped writing," she replied. "We always received a letter on June 9th, every ten years."

"Sigursdsblot," I recalled, a smile spreading on my lips and then quickly fading. "But not this year?"

"No. Nothing came." She moved to the window, the cars whizzed into a blur of color outside. The heavy metro traffic weaved its way around the downtown construction zones.

"He is still with us," I told her. "He does not have the courage to end it himself."

"How do you know?"

"I made him, Aleksandra. I know everything about him," I remarked. "And I know where he is."

"Are you going to him?" Wesley asked, entering the room and sauntering over to a corner chair. He plopped down, put his feet up, and laid the Chicago Tribune in his lap.

"Why should I?" Moving to the fire, I relit the dying embers. The quarry-stone fireplace encapsulated the vermilion aura, only the fire's warmth escaping its embrace.

"Because you will," he replied opening the paper to the business section and discarding the rest into a pile on the floor. "You cannot just leave people to themselves."

"Maybe I will this time," I told him, "Maybe I do not want him back after he helped shut me away."

"It was for your own good, mother," said Aleksandra.

"Who were you to decide what was for my own good?" My voice boomed over the subtle roar of the traffic below. "You stood there; you let him take me away!" I glanced toward Wesley, his paper now in his lap, his eyes focused on me. "And Aksel stood there too, holding you back!"

"You needed rest, Bree," Wesley said as he moved the paper aside and stood, walking toward me. "You were losing yourself."

"I had already lost myself, Wesley!" I boasted. "That happened the day you turned me." I moved away from his outstretched arm and walked to the window. Hundreds of years had progressed around me as I slept. Now I lived in this fast-paced world, ignorant to its ways and terrified, as I knew I did not belong here.

I went into the kitchen with its vivid track lighting, its stainless steel accessories, and throngs of metal gadgets and things that whirred, purred, and came alive with the addition of electricity. The tangerine walls were too bright. The checkered floor with its shiny black and white tiles swam as I walked onto it, my feet causing an absurd rubbing noise in my new flip-flops. My toes were naked to the world, and the lighting and toxic color palette highlighted my feet's brilliant whiteness, the blue Twilight Kiss nail polish only adding to insult.

This era of man hid nothing from the world. And there was a garishness to its honesty and open-book ways.

Aleksandra followed me. "Why do we need all this stuff?" I asked her. I picked up a blender, pressed the buttons until the motor whirred to life, the sharp blades crushing the delicate air around it. "We have no need of these things!"

"It is part of the illusion," she replied. "We had mortal fixtures before, mother."

"Yes, but this is excessive."

"Our status requires us to keep up appearances, more so than in the past," she said, unplugging the blender. The motor stopped. The room was quiet again.

"You had Parisian rugs in Russia and fine China. And no expense was spared in England, why should our habits change now?" she continued.

"I do not like this time," I told her.

"You will get used to it."

"What if I do not?"

She walked out of the kitchen and I followed. "You will," she replied.

Eventually, that is what I did. I became accustomed to the whizzing around me, but never got comfortable with it. Instead, the whizzing and the buzzing grew constant in my head until it pulsated and quaked my insides, and I felt the little peace sleep had afforded me was slowly eroding away.

Winter came to Chicago, and as the snow piled on State Street, I pondered Aksel's absence. The making of our kind, that process of transferring blood and memories, creates a constant link between the maker and their kin. The blood made his thoughts mute to me, and I could not feel him nearby, but I could sense him in the universe.

On an early December evening, just shy of Christmas, I sailed through the city, the snow clinging to windows, collecting on the rooftops. Children skated merrily on Navy Pier, their parents frantically finishing their holiday shopping. As I touched down near the closed-up vendor booths, now covered in a rich dusting of powdery whiteness, a few of the children glanced my way. Their attention quickly returned to the icy rink and to catching snowflakes on their outstretched tongues.

The fountains leapt through the foliage, while lights cascaded onto the palm trees, their leaves glistening beneath the glass ceiling, as I walked through the Crystal Garden doors. A gust of heated air greeted me. The shops boasted holiday specials that hungry out-of-town shopping groups eagerly consumed. Shoppers pushed and shoved their ways through the busy corridors, in and out of crowded shops, and rested their weary feet in mediocre restaurants, placing too much trust in overworked waiters.

Something had lured me to the pier that night, to the bustling tourist epicenter. I thought it had been Aksel. I thought, for some bizarre reason, he was near. That he had returned to me, to face the wrath I was sure to release. But, I did not find him amongst the crowd, and near dawn, I abandoned my search. What lured me to that pier remained a mystery.

Sailboats returned in throngs once winter thawed into a temperate Chicago spring. Joggers trekked along the shore in droves, sweating in unison, their panting a celebration of renewal. Children walked hand-in-hand with their mothers or sprawled out on fleece blankets for picnic lunches in front of Buckingham Fountain.

But that was under the brilliance of day, and we saw this as a movie played out on the ten o'clock news. The mirage of a gorgeous spring day in downtown Chicago busted by the realism of a mugging on Michigan Avenue, and a reminder that with warmer weather comes an increase in crime.

When the sun retreats under the horizon and the buildings sway in the moonlight, Chicago comes alive. And after a long, brutally cold Midwestern winter, the restless were about to shake loose the cobwebs from their dusty bones. As much as Wesley and Aleksandra had looked for Aksel, only I knew how to find him. Now he, too, was coming out to play.

TWENTY-THREE

By nightfall, the blistering July swelter had turned to a muted stifle that stuck to your skin as you walked the streets. The dew clung to your hair, moistening the strands, plastering them to your face. Tourists walked along the lakeshore, stopping to snap pictures of the sparkling skyline; the heat doing little to deter the constant pattering of boisterous foot traffic in downtown Chicago. Their camera flashes blended with the city streetlights, mingled with headlights, and danced with starlight, as all weaved a glinted tapestry on the glass windows.

The subtle wind rolling off Lake Michigan did little to offer the city a reprieve from the summer's venomous torment. Crowds continued growing on Navy Pier, the inebriated – or slightly so – passengers awaiting voyages on the few skyline boat tours running that evening. The shops showed no signs of slowing in their patronage. It would be a profitable night, the July heat keeping the tourists until closing time forced families and young people alike to retreat – the latter seeking refuge in noisy nightclubs, while the first only dreamt of those wild, carefree days.

I watched a crowd board a small yacht, waiting to go onto the lake. On board, a man waiting, ring in pocket, ready to ask the dainty blonde-haired woman next to him to be his bride. It would be a surprise.

I had to smile at the thought of a surprise – something so simple. Those things no longer exist for me.

There are no surprises left in my world. There are only certainties. I will wake to greet a new nightfall. I will feed from the living. I will kill again. No surprises.

The pier was not where I was supposed to be that night, though.

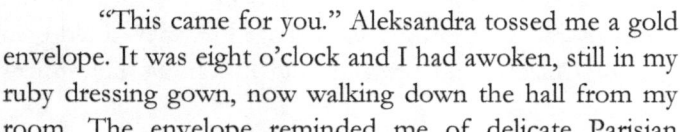

"This came for you." Aleksandra tossed me a gold envelope. It was eight o'clock and I had awoken, still in my ruby dressing gown, now walking down the hall from my room. The envelope reminded me of delicate Parisian sheets beneath my fingertips, the sender having spared no cost. Turning it over, my fingers ran along the embossed letters. "Fancy," she remarked.

"It is from the curator at the Field," I noted. Her eyebrows arched as her slender arms stretched toward the ceiling. I followed her into the living room as the automatic lights flicked on. Wesley walked past us, pressing a button for the drapes to part.

State Street unfolded before me, the colored lights, the movement of people, of life circulating below. I shut out the thoughts and watched them move before me as ants, miniscule and pathetic. I could crush them. As I sat in my tower, I owned them.

"How is Peter?" Wesley asked as he lit the fire. He sat at the corner desk, opened the laptop and began fiddling with some financial documents. Aleksandra moved to his side, pointed to the screen, made a few remarks out of my earshot, and then walked to the bookcase where she stood for some time before removing a copy of *Psychology*.

"Not sure. I haven't seen him in a few months. He took his wife to Ireland for their silver anniversary," she replied.

I continued watching the ants below. I could smell their sweat through the distance, through the thick panes of glass. Weakness married the despair in their veins, their blood a thick river of rapids calling for me to tame it with my kiss. Peter Templeton and his wife Barbara were big ants. She was from old money, and he was from an old scholarly family, from England. Together, they could own half of Chicago and probably did in various investment deals.

As I watched the ants below, my fingers sliced through the gilded envelope. Inside was but a single sheet of ivory cardstock, its crimson lettering embossed into a bold, raised print.

"The Field Museum will be hosting an exclusive Vatican exhibit," I noted, flatly, as I slid the invitation back into its envelope.

"Are you going?" Wesley asked.

"There will be a private screening of a special by-invitation-only portion and I am to be the curator's special guest," I replied.

"Is that a yes?" Aleksandra asked.

My shoulders hunched, I turned and left the room. Something did not feel right.

That had been three weeks ago. The invitation has sat since collecting dust on my nightstand next to a bottle of Imperial Majesty perfume. Every night, the torn envelope stared at me. My fingers traced its satiny edges. My eyes read over the embossed lettering. Each night I searched the invitation in hopes of discovering why it made me feel uneasy. Why did the thought of going to this gala prickle my skin and trouble my mind?

Being a museum patron, I attended most nightly events. My money ran as free as the expensive French champagne that the benevolent Chicago elite lapped up into their greedy mouths. Only a few, like me, would ever send in a check, and even mark it for an anonymous donation. Most of the people at these galas wanted accolades.

As they exited limos, their cheesy, falsified whitened grins flashed greedily toward the wanton cameras. As they ascended the marbled steps, they reached for only the hands of prominent people. They spent their night rubbing noses and hobnobbing with congressmen and senators and television stars and anyone who could *make things happen*; and they were all too eager to drop in their donation amounts. "Yes, we did have that situation with our plant in China – had to lay off three hundred workers, but these are priceless Italian relics! We could not see donating anything less than our usual two million."

"You can always wear your Prada," Aleksandra said, entering my room. I had been fingering the invitation, examining it. "Why are you hesitating?"

"Something feels off about this," I told her. I placed the envelope back onto the nightstand and sat down on the edge of the bed. The cobalt velvet bedspread yielded to my weight as I traced wavy lines in the fabric.

Aleksandra moved to the corner cedar wardrobe where I kept my elegant gowns, opened the heavy doors, and began thumbing through the massive collection. Many of the dresses were now antiques, and she took special care not to disturb the oldest gowns near the back.

"You should have these preserved," she remarked, as her fingers slid over antique lace, "or put them in a museum."

"Look around," I laughed, "this place is a museum."

Remnants of ages past – a painting commissioned from Titian, a bust from Michelangelo, various vases and trinkets and tapestries from castles, and royal seals in glass cases – on display. To the world, this was a display of wealth, but to us, it was a scrapbook. It was our photo album, our history.

She pulled the coral, sleeveless, mid-length Prada from the closet, held it toward me. Frustrated, she placed it back into the closet. "You are hard to dress, you know?"

"Just get my night clothes," I told her. "I should not go."

"Because of a feeling?" She continued to rummage through the closet.

"You are being ridiculous, mother. Peter will be offended; he invited you for a personal screening. Those do not happen all the time." She finally selected two dresses and tossed them onto the bed. "Try these and pick one."

An hour later, I descended in a darkened area near Soldier Field and walked toward the lit museum. Limousines and town cars lined Museum Campus Drive. Headlights blended with spotlights and blurred with flashbulbs as the Chicago elite stepped from their vehicles and entered the venue.

My vintage Gucci scoop-neck gown trailed behind me, the coral fabric enveloping me in wispy Italian lace. Tiered diamond studs hung from my earlobes. My lips were dressed in a dusky rose with my eyes a shadowy gray, lined in silver; a slight hue of Imperial Majesty, a smoky chestnut marrying the floral rose water, clung to my skin as morning dew clings to a blade of grass.

The flashes were blinding as I walked past the car processional and ascended the marbled stairs. I shielded my face from the photographers, as Peter's assistant, Jody, a verbally expressive graduate student, greeted me at the top and ushered me in.

"Peter's been waiting for you," she said, handing me a program. A Byzantine era cross, gilded and jewel encrusted, stared back at me from the booklet - *God's Treasured Jewels: A Special Vatican Collection.* A better title would have been – *A Garish Abuse of Power Through Time,* I thought.

"Waiting for me?" I smiled as we passed the senators from Illinois and Michigan.

"In his office," Jody explained as we weaved through the main hall. She pressed down on the staff elevators and, sliding her key card, we entered. She pressed for the basement and we descended into the somber, sacred chambers where history slept waiting for its glorious reveal. A section of Grecian urns greeted our descent, the doors opening to their hidden lair. Racks upon racks of fragile pottery was being restored by the best in their field, working diligently for the masses to gawk and awe and never fully appreciate what it took to bring that treasure to them.

"What rare find has he come across this time?"

Jody chuckled at my question. Peter had a penchant for discovering rare artifacts that both interested me and secured my pocket book. Most often, these items remained in the Field, endowed to the museum for future generations to enjoy. Then there was the treasure of a sentimental nature that I would have him seek.

"Usually he tells me, but not this time," she said as we turned toward the Egyptian restoration section. A shipment of Greco-Roman period Egyptian artifacts had recently arrived. Large shelves contained items still waiting for cataloging. "It is this Vatican collection, something about it. It's not sitting with him, Bree. Honestly, between us, he is not himself."

Peter's office was behind a drab, grey door. Jody's cell beeped and she left to return to corralling Chicago's elite.

The knob turned easily in my hand, the door giving way to a dimly lit office. "Peter, if you wish to be mysterious, you should lay off the cologne. I can smell you down the hall." The door shut softly behind me.

"Hey, you gave me this stuff. If you did not like the smell of it, you should not have bought it." He rose from behind the desk, stepping into the dim aura of the desk light. I moved to the wall and flicked the light switch and the room filled with a sickly neon glow.

"I didn't tell you to bathe in it," I tossed him a smile. "Still, I guess it is an improvement over that musty wet-dog odor you had been sporting."

"Hush, the wife spent good money on that cologne in Germany," he said, laughing. "Oh, it was awful, was it not? The guy who sold her that must have been a real looker!" He moved to the chair next to his desk and cleared a stack of books and papers from it. He removed a handkerchief from his back pocket, dusted the chair, and then offered me a seat.

"What is so important about this collection?" I smoothed my dress as I sat.

He opened the top drawer of his desk as he sat down and removed a small red box. It was no bigger than a ring box but aged, its hinges rusted and its velvet cover worn. Branded into the velvet was the papal seal, the triregnum, a crown with three levels, resting between two crossed keys. His thumb rubbed firmly across it.

"This item was not cataloged when it arrived on loan from the Vatican," he told me as he handed over the box. "We immediately reported it missing to our insurance company and to the Vatican's. I suggest you take it and make it disappear."

"Peter, neither of us trade in black market wares; that is not who we are." I held the box out to him. He forced my fingers round the box and placed his hands around my own. "I am not selling it, Bree."

"Peter," I whispered. There were people approaching from the hallway – Jody and Barbara. They were laughing; Barbara had had too much to drink and it was far too early in the evening for that.

"You will want this," he said as he stood, adjusting his tuxedo jacket. He took my purse and put the box inside it. "Open it when you get home. There should be a package coming to your house tomorrow night, by messenger, sign for it."

"If you are in trouble," I told him, but he cut me off. Jody and Barbara walked through the door.

"Of course we find you two here," Barbara announced as she barged through the door. The twiggy, grey-haired elfish woman was resplendent in her Versace cocktail gown, the red silk hugging her body, but alcohol did not suit her. Jody's constant vigilance was required.

"The donors from Northwestern want their tour, Peter." She clung onto her husband, much to Jody's relief.

"I have tried stalling them, but they are insistent, sir," Jody explained, apologetically.

"It is not a problem." he nodded toward me, smiling. "Save me a dance now, Bree, got it?"

"Who else would I dance with, Peter?" I laughed as we walked from the room. I clutched onto my purse as if guarding a bomb. "All my dances are for you, as long as Barbara's fine with that."

"Oh, Barbara's not going to mind," Jody whispered as the older couple walked in front of us.

"I have a feeling you are right," I replied as we gathered on the elevator and ascended into the Field Museum main lobby.

TWENTY-FOUR

J ust open it."
Wesley tossed the packaged onto the desk. It had arrived the next night, just as Peter promised. Aleksandra had signed for it, and she and Wesley had patiently waited for me to return from wandering the city with my mysterious box in tow.

I had fingered that box as I walked down West Ontario. A group of female tourists passed, their purses clutched tightly to their exposed chests. Their stiletto steps screamed on the pavement. They paused before entering The Red Bar Comedy Club, and all three women glanced at me before opening the door. My hand moved from my pocket as I waved and walked away.

A summer rain drizzled down, glistening Dearborn Park as I walked by. A couple huddled together walking a terrier, their oversized shared umbrella swaying in the lakeside breeze. Our State Street pent house was but a stone's throw from here; the light from the Study filtered through the cracked drapes.

I watched my apartment from a park bench, the rain beading against my vinyl raincoat, the lavender fabric melting into the graying Chicago sky. The study's drapes slowly opened, Wesley stood behind them, easing them away from the glass. His mouth moved freely, laughing and forming a perplexing smile before turning away. Light from the television flashed in the room and I could see his feet peaking near the edge of the couch.

I waited until the messenger rode away on her bike, the satchel now lighter from delivering my package. As her yellow jacket disappeared down State Street, I crossed at the crosswalk, the door attendant letting me in.

"A package just arrived for you." The attendant rushed past me and grabbed the padded manila envelope resting on the security counter. "I was just about to take it up."

"I have good timing then. Thanks, Bill."

Taking the package, I entered the elevator and ascended. The metal box swiftly climbed to the pent house apartment and I heard Aleksandra and Wesley talking in the foyer before the thick doors opened. They were arguing, which is something they seldom did.

"This is not your decision to make!" Aleksandra was holding a ripped envelope, a letter inside. "Now what am I supposed to do?"

"You could speak at the conference, as you are scheduled to do, and thank me," Wesley replied in a huff. "North Western's getting a generous grant for this."

"My research is not ready to be presented!" she stammered. "Mother," she turned toward me as I stepped from the elevator, "talk some sense into your brother."

"Oh, I am not sure that is possible," I chuckled. "I have never been able to talk much sense into him." I walked into the study and she followed. "Just present your preliminary findings; that should be enough. And send a research assistant."

"They are expecting more than preliminaries, especially if we want to secure that grant funding,"

Aleksandra said as she fell onto the settee. "Is that it, then?" Her eyes moved to my hands.

Wesley came into the room and walked to the window, looking out on the busy street below. "What is in Peter's mysterious package," he asked. "Have you opened the box?"

"No."

Slipping the rain slicker off and hanging it to dry near the door, I moved into the study and sat down, placing the package on my lap. Reaching into my pocket, I pulled the red box and traced the papal symbol with my fingers.

"Why would Peter risk his job for this?" I whispered. Dropping the box into my lap, I grabbed the envelope as Aleksandra and Wesley watched. "There is no sender identification and there should be."

I tore the serrated tab and found a single sheet of white paper inside. Taking it from the envelope, I rose and walked to the fireplace, my back to Aleksandra and Wesley as I read.

The writing was in ink, smeared in spots where the writer had hurried or written with great emotion. My eyes began to water in the beginning as I read, "My dearest Bree," and were nearly blinding me by the time I reached his name at the letters end.

"Bree?" Wesley moved to my side but I shrugged him away as I moved to the sofa and retrieved the box.

A portrait in my likeness lived within the velvet box – surrounded in opal and rich gilding, and blood stone set into the bottom of the amulet. I traced the face and saw him – watching the papal palace, observing strange rituals, observing the construction of this piece; observing as a skilled artisan painted my image on the jewel. Then I watched as he snuck into the Vatican and snatched the amulet, tucking it safely into the velvet box.

As I slept, he researched. He watched.

Wesley snatched the letter as it fell from my hand. I sat with the amulet, rubbing it repeatedly. As he stood by me reading, Aleksandra came near and read over his shoulder. She gasped. "What does this mean?"

"I don't know," I told her. And it was the truth. The letter. The amulet. They introduced more questions than I had had the night Peter thrust the box into my hand. "But I know where to find them."

"Where did you get this?" I tossed the velvet box onto his desk. The box skidded across hitting a stack of papers before stopping. He looked up, exhausted.

"We cannot talk about that," he said grabbing the box, quickly standing, moving to my side and shoving it into my purse. "Put it away."

"Peter," I glared at him as she returned to his chair. The man shook beneath his collared shirt, the top two buttons undone, the tie loosened and hanging gingerly around his neck. His hair was tasseled and unwashed. Bags collected under his eyes, the thick glasses not hiding them. And peppered stubble adorned his chin. The remnants of his last meal lay scatted on the desk.

"You need to sleep." He shuddered under my touch as my hand rested on his shoulder.

"I have too much to do still," he said.

"Why?" I asked. "It can wait till tomorrow. I want answers."

"No," he replied. Glassiness crept into his eyes as he looked past me. "No." He shook his head and returned to the computer. His fingers busied themselves at the keyboard.

"What are you doing?" I asked. When he did not answer, I moved behind the desk to watch. He was moving files to the recycling bin. When he noticed me behind him, he opened a document and typed "they know," then quickly deleted the words and then the file.

Peter retired the next day and took his wife on a cruise around the world. The same party that sent me the letter and the box sent him a generous sum of money for his troubles. A registered letter arrived to each Board of Directors, mine including a personal note, insisting this decision had been in the making for ages. I knew better, though. The Vatican knew the amulet was never lost and they were seeking it. Peter knew this, and so he fled. They would be hunting for the sender and for Peter. And so would I.

But Peter's sudden absence didn't go unnoticed after a string of fictitious and anonymous emails found themselves in a reporters inbox. The Chicago Tribune, not one to shy from a scandal, ran with the story of the curator's mysteriously abrupt resignation and missing artifacts until all avenues of investigation were exhausted. We did what we could to silence the rumors, but it had to run its course. By mid-January 2006, when not even the paper's best-hired private eyes could track Peter down, the story fizzled.

The Field's newly hired curator, Melanie Davies-Whitaker, a staunch defender of antiquities conservation from The British Museum, eased into her role and took up the efforts to eradicate any staff-bred rumors. She brought in her own staff from the British Museum to oversee the transition of the Queen's Royal Jewels exhibit. They then left for the British Museum's Tell el-Balamun dig site –

with two Field anthropologists assisting. Davies-Whitaker had asked Aleksandra to go but she refused. When she called the second time, though, Aleksandra was mute, leaving Wesley to reject the Field's offers. Science, Aleksandra said, did not dwell in the past.

Unlike Aleksandra and Wesley, I distanced myself from the museum during the investigation. Whatever secret the amulet held – whatever power it contained – I did not want Peter's leaving to be in vain.

Once, in my weakness, I ventured to the broad granite steps. But I dared not ascend.

Not until I was invited back into those granite halls and rooms filled with ancient treasure.

"Call me Melanie," she said, "please. I insist. After all, the staff leaves the impression that my predecessor thought highly of you." She waved her hand toward the chair. "Have a seat," she urged. "Please, you must."

"How can I help you, Melanie?" I asked. It was gravely disconcerting being in his office – *Peter's* office – with her seated behind his mahogany desk.

"It's this," she said as she handed over a small rectangular box. It resembled a shoebox with Peter's name scrawled on the top in black permanent marker. "I held on to his effects in case he returned for them. But since his instructions clearly state to do so, I'm releasing them to you."

I lifted the lid and began thumbing through the contents. Nothing important: a Harvard felt tip pen, moleskin journal, and miscellaneous office goods. "You could have couriered this to me," I noted.

"Yes, but the other board members thought a face-to-face would be best," she replied. "You were absent from the welcome breakfast. And you *never* come in!"

"I'll make more of an effort to be here for the next gala," I said as I stood and extended my hand. I clutched the box to my side.

"Please do," she replied as she escorted me out. "I speak for the Board of Directors; we don't want you being a stranger."

"Of course," I replied, smiling as I left.

I would have stashed the box away had it not been for Aleksandra's curiosity. Her hungry hands sifted through its contents. She removed each item, twirled it in her hand, and eventually plopped it next to her on the couch.

"There is nothing here but desk clutter," she said. "Why didn't they toss it?"

"He left it in my care," I replied. I sat down at the desk and opened the laptop. The screen emitted a vivid neon glow as the machine woke from hibernation.

"Green this week?" I remarked, my fingers tapping at the keys.

"Mother, what does this key go to?" she asked. She held up a tiny brass key.

"Safety deposit box?" I speculated as she walked the key over and placed it in my hand. The metal was cool.

She pointed to the journal. "I would get reading," she laughed. "Or hire an assistant to phone every bank in the city."

There had been no need for assistants or phoning banks, however. Peter had revealed the location within three sentences: *I had a meeting today with a scholar at Union Station. We discussed Dante's Inferno – the 8th Circle. Bree was a no-show.*

There had been no meeting, but we had discussed Dante. We had discussed, in length, the eighth circle –

fraud. In graduate school Peter had painted a scene from Dante's *Inferno*, where Dante and Virgil descend into the eighth circle of hell, riding upon the back of Geryon – a winged, shape shifting monster. He had given me that painting. He knew I would understand the reference.

"I know what this key opens," I told them. Wesley and Aleksandra were sitting together on the couch reading, as I entered the Study.

"How?" Aleksandra asked.

I held up the moleskin journal. "He left me clues!"

"Going on a treasure hunt, then?" Wesley asked, his eyes not veering from the newspaper.

"That I am."

A dusty snow fell the night I left for Union Station to retrieve the contents of Peter's locker.

D8: Dante's 8th. It stood stacked on top of its partners, locked and abandoned. Heartbeats and mindless thoughts droned past as I slid the key into the lock. Three lockers down a slender man approached in a three-piece business suit, slightly wrinkled from a day's train travel. His locker door swung open and he shoved in a laptop case before closing it. What should I do with a four-hour layover, he thought. He walked away, key in hand.

Waiting until the crowd around me dispersed, I opened the locker to find a new moleskin journal. There were scribbles here and there, passwords for Peter's emails, and the override for his home security system. Did he need me to sell his house? I stopped thumbing through the book and tossed it into my messenger bag. The snow was beginning to fall more heavily now. The city's homeless would take to shelters soon and I would lose my chance for an easy feed.

Outside the train station, I ascended and flew a few blocks before spotting a woman huddled under a filthy, flea ridden blanket. The stench of urine permeated the air while the soft whimpering came from the small child sleeping in her lap. As the duo slept, I fed from her and left behind one-thousand dollars tucked into the woman's shirt. And another tucked into the child's pajama top.

The snow was a white blur by the time I got home. The scorching fire raged inside warming the study. I tossed the book onto the desk and rubbed my hands over the amber flames. The flakes outside stuck to the windows before melting and running down the glass.

"What is in the journal?" Wesley asked. He had been reading the Tribune from his chair.

"Passwords."

"To?" He put the newspaper down.

"Random e-mails and the security system for Peter's house on the North Shore," I noted. The flames licked the granite fireplace, the wood crackling sending sparks into the darkness. "What does it mean?"

"Maybe he needs you to cancel his newspaper subscription," Wesley laughed. He stood and walked to the desk picking up the journal. He looked to me and waited for me to nod until he opened the soft, brown cover. His fingers thumbed through it, venturing farther than I had.

"They are watching," he whispered.

"Excuse me?"

Wesley turned the book, his index fingers separating the pages, and showed me a page with the words *they are watching* scrawled near the top, with my name and a date and time written on the bottom.

"July 10th, 8:30?" Wesley asked. "Does that mean anything to you?"

"Not that I recall." The main door opened and Aleksandra yelled into us; Wesley let her know we were in the study.

Entering, she tossed her Gucci lab bag near the door, kicked off her black, last season Prada pumps and plopped onto the settee, tossing her auburn hair over the back and stretched out her legs. Wesley closed the book around his index finger, leaned down to place a genteel kiss on Aleksandra's forehead, and then resumed his search for more clues.

"If that lab's alarm goes off one more time, I'm hiring a new security company," Aleksandra remarked. "This is the third time this month I've been called to reset it because they've set it off!"

"July 10th," I tossed into the atmosphere along with a throw pillow aimed at her face. She caught it and sat up.

"July 10th at 8:30 – where would I have been? Do you remember?"

"July?" she asked. She moved to the desk and pressed the button on her laptop. A few seconds later, the screen lit up with her multi-colored DNA sequence wallpaper. Aleksandra opened a calendar document and flipped back to July. Her studious eyes roamed the spreadsheet, combing through the various engagements.

"I am not finding anything noted for that date," she said.

"Perhaps it was an appointment he planned on making," I wondered aloud.

"Wait," she said. She was now looking at an Excel spreadsheet. Her fingers were gracing the arrow keys, moving frantically between the up and down keys. "On July 10th I have a check written from your account to The Field Endowment."

"The night of the Cranston Expedition Fundraiser," Wesley realized. "They were watching that night."

"Who was watching?" Aleksandra asked. Her voice raised an octave as she turned from the computer.

"The Vatican."

"The Vatican!" Wesley nearly dropped the book. Aleksandra sat down at the desk, her pale complexion somehow a shade paler. "Why is the Vatican watching someone?"

"They were watching Peter. They wanted the amulet back and they did not believe his cover story – that it had gone missing en route."

"They must have been watching that night," Aleksandra said. "That is why he left after he gave it to you. Now they'll be watching you; they'll be watching us!"

"You must go to him now, Bree," Wesley said calmly.

"I have been trying to locate him, this whole time, but I do not know where to start!" I snatched the book from his hand and thumbed through the pages. "It is all in code!"

"Let me see it, then," she said. Aleksandra took the book from me and began turning pages, her fingers tracing the letters. Three days later, she came to me with a page marked. "How does this sound? 'Booked a cruise to Norway. Will depart at 9 am – sharp – no luggage required. Passport – check?'"

"You're grasping, Aleksandra," I said.

"Grasping?" she said. "Perhaps, but what do you have to lose?"

TWENTY-FIVE

The Norwegian winds are icier in January. They whip off the water that laps and licks near the rocks of my abandoned cavern home. The overgrowth and mossy covering still shrouding the door, which had only been slightly disturbed not too long ago when I awoke. Now, nature once again concealed that which human hands had once built into the mountain.

This had been my fortress in the fjord, my Norwegian paradise. This had led to two new beginnings and an end. Now ghosts from my past had reappeared to haunt me in trinkets and religion. Those ghosts lured me to the cobwebbed sanctuary where I had slumbered, bleeding into time until the future became the present.

My hands held Peter's journal, the page open to the entry Aleksandra found the night before. Scribbled in the corner in tiny, faded penciled letters, was a cryptic "Booked a cruise to Norway. Will depart at 9 am – sharp – no luggage required. Passport – check.?" Alone, rather in insignificant scribble, perhaps just a thought on a possible excursion, but then my eyes caught a faded word written across the page – "ekki" – and I knew the code was for me.

Ekki. The first time he called me that I was in the Egyptian exhibit at the Field. There was a gala that evening, raising money for a children's charity. This was shortly after I awoke and the world was new. As I walked amongst the artifacts, I felt part of them. Out of place and out of time, and strangely on display.

He approached me from the shadows as I emerged from the Field's replica pyramid, his scent betraying him as it always would. Aleksandra was behind him. She introduced the older man whose hair had silvered and whose suit had dust from the archives clinging to its lapel. He lived for his work and wore that fact proudly.

"Ekki," he remarked as he fearlessly took my hand in his, kissing it. "And with golden hair, as well, Aleksandra, it is enough to make the god's jealous. The Sumerian's would quake at the site of her, of any of you walking ekkimu." Then he laughed as Aleksandra took his champagne glass away, handing it to a passing waiter.

"I think you have had enough," she whispered.

"An ekkimu?" I asked him. "You think I am a vampire?"

"I know you are a vampire," he replied, his eyes darting about the deserted exhibit.

"Vampires do not exist," I told him, smiling.

"Do not be silly," the silver haired curator replied as he grabbed a lobster ball from a passing tray and stuffed it into his waiting mouth. He pointed to Aleksandra. "She told me," he said between bites. He laughed again, this time a joyous laugh that drew eyes from the few others in the room. "And my antiquities professor said the Sumerian's were full of it, that vampires did not exist. A plague, he said, wiped the buggers out! Guess who is a pompous blowhard now!"

Ekkimu. The word for vampire in ancient Sumerian, which when shortened to Ekki, became his pet name for me. In the little time I knew him, I grew fond of Peter. He and Barbara threw elegant parties in their North

Shore home, opening their beachfront veranda to a select few of which Aleksandra, Wesley and myself were always included. It was not long before I became as generous as my brother and Aleksandra, bestowing thousands on collections and funding expeditions.

Peter had never asked me to turn him. Aleksandra admitted that he had asked her only once. She refused and he understood, and that was the last time he mentioned her peculiar state.

Neither Peter nor Aleksandra would tell me how the pair met. A dark secret hung between them, binding them in a bond tighter than blood. I would have never found out had it not been for him telling me, though. He thought I should know.

"She was dying, Bree," he told me. It was at a private dinner, celebrating his grandson's graduation from Vassar. "Judith had acute lymphoblastic leukemia. They tried treatment, but her blood never responded and the cancer spread."

The pain dripped from his forehead with each droplet of sweat that beaded and rolled down, falling onto his linen suit. The May heat was unseasonably, warm that year. Wesley and Aleksandra were inside with Barbara. The three were talking with Colin, Peter's only son and Judith's father.

Colin was a younger copy of his father, hair a darker brown, though, and a few less lines creasing his brow. But the resemblance was uncanny. The near loss of his only daughter wore heavily on him, and it played in his hazel eyes. Her face, solemn and fixed forever in time, imprinted on his pupils from that last moment he saw her lying in the hospital bed. You could see it when you glanced into his eyes. It was there with the memories of his father rushing him from the room, of Judith's shallow breathing, her sunken cheeks, of her fever that spiked near dawn. There were too many memories haunting Colin from that night. Too many hurtful memories leaving an acrid taste in his mouth that the red wine could not drown.

"Aleksandra's a fixer, Peter." The sky was clear; the stars were bright over the lake.

A few sailboats were still out near the shore, their lights bobbing with the waves. The coastline cracked to life with Peter's family and friends. Groups gathered, huddled near fire pits outside. For those not risking the mosquito bites, the living and dining rooms, lit by chandelier and opulent candlelight, served as recluse spaces for conversation between friends.

"Fixed?" he asked. His gazed remained on the stars. "Can you really call it that?"

"It was her choice." I took his shoulders and turned his face until his eyes met mine. "Aleksandra gave her a choice, Peter. Would you rather have let her die?"

He turned away, his eyes squinting back tears. He looked into the living room through the glass curtain wall and watched Colin engaged in conversation. "He knows," Peter said, gesturing toward Colin.

"That she is a vampire?" I asked.

"No," he explained. "He knows she is different. He knows she did not go into remission because of Aleksandra's protocol drug! And he is right, Bree. She *is* different. She would have never missed her brother's graduation party. She would not have missed his graduation! She's no longer our Judith."

"Peter, Aleksandra knew what she was doing," I said, lowering my voice to a whisper as a couple approached and exchanged a few pleasantries before making their way onto the beach. "Judith knew, too.

Aleksandra prepared her as best she could. She had days, left, if that, you know this."

He was quiet for a while as we both gazed out onto the beach, the fires dying into soft halos of warmth. Car engines purred to life in the driveway, their lights blooming in the darkness. The party was dying down and Colin was moving his mother to her bed; she was tipsy.

Finally, when the veranda was deserted he spoke, "That's when I found out she was a vampire, Wesley too." Silence fell once again.

Colin and his son, David, could be heard escorting guests to the front door. David was on his cell phone, calling for a taxi.

"Aleksandra came to me the night Judith spiked her last fever, the night the doctors said she had, maybe, two days left. Everyone had left for Colin's and I stayed behind, to hold my Judith's hand, and when I went to check my work e-mail from the laptop, your sister had sent me a note. You know what it's like when a good friend catches you at a vulnerable moment?" he asked. I smiled and nodded. "I think I replied with a novel! Every memory I could recount, from Judith's first steps to graduating Oxford."

"I am sure she read every word, too." A letter that personal would have demanded no less.

"I hit send, got up to stretch and decided to walk down to the cafeteria for some coffee. I was gone thirty minutes, Bree. When I returned, Aleksandra was standing at Judith's bed side," he recalled.

That night, Aleksandra revealed herself to a startled Peter, and nothing was ever the same between them. The family released Judith to hospice care and Aleksandra took over as her physician, coming from Northwestern with a new blood augmentation protocol that could save her life. That is what it did. Two nights later, instead of dying, Judith climbed out of her sick bed a new woman.

The journal felt heavy in my hand as I stared at the overgrowth covering the entrance to my old sanctuary. Even though I could not hear his thoughts, I knew he was behind that clad iron wall. Behind that set of intricate locks and down the staircase, he was waiting for me. He would wait forever if he had to.

A gust of wind stung at my eyes and I shielded them with my sleeve. The fleecy parka rubbed against my cheek, the ivory fabric washing against my skin. Snowflakes started falling against the wind as a storm set into the fjord. I walked with trepidation to the entrance and brushed away enough covering to open the lock. My fingers slid effortlessly over the combination with my eyes closed.

The door creaked open, and heavy trails of dust flittered in the air as the light crept in. The main room was dark once the door shut behind me, except for the sliver of light skirting the panel leading to the inner sanctuary. I followed this light and fumbled with the heavy locks. The door was built into the floor and, when I lived there, was cleverly hidden by furniture. Now dust concealed its secret levers and switches, its locks and pulleys. Time had forgotten this place and there was no longer a need to hide the sanctuary.

Managing the last lever, a cumbersome brass invention that unlocked the final lock, the panel clicked and slid open. A cascade of candlelight warmed my weary eyes as I descended the stone staircase.

The flames licked at the walls, charring the stones as candle wax spilled from the narrow niches. The wax collected in cooled piles on the steps below and melted against my satin Gucci platform boots.

My fingers felt the amulet in my pocket, the hardness heightened by the cold, Norwegian air. I turned it over in my palm, clutching it and tightening my grip upon the trinket. A musty odor rose from the inner sanctuary, and as I got closer, the amulet grew warmer with my touch. Slowly, I pulled the amulet from my pocket, glancing at my likeness staring back, and then I slid it tightly into the palm of my hand. I secured it there, and slid both back into my pocket.

Candlelight engulfed the sanctuary, tiny flames saturating the ledges with their incandescent auras. His back was turned to me as I entered. My linens still graced the bed, the azure satins, and velvet cream pillows imported from England. They were relics sent from a long past time, buried and forgotten here. My hand reached out toward the bedspread as I crossed the room, my boots tapping at the floor as I walked.

Dust and time tarnished the satins smoothness. My fingers ran along the rich embroidering, the faded flowers, the delicate stitching, and a thick smudge of dust clung to my fingertips as I lifted them away. As I looked down onto my fingertips, he turned and I felt his eyes bore heavily down on me.

"They woke you," he said, stepping toward me. He stretched his hand outward and brushed it against my cheek. My eyes followed his fingertips travel toward my lips. He ran his index finger over them until they parted.

"You stopped writing," I replied. "They did not know what else to do. And they did not know how to find you."

"And you did?" He sat down on the edge of the bed, his lanky Norse legs dangling over the platform edge.

"Why did you stop writing?" I asked. "Was it because of this?" Pulling the amulet from my pocket, I handed the jewel to him and watched as he shrank back onto the bed in fear. "Aksel, what is this?"

"Bree," he began. "This is yours. Keep it and hide it. I cannot have it!" He threw it toward me, the amulet landing onto the bed with a soft thud. Billowing clouds of dust rose from where it landed.

"The Vatican is after this! A good friend of mine had to leave his position at a museum because of this, Aksel! What is it?" I demanded. I retrieved the amulet, inspecting it as I sat down next to him on the bed. My face stared back at me, eerily smiling.

"It is a good luck charm," he said. "That is all. But the church believes the amulet is witchcraft."

"Witchcraft?" I turned the amulet over. The underside revealed the emerald beneath. "Even so, why does the church care? If they thought it was black magic, they would have destroyed it."

"This amulet belonged to Pope Julius II," he explained. "In his journals, Pope Julius II wrote of a mysterious woman with golden hair, who roamed the papal temple at night. And when, one evening he spotted this woman, he called for guards and she rose into the air like an angel."

"That was me," I said. "After I left you with Evelyn, in Hungary, I went to Rome."

"He wrote that you were the devil; that you had come that night to tempt him," Aksel said as he eased toward me on the bed.

I looked closer at the image painted on the amulet. "What is it for then?" I asked him, holding it up to the candlelight.

"Apparently it wards away evil. That is why they painted your face upon it," he explained.

"We are not evil," I told Aksel. I stood and paced the room. "We are something in between. This proves that."

"This proves nothing because this amulet is worthless," he insisted. He came to my side and stopped me. "I went through a lot of trouble getting this from the Vatican, Bree."

"Why?" I asked him. "If this is worthless, then why bother?"

"Do not ask questions, please. Just listen and take a silly trinket from a silly old man. And promise me you will keep it for good luck."

"Aksel, my friend committed a crime and lost his job for this amulet. And I had to hunt you down via cryptic clues in a journal because you stopped contacting Aleksandra and Wesley." My voice echoed off the stone. "They woke me up because of this."

I held it to the candlelight and rubbed my finger across the face again. A painted visage smiled back. "All of this trouble for a good luck charm? This is not like you! Wild goose chases… drama… mystery. Fine, maybe it is you, but I deserve answers! I deserve my oldest friend by my side when I wake!"

"Bree," he said, taking my head into his hands. His eyes met mine and I remembered the pain I felt watching him as Wesley placed me in the sanctuary. How he held Aleksandra from me. "You are right. This is not like me. So, just trust me. Please? Hold on to it. Keep it safe."

"Safe from what?" I asked. "Safe from whom?"

"You hold great power," he whispered, "and there are those who will use it against us. Against you."

"The Vatican?" I asked as I searched his eyes. They revealed nothing.

He looked away. "Keep it with you," he instructed. "And keep it safe."

"Aksel, please?" I begged.

"No questions," he said. "Just trust me."

TWENTY-SIX

Good luck. If that amulet meant to bring such a thing, it never did. Aksel moved in to our State Street pent house, taking residence in the upstairs study. Even though he lived among us, he was seldom there. He was shifty, like a shadow, moodier than I remembered him.

I never wore the amulet. It remained in its velvet box, tucked safely away in my nightstand. Collecting dust among other trinkets, it lived there until Aksel returned each month asking me to fetch it. He had to see it, to touch. He had to feel it beneath his own weary fingers.

He came just last month and loosened a tiny ruby from its outer edge. I watched him pocket the jewel and then walk onto the balcony. He dangled his lanky arms over the rails, the traffic blurring below, its incessant hum irritatingly sweet that evening. The cool, October air blew in a soft gust as the jewel teetered in his palm.

"What are you going to do with that?" I asked, coming behind him. His visits were more frequent that month. Since I had found him that past January in my old Lofoten home, he came to visit every month and only stayed for two nights. Yet in October, he came on the first and stayed longer. He lingered, sleeping in his guest room during the day and skulking around the apartment at night – traipsing from room to room, gazing from window to window, and fidgeting any time he sat too long. He only left long enough to feed, and even then, only every few nights.

"They know where you are, Bree," he told me. "They know where we all are, now."

"It is the Vatican, Aksel," I told him. "You are foolish to believe you were ever invisible."

"I may not have been, but your friends were," he replied. He fingered the jewel, placed it in an envelope, sealing it. I grabbed at his arm. "They have Judith," he said. "I think I know where they are keeping her, though."

"Rome," I told him. Turning, I walked back into the bedroom. I glanced at my cell phone; the slick white contraption once felt unnatural in my hand. I thought of calling Colin, of warning him. But anything I could have said would have sounded absurd.

"We have to get her back," I yelled to Aksel. "You have to get her back! Colin almost lost her once; I cannot watch him lose her again."

"Stop, Bree, just stop," he said, placing his hands on my shoulders. "They are not in Rome. They are here... in Chicago."

Colin's Albany Park apartment door was unlocked, his living room window cracked open, the wind scattering desk papers to the floor. He should have been holding office hours that evening until eight. It was his one late night that month as Chancellor of the English Department, to meet with students at North Park University, but he was not at his office. By the time I arrived, a line of distraught undergrads had already collected outside his door. They rushed the door, their banging fists striking the glass. Some slipped term papers under the door and walked away, eager for a night of collegiate mischief – or extra cramming time for Colin's next test.

His office was locked, though, unlike his apartment. Colin was a cautious man. I had never known him to make such a callous error as this. Albany Park was one of Chicago's quieter neighborhoods, indeed, but still a college campus, and still in Chicago. One should not feel comfortable leaving their home unlocked with a window ajar.

The door creaked on its un-oiled hinges as I swung it open, gingerly stepping inside. Other than the papers that had blown off the desk and onto the floor beside it, nothing looked out of place. A half-eaten bowl of chips sat next to an open and empty pizza box on the coffee table. Throw pillows were strewn into a heap near the television. An empty pop can was on the floor next to the couch. A musty odor clung to the air despite the open window, and a pile of laundry peaked itself from behind the corner leading into the apartment's bedroom. Exactly what one would expect from a divorced-bachelor.

Colin's wife, Morgan, a theatrical arts teacher, left him for a thirty-something, up and coming Wall Street Day Trader, and moved to New York to reclaim her lost youth. She snagged a part in a pathetically received off-Broadway play. To be supportive, before she fell ill, Judith flew out to see it. Even she could not sit through both acts. Morgan was no match for the Big Apple's bright lights, and her career remained off-off Broadway.

When Judith returned without her mother, Colin realized there was no hope in reconciliation. The woman he had fallen in love with in Paris during that French class trip in college – whose eyes had sparkled in the moonlight as they looked over the Seine, and whose wavy hair distracted him from Notre Dame's gothic spires – was no more. Her tutoring was a salvation, boosting his tragic failing grade to a meager passing one. She threatened midway through their tutoring the first semester to drop him if he did not pay attention, but her eyes were too distracting. He struggled but, in the end, finished the second semester able to go on the class trip. And by then, they were falling in love.

Colin had purchased a bottle of Parisian cologne on that school trip. Foul smelling stuff, actually, but Morgan adored it. He would wear it for her and his belongings still carried the scent – faint but traces remained. They were afterthoughts, aromatic memories to haunt my senses, to remind me that something was dreadfully wrong.

I caught the faint wafting of his cologne in the air as it moved past me, but I did not smell him move with it. His heartbeat, his blood, was not present in this room. Nothing living moved here. The streetlight illuminated the desk and shone off the aluminum pencil holder, its smooth grating letting the light pass through. I could see painfully well in the dimly lit room, where the darkness would blind a human.

A human, I knew, could not walk in this blackness. Not undetected. A human would stumble. A human would catch its toe on a door jam, or smack itself on the edge of a chair, wincing uncontrollably. A human cannot help, after all, doing so when they are in a tug-of-war with death.

"I smell you," I said into the darkness. "You should not be wearing his clothes. They betray you."

"They are all I have left," she said, emerging from the shadow. Judith wore his Blackhawks jersey over her t-shirt and jeans. Her blonde hair was pulled away from her face in a ponytail. Wisps of hair escaped, framing her cherubim face.

"You look better than the last time I saw you." I stepped over the pile of laundry as I moved to hug her.

Her arms were unsteady around my shoulders, the tears quickly coming before I even embraced her.

"I told dad my secret," she admitted, whimpering into my shoulder.

"He probably did not believe you." Taking her hand, I led her to the couch and forced her to sit next to me. A *Writer's Weekly* stuffed between the cushions pinched my thigh before I removed it. I plopped it onto the coffee table. "Your dad needs to hire a cleaning service."

"He did not believe me," she started.

"But I insisted. 'I am!' I kept shouting it, Bree. 'I am a vampire!' I kept shouting it! And he was trying to calm me, so I showed him my fangs," she said, hanging her head. "He thought they were plastic."

"Why did you not leave it at that?" I asked.

"I needed him to know," she said. "I am not sure why, but I did. He is my father. I was dying, and now I will never die. And he needs to know why."

"No, he does not. You know how much trouble you are in now!"

"Well," she whispered. "The cat is out of the bag; he saw me."

"When?" Her face turned to mine, her eyes squarely looking into my own.

She gestured toward the open window. "I left and came upon a student. He was coming to see my father. I fed from the kid and dad saw me. When I realized this, when I heard him scream my name, I rushed back here, but he ran out. I have waited here since, but he has not returned."

"Where could he be?" I asked.

"I have no clue!" she replied. "I phoned my brother, some of my father's friends, no one has seen him."

"He is still in town," I said. "I think I know where. Just stay here."

There was a coffee shop near campus where the college students gathered, their laptops and books cluttering tables, coffee mugs filling the empty spaces. This was the official "cramming" spot, where students ran for the mid-term and finals half-off specials. While the other coffee haunts closed shop at ten, this one was open all night during testing weeks, catering to the profitable, caffeine-addicted student clientele.

The day-glo neon lights stung my corneas as the glass door slid open, the aroma of freshly ground espresso welcoming me. He sat in a corner booth alone, his back to the door. Surrounding him were students hunched over their lattes and frappes, their steaming and blended vats of caffeine with added shots of energy, peering into lit laptop screens, their highlighters moving over passage after passage. Some were, despite the rooms energizing caffeine haze, teetering on the verge of sleep.

Smiling at the weepy-eyed barista behind the counter, I walked toward his table and sat across from him. He cradled his head in his hands; his cheeks pale, and his eyes bloodshot. The untouched espresso had grown cold. I took the cup from the table and he barely noticed.

"Can I get a fresh one of these?" I asked the barista.

"Will the professor be okay?" asked the short brown-haired woman as she pressed a button on the large coffee grinder. The aroma of freshly ground beans permeated the shop again. "He just looks so... sad." She made the espresso machine whirr and buzz, blending coffee and water, producing clouds of steam.

"He will be just fine, thank you," I replied, handing her cash. "Keep the change."

I placed the steaming brew before him and he straightened up, smelling the brown liquid as he took the cup. "What are you doing here," he asked.

"What are *you* doing here," I returned. "Judith's waiting for you."

"I know," he said between sips. "I think she killed my student," he whispered.

"I think she has done more than that," I told him.

"What do you mean?" he asked. "And how did she kill him, Bree?" His voice was warming with the espresso.

"Quiet down," I urged him. "She told you, Colin."

"Oh, right," he chuckled. "She is a vampire. Bree, please be straight with me. My father speaks highly of you, of Aleksandra and Wesley. Stop lying to me and covering for her, it only makes you an accomplice. What I saw tonight," he began, "was that poison or a small gun in her pocket with a silencer?"

"First, he is not dead," I told him. "Aleksandra would have taught her not to kill unless she needed to. Second, Colin, your daughter *is* a vampire."

"Bree," he began, but I shushed him.

"Colin, Aleksandra did not cure Judith with a treatment, she cured her by turning her undead."

"Really? And how did Aleksandra become a vampire?" he said, sipping his espresso, not believing me; not wanting to believe me.

"I turned her," I told him. "Her father was a Russian prince and he passed away. When Aleksandra came of age, she wished for this curse. Do not ask me why."

"Have I officially cracked up now?" he asked. "I would have to be a bona-fide whack job to believe you!"

"I am being completely serious and honest with you." I pressed my back against the wall. The students remained hunched over their work, oblivious to the bizarre nature of our conversation. "Why would I make this up? What would I gain?"

"Judith must want something," he replied. "I may be her father, but I cannot lie for her."

"She wants her father's love!" I attested, firmly. A few eyes diverted from their laptop screens, but quickly returned to their studying. "And she desperately needs it right now. You do not realize it, and I know she doesn't, but your daughter just made some powerful enemies."

"The police? Of course, she did, and rightfully so, Bree."

I shook my head. "What do you mean, then?" he asked. He drained the last sip from his espresso and placed the cup on its saucer. He scooted the dish to the table's edge, signaling to the barista to fetch the soiled porcelain.

I waited until she left, then lowered my voice and leaned across the table toward him. "I came to see you tonight because a friend of mine worked with your father a while back to steal something from the Vatican. Your father gave this item to me before he retired and now the Vatican wants it back," I told him.

"Well, give it back," he said. His eyes shifted about the room.

"It is not that easy and I cannot tell you why," I replied. "My friend came to me tonight; he said the Vatican had Judith here in Chicago. That is why I came to your apartment."

"They had Judith?" he asked. His voice seethed with fatherly concern.

"Because Judith's a vampire now, they must think she is linked to this thing too. They wanted the amulet your father stole from the Vatican collection," I explained.

"You are back to this vampire concept, then?" he asked.

"It is not a concept, Colin!" My frustration grew more each moment he argued with me. Most people feared me once they learned the truth; I had never had someone argue the existence of my kind to my face in this manner.

"Yes, I understand," he began. "I have seen the television special on cable. It is a religion now. Or, excuse me, an alternative lifestyle. Whatever," he waved his hand in mini circles near my face, "Do you drink blood or suck people's happy thoughts? Is that what she does now, Bree? She kills for blood?"

Seeing no other way to get through to him, I stood and moved to his side. Tugging at his collar, he rose from the chair; his face contorted. "What are you doing?" he asked, bewildered.

"I am answering your question," I told him. "I suggest you do not fight it, or this will hurt."

My arm embraced him, my strength surprising him as he struggled. My finger grazed against his stubble as I traced his jaw line, slowly moving to the jugular. It pulsated beneath my cold touch, the rushing blood a symphony to my ears.

I bent my head, licked the saltiness from his neck, and whispered, "Have you figured out which type of vampire I am?" Choosing a small patch of skin over his pulsating jugular, near the shoulder line where the neck was tender, I sucked until it was pink and then sunk my teeth into waiting the flesh.

The blood flooded my mouth as images invaded my brain. A young Colin skipping rocks on the pond, climbing trees and learning Greek. There were flashes of college, of falling in love in Paris. These were followed by him and Morgan getting married, then came children and teaching, and divorce. His blood sang to me, played with me, danced with me. His blood calmed me.

Drinking from him was like drinking from a brother until I started pulling away. There was a flash from a winter's gala at the Field Museum, a political fundraiser. This was shortly after I awoke and I was new to Chicago, new to this new age. He walked up to me that night, we shared a dance; and when he asked for my phone number, I fled. A dozen long stem roses and the W.B. Yeats poem 'The Song of Wandering Aengus,' scrawled in freehand, surprisingly arrived two days later from a secret admirer.

"And someone had called me by my name," I said as I withdrew. I was dazed from his blood, and from his secrets.

"It had become a glimmering girl," he whispered, slumping into the chair. "How could you not know it was me?"

"Aleksandra told you my favorite poet." I glanced around the coffee shop. The students remained locked in their studies, the barista smiled at us. "Clever girl, but she never signed your name. I had no idea who the flowers and poem were from."

Grabbing his coat from a nearby hook, I tossed it to him. "How do you feel? We need to get back to Judith. She is in grave trouble, Colin, and I do not think she realizes how serious this is."

"Wait," he said, grabbing onto my arm. He glanced around and then leaned in. "Am I, you know, a vampire now, too?"

"You are so daft."

The barista smiled as we walked past the counter. "Way to go, professor!" she remarked. A few of Colin's students whistled as we walked out, the door swinging behind us.

"You seem to be popular, now," I told him.

"It seems so."

TWENTY-SEVEN

The years I have lived have taught me one thing, survival wears down, and it does not build up. I used to tout that nothing could weaken us. That the years and the blood would strengthen us; provide us with knowledge and power. That, I now know, is an illusion.

From the outside, we appear omnipotent, godlike to mere mortal beings. Yet we are just as shallow and scared as humankind is. We walk the same streets, cowering in the same shadows. We fear being discovered, having our miserable lives snuffed by the sun's golden rays. Despite the fact we are miserable, as you are, we would not willingly step into the sun. No more than you would willingly step off a bridge or put a bullet to your head. We have no desire to end this existence, and so we cower in fear that that thin veil between our worlds will be pulled away.

What would happen then? Would humankind accept us? Not a vampire culture that Hollywood has mass-produced, where vampires are cuddled and coddled, and sparkle with ripped abs, romanticized and adored as playthings for a bored public. Or the subculture where teens drink from pricked skin while lying atop tombstones, gowned in morbid black clothing, their faces painted grim shades of gray and white, as they sip wine and read Gothic poetry – paying homage to god's Poe and Byron. What would happen if society were introduced to real vampirism, to our power and knowledge? Could it handle that? Could *we* survive that?

The past four weeks leading up to tonight have moved in rapid succession. As much as I have tried to stop the inevitable, this is the only conclusion I have arrived at. My dear family – and all who may come to read this tale: When you read what is to follow, please remember I have meant no one during this journey harm. I should have died mercifully in that convent with Sister Veronica and the other sisters. I should still be asleep. I should not be here now, and this is not my war. But I am ending it. Tonight.

Please forgive me.
Please. Forgive me.

The window was still open as we neared his apartment, the glow of Colin's headlight glinting off the glass. Judith was still there, as I had instructed. She sat on the couch, patiently waiting. Let me do the talking, I had insisted. He was still too stunned to protest. How he had managed to drive the three blocks to the apartment astounded me, but he had insisted on doing so.

Judith remained seated when I flipped the living room light switch. She met her father's dazed glare then turned away, pain seethed underneath her determined brow. Colin sat down across from her in a broken down recliner, his eyes downcast.

"Judith, you have put your father in danger coming here." I removed the pizza box and sat down between them on the edge of the coffee table.

"They said he had it, Bree," she said. "I didn't even know what they were talking about! But they said if I could get it, bring it to them, they would not kill him. And I thought, well, if they were going to kill him, I wanted him to know the truth. I wanted to meet their demands and save him! Would you not have done the same?"

"Kill me?" he asked. His startled eyes stared into hers and then into mine.

"He does not have it," I told her. "Colin, they don't want you," I assured him, "They think they want you, but you have nothing of value to them."

Colin slumped into the recliner, the leather crackling beneath him. "What do they want?" he said.

"This," I said grabbing the amulet from my pocket, holding it out to show him. The dim lighting did not do the amulet justice and the jewels surrounding the portrait barely sparkled. I shoved it back into my pocket as he reached for it.

"What is that, Bree?" Judith asked.

"Those men want that awfully bad. They knew they were capturing a vampire, and still they were persistent. It must be worth a lot to them," she said.

"It is a good luck charm; that is all the information I have." The hardness of the amulet paralleled the truth; the Vatican would not stop until they had it back.

She stood from the couch. "They did not let me go, Bree." She turned her back on me. "I had to kill my way through five men. They were going to kill me! I had no choice! What is Aleksandra going to say?"

"She will be proud," I whispered. I stood and embraced her as she trembled in my arms. Colin sat, his jaw slack, his eyes widened. "We all have to kill, eventually; no matter what she has taught you. But we must choose to do so discreetly, and for the right reasons. Those men,

Judith, they were dangerous. They were bringing this on themselves, and they knew that."

"They were from the Vatican, Bree!" she remarked. Her voice quivered. "Men of God! Whether you believe or not, those are powerful people and an enemy I do not wish to have."

"Nor do I," I replied, "But we have no choice, thanks to Aksel? He brought this amulet into our lives. And he has created this mess, and, like always, I have to clean it up!"

She ran her hands through her hair, loosening the tight ponytail and tossing the hair band onto the floor. Ash blonde, shoulder length locks fell as she scratched at her temples.

"Where do we even begin?" she asked. "I can take you back to their hotel but they are all dead. The rest are in Rome, at least that's what I gathered."

"I am not going near Rome. If they want this amulet, they have to come and get it," I said.

"This is unreal, just think for a minute," Judith noted. "That's no good luck charm, Bree. The Vatican's acting as if you hold Armageddon in your hands."

"I am beginning to think you're right, but I have never been able to get the truth from Aksel," I admitted. "To be honest, I do not believe he knows what it truly does. He believes it is powerful, and from what I can tell, the Vatican does as well. But why? I have no clue!"

"One of them was on the phone," she said. "Whoever's behind this is convinced that trinket is a key of some sort."

"A key?" I asked.

"That's all I heard," she said. "A man's voice, in Italian, 'Get the key!'"

Judith paced over to the window and looked out onto the now vacant street. "If we are going to move him to your place, now is the time. He is going to be safest there; do you agree?" she asked.

I glanced at Colin. His head hung, his chin gracing his chest, his tired eyes reddened from the tears. The heaviness gracing his face was familiar; it showed a burden drenched in despair, in fear, and in pain. He had appeared this way sitting next to Judith's hospital bed the night before Aleksandra turned her. Seeing him like this was agony.

"Am I going to die?" his voice cracked.

Judith turned and rushed to her father's side as his body trembled, the shock of revelation wearing off. Reality now stung through with its icy tentacles; it was time for him to leave the old, naïve, safe world behind.

"Am I going to die?" he asked again. "Be honest with me."

"Not as long as we are with you," I replied.

Outside, Colin's hands trembled as he reached for the door handle. Judith snatched the Lexus's keys from her father's hands and steered him toward the back. Besides the vacation cabin on Lake Placid, the sleek, silver Lexus was the only luxury item Colin managed to walk away with in the divorce settlement.

Colin sat silently in the back, his hands cupped in his lap, his bottom lip curled beneath his teeth. I climbed into the front beside Judith as we pulled out of the apartment building and eased away from the campus area. It was late that evening and campus security was in full patrol.

No one spoke until we were on the Dan Ryan Expressway. A drizzling of rain collected on the windshield, enough to run the wipers, and enough to break the silence.

"Why do they want you?" Colin asked me. The back seat was pitched black, his voice rising from the shadows. The occasional headlight betrayed his existence. "What could you have done to the Vatican?"

"The Vatican," I began, but I could not answer him. How could I begin to answer such a complicated question? "They do not want me, Colin." I tried to clarify, "They want Aksel. Or they want the amulet. I'm not sure which anymore."

"Then why do they not just go and get him and leave us alone? Or you can hand over the amulet?" Judith asked. She was passing a semi trailer and swerving into heavy traffic. She flicked on the radio and hit scan. The radio ran through the stations, blurring random strings of talk and music, until a weather report caught her attention and she smacked the scan button once more. The meteorologist was calling for a thunderstorm with golf ball sized hail.

"Of course, we get caught out in this. Why did we not fly him in, Bree?" she whispered beneath the drone of rain pelting the glass.

"That is what he needed, because he is not spooked enough, Judith," I remarked.

"You still did not answer my question," she demanded as she swerved in front of a late model Jeep. The Jeep beeped and slammed on its brakes. "Why not give Aksel up?"

"Judith, we are not going to need the Vatican to kill your father with the way you are driving! Slow down!"

Judith eyed the rearview mirror, then her side mirror. She made a shape right off onto the shoulder and turned the headlights off. "Dad. Bree. Do. Not. Move," she whispered. She and I watched through the side mirrors as a car parked behind us. It turned its engines off and waited. Minutes passed and then three figures stepped from the car and began walking through the storm toward our car. Judith placed her fingers on the keys, started the car, and sped into traffic.

Our lights were not on as Judith swerved onto the Dan Ryan. A flash of lightning blazed the sky a yard away, blinding the teenage girl driving the minivan behind us. She had been going fifteen over the speed limit already, too fast in this weather to avoid hitting us. The front end of the minivan collided with the back of the Lexus, flipping the town car up and over the slippery road. We flipped into the air and rolled over a semi-truck and four cars before coming to rest in an embankment.

"Colin," I shouted into the Lexus as I climbed from it. We flew out into the dark, stormy night as the vehicle flipped and rolled over the cars. "Colin!"

Judith struggled with her father, trying to free him from the back seat, but could not. The backdoors were stuck, smashed from impact. The gnarled metal mixed with shards of glass and beading rain as cars slowed to avoid the scene. Skidding tires met with a symphony of horns and shouts from cars down the road, a couple passerbies running to help.

Neither of us could pull him over the backseats in time, his unconscious body slumped and freely rolling in the rear of the car. At the last minute, against her will, I pulled Judith from the car, leaving Colin for dead.

She screamed into the air, her voice a primal howl into blurring traffic whizzing by. She shoved past me and sat down in the grassy ditch off the side of the freeway. We were safely removed from the wreckage, but still close enough to see the sparks as they freed Colin from the car;

and as the paramedics worked on his body. They were inserting an intravenous line in his arm and securing his neck with a cervical collar. Lights and sirens painted the night sky. Traffic stopped, and, even with the rain, people stood outside their cars gawking at the wreckage.

"My dad, Bree, that is my dad on that stretcher." Her voice was remote and distant. "He is dying." Sitting next to her, I wrapped my arms around her shoulders, holding her close.

"I should be with him," she said. "We should go to the hospital."

"No," I told her. "There is nothing we can do for him now, Judith. Going there will only risk our safety. It will risk his."

"But he's my dad; I cannot let him die alone!" She stood, brushing wet grass from her pants. Her soiled clothing clung to her as the storm picked up, thunder clapping in the distance. The downpour suddenly increased as the ambulance sped away and cops directed traffic around the wreckage. "You can stay, I don't care. I'm not giving up on him."

"Do not go, Judith," I insisted. "This is not going to be easy."

"I have seen death, Bree."

"I know." I reached for her but she shrank away. "But this death will be too close to you. Those deaths – those close to us – they change us and we should not see them. We should not experience them."

"Why should we fear change? Fear death? If he is to die tonight, why should I fear being by his side?" she argued. "This monstrous blood has changed me, but it hasn't stripped from me every ounce of my humanity. I can still love my father! I can still cling to the hope that he's not dying in the back of that ambulance!" The rain trickled off her ruby lips, the droplets cascading with each syllable.

"Judith," I began, "now is not the time to argue and philosophize."

"You are right," she interjected. "Right now, I need to be with him, not arguing in a sloppy rain storm on the side of highway!"

Judith turned, watching the police cars working to clear the scene. The ambulance was on its way to the hospital; its sirens blared through the heavy traffic piling up on the busy Dan Ryan.

"Judith," I whispered, tugging at her sleeve. "Come away from the road. Look." I motioned toward a car parked nearby, off the shoulder, its lights off. "It's them."

"You're right," she said. "I hear them, too."

"Listen," I told her. "We need to split up and meet up at the apartment. Do not go to the hospital. Please, Judith. I know you want to be with your father, but these men," I told her, "if Colin is not already dead, they will kill him for sure."

"I love my father too much to jeopardize any chance he has, Bree," she said. We watched a flicker appear in the front seat of the car as the driver lit a cigarette. "Do you think he has a chance?" she asked.

"I do not know," I admitted. "I would not get your hopes up, Judith. The head trauma involved... I do not have Aleksandra's training, but even I know the mortal body's limitations."

"Why can we not kill them now?" she asked. "There are only a few of them!"

"I do not do an eye for an eye, Judith," I told her. "That is not the way you should base your immortality. Plus, we need to know who they are working for."

"They are working for the Vatican. I found out that much already!"

"The Vatican is not a mom-and-pop organization, sweetheart." My voice boomed over the traffic's ceaseless roar. "Do you really think the Pope himself signed your father's death warrant? I think not. Someone is behind this, and I doubt it is the big man on the throne. I intend to find out who and why. Then I intend to end this war."

"Then interrogate them," she insisted. "Interrogate them as they interrogated me."

"Did they get information from you?" I asked. "No, they did not. And we would not get any from them. The Vatican only hires the cream of the crop, Judith. These are trained men. If we even approach that car, I bet they will have a self-destruct in the works. Cyanide. A bullet to the head. Take your pick."

"What do we do then?" She stared at the car, the cigarettes glow now extinguished. Cars whizzed past on the freeway, oblivious to the insidious nature of the stalled vehicle's passengers.

"We run, we meet up, we distract them," I said. "Then I figure out what the amulet really does." I fingered the amulet again, the coldness pressing against my jeans. The storm was moving off the lake as the rain began to ease.

"Aksel knows, he has to," she said.

"He knows something and it is about time he tells me," I said as I took off for the north of Chicago. She took off for the south to lead our stalkers astray.

TWENTY-EIGHT

The storm carried me toward the shore as I traveled north before turning south, heading into downtown Chicago. Buckingham Fountain shimmered with moonlight, tourists surrounding its gate now that showers were fading. As the rain ceased, the Chicago nightlife began. Vendors opened umbrella-clad food stands while street performers – guitars and saxophones in hand – staked out their corners, collection boxes ready for the evening's offerings. Soothing jazz mingled with rhythmic folk, just blocks from each other.

October evenings in Chicago can be a transcendental experience, especially after a fall storm. The scent wafting in from the lake after a storm cleared was always the sweetest. The way the shoreline soil felt saturated from the rain, squishing beneath my naked toes, tickling my feet was almost sensual. The skyline, lit up as a beacon, its buildings alive with movement and purpose and all dressed in shimmering glass and steel. The city, cooled by the autumn breeze, yet still showing no signs of slowing.

I circled Buckingham Fountain, observing the tourists snapping pictures as the lights at the fountain's base changed colors. A canceled concert on Lincoln Park Zoo's south lawn was causing overflow traffic in the area. Out of town concertgoers – their hotel rooms booked months in advance – were stuck in the city overnight. They wandered downtown on their impromptu adventures. They tossed cash around hip bars and comedy clubs, padding the wallets of Chicago's many cabbies.

My eyes had scanned the nearby streets for the car that was following Judith, and Colin and I on the Dan Ryan. I had tried flying low enough so they could follow me, but still high enough to avoid drawing attention to myself. Now I feared I had concealed myself form my stalkers too well and pulled them onto Judith.

Finding a park bench near a crowded corner along the shoreline, I sat and waited. Across from me was a cart hawking tee shirts of the skyline, all ridiculously marked up. A couple tourists were perusing the cart's wares but were not buying the cheaply made garments. They would be flying off the shelf come June, but in the fall and winter, tourists were discriminatory with their tastes and tighter with their cash.

Ten minutes elapsed, and with no sign of the men, I strolled past the t-shirt vendor and into the welcoming darkness along Lake Michigan. I trailed the shoreline until I was certain no one had followed, and ascended into the dewy clouds – the vapors concealing me. The moisture stung my skin as I climbed further, reaching higher into the star-lit sky before perching atop Willis Tower.

One-hundred and ten floors above Chicago, the ants scurried below. Watching traffic wrap around the city, horns blaring while tires squelched across freshly wet pavement. The thoughts of thousands hummed through the air, flooding my brain as I fought them away. I needed to hear those men, the men who had been after our car. I needed to hear only those men and the thoughts of countless Chicagoans struggled to bleed through.

Sitting atop the skyscraper, the wind howled against me as I braced onto the buildings antennas. Clearing the static and noise, the humdrum from the greedy ants, as they scurried about took skill. And time. If the men had followed Judith, if she had remained lower, pulling them, then I would have the time; time to make their thoughts betray them.

For over an hour, I sat atop that tower as the wind pelted me, threatening me with its constant barrage, when finally I heard them. One man, a smoking man, repeated my name under his breath. Their car abandoned its course – whatever course it was on – and the men were heading toward my State Street apartment. They knew where I lived. They knew what I was. They knew how to kill me.

Approaching from the south, I spotted their car parked along the street. They were inside, the three men, one of them striking a lighter – the petite flame singing the cigarette's tip. They casually sat awaiting dawn's golden crest, when they would cowardly sneak into the apartment and slay each of us – Aleksandra, Judith and myself, as we slept. It'll be done in a snap, thought the one in the back seat as he popped an M&M in his mouth. The man passed the bag to the smoking man, who then shook a few candies into his palm and crumpled the empty bag, tossing it out the car window.

They laughed at our perceived security. They mocked our lives, these young men. Their lives were but hiccups compared to my own. They felt they had lived, had seen war, had loved women and slain great men. They knew nothing of love, of war, or of greatness. They were but blemishes, superficial and insignificant.

Swiftly, letting the wind carry me into its cusp, I sailed toward the men's thoughts. Stopping a few yards behind the car, concealed in an alleyway, I watched the one man light another cigarette. The blue flame briefly illuminated the front seat as the driver next to him rolled his window down. The back driver's side door flung open, a man stepped out coughing loudly. "You're gonna give us all black lung, Charlie; give it a rest!"

"Get inside, son. Are you stupid?" growled the driver as I watched the backseat passenger climb in and close the door. "You have no clue what we are dealing with, so stay put and follow our direction."

"I am over sittin' in cars; sittin' in buildings; sittin' and watchin'. We found the apartment, no? Why not go in and do what we came here for?" the backseat man asked.

"These one's are too old, kid; we can't go rushing in there," the smoking man replied, taking a drag on the cigarette.

"Vampires are vampires, Charlie," backseat man replied.

"No, they are not," huffed the driver. "This will not be another Paris, Bobby."

"There was thirty of 'em!" replied backseat Bobby.

"Thirty young ones are nothing compared to one elder, Bobby. And we are up against at least two – possibly three."

"Elders, young ones – vampires are vampires," backseat Bobby sighed, opening the car door and stepped out once again. "I need some air."

Moving from the shadows, I seized the man, sinking my teeth into his tender flesh. Charlie's Marlboros lingered on Bobby's olive skin, the odor of cheap tobacco mingling with his expensive Italian cologne. His blood was a pungent concoction leaving a luscious taste on my tongue reminiscent of honey and figs and sea salt, with a forethought of garlic and gypsy wine.

When he was near death, I released him. As his body slumped to the ground, the driver noticed his partner's head violently smack against the car door. "We have company," he pointed as the other men turned. The cigarette man took a final drag from his Marlboro before tossing it from the open window. All three men stepped from the car.

"See your partner?" They eyed the man slumped on the ground, the wounds on his neck still bleeding.

"Who sent you? Why are you after the amulet? What does it do?"

"We don't know what the amulet does," the smoking man replied. He pulled the red and white pack from his shirt pocket and withdrew a cigarette, tapping it against the cardboard before tossing the slender stick of tobacco onto the ground and smashing at it with the tip of his boot. "We were not paid to care, just to bring it home."

The man walked around the car as he placed the pack of cigarettes back into his shirt pocket.

"Where is home?" I asked. He paused near the trunk, cautious to keep his distance from me. "Who wants this amulet enough to kill for it?" Their blatantly insulting glares traversed the darkness.

"Did you not hear me?" I called out to them.

"Who sent you?" Rushing to the driver's side, I clutched his throat. Raising him into the air as the other two watched, I cried out again, "Who sent you?"

"He sent us," a weakened voice whispered behind me. The man slumped on the ground had regained consciousness and propped himself against the car. "The father," the voice continued its raspy whisper fading as the man's heart struggled.

"Which father?" I asked him, kneeling beside his near lifeless body.

"You know him," the man with the cigarette spoke from his position near the car.

He was in his private chapel reciting evening prayers, his voice thick with ancient Latin. I watched him from the balcony. The Vatican Archivist knelt at the altar. The small room just off his bedchamber aglow with the soft light of a modern bulb, but its placement concealed. Prayer candles aided the natural, peaceful ambience one would expect from a prayer room, the familiar scents of incense did not hurt.

His back toward me, I entered past the velvet curtains, the ruby fabric billowing in the wind. I stood in the corner as he finished his prayers. His words were mere whispers, inaudible to another human unless they were next to him. For me though, I could hear those words, that ancient tongue, from across the ocean. Being in the room with him now was an amplified reminder of my past. The closing *amen* stung into my heart as a knife's blade would feel piercing your mortal flesh. Was I so removed from the world that these words, which I once recited with sincere earnest, now caused me excruciating pain?

His weary knees cracked as he rose from the floor.

"They are all dead," I admitted. This marked my first confession since Bergen, if you could consider this a confession.

Clambering to his feet, he flipped around, eying me suspiciously. He rushed to the hallway door, reaching for the bell that hung near it; but I met him there, seizing his hand before he could grasp the gold cord. He pushed against me and I shoved him back into the altar until he relinquished. "Dedo," he whispered as I released him. He stumbled to his feet, holding his arms against his chest. "I knew this day would come, just not tonight. Will you allow me first to prepare my soul?" he asked.

"I am not here for your soul." The door to his bedchamber was ajar. Opening it, I walked through and then sat down on a settee beneath a painting of St. Bridget. "I have the amulet," I admitted as I fingered the jewel in my pocket. "Is it really worth all the blood that has been spilled?"

"Blood?" the old man whispered, the years of church service showing on his wrinkled face, his snowy hair betraying the calm exterior he flashed to his papal father. Being the Church's Archivist – keeper of records and secrets – wore heavily in his eyes. The sacrifice of love and of having a family, were becoming tempting regrets as he neared death's natural door. And he earnestly prayed to erase the guilt of these Earthly temptations from his heart.

"There was never meant to be blood spilled." He shuffled into the bedchamber, sitting on the edge of the bed, its springs creaking beneath his weight.

"Someone dear to me lays dying tonight because of this, father." Pulling the jewel from my pocket, I dangled it before him letting light reflect off the rubies.

"Your men have stalked the ones I love, my family! They have threatened my peace, my joy, and for what? For this? Tell me what is it – its purpose. Why am I here?"

"The man was supposed to have it," the archivist replied, his eyes trailing the amulet as I placed it back into my pocket.

"What man?" I knelt in front of him, my face inches from his own. "Father, did this belong to someone?"

"It belonged to a Holy Father," he replied, looking up at me. "Once...Can I hold it?" he asked, "Just once.

The amulet is a legend, one I never thought I would ever see." I reached into my pocket, fished out the amulet, and slipped it into his shaking hand. His palms quivered as he held the piece, his fingers unable to grasp it. "When I saw this on the manifest shipping to the museum, I never dreamt it was *the* amulet. Honestly, I thought it was but a legend passed down amongst the papacy."

"Why are you telling me this?" His candid reflections surprised me. He handed the amulet back and walked out of the bedchamber through the chapel, traversing toward the open balcony.

"I sent those men to retrieve the amulet," he admitted.

"I know, that is why I am here," I replied.

"No," he insisted, "you are here because blood was shed! You said so yourself. Blood was shed but not of my doing. I did not send people to murder you or anyone else."

"You cannot erase what has been done. You must make peace with your demons and ask for forgiveness."

"I charged my undersecretary with the task of retrieving the amulet. Mistakenly, I told him to pursue it at all costs. Francisco is too naïve for such a task, I see this now," he explained, "I signed the document of transfer, allowing that amulet to leave the Vatican vault for the American museum. Everything that has happened since – the murder – that has not been of my doing. My mouth did not order those commands," he said, tears staining the creases of his weary eyes.

His footsteps pattered across the smooth Italian marble as he walked into the bedchamber and sat in a chair near the window. The sky overlooking Vatican City was crystalline that evening – cloudless and lit with the brilliance of a billion stars. Standing there, I realized the

Vatican had remained as constant as the sky, both permanent forces orbiting each other, battling for attention in a world too busy to see the beauty each had to offer.

"Those murders, I am responsible for them," he said, his eyes glistening. "One day, I pray I will be forgiven for my transgressions," he finally said after we both had become lost in the starlit sky.

"Father, can Francisco be working with someone?"

"Conspiring against the Holy See?" he gasped. "I think not!" His eyes shifted back and forth, moving in unison with his head. "At least, I pray it is not so. Someone forced him to commit this crime."

"Those men were acting – slaying, father – on behalf of a higher authority."

"I was not that authority," he said. "And I can assure you, blood was not shed under my command, or that of the Holy Father."

"No," I said, "it was not your pope." I turned. "It was your Francisco. I can see his face in your thoughts. The men who harmed my friend – that was the same face. His face…"

"You must destroy the amulet, then. That is the only way."

"Destroy the amulet?" My fingers rested against the smooth jewels in my pocket, the cold hardness. "Why?"

"You cannot let Francisco get it back," he urged. "If the papal legends are true, then it is more powerful than anyone can comprehend."

"Then it is not just a good luck charm," I laughed, fingering the trinket.

"It is a protective hex." His voice flattened to a gruff whisper and I moved closer to him from a spot across the room.

"At least, it was supposed to be. Legend says one evening an angel came to visit a pope, but that night he had a revealing dream. This angel was no angel after all, but a demon in angel's clothing. So he summoned a maiden who dabbled in the occult, procured a protective hex; and then he sentenced the maiden to hanging. Her crime: witchcraft."

"If it is protective," I asked, pulling the amulet from my pocket and examining the portrait painted in my image, "how can I hold it? Should it not burn me or turn me to stone, or something?"

"That is the secret," the archivist replied reclining back into the chair, "As they were looping the noose about her neck, the girl told the hangman that the amulet would never protect the pope, but only the one whom he wished to ward away. The paint was already drying as her lifeless body swung from the olive tree, and the spell was cast."

"That is an amusing story, but how am I to believe any of it?" I tossed the amulet from one hand to the next, the image smiling back at me.

"It was but a legend here, as well. Then again, you and your kind were legends, too," he noted. "Then the amulet was stolen and the records say the guards entrusted to its care were drained of blood. For me, this confirmed both."

"You believe in my kind, then?"

"It's been the archivist's duty to know Church's enemies," he asked. His hands no longer shook as they rested at his side.

"We are not at war with you, pull back Francisco and we can be at peace, Father," I urged him. "The amulet is safe in my hands."

"No!" He rose and came to my side, any fear of being near me now replaced by his urgent need to destroy the amulet. "It must be destroyed. You must do it, I cannot. It's impossible."

"Why?" My hand upon his shoulder startled him and he shrank away. "Father, why do you fear it so?"

"Previous archivist's had been tasked with finding the source of the amulet's power. One archivist was close, and even began alleging it's not a cursed stone. But in 1878, his notes and the amulet were shoved away in a collection of journals and papers in the secret archives."

The man jogged toward a personal writing desk in the corner of the room and took a small gold key from a drawer. He went to the wall near the chapel entrance and removed a curtain, revealing a small safe. Inserting the key, he opened the safe door and took out a petite leather-bound notebook. "I'd only begun sorting through that section of memorabilia – for archivist eyes only – when I found this."

"Can you read Latin? It is all here! I could not believe the words when I first read them. They were all running experiments on the amulet. These former archivists were hiring men of science to study it!" he shook his head and handed me the notebook. "There are references to a weapon, but I do not understand it. Francisco does, his father was a magnificent German engineer – a brilliant man. If he is hiring mercenaries, and under the authority of my name," the archivist paused, tears rushing his eyes, his voice choking behind the admission of betrayal, "then he cannot gain possession of this amulet."

TWENTY-NINE

Certain clarity comes with soaring through an October sky. As the chilly autumn wind whipped through my hair, thoughts turned to a simpler time when I could feel the sun on my cheeks. When the world was limited and time finite, my future decided.

The golden pre-dawn horizon chased me toward Chicago as the city's bustling skyline welcomed me. October on the lakefront in my State Street high-rise, overlooking the ants scurrying below, living their glorious little lives – that all seemed like eons ago. Clarity. That is what my trip to Rome had given me.

The State Street apartment was dark when I arrived. Judith waited in the study, sitting in silence near the fireplace, her back to the wall. The curtains were drawn, the fireplace unlit and the lamps off. To the outside world, it appeared no one was home. And if Francisco was sending reinforcements, this was the message I intended to send.

"Is it safe to go to the hospital now?" she asked as I entered the study. Her hand moved to the light switch but I cut her off, moving to her side swiftly, catching her hand, slamming it against the wall before releasing it.

"You bled them dry, Bree!" her shrill voice pierced the blustering Chicago traffic. "I watched from this window." She moved to the window and swept aside the shade. Crime scene investigators had swarmed the area last night, their yellow tape marking a perimeter around the car and its bloodless inhabitants, she explained. "I watched knowing they would not find anything. I watched hoping they would not find anything."

"Even if they did," I remarked, coming up behind her, "the one behind this will bury it." I told her where I had been while she slept – the information I had uncovered.

"What can we do now?" she asked, her voice trailing off, the exasperation evident in each syllable.

"I have to find Aksel," I replied. Removing the amulet from my pocket, I held it against the moonlight before she released the shade, once again bathing the room in blackness. "It all centers on this amulet." I pocketed the jewel, fingering its coldness. "He knows more than he is willing to say."

"What do you need me to do?" Judith sauntered to the desk and sat down, fumbling through the drawers. "Maybe he will confide in me, Bree. If I tell him what happened, what happened to dad, maybe Aksel will end this nightmare for us all."

"No, Judith." I headed for the front entrance. She followed as we neared the apartment's front door. "He is my problem and it is my face on the amulet. It seems destiny, although I do not seek it, that it is my war to fight. I will question him. Go be with your father now; he needs you, my dear."

"Bree," she shuffled over, placing her arm around my shoulder, pulling me tightly to her, "promise me one thing, please?" My eyes met hers as a tear slipped into the corner of her eye where a bit of dust still lingered from last night's flight. "Promise me you will end this."

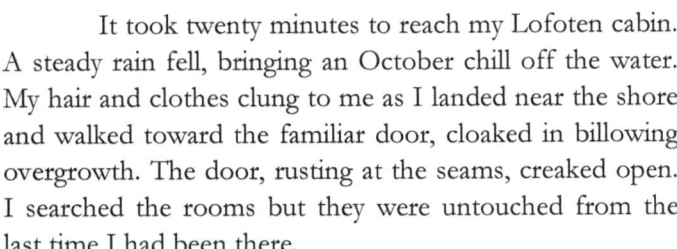

It took twenty minutes to reach my Lofoten cabin. A steady rain fell, bringing an October chill off the water. My hair and clothes clung to me as I landed near the shore and walked toward the familiar door, cloaked in billowing overgrowth. The door, rusting at the seams, creaked open. I searched the rooms but they were untouched from the last time I had been there.

The candles circling the bedchamber caught aflame as I sat on the edge of the bed, the covers still rolled back as if I had just awoken. "Aksel!" My voice echoed off the stone chamber, carrying itself up the barren staircase as candle flames flickered in its path.

Rising from the stone steps, the brisk air, rushing through the open door, greedily greeted me. My mind churned as the rain pelted my face. I fumbled with the locks, the rusted hinges threatening to disintegrate with each movement. As my eyes once more beheld the Lofoten cabin, the billowing overgrowth now completely covering the door, my feet lifted off the sandy shore.

Norway's villages and bustling cities, greatly changed since I last flew over them, blurred beneath me. The rain eased slightly but the wind showed no signs of relenting as I neared Trondheim. The city's buildings were alive with activity; its glass towers hovered above me as I landed.

I landed on that cobblestone street, now paved with asphalt. The inn was still there, standing across from the tavern, which held the same name it had back when I first found him. There were no lights on, the room was vacant, and he was not in there. I walked toward the shore, as I had on so many nights when I lived in Norway. The wind still bustled, knotting my hair.

The tide came in quickly, my boots sinking into the sand as I walked. His silhouette graced the shoreline. He sat in a beached boat, a fire smoldering nearby. His hands rubbed the woodcarvings. He was remembering that life – a simpler time, and innocent time.

"Do you wish now," I whispered, walking up behind him, "with all you know, everything you have been through, that you would have stayed in your cabin? Do you wish that you had not come out that night and spoken to me on this shore?"

"No." His head hung, his hands grabbed at his hair.

"Then why are we here?" The bench next to him was narrow, but he did not move over. He barely noticed I was there. "Why did you come here?"

"I came home," he whispered raising his face, blood tears staining his cheeks. "Bree, I came home to die."

In the moonlight, I saw them now, the carvings. They were of his making. He had been coming here for a while now, coming to work on this boat. In the Viking tradition, they chronicled his life, to help him achieve death.

"You don't get to enter the void yet, Aksel," I demanded. "That ending is for cowards."

"It is the only way to get them to stop, Bree," he said. He faced me and took my hands. "This is not how I saw us ending… or me ending, really."

"Just tell them to stop." I removed the amulet from my pocket, tossing it at him. It clinked in the darkness as it struck the boat's side. "Give them back their cursed amulet!"

"Pick it up," he said, his words flat against the sea air. "Put it away," he spat.

"Now you have me regretting ever stepping forth on Norwegian soil, Aksel. Why must you be so infuriating?" My foot kicked, sending sand into the flames so the wood crackled and sparks shot out into the atmosphere. I watched as they sailed away and I longed to ride along with them, ride away from Aksel and his amulet.

"Why must you always return to me, return to me and bring into my life such… heartache?"

Tiny fiery tongues licked the obsidian sky as I watched Aksel rise and walk from the boat. He picked up the amulet, dusted it against his pant leg and stared into the painted face. His thumb rubbed gently against the portrait.

"I painted this with my eyes closed," he remarked.

"You painted it?" I began to walk toward him, but his eyes warned me to stay back. "The legend of the witch really is a farce."

"The legend never named the painter, actually, and so those who have told the story, through time… the pope's, the archivist's, they have all assumed it a witch," he said, his eyes not once leaving the amulet, "But I painted it, once I found out what the amulet did, and who it was intended for."

"What about the angel and the girl? The legend?"

He turned, his eyes glossed in a veil of red. "Legends, cleverly weaved legends. In an ignorant time, it is easy to weave such lies, Bree. You know this. After all, you taught me well."

Going to his side, I took the amulet from his fingers; his vacant, colorless glare reflected back at me as I did. The jewel was cold, from both his touch and the icy Norwegian air. The waves roared, crashing against nearby rocks and the fire swelled despite the wind's surge.

Growing closer to the fire, I stared into the face on the amulet and it stared back at me. Time stopped as the embers near my feet crackled. I considered tossing it into the fire, but knew he would throw himself into the flame to rescue it.

"Aksel, the archivist thinks this amulet is a weapon," I said, facing him. "But the legend… is it all a lie and innocent people are dying over a Vatican artifact? Aksel, Peter had to give up his entire life in Chicago and Colin," I choked back a torrent of tears, "Colin's on life support after the men who seek this mowed us down on the Dan Ryan the other night!" I held the amulet up to the firelight so we could both see the portrait clearly.

"Whatever legend is behind this, whatever magic the archivist's secretary believes exists inside it, he is not just after us now, Aksel! Tell me; what will happen if he gets this amulet and finds out it is useless? What then?"

As I spoke, my words frantically spilling forth, Aksel snatched the amulet. When I finished, he fingered the amulet, glanced at it once more and then placed it in my coat pocket. "Trust me, please," he said.

"Why should I trust you?" I demanded. "Nothing since I have awoken has made sense!" I removed the amulet, clasping it and brought it to my face. "This, Aksel, this doesn't make sense! How many people must die for this amulet? How many more people have to die for this legend you have created?"

"Bree," he whispered, his voice shaky, "I promise, one day you will understand." He walked to the water's edge turning away from me. "One day, you will understand why I have awoken you now, why I have interrupted your slumber. One day, my precious, you will thank me."

I pressed on, "I want answers now, Aksel, not in the future!" Stepping closer, I waited for him to turn but he refused to face me. "I will throw this amulet into the ocean then!" I screamed.

"Why are you so stubborn?" he hollered, swiveling into view. "Why can you not just trust me?" he asked, walking toward the bench.

"Why can you not trust me, Aksel?" I bartered in return. "Trust me with this amulet's secret."

"It's complicated," he said.

"I don't like the sound of this," I replied. I sat next to him and he placed his hand in mine.

"You must protect it, Bree," he begged.

"Do I have a choice?" I asked, already knowing the answer. "But," I began as I glanced toward the boat, "you don't have to destroy yourself because of it."

"I do," he said. "It is the only way to protect you."

"I do not understand, Aksel."

"I don't ask you to understand," he said.

"Why is it this way with us? Always!" Taking his face into my hands, I stroked his firm cheekbones and traced the angle of his jaw with my index finger. "What have you done, my old love?"

His hand reached into my hair, his fingers gently stroking the strands. "I remember the first time I saw you by these shores. You were breathtaking, and then one night you slipped into the water and disappeared into the rocks." His voice trailed as his eyes lingered toward the same rocks. Not too far from the shore where his cabin once stood was now a fresh fish mart, of course now closed for the night.

"Day after day, night after night, your face bewitched me, Bree. Your eyes, your hair, your flawless beauty… the moonlight bathed you in incandescence. "

"I was finding my way in those days." The fire crackled as the memories surfaced. "I had just left Wesley.

I had never been on my own, and did not know how to be on my own."

"You did not stay on your own long," he remarked.

"I should not have made you so quickly," I admitted. "I had no idea what I was doing!"

"We were newlyweds," he laughed. "Neither of us were prepared for what was to come, so we floundered along, learning as we traveled."

"And making mistakes along the way," I noted, squeezing his hand. My voice quaked, "Was the amulet a mistake, an experiment or enchantment gone wrong, Aksel?"

"No, but you will still hate me for it," he said. His back stiffened, and he released my hand as he stood. "Bree, please listen to me," he said. "Some powers are far too great for one person to possess. You must keep it close to you at all times." As I began to protest, he placed a hand upon my shoulder. "If you have ever loved me, if you love me now, promise me you will keep it close."

"Aksel, of course," I whispered.

"Bree, do you trust me?" he asked. His eyes melted into mine as he stared at me. "Do you love me?"

"You know I do." Clutching onto his head, I grabbed at his hair as his body trembled. I pulled him closer, embracing his bulky frame. His muscles quivered beneath my touch while he sobbed, the tears collecting on my shoulder. "What do you need me to do?" I asked.

He pulled away, the anguish seething from his grief stricken eyes. "I need you to be with me when I go. I don't want to be alone."

If the night were not already dark enough, his words would have removed every ounce of light from the starlit sky. The moon itself wept as the stars heard Aksel's words, plunging themselves woefully into the icy waves below.

"I have sent word to the archivist's secretary," he explained. "He believes I have the amulet now and I am destroying it with myself. Yet this is my third fire and I have not found the courage to throw myself on the embers."

"This is a foolish plan! The man is deranged. He believes this is a secret weapon, some ultimate power, and he is not going to stop because you are dead."

"Just help me, please?" he asked. "And be with me."

"I cannot." I stepped back.

"You must," he replied.

The wood crackled as the orange and red flames licked the night air, his face aglow in the fires warming aura. The memory of Aksel next to the cabin fire when we first met, when I thought his bearskin bedding was alive from the firelight, of all the firelights that had warmed our faces over the years... those memories faded as I looked at him now.

"It broke my heart, Bree," he whispered, "when you had to sleep. There was so much uncertainty. Would you ever wake? Would you be the same? Then she came to me – the girl. She helped me search for this amulet, all those years you rested. She helped me learn its secret. She said it was time to wake you. That's how I knew you would come tonight, how I knew I didn't have to be strong. She said you would be strong for me. You have always been strong for me."

"What girl?" I asked.

He pointed in the distance where the firelight met the creeping darkness. There approached the dull outline of a wavering black dress. The cover of shadow hid everything else but the subtle aroma of lavender and linseed oil wafting over the fire.

"She helped you find this?" I pulled the amulet from my pocket, fingering the cold stone.

"It is time. If she is here now it is because they are coming!" He leaned forward, grabbed onto my waist and whispered into my ear, "Trust me and keep it close, no matter what happens."

I whispered, "Good-bye my love," as I sunk my teeth into his hardened veins. His skin was leather to my fangs as they pierced the flesh, the cool liquid unlike mortal blood that gushed warm and freely into my mouth. Aksel went limp in my arms as I drained the old blood from his body. I choked each ounce down my throat as his arms, clinging to their last bits of strength, grabbed at my sides. His nails dug into my clothing, ripping my shirt.

"Bree," he coughed, "it is a weapon."

"Aksel," I pulled away, gazing into his motionless face. "Aksel!" But his body started breaking, turning to dust, pieces disintegrating beneath my touch, mingling with the wind and riding out on the waves and into the obsidian sky. Speechless, I watched as he scattered away from me for all eternity. Then he was gone and the scent of linseed oil and lavender remained to comfort me, once again.

THIRTY

The crystalline orbs stalk me, taunting me from their inky prison. Their starlight is already fading as I lament the passing of this night. Each orb cries with me, pleading for its release from this world, from its own immortality.

The feel of Aksel's skin – the iciness of his breath against my cheek – I can still sense him there. The hell in his eyes – the cold, isolated glare. How he stared at me with his haunted, desperate gaze, begging me to keep the amulet safe. Hidden. Close.

That amulet. So secret and mysterious. I had more questions now than I did before I spoke with Aksel. Now he was gone.

He was gone.

Once again, the image of his essence scattering out to sea was there before me – a never-ending nightmare. As the wind now carried me home, the stars tormenting me with their joyous vibrancy, I could not erase his face from my mind. I closed my eyes and all I saw was his face breaking into a million fragments and scattering into the void, spreading beyond my reach.

The image – now scorched into my corneas – was a wicked reminder that I had murdered the man I loved to protect an amulet I knew too little about. That thought sickened me.

Chicago traffic was but a muddied puddle of reds and whites weaving across the asphalt below as I landed on my balcony. My body shook, his blood ashes staining my clothes. The damp Norwegian sand coated my ecru slacks and tan boots. My windswept hair clung to my tear stained face, knotted from the tumultuous Norse currents.

The fire already raged within as I stepped off the balcony and entered the study. I moved to the heat, watching the glowing orange and red flames dance off the logs. The white ash cascaded from their woody home, revealing a seething hotness below, waiting to refuel the fire. My hands, weary from their travels – from their devilish deeds – licked at the flames for warmth.

"Mother?" Aleksandra whispered, entering the room. Eagerly, I wiped the blood tears from my cheeks and turned. "What happened?" She rushed to my side and began smoothing the knots from my hair, and tracing the tears in my shirt with her fingers. "Where have you been?" Her fingers glazed over my tear-stained face, then down again to the blood splattering my shirt. "What have you done?"

I pulled the amulet from my pocket and held it to the firelight. "I need to know what this is," I said, my voice hoarse. As I spoke, the taste of his blood's potency grew in my mouth. The remnants still coated my tongue, its spiciness reminding me of him. My body convulsed from the memory of my lips upon his neck.

"Mother, what happened tonight?" She led me to the settee. I sat there with the amulet in the palm of my hand, stroking it, hoping it would tell me its secret. "Mother, please tell me," she urged. Her hand reached up, loosening the knots.

"Aksel has gone into the shadow." I closed my eyes hoping that would make reality hurt less. However, it did not.

"What?" She rose from the settee. "How?" She moved to the window, averting her eyes. Her hand moved, wiping the tears from her face. The sound of sirens screeched in the distance as a full onslaught of emergency personnel flew down State Street. "Where did it happen?"

"Norway," I told her.

"I am so sorry, mother." Aleksandra walked to the desk and grabbed a tissue. She blotted at the tears. "Did you," she began but hesitated, "did you try and stop it," she asked.

My eyes remained on the amulet. "No," I admitted.

"How could you not?" She rushed at me stopping in front of me. Her hand grabbed a hold of my chin, pulling my face toward hers. Her eyes met mine until she saw the pain residing within. Then she released my face and backed away. "Tell me you did not."

"Aleksandra," I began, "he wanted it."

"Mother! What happened?"

Rising from the settee, I walked toward her. "Do you think it was easy for me to help Aksel? He was my first, Aleksandra. My first! My beloved! He didn't really want to end his existence, Aleksandra; he *needed* me to end it. I will never understand why. And I do not need to! No one needs to!"

I turned away from her. My eyes burned with him telling me good-bye. The rawness of the moment crushed me now as I stood in my posh high-rise, surrounded in opulence. The rawness of his sacrifice stung as the amulet's hardness creased my palm, the jewels cutting into my flesh because I held it too tightly. Reality, in itself, was raw.

"He *needed* me to do this for him," I told her. "And when you love someone, you show them mercy, my daughter— you grant them that."

"Aksel's gone," she whispered in disbelief. "I cannot fathom this."

"He was running because of this amulet." I opened my palm, the flesh now branded with the jewel's imprint. "Whatever curse surrounds it continues on."

"What does it all mean?" she asked. "Peter, Colin, Aksel, how many must martyr themselves for that? Why is it so important?"

"He said it was a weapon, Aleksandra. What kind of weapon can an amulet be? Aksel and the Vatican may be convinced of such, but I am not sure," I admitted. "But I know one more person who can tell me the truth," I assured her, tossing the trinket into my pocket.

"Well, I sincerely hope you get those answers. And soon. Colin is not going to make it; Judith is pulling his life support tomorrow night. If Aksel and her father's deaths were in vain, she is going to make this a personal crusade. If Francisco wanted a war, mother, he is about to get one."

"I am not about to bring a war down on this city," I told her, "Or anywhere for that matter." Chicago bustled with life, its inhabitants – infectious, soul-filled ants – scurrying about oblivious to the detrimental drama unfolding before them.

"Go to Judith and Colin tonight, please. She should not be alone," I told her. "Go and calm her. We have lost one of our own. We could lose another before dawn approaches. But we must, nonetheless, say farewell to him at nightfall. So let them not talk of war tonight. Tell them, Aleksandra. For his sake, tell them. Tonight, we shall have peace."

"I will," she said. "Wesley is already there. Come with me," she urged. "You should not be alone."

"Please leave me to my sorrow tonight." I rose, kissing away the soft plum blush dusting her cheek. "Let me mourn him, just for tonight. The reality is now eating me. I have slept so long without him, but now knowing that I will always be sleeping without him…"

"Find comfort in the darkness, in the silence, if you must," she said, hugging me, "But do not let it swallow you whole. Do not go into the shadows yourself because of this. The others, they will understand as I understand. You will see. Say good-bye to him tonight and I will see you tomorrow."

Aleksandra walked onto the balcony and ascended into the chilly October night. I walked to the desk, opened the laptop, and found myself cloaked in the computer's brilliant green glow.

Two hours had passed since Aleksandra left while I sat penning this account. Laptop keys crunched eagerly beneath my fingers as I feverishly typed. Dawn would soon approach.

Each page trickled from my memory, the images as clear as if I were seeing them in front of me. I could touch them. I could violate these points in time as the blood had violated me. There I was in the convent. My throat throbbed as Wesley's teeth sunk into my virginal, mortal flesh.

There was Aksel: alive, his body glistened beneath the cascading moonlight as he walked along the shoreline, his barefoot toes skimming the frigid water. The wet sand was mushy as it invaded the crevices between my toes when we walked the Norwegian shore. His mortality seduced me as the moonlight danced off his tanned flesh.

Swiftly, the pages multiplied as my immortal existence spilled across in black and white boldness. Viktor. The twins. Mavra. It pained me remembering how mortal he had been. How mortal they had all once been. So alive. So precious.

Viktor's mortality energized and completed me. He was everything to me.

It seems as if those priceless nights spent listening to his heartbeat were a thousand years ago, not hundreds. And I ache to hear that heartbeat again, to close my eyes and hear its rhythmic cadence in my ear. I long to feel his lips press upon mine. To feel his bold Russian arms about my waist, reassuring me that mortality and immortality have a purpose. Writing about him brought him to life on the page. For a brief second I saw him before me. Yet when I reached out to hold him, he faded into the shadows.

Everything must die as he died.

The night wore on, the stars constant in their brilliance as the Chicago traffic slimmed. The pages caught up to the previous night, to that last fateful night with Aksel. In agony, my body quivered. I had murdered him. I had confessed my sin.

The *Moonlight Sonata*'s haunting first movement began as Beethoven's piece queued on the Internet radio. The music turned to the past while I turned to the present. The pages piled on the computer screen, filling with ghosts and demons. The amulet rested near me on the desk, its image staring blindly.

Picking it up, I rubbed my thumb across the portrait. "Who are you?" I asked the smiling face. Its agelessness haunted me.

"You know who that is," a voice replied from behind. The air in the study morphed as the fire finally died out. A mist blew in from the cracked balcony door replacing the musty smell of ash with a subtle, but unmistakable, aroma: lavender and linseed oil.

"Or do you remember her?" Sister Veronica's words sliced through the sonata's flowery second movement. "The girl painted on that amulet, her face drove away the black petulance. As its poison annihilated those we loved, she persevered. She cared for the sick, the dying, and the homeless. Her merciful hand was ever ready to steady those in need."

"People change," I hissed. The song ended. I slammed the laptop shut and rose, pressing toward her. "The blood has a way of doing that."

"Being a vampire changed you, Bree," she remarked.

"The blood... being a vampire... the two are one." I sauntered to the window and placed my hand on the glass. Despite the October chill, the window felt warm to my unnaturally cold hand.

"I am a monster, Veronica. You can sing me to sleep, keep me there for a thousand years, but it will never change that."

"You are not a monster, Bree," she whispered. "The blood does not control you, not like it does others. Aksel knew that." Her eyes moved to the desk. "That is why he gave you the amulet."

The room spun as Veronica moved to the desk and grabbed the trinket. Her prayer beads swung as she walked back to me. The amulet caught the moonlight as it sat in her palm, her outstretched hand coming closer.

"It is a useless token, right?" I spat, taking the amulet from her. "Vatican hocus pocus. Just because one man believes it has powers, does not make it so."

"True." She turned, the blackness of the habit blending with the shadows as she moved to the couch. Sister Veronica smoothed her scapula as she sat. Her fingers twirled the prayer beads and she glared past me. The wood beads clanked together beneath her fingertips. "But it is powerful, Bree. To those who have faith, it is a weapon."

"Faith?" I asked her. "Faith in what?"

"Aksel had faith in the magic that made that amulet. Francisco has faith in how he can exploit that magic – turn it into a weapon. Giving the amulet to you was the only way Aksel could stop him. Now you must have faith. I cannot tell you in whom or what, but you must find that out for yourself."

"Great sacrifices have been made because of this amulet, and you come to me speaking of faith!" I growled. "What does it do? This trinket, what is it for?"

Sister Veronica's face grew ashen and her eyelids fell. "It protects you."

"I am a vampire! I have no need for protection!"

Sister Veronica rose from the couch, walked toward me, and stood glaring into my eyes. "Yes, my friend, you have always needed protection."

"From whom?" I laughed. "Francisco? Not even the archivist... or the Pope wants me dead. The archivist wants my help! If the archivist finds that coward first, he may fair a worse fate than if I had found him."

"Not a person," her cold voice whispered breaking my laugh. "A thing."

Her feet moved to the balcony door, opened it, and beckoned for me. "Come with me my old friend. We have much to discuss."

THIRTY-ONE

We are all stories in the end. When found wanting and desperate as we lay dying, it all comes down to moments lived. Sad moments. Happy moments. Indescribable moments. They are all just that – all too fleeting. When that final moment comes, we reach out, hungrily, struggling to hold on to the last second, to remain. Yet we cannot stay. We must not. That is not how stories end.

Inbound traffic was already backing up on the Dan Ryan as I flew over the pre-dawn city. The people of Chicago were beginning to wake, eager to face the new day. These mortals below labored under the false pretenses that they were safe in their gated homes. They believed their doormen, bodyguards and handguns offered protection. When all along monsters flew above – walked amongst them – threatening their mortality. Their alarm systems and steel doors – their weapons – were no match for our kind.

There were but a few stragglers in the hospital lobby at that hour of night. Only three hapless, hung-over souls remained near the hospital's cab-call desk – a deserted area this time of night. Two women – in their mid-twenties – hunched over armchairs in various states of despair, their vomit-covered sequined club wear clinging to their wasted bodies. Their driver, a solitary man sat beside them, covering his face with his coat as I walked in. His body slumped with the weight of a night's indecisions and cheap liquor. He reeked of beer and stale chips, of cigarettes and drug store perfume.

I walked past the trio – their thoughts still focused on their drunken exploits – and headed to the elevator. The ICU was on the sixth floor and the elevator nervously hummed and clanked as it snaked its way up the shaft. A fluorescent, disinfectant glow greeted me as I stepped off and into the isolated ICU floor.

The specialized ward, with its glass rooms fashioned in a semi-circle pod, had an octagonal nursing station in the middle; the nurses pressed behind computer screens like sardines in a tin can, diligently monitoring life signs. The gentle hum of ventilators within the ICU bubble vibrated the glass, but only my ears could detect it.

As I reached for the buzzer, my other hand felt the amulet in my right pocket. Its coolness reminding of Sister Veronica's defiant stare as the October wind whipped at her veil. Those comforting talks from our youth – sitting near the fountain, our toes dipped in the lake – had come full circle. She had returned to me, my friend, my confidant. Somehow, Aksel had brought her to me. Through the expanses of time and space and death and life, she was here. My guardian angel, through an amulet she came. Now I knew what I had to do. And why.

The buzzer's sudden sting pierced the stillness pervading that hospital hallway. Inside the glass walls, the ICU machines beeped and ventilators purred. Yet outside, the only noise was of the nurse's, "Can I help you?"

"I am here to see the patient in room 149, please."

The door opened with a click and I walked through, the aroma of sterile alcohol and hospital grade tubing violating my nose with its eye-stinging potency. Colin's room was the second on the left. Dimmed fluorescent lighting bled through thin, patterned drapes, now drawn over the sliding glass doors. A place card taped near his room number signified he was terminal – not going to make it – left for dead.

The door swooshed as I opened it, yet the others did not turn their glance from Colin's motionless body. Judith clung to her father's side, her hand entwined in his; ruby tears adorning her cheeks. Wesley and Aleksandra stood near the window watching the city wake. Death was nothing new to them. I walked to Colin's side, looked into his near-lifeless face and then beheld Judith's innocence. Despite the blood and its power, she was far too young to know this pain – to feel the raw ache this death would bring into her life.

"Wesley, Aleksandra," I said as they turned, "take Judith away."

"No!" She looked up, startled. "I am not leaving my dad!"

"Wesley, do it." As Wesley came closer to the bed, Judith held her father tighter. "Judith, go with them; do not fight me."

"Mother, please; do not deprive her," Aleksandra begged. "You do not have to do this! He will be dead before morning. Just let him pass naturally. For her sake, please."

Wesley met my stare and then lowered his glare, diverting his eyes instead in Aleksandra's direction. "Trust your mother," Wesley whispered. "She knows what she is doing." He moved to Judith's side and placed his hands on her own.

"Aleksandra, stop him!" Judith urged as Wesley pulled her arms free. "Let go of me!" she yelled, thrusting her body weight against him as she held tightly to her father, "Wesley stop! Let me go! Get off me!"

Aleksandra glanced up, glaringly, and I held her stare. "Do as she says, Judith," she instructed.

"But I cannot leave him! Please, do not make me leave him! He is dying, Bree," Judith plead as they led her near the door. "Give me this time with him. Please, Bree, this is all I will ask from you; just let me have this time with my father. Please?"

"Take her away," I told them as Wesley pulled her sobbing from the room.

Lying in his bed, Colin was but a mass of organs and blood and tissue. Tubes nourished him. Machines breathed for him. Doctors kept Colin alive.

Reaching up, I silenced the alarms and sat down next to his bedside. The chair creaked beneath my weight, yet he remained unresponsive. There was less than an hour left until the sun crept over the horizon. The dusky light wafting through his window casted shadows over his graying face, and he already appeared dead.

Peter would not recognize his son, lying here lifeless in a hospital bed. Colin's own students – who just days before had heard him lecture on Yeat's - would not believe this man was their great teacher.

I grabbed his hands, stroked them beneath my grasp. Their warmness startled me.

"The silver apples of the moon, Bree," her voice whispered from the far corner. An obsidian sliver snaked into view as her habit caught the moonlight.

"The golden apples of the sun," I replied. "How did you know?"

"I know everything," Sister Veronica whispered from the corner. "I know he is dying, just hours now."

"But that… that poem, that is ours," I spat. How dare she come into his room, as he lay fragile and exposed, and defile our friendship. "That is something we will always have," I whispered, turning back to him, my eyes falling on his withering body.

"Bittersweet endings, professor, you always lectured about them. He hated them," I said turning to Veronica.

"He preferred a real, gritty page turner. Life, he would say, it is not full of happily ever after. Now he is living it, is he not? He does not get a happy ending." She did not reply as my eyes traveled over Colin's ashen face.

"I wish I could share with you those golden apples, those silver moons. Or hear your voice recite Yeats and Joyce until you are blue in the face."

"You could, you know," she whispered. The habit rustled as her shoes clicked against the hospital linoleum. Her hand pressing into my shoulder felt real, felt solid. "He was not going to stop searching for you, holding out hope."

"No, he didn't." Recalling the roses, the last line of Yeats' poem attached. That had been years ago, after meeting the night of the Field Museum gala. "But I cannot turn him."

"It is what he wants, Bree," she whispered as she leaned over his face. Her fingers slid across his brow. "It is what he has always wanted."

"He did not even know about us until now, and now we are in the midst of chaos. And he is terrified," I spat. "This is not what he would want. It is what you want!"

"He wants to be with you, Bree," she said. Her haunting glare ate at me. "As he lies here dying, as he listens to us right now, his soul is crying out to you. Listen to him! He wants you! He has always wanted you!"

I closed my eyes, listened for his thoughts. Behind the ventilators drone and the IV dripping, his mind hissed and whispered. After the hours Wesley and Aleksandra sat vigil in this room, they had not listened to Colin – to what he needed, to what he wanted.

Gasping, I opened my eyes. "How did we miss this?"

"It is easy to miss a dying mans last words when you are not listening for them – or you do not want to hear them, Bree," she replied. "Will you grant it?"

"I... I cannot." I slumped into the chair. "How can you expect me to do this, Veronica?"

"You must! It is his dying wish!" she demanded. She came toward me with an unworldly swiftness. I knocked into the hospital bed as I stood from chair, Colin's hand flopping to his side. .

"He will die," she said, "and it will be your fault."

"The car accident killed him," I spat, "not me. I could not turn Mavra, or Viktor, and I cannot turn him."

"You caused the accident," she retorted.

"The amulet caused the accident," I countered. "So it is Aksel's fault."

A lump grew in my throat as Aksel's name surfaced. Blaming him for such an unfortunate circumstance was shallow and pathetic. One death from the amulet, and the night was yet to be over. The burden he left burned a hole in my pocket.

"And, my old friend," she came to rest her hand on my shoulder once more, a tear in the crease of her eye, "who made Aksel? You have the power for a reason, use it," she whispered before fading as a mist before my eyes.

With my right hand securing the amulet, I hovered over his body. With my left hand, I removed the ventilation tube and crooked his head to the side. My teeth pierced his salty flesh and I thought I heard him grimace beneath my tight grasp. His life splashed in, each searing ounce filling me in this chilly pre-dawn hour, warming each cell as I stood holding him above the hospital bed. Blood droplets collected on the starched, fitted sheet, the powder blue blanket already stained from the ventilator fluids.

His body went slack in my arms, his legs drooping on to the bed below. I closed my eyes and let droplets of my blood from my bitten wrist drip into his mouth. I waited, fighting exhaustion as his blood mixed with my cells, rehydrating me.

Images scrolled furiously before me. Their vividness was blinding as each flash revealed another secret from Colin's past. There he was, a little boy, his knee scraped against the sidewalk. A bike now lies askew in the middle of the lane as a group of kids taunted him. The next drop framed him as a teenager hidden in a darkened library, submerged in a sea of books.

Instead of studying economics, he studied the red head with emerald eyes the next table over. His first kiss, with the fiery red head, that came with the next drop. Then as his breathing grew shallow, and his heartbeat slowed, the memory of Judith being born. Highlights and memories cascaded with his blood, one after another until his body collapsed in my arms.

Looking down on Colin's broken body, I remembered how Judith had just been there. Moments ago, I had torn her from her father. I forced her from this last hour with him.

I had done that.

Sitting next to him in that hard visitor's chair, I recognized death's shadowy veil nearing him. Death was there for Colin, to claim its prize. With his ventilation removed and nearly all his blood gone, I was surprised he still held on. He mocked death's vicious scythe.

Then he turned. His body seized in a moment of breathless abandonment. As I stood and backed against the wall, what little color he had leached from his skin. The waxen vampiric complexion spread, quickly erasing the deathly ash. His limbs twitched and fluttered; his eyelids blinked.

He held out his hand to me and I went to his side, grasping it. It was cold now, his hand – unearthly cold. Gone forever was that mortal heat, which even in sickness a body retains.

"Our poem, Bree, you remember?" he asked, his voice deeper with the blood.

"Of course, Yeats' 'The Song of Wandering Aengus'. How could I ever forget that?"

"You are *her*," he said, sitting up. "In the poem, you are the girl and I am the poet. I am old now and I have wandered through hilly lands and hollow lands, looking for that girl who got away. Now you returned and saved me."

"You left me no choice, Colin."

"And now I will 'kiss her lips and take her hands,'" he recited.

"And walk among long dappled grass," I replied.

"And pluck till time and times are done," we recited together, "the silver apples of the moon, the golden apples of the sun."

THIRTY-TWO

Remember the plague?" I asked Sister Veronica. "Remember how it robbed us of our childhood, stole our families?"

I had returned to the State Street apartment after turning Colin, and after phoning Wesley to come fetch the newly formed, immortal poet. Now I stood on the balcony peering over the street as traffic slowly filtered into the city. The morning commute snaked past as the sun peeked over the horizon. A sliver of its golden warmth winked behind the steel and glass monstrosity across the street.

Weakly I spoke to Veronica, and to the universe, and to anyone who could answer, "Why did we survive?"

"Each life has a purpose," she replied, her voice steady behind the traffic's vibrations.

The dawn light's glow warmed her pale complexion, and her pupils were now orbs of rare ebony within their white settings. My hand crept toward her cheek, reaching eagerly to stroke her milky, glistening skin. She veered away, turning her face so the corner of the habit grazed my hand. The fabric – the rough, aged cotton – felt solid as it brushed against me.

"We were chosen, Bree. We had a calling, a reason to live beyond that wretched pestilence." Her wary eyes gazed into mine as she faced me once again, then they fell to the horizon.

"Then why am I here? Answer me that!" I demanded. "Find the scripture that says be obedient, be pure, sacrifice and you will be rewarded with an eternal curse! Show it to me, Veronica!"

Veronica's lips pursed as she slid the balcony door closed. The glass made a subtle, nearly inaudible thud as it met the wall, and then she locked it. The curtain ruffled, billowing against the spotless glass before settling and obscuring my view of the study.

"I died twice the night Wesley took me, Veronica," I feebly whispered as I watched the sunlight play on the windows around me. There was warmth in the air, hanging like a palpable cloud. This was warmth I no longer remembered, or had forced myself to forget. I inhaled the dawn – my eager mouth open to the crisp morning – and found the air a bittersweet reminder of my sacrifice. The air soured against my lips and turned rancid as it stung my tongue.

"After he turned me I looked back at the convent," I continued, watching the sunrise. "We were miles away on that hill in the abandoned castle overlooking the creek." She smiled in remembrance. "I could see the candles flickering, Veronica. All that distance away... what, five miles? – I could see them and I heard the sisters crying and praying. Some were weeping – openly weeping, Veronica. I had never heard them do that before – crying out to God with raw agony bleeding in their voices. The lights, the sounds, it was as if they were happening next to me. Then I realized you were not at mass."

Veronica's eyes softened and her head bowed as my skin warmed.

"I worried you had been blamed for my escape," I admitted. "But when Wesley told me you were confined to your bed with grief, I died yet again."

"Those were dark days," she whispered.

"My life only grew darker, I am afraid," I whispered, glaring at the sun as it threatened to breach the building shielding me. "That day stained my life deep ebony, my friend, and there is no lightening it."

"All the light you will ever need is with you now, Bree," she said, her hand coming to rest itself on my shoulder. It was a comforting notion, giving what was about to happen.

"Stop," I quivered, "it is too late for hope, for comfort."

"It is never too late for hope," she said. "You have had the answer all this time." She reached into my pocket and pulled out the amulet. Reaching for my hand, she unclenched my fingers and placed the cold, jeweled circled antique in my palm. "The answer is within, Bree; just use it."

Bringing the amulet to eye level, it gave its age in the growing daylight. The jewels glistened, but the portrait – my portrait – showed a slight fading. Tiny cracks ran along the portraits surface. Years of fondling had worn the varnish and rust grew at its clasp.

"He left that to you for a reason," she said with a new urgency. "And you cannot let it fall into the wrong hands."

"They are taken care of." My eyes glanced to the shut door, and then shifted to the growing daylight. My flesh grew with an uncomfortable heat.

"Don't be too certain," she spat.

She urged, "An obsessed man can be tenacious."

"I do not have a choice then, do I?" I asked, resigning to my fate. Why had I not questioned Aksel more? Why had I not forced him to tell me everything about this amulet?

"What on Earth possessed Aksel to make this curse – this weapon? What was he thinking?"

"Curse? Weapon?" Her voice softened. "He loved you. He stopped at nothing to protect you, Bree."

"He has done a swell job protecting me with this, has he not?" my voice boomed. "This amulet has caused more damage than protection."

"How so?" she asked.

"Are you serious?" I stepped back and the balcony railing cut into my back. "Countless mortals are dead and I forced this curse on a dying man."

"Mortals die every day, every minute in fact." She gestured to the street below, now congested with morning traffic. Honks and hollering – the orchestra of a busy, midweek city's solemn requiem – gave her gestures audience.

"Car accidents, heart attacks, by their own weak hands, mortals perish," she continued, "And you did not force this curse on Colin. You heard his thoughts; it is what he wanted. Bree, human lives, they are insignificant. They are here today and gone tomorrow. And you know this. You understand this."

"Their lives are not insignificant, Veronica," I groaned through stiffening lips.

The sun was nearly over the buildings now, its heat seering my skin. Moving to the balcony's edge and gripping the handle, I peered into the growing sunlight. It was a phoenix, rising into the sky aflame and anew, mesmerizing me as it climbed higher. The light seared my eyes, yet I could not turn from the orb's glow or the orange aura surrounding it. The blueness of the sky, the muted whiteness of the clouds, it had been too long since I had seen such raw splendor.

"I watch them hurry, scrambling to start their lives before the sun is even up," I said, not peeling my eyes from the sky.

"Such purpose, such drive and spirit. They are raw, Veronica, and passionate, and innocent creatures exploding with history and virility. And no matter what horrid circumstance life throws at them, they persevere. My kind? We cower in the shadow like rats hoping to not be discovered for the monsters we truly are! These people below, they rally and fight; they love and argue. I admire humanity, more so now that I have the blood than I ever did when I was human."

"Then you know what you must do." Her lips pressed against my burning cheek and I winced.

"It has to be done," I said. I looked away from the sky and angled my head down State Street, taking in the city now bathed in a golden aura.

"Destroy the amulet, my friend."

THIRTY-THREE

October 22, 2012

In a darkened room – partitioned from the study where they seldom ventured – Aleksandra and Wesley left a motionless, hardened shell of a matriarch. Bewildered, they placed Bree's body in the room, laying her on a relocated settee. Judith and Colin came, and the four were aghast at the site before them.

"Her skin is rough. Feel it," Aleksandra whispered. "Wesley, what happened to her?"

Bree's skin was granite beneath Aleksandra's touch. The sun's heat emanated from the matriarch's cheeks, and it singed Aleksandra's fingertips. She winced with every touch, bringing the sore tips to her mouth to lick the heat away.

"She's burning up!"

"She was on the balcony," Aleksandra continued. "Feel her!"

Wesley flicked on the lamp and held his hand to Bree's face, immediately withdrawing it. In the lamp's light, the matriarchs delicate, honey drop curls were incandescent, roughened ringlets. Her tightly drawn lips were cracked and blood stained. Her once milky skin lay taut, spread tight against her bones, threatening to rip its new tan. As broken as his sister was, Wesley thought, studying her, something about Bree ringed with a vague and sickening familiarity. She appeared strangely human.

"She went into the sun," Wesley said, his fingers smoothing Bree's hair.

"How could she have? Wesley, she would be a pile of ash." Aleksandra crouched to the floor, resting on waiting knees beside her mother's body. She clasped Bree's hand and let the heat warm her skin. "We have both seen a body burn. That is an unspeakable horror – one I will never forget. But it does not do this."

"I have no other explanation," he conceded.

"What is she clutching?" Colin stepped from the shadows and pointed to Bree's left hand.

Gnarled into a tightened fist by the sun, Bree's fingers snaked around an obscured object resting in her palm. Colin leaned over the matriarch's body, delicately taking her hand in his. Her hand was delicate porcelain beneath his grasp as he tried prying her fingers loose. When that failed, though, he grew eager in his approach, forcefully grasping at the fingers. Judith pushed him aside when she heard a wee cracking.

"I almost had it!" he growled.

"You almost snapped her finger off!" Judith said. She then ran a finger over Bree's left hand feeling for damage, and sighed with relief when she found none.

"What do we do with her?" Colin asked. "I mean, is she alive? Is she dead?"

"We care for her," Aleksandra blurted.

"Aleksandra, feel your mother's skin. It is scorching. She went into the sun. I cannot explain why she did not burn, why there is not a pile of ash greeting us on the balcony. I am certain Bree will not be waking from this coma. She is no longer with us, and you must let her go." Wesley placed a cautious hand on Aleksandra's shoulder.

"How should we do it?" Judith asked, her voice dripping with sugary kindness. "Do you want me to phone around?"

"I'll have a mausoleum constructed," Wesley said, gazing at Alexandra stroking her mother's arm. "That will give Aleksandra time to say her good-byes."

They left, turning the lights off as they went. The matriarch slept in the darkness, in the cold, quiet of night.

THIRTY-FOUR

Six full moons had danced across the sky since Bree stepped into the sun; their silvery brilliance illuminated the heavens, bathing the world below in mysticism. Chicago – the city and its people – whizzed and whirled in constant rhythm – a teaming, unstoppable life force unaware of her sacrifice. Winter came and ice clung to the tree branches as the city froze. Lake Michigan slumbered, its frigid waters lapping at the shoreline – eager for warmth. Everything slept.

Then dawn broke.

April 13, 2013
Daybreak

Salmon droplets grew on Aleksandra's skin as she thrashed about the bed, staining the satin sheets with her blood-sweat. An endless unlit tunnel stretched in front of her. The air swirled, twisting her hair and stinging her cheeks as the earth quivered beneath her stocking feet.

Something lured her forward into the abysmal tunnel, urging her into the ghastly darkness. She stretched her arms forward, desperately reaching for the walls but recoiled as something slithered near her feet – just as her fingertips reached the slimy brick. The slithering heaviness pressed against her toes, leaving Aleksandra shivering in the moist darkness, unable to see the source.

Aleksandra fell forward onto the moving earth as she vainly attempted to grasp for solid brick. The ground skittered beneath her palms. The wind ceased. All was quiet but the subtle sound of shifting dirt. Aleksandra took the wobbly soil into her palms, smoothing it between her fingers. The odoriferous particles slid against her fingertips with the smoothness of Italian silk. She felt them eagerly slip from her hand and return to the waiting ground.

In the stillness, as nothing moved – save for Aleksandra's fingers and the few particles slipping from them, she felt a warm presence pass near and a lightness press upon her shoulder. She winced as the lightness, or perhaps a pain – it had been too sudden to be sure – lifted. Aleksandra grabbed at the spot, removing her hand from the stinging shoulder. A single drop of crimson rested against her milky fingertip.

Standing, she whispered into the void, "Is someone there?"

The only reply was a shallow whirr from the far end of the vast blackness.

"Hello?" Aleksandra urged, "Is someone down there?" Her voice echoed in a muted reply.

Aleksandra stood and took a shaky step forward as a heavy, blanketing mist grew to encapsulate her. A bony hand reached through the carpet of gray, and Aleksandra panicked. Her scream was raw and animalistic, a scratchy, deafening howl that reverberated off the bricks. The hand thrashed and turned as its disembodied master listened for screams. Then the hand clutched Aleksandra's leg and held it fast, forcing her down. The ebony void shimmered and wavered as the arm pulled Aleksandra down into the thickening fog. That noise – a hum, a whirr, a blurring, mind-numbing whisper – swelled, edging its way toward her.

Aleksandra fought and thrashed, digging into the hand and howling into the darkness.

April 13, 2013
Nightfall

"Aleksandra!" Wesley safely screamed from his side of the massive king bed. He grabbed the overstuffed body pillow lying between them, now mangled and soaked with Aleksandra's blood-sweat, and tossed it on the floor.

He grabbed her at the shoulders and shook her. "Wake up! Aleksandra! Wake up!"

Dizzied and unfocused, the room blurred into a muted orange nightmare as Wesley flicked on his bedside lamp. Aleksandra clutched at the new white and tangerine striped comforter, her sweat marring the new Italian satin.

"What is the matter, my love?" he asked, bending his head to kiss her neck.

Her voice quaked. "It was just a nightmare," she sighed, "nothing to worry about."

Aleksandra felt Wesley's moist lips on the nape of her neck, followed by the sharp point of his index finger against her shoulder.

"You're bleeding," he whispered.

She reached up and felt the scratch – recent, fresh.

"That must have been a wild nightmare, my poor amore." He held her tighter.

She broke from his embrace and pulled the soiled covers away. Aleksandra stood, her legs quivering. She eyed the bedroom floor for signs of quivering and slithering, for shaking and movement, for foul smelling dirt.

"Are you sure you are alright, Aleksandra?" Wesley called from the bed. He was gathering the bed sheets, the coverings, the pillowcases, all drenched in blood-sweat.

"Do you think she is still in there, Wesley, locked inside?" Aleksandra asked, her voice a nearly inaudible whisper.

"It does not matter what I think or what I believe, Aleksandra," he replied walking to her side, placing his hand about her waist. "There is no surviving the sun."

Aleksandra's head dipped, her chin skimming her chest. Her luminescent hazel eyes closed as a tear dropped, collecting on her white sock. There was a brown smudge peeking from her toe lines.

She looked up. "I must go to her."

"Aleksandra," he said, grabbing her shoulders, pulling her to him, "don't hold on to her. Let her go. She would not want us like this, mourning her, tending to her like an idol, keeping her like a household fixture to view when the mood strikes. If you want a pet, my love, get a house cat."

Aleksandra glanced at the smudge, remembering the coldness, the hardness of the earth. She turned her palms over and eyed the silt-lined roadmap the quivering ground left in her palms. Aleksandra closed her eyes and deeply inhaled the fragrant remnants, and she brought her hands to her face. With a vague and eerie recollection, she felt the rush of wind sweeping through her hair and the vibrating hum cascading through the tunnel. The black, endless tunnel...

Her arms slid to her waist as she opened her eyes and pulled away from Wesley. Aleksandra turned and left the room, leaving him calling after her.

Firelight graced the study as she entered. Wesley soon followed, dropping himself at the desk. Electronic light christened the room as the laptop booted. Aleksandra approached the balcony but could not grasp the doors handle. The firefly stars danced brightly in the summer sky, playing brightly against the Chicago skyline as Aleksandra peered out the expansive glass window. Her hand slipped from the handle, moving to the glass.

Aleksandra pressed her body against the cool glass wondering how it had felt to stand in the sun's blaze. The moon – high in its orbit – paled against the sun's golden brilliance. Its grey coldness was but a weak shadow to the creator's favorite child. How had the seering sun felt against her mother's skin? Why had she done this?

"Don't question what we will never know," a man's voice spoke behind her.

Aleksandra turned as Judith and Colin entered. Wesley stood.

"She chose to taste the sun without me, Aleksandra," he continued, sitting down on the green velvet couch near the stone fireplace, "and we shall never know why."

"If only she had talked with me," Aleksandra whispered, returning her gaze to the starlit summer night.

"About what?" Wesley asked. "You chose this life, Bree did not. It has always been a treacherous journey for her, and now this business with Aksel. Eventually, Aleksandra, the load becomes too heavy to bear."

"It's the amulet, Wesley," Judith chimed in. She stood at the fireplace, her hands hovering over the rising amber flames. Crackling sparks eagerly shot toward her fingers, but faded before they reached her silver-polished nails. "Francisco chased us all over Chicago, nearly killed my father, surely she felt responsible."

"Bree was a fighter," Colin stated. "She would not have done what she did unless there was no other option."

Aleksandra turned from the window. "How do you know my mother so well as to make a statement like that?" she spat. "You barely knew her!"

"Aleksandra," Wesley whispered, coming to her side, reaching for her shoulder. She shrugged him off.

"Do not ever pretend to know her." She glared at Colin, her face but three inches from his. He could smell the musty scent of sleep still lying heavily on her tongue.

"But I do know her," he responded, an eerie, unearthly calmness in his words. "Her blood is in my body. She lives on in me. She lives on in you, too, Aleksandra."

"You are supposed to be dead, Colin. I am sorry, but we left you with mother. We left you to die." Aleksandra explained. She turned and sauntered to the fireplace, her eyes glossing over with red-tinged droplets. She ran her finger along the cool granite mantel, tracing the veins as if the lines traced into the recesses of time and could return Bree to her. A solitary ruby droplet fell down her cheek and her fingers stopped it at the chin, wiping it away.

Colin rubbed his eyes, and then smoothed his palms over his mouth before letting his hands fall into his lap. He clasped them tightly. His eyes remained closed. "What do you mean," he whispered.

"Bree was there to kill you before a natural, painful death took you," Judith admitted. She sat beside her father but could not bring herself to hold his hand, or place his arm about his shoulder. She remained distanced, the blood building a chasm between them. "I cried, fought them, tired to resist. They forced me to leave, though, in the end."

"No," he replied.

"I am sorry, Colin, but it is true. That is how it happened," Wesley admitted. "What Bree did after that, why she turned you, we do not know. And we will never know now. Those answers, unfortunately, we will never be able to provide you."

"No," he insisted, "there were two when I turned."

"Two what?" Judith asked.

"Two women," he explained, his voice quickening, "speaking in the room before Bree turned me. There was someone with her. I am sure of it."

"Dad, no one was with her," Judith insisted. "We had all left." She paused. "Perhaps it was a nurse."

"No," he urged as he stood, "the woman in black."

"You were in between worlds, Colin," Wesley said, his voice steady, even.

"You'll see and hear many strange things when your body is dying and your soul teeters in between worlds," Aleksandra tried to reassure him. "I had nightmares for months after I was turned, and it's not surprising you had them while dying."

"No!" he boomed. "I know what I heard, Aleksandra. She had come to me before, on the road, in the ambulance. She told me I would not die – that I would never die," he said, his voice softening. "I believed her. She frightened me, but I believed her."

Judith's eyes shifted to the flickering firelight as he spoke of the horrific accident. That chilly October night that had changed the course of all of their histories. She recalled watching from the roadside as the red and blue ambulance lights blurred in the hazy rain. She and Bree could not even follow, could not be at his side. Francisco's men stalked them from the shadows, inching closer as the wetness fell.

"My body was failing," he continued, his voice luring her to the present, "but then there was her voice again. In my mind, I could see her. The woman in black."

"Father," Judith whispered, "stop. There is no woman in black."

"No," Wesley said coming near, perching himself on an ottoman diagonal to the sofa. The crinkled Corinthian leather creaked as he sat down, and he grasped onto the worn edges and leaned in. "Tell me."

"She was always surrounded in black and faceless, but her voice was delicate," Colin began. "The pain had become intolerable. My heart, my lungs – I could feel them failing, but my mind never stopped feeling every tiny prick, every ache. I could handle no more. In the ambulance, this woman bathed in black hovered near, telling me to hold fast, that I would never die. Every tube, every procedure – I remember it. The doctors said I was not aware – even Aleksandra agreed, but the woman in black let me see," he recalled.

"Judith, my daughter, I could not watch you weep at my bedside. Eventually, the pain and heartache she forced upon me became too much. I lay that night in October -- the night Bree came – wanting more than anything to be pain free... forever."

Aleksandra slipped from the room as Colin spoke of the Woman in Black in blurred detailed. Her bare feet pressed into the Berber carpet running to Bree's secret chamber; its oatmeal blend matching her pale skin. She slid the door open and turned on the light. Bree laid motionless, solid, tan.

"Mother," she whispered, closing the door behind her.

Aleksandra walked to the settee, knelt beside the Matriarch and, reaching up, carefully stroked her mother's hair. A sea of artificial neon drowned Bree in its obnoxious yellow glare; it swam on her skin, dripped fluorescent gold from her hair and tinged her ruby lips a rusty brown.

"He will move you," Aleksandra whispered as she smoothed Bree's locks, "and soon." She let her fingertips glide over Bree's warm skin. Her fingertips gently inched their way toward Bree's lips, cracked and refusing to part. Bree's body retained a smidgen of the sun's warmth from when the Matriarch had stepped into the day light last October.

Tears pooled in Aleksandra's eyes and she laid her head upon Bree's chest. The eerie warmth comforted her. "Mother," she whispered, "I need you."

THIRTY-FIVE

June 20, 2013
Evening

I t's been ready for weeks now," Colin whispered in Aleksandra's ear. "He will move her and you cannot stop him."

"He cannot take her," Aleksandra wept. She held tightly to Bree's hands and stroked the matriarch's fingers. Tiny cracks ate at Bree's nail beds; their crystalline surfaces were sun scarred, marred – each a murky white with muted grey ribbons across their tips, wave like and wispy.

"This can be her tomb," Aleksandra begged. She lowered Bree's hands, gently placing them to rest in the matriarch's lap. They creased the satin throw Aleksandra had delicately placed across her mother's lap, trapping in the unnatural warmth.

"We can keep her. This is where she belongs," she argued. "Ask yourself, would you want it any other way?" She turned, facing him, ruby droplets christening her cheeks.

"It is not for me to answer, Aleksandra. This gift is far too new for me to comprehend how Bree must have felt, what turmoil she must have experienced to do this to herself," he replied.

Colin inched into the room, sitting down next to her. "Wipe your tears," he whispered, handing her a handkerchief. "We will figure out this mystery. The amulet, Aksel, Francisco, how they are all connected, but we must let her sleep now; let her rest." Colin reached forward and brought the cloth to Aleksandra's tears, dobbing them as they formed anew.

"We owe it to her, out of respect. Bree would not want to be a museum piece. And somewhere, in here," his finger gravitated to Aleksandra's forehead, resting between her eyes, "you know I am right, Aleksandra."

"But mother does not feel gone, Colin," she whispered, returning her gaze to Bree. The matriarch lay rigid and motionless.

"She is," he urged. "She is and the sooner you accept that, the better off you will be – we will all be."

Colin stood and left, a muffled scratching echoing from his corduroy pants as his legs rubbed against each other. She heard the familiar sound ebb as he walked down the hall and into the Study. The door creaked as he opened it, and softly clicked, catching on a raised edge of carpet as it closed behind him.

"Mother," Aleksandra wept, "I have sat here for weeks waiting on answers – waiting for signs – and you give none. You are lifeless and silent, and it terrifies me. Do you not see Wesley is going to take you from me? And I can no longer stop him!"

She clasped Bree's hand, caressing the palm, and slid her fingers over the matriarch's skin. Her thumb ran over the smooth, muted, beige flesh; as the sun's deep burn faded, a tinge of olive tint lingered. Her icy fingertips rubbed Bree's fingernails, their warmth still a troublesome puzzle.

Aleksandra laid the hand down – fingers first, followed by the palm – returning it to Bree's lap. That was when she saw it. It was a spec, a smidgeon, really. An insignificant thing to miss, yet she had. In the countless times she had caressed those hands and cleansed that skin, she had not seen this; nor had the others.

Aleksandra took the fingers to her lips, inhaling the spec's aura. Her tentative lips parted, quivering as she slid the bronzed finger past them. She licked the speck and sucked the fingernail, tasting the unnatural warmth singeing her tongue. The taste was unmistakable.

Blood.

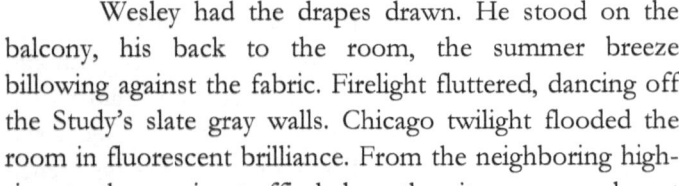

Wesley had the drapes drawn. He stood on the balcony, his back to the room, the summer breeze billowing against the fabric. Firelight fluttered, dancing off the Study's slate gray walls. Chicago twilight flooded the room in fluorescent brilliance. From the neighboring high-rises to the passing traffic below, the city was complacent and oblivious.

"Did you see it?" Aleksandra shouted, walking in. "Tell me, Wesley, did you see it?" The window glass rattled, the thick panes creaking as they settled.

Colin stood from the settee. "Aleksandra," he began, trying desperately to intervene, to assist. Aleksandra's hand rose into the air, steadily, her icy glare boring into him.

Colin took three steps forward toward Aleksandra, hands outstretched to calm her, before hearing Judith gasp. He had no time to look down; Aleksandra lured him into the air, dangling him there suspended in mid-air like a cat playing with its prey, before thrusting him backward. She smashed his chest into the granite fireplace, stunning the room and crumbling the finely crafted Italian architecture – granite now littering the carpet.

"Wesley!" Judith shouted as she clamored to her father. "Stop her!"

Wesley steadied his steps, creeping toward his mate. Her eyes were afire and fixated, yet hauntingly vacant. He had felt hope in the warm, early summer air. A dense aroma of change clung to the coming humidity. He had tasted it in the breeze wafting off Lake Michigan. Yet a nightmarish hurricane of turmoil and agony preceded all hope now.

"Did you see it?" she continued, walking to him. "Did you see it and not tell me?"

"See what, my love?"

"How could we have been so blind!" she lamented. "You saw it, Wesley! And how could you keep it from me?" She blasted, turning to Judith. "Of all people," she whispered, her head whipping back to face Wesley, "how could you?"

"Aleksandra," Wesley whispered, reaching out, grabbing her shoulders.

Aleksandra's arms encircled him. She gripped at his shirt fabric, grasping fists of the cotton with one hand, and securing a belt loop between her middle finger and thumb with the other.

"Don't be coy," she snarled, hoisting him high.

Wesley desperately fought against her – his grip on her shoulders tightening, his fingers digging into her icy flesh. His feet dug into her shins, crawled eagerly up her thighs, slammed into her groin and ferociously punched into her stomach. His fingers clawed at her throat and pounded against her breast. She carried him backward, still, toward the window, driving his body into the glass.

Her hand slithered up his chest, snaking its way to his throat. She fastened her grip, pressing him against the window – the glass splintering behind him. "Did you see it?" She hissed.

"Have you seen the void?" Wesley cried. "Where did your dreams take you? Oh, my love, don't let Bree's madness eat you. Put me down; don't give in to it."

"Fight it," cried Judith.

"Why?" Aleksandra hissed. "The void…I must fight for her. She needs me." The glass moaned as she pressed Wesley firmly against it. "Did you see it? Did you see it and hide it from me? My *love*?"

"Did we see what, Aleksandra?" Colin cautiously creaked from the rubble. He stood, brushing debris and ash from his corduroys.

"The blood."

"What blood?" Judith whispered.

"Aleksandra," Colin questioned as he approached, stealthily, as if he were a cat hunting a mouse, "where would we have seen blood?"

"On mother," she said her fiery glare softening. "Mother has blood on her."

"Why does Bree have blood on her," Colin asked.

"Aleksandra, where did the blood come from?"

Aleksandra did not answer, her gaze fixed on the approaching poet. Colin was near to her now. Closely he inched, his feet gliding their way to her.

"She is still with us," Aleksandra whispered, in a trance.

"No!" Wesley's voice shook the glass once more. "Aleksandra, listen, she is not. Let her go!"

"She needs me," her voice was a nearly inaudible whisper. "You'll never understand."

Colin grabbed Aleksandra's shoulders. He tried loosening her grip; tried prying her off Wesley, but her hold was unyielding.

Her left hand released Wesley's belt loop, snaked up, and clutched Colin's sweater.

Colin resisted, and he thrashed and squirmed before she flung him aside. He landed against the glass, sliding to the carpet. Judith, watching, sat down, folded her hands, hiding them in her lap, and bowed her head, wishing to become invisible.

"Aleksandra," Wesley whispered, "I'm moving her to the mausoleum tomorrow night. I must find a way to save you."

Aleksandra met his glare. A cloud of dreadful unease fell as her piercing-slit eyes stared into his. Then her eyes widened slightly – enough to make each of them cower.

"Save *me*?" Her timber swelled. She closed her eyes as Wesley's body rose toward the ceiling, barely scraping the white plaster. He reached up, stabilizing himself, trying to press against it and propel himself down. But he was adrift and helpless.

"Put me down," he whispered, his body now floating toward the open balcony, past the billowing curtains and into the welcoming Chicago breeze. Aleksandra followed it. Toe-to-toe she walked, her eyes steadily affixed on the prize before her, her hand not dropping as he hovered perilously over the rail.

"You need saved," she whispered.

Wesley howled, "Stop!" He thrashed and wailed and plead, and still he hovered while she stared him down with intense frigidity. His cries slowed the State Street traffic and hushed the incessant Chicago drone, and horrified all in the room.

"Aleksandra," Judith shouted from inside, "stop this! Please, stop!" The young one urged.

"You will not move her," Aleksandra shouted. "Do you hear me?" Her eyes darted between the three – Wesley hovering over the balcony, Judith standing in the room's center and Colin slumped against the glass, knees drawn and head cradled in his hands.

"The first one to even touch her will feel sun fire, and you will not be saved from its hellish kiss," she hissed, lowering Wesley's body and resting him on the balcony's platform. "My word is promise, be sure of that," she spoke, turning to each of the three. "You will be ash, even if I have to burn with you."

"Tell me," Aleksandra demanded, landing on the balcony, thrusting the palatial curtains aside, "are you ready for this war?" A night had passed since she left Chicago yet it could have been days.

He turned from the opulent altar, its aged patina and jewel encrusted edges glistened in the darkness of nightfall and candlelight. His jaws slackened as she approached and clutched his pallium, pulling the fabric back. The archivist slipped toward Aleksandra, his feet shaking as he ended in her embrace.

"I ask for no war," he replied.

She pressed his body into the altar, disturbing the linen neatly laid upon it. "Yet you start one."

"You are mistaken," he whispered, bravely, his eyes unblinking, staring into hers. "We are trying to end it."

"Your words are hollow, old man." Aleksandra released him and he grabbed the altar's edge, steadying himself and calming his quickening breath.

"All wars have martyrs, my child; your mother was no exception," he spoke. "The only difference: She understood the consequences if she failed."

"You speak in riddles," she spat, "You speak in lies!"

An envelope's crisp edge grazed her palm as she turned, facing the balcony. He pressed it into her hand and curled her fingers around it.

"Riddles are only riddles until they are decoded, my child. Now, go."

THIRTY-SIX

June 25, 2013
Evening

Sparks of grey-light shot from the moon, dripping silver shadows onto the rippling summer waters; and for a moment the world – that strip of beach, Chicago, everywhere, stood still. Aleksandra waded along the shoreline, letting the cool lake waters brush against her invading toes. The murky lake concealed the chipping eggplant lacquer; and the distance from city lights hid her unfed ivory skin.

The envelope was safely beside the parcel, both secure in the melon Louis Vuitton satchel at her side. Her fingers had traced each pen stroke on the letter inside that envelope. She had inhaled the lingering scent, tasting the dullness of lavender laced with linseed oil.

"Riddles," she had grumbled, opening it five nights ago. She had landed on the outskirts of Vatican City, taking up residence in a crowded café. She ordered little and ate none of it, tossing bits here and there to the waiting birds approaching her street-side table. They pecked at the crumbs, their beaks tapping the worn stones in tympanic rhythm.

The candlelight glinted through the wine glass, a warm burgundy glow swelling over the envelope as she sat eying the café's guests. The man with his wife, the family on vacation, all too consumed with their own trivialities to notice her. Their conversations blurred with the passing traffic, the whizzing motor bikes and honking horns. It neared eight, the dinner rush was en route, and the city was just beginning its nightly ritual of color and sound.

She had slid her finger beneath the crimson seal and opened the flap letting the envelope fall open. Aleksandra had removed the letter and resurveyed the crowd, wanting to be cautious, until her eyes drifted to the paper. A series of coordinates appeared on the bleached white page, and taped beneath it, a shiny, metallic key.

I have a code, Aleksandra had thought, as she punched the coordinates into her phone's mapping program. She tossed it all – the phone, the parcel, the letter – into the satchel and slipped into the shadows behind the café. She ascended, the bag flapping wildly as she savored the Mediterranean air brushing against her cheek.

Now she treaded the shore, slicing the still water with her feet, leaving depressions in the smooth sand. Droplets of moonlight kissed her amber locks, while the subtle lake breeze picked up each strand, twirling them. She walked out into the water, wading into the lake until her calves were submerged. And she stood clutching the satchel and looked up into the summer sky.

She had seen those same summer stars in her childhood. She had seen those same constellations – Cassiopeia, Sygnus, Scorpius – every summer evening since. It will continue to be so, an unchanging sky, Aleksandra thought.

"These riddles, mother," she spoke into the darkness, "I'm chasing and fighting and I know not what for! And now this?" Aleksandra clutched the satchel drawing it to her chest. She held the leather bag to her bosom. "Why this?" she whispered. "Why me?"

"In times of great peril, you must have faith," a voice called from the shore. A darkened figure stood near an embankment, shielded from the moonlight.

Aleksandra's grip loosened on the bag, letting it hang at her side as she ran toward the figure. The wet sand squished between her naked toes, and soiled the hem of her jeans. But despite her vampirish quickness, in the three seconds it took Aleksandra to reach the spot on which the figure first appeared, it had vanished.

The designer bag slid across the flagstone and through the open balcony doors with a thud startling Judith. She leapt from the couch, the new James Patterson thriller falling to the floor. Aleksandra followed, her feet touching the balcony's edge as Wesley rushed into the room.

The hearth slumbered against the wall, its womb void of oak logs popping and whistling, sending their chorus skyward into the obsidian night. The sticky June air clung, though, to the ash-stained belly, appeasing the beast with humidity for the time being. And what had been a faultless marble façade was now cracked and shattered. Aleksandra winced at the marred fireplace with disgust as she walked through the room.

"Where have you been?" Wesley demanded, clutching at her arm as she moved past, but it slipped through his grasp. "Aleksandra, wait!"

"What's this?" Judith asked, pulling a thick manuscript from the parcel lying at her feet. She began thumbing through it as Aleksandra walked from the room. "Wesley, you should see this," her voice trailed, looking up to find him following his beloved.

"Wesley!" Judith shouted, leaping from the couch, the manuscript in hand. She trailed after, following their voices.

"I do not owe you answers, Wesley," Aleksandra whispered, kneeling at Bree's side. She took the matriarch's hands into her own, kissing the milky fingertips.

"Oh, I believe you do," he replied. He hovered over her, glaring. "Six nights ago you attacked us and disappear only to return, and you expect us to roll over?" His voice shook the small room. "You expect there to be no questions asked, for everything to be as it was, but it cannot be that way!" he shouted. "And you know this! How can you not? How can you come back..." his words trailed off as Judith entered, eyeing him.

"The answers you seek, Wesley," Aleksandra spoke, her eyes not veering from the matriarch, "are not mine to give."

"I believe this may be of some help," Judith intervened, thrusting the bound papers at Wesley before he could reply. He closed his gaping mouth. "We should read it, Wesley," she urged, crooking her head toward the door.

"I understand now, mother," Aleksandra was whispering to the olive-skinned matriarch. She ran a palm over Bree's hair. "I understand."

"Yes," Wesley whispered, glancing from Aleksandra to Judith, and then to the manuscript, "Let's."

A bone-chilling wail pierced the darkness startling Aleksandra. She awoke bathed in a black mist, its ethereal moistness blanketing her skin. The ground quivered beneath her bare feet and she stumbled, falling onto her knees. The soil slithered and nipped at her fingertips. The mist shimmered and turned cold, tickling her face as the wind gusted with each wail, blowing the darkness aside.

Her knees sank into mud as the wailing grew to a muffled howl. "Hello?" She called out to the void, the mist dissipating as she met brick.

The wind blew wildly, blowing locks of her hair astray, tossing them this way and that as she traced her fingers along the tunnel's exterior. Memories of that nightmare, of that scratch....

It came again, the wailing. From the tunnel's rear, it snowballed into a wild howl reverberating in her ears. The ground no longer quivered as the slithering at her feet ceased. The mist hung above her, its shimmering dulled. The brick felt oddly warm to touch, warm and slimy.

Aleksandra let her fingers trace the bricks as she closed her eyes and advanced inward, down into the waiting chasm. The musty bitterness of decay, growing heavier the farther she walked, stung her nose. She walked, trudging through a viscous liquid, with the sinking feeling of something crawling between her naked toes.

"Hello?" Aleksandra called, thinking she had heard someone whispering behind her. She turned quickly, groping at the darkness yet felt only the stale air.

"Hello!" she shouted. "Is someone there?"

Aleksandra kept turning, wildly groping at the wall, at the air, until she fell against the brick. A subtle rumbling grew near and she tensed, flattening against the wall. A soft breeze followed, brushing against her before the ground began to the quake. The slithering began anew and, while she could not see it, she felt the mist envelope her.

Aleksandra turned, hugging the brick, her body quivering. She began slowly following the wall, inching herself out of the tunnel. She willed herself to wake up, to make the mist dissipate, to make the slithering and quaking stop. But it was to no avail; there was no reprieve from the darkness. Aleksandra had not gotten far when she heard the whispering once more. She turned and called out, but again, no reply.

"Mother?" she asked, cautiously, quietly. "Is that you?"

Aleksandra waited as the wind slowed and the mist cleared. She waited as the slithering and quaking ended. She waited in the darkness, but got not reply.

"Is that you?" she said. She turned her face – tear-stained and soiled – from the unknown. Aleksandra pressed her palm against the tunnel's wall and started for the entrance.

"No!" Aleksandra screamed. A stabbing pain stung her calf, and a hand – a claw-like, roughened, bony appendage from the feel of it against her skin – seized her leg.

Aleksandra reached down into the mucky earth, desperately feeling for her assailant. "Let go!" She howled. "Let me go, now!" She thrashed, kicking as her hands fumbled through the skittering mud.

Aleksandra managed to flip on to her back, wiggling her body. Aleksandra's attacker lost its grip as she flipped. She scrambled frantically onto her knees, unsure of her bearings. She knew she had to run, and she had to run now.

Aleksandra's left foot rose, but found no solid footing as it landed on the slithering soil. Aleksandra willed herself to fly as she struggled. Fly, she thought, fly out of this forsaken tunnel. Instead of soaring into the shimmering

mists, and then waking to the bustling Chicago night, Aleksandra planted, chest first, in the muck.

She rolled over and sat up. "What do you want?" Aleksandra hollered, her words echoing in the blackness. "What – tell me – NOW – what do you want!" she stood, shouting into the void.

Aleksandra turned, feeling a presence slither near, hearing whispering in her ear.

"I cannot hear you," she sighed. "I cannot help you if I cannot hear you."

The whispering grew louder, but it was still whispering; still noise.

"Please," Aleksandra's voice softened as she twirled in slow, dizzying circles, speaking to the vastness surrounding her, "I want to help."

All went still and quiet, and Aleksandra no longer felt the presence, no longer heard the whispering. Then she felt a firm pressure against her back, moving suddenly and too quickly for Aleksandra to fight its source. It clutched at Aleksandra's head, grasping a wad of her auburn hair. It yanked her head back, squeezing the knotted locks in its grip; burning her scalp.

"Help…," a rasping whisper bled into Aleksandra ear. "Help me."

THIRTY-SEVEN

June 26, 2013
Evening

I s that the amulet, then, you know… what she's clutching on to?" Judith asked.

"I guess so," Wesley replied. The three of them had read the contents of Bree's bound papers, and then reread them upon waking the next night.

"Was this her farewell, then?" Colin's voice cut the tense silence eating at the room.

"I guess so," Wesley whispered. He leaned against the cracked mantle, his shirt catching on the stone. There was a scuffing noise as he shifted loose. He held the manuscript to his chest, protecting it. Too many memories pressed against him, he thought, and too many secrets.

Chicago's chaotic nightly symphony – the traffic, the people and the lights – existed beyond the study; beyond the marred mantle and the leather back chair; beyond the frightened fledgling caught in a conspiracy and a man with a second lease on life. Humanity sprinted below with careless abandonment, and the all-seeing eyes housed in the State Street penthouse above were for once unconcerned.

Colin stood from the sofa and smoothed his jeans. "I told you I heard a voice," he said and then walked out onto the balcony.

"What voice?" Wesley asked, following him. He peered over the railing and then turned his back to the hustle and bustle.

"From the hospital." Colin watched the traffic below. "The female voice I told you about; the woman who was with Bree when she turned me."

"Dad, there could not have been anyone else with you two," Judith said, easing her way out. "We have been over this."

"You were not there," he replied without turning.

"Neither were you really," Wesley reminded him. "You were on death's bed."

Colin dropped his head, letting his chin graze his chest. His hands clutched the railing.

Judith reached for his shoulder but he shrugged her off. "Bree wrote that the woman was there. Sr. Veronica! She called her that, yes?"

"Yes," Wesley whispered.

That name seared through the pages held against his chest, through his ecru polo, and into his ashen skin. He had suppressed the memories of Sr. Veronica helplessly dying and longing for her friend. Surrounded by her betrothed kin, in her heart Sr. Veronica was alone without his sister. He remembered hearing Bree's name and rushing to the convent, hopeful. There lay this face, a face from his childhood, clothed in a black veil. She had reminded him of Bree before he had tainted her with the curse. Sister Veronica's soul was ready to escape, but her heart yearned for comfort. He had provided that. That – after all these years – was his secret. That was his curse.

"Death, grief, it is a trickster, Wesley," said Aleksandra from the Study door, her jean bottoms soiled from the previous night's journey. She had slept beside Bree, unable to leave the matriarchs side. She smoothed her twisted auburn hair and loosely piled the strands in the back of her head. She secured them with a clip from her pocket as she walked onto the balcony.

"We are all tricksters, are we not?" Aleksandra asked. "That is what we do? We paint ourselves, walk amongst the living. Parade and prance for them, adore them. Then we slay them." She walked to the ledge and peered over it, staring at the smooth ribbon of traffic trickle past.

"Watch the river of ants, Wesley. Watch the self-centered, mindless herd scurrying about their finite lives, always fearing what they cannot see. They worship money and nothingness, beauty and pride. They pray to hypocritical gods. They are puny and worthless."

"Where is this coming from?" asked Wesley. "You have always cared for humanity. We all care for humanity."

"We are monsters!" She howled as a summer breeze blew through her hair. "We hunt them and feed from them."

"My love," Wesley whispered. His head drooped and his fingers wrapped tighter onto the iron railing until they appeared to merge – flesh and metal, married together. "I never thought this day would come, not for you. Not to us."

"Wesley, what is wrong?" Judith asked from the opposite side of the balcony. She edged closer to Colin. And Colin edged closer to her, the one reaching out for the other.

"Aleksandra is slipping into the veil. Just as Bree did," said Wesley. He reached forward.

"You are wrong, my love," she hissed. "So wrong!"

"Losing Bree and then reading her manuscript, it has been too hard on Aleksandra," Wesley said, turning to the others. Crimson tears pooled in his eyes, and his voice quaked. "We have no other choice."

Wesley and Judith made preparations while Aleksandra holed up in Bree's room. Two weeks passed and Aleksandra remained, unmoved and unfed. Wesley watched from the doorway as she spoke and sang to Bree. Nights belonged to her voice, and Judith began leaving at nightfall to escape Wesley's maddening pleas and incessant humming.

"Do not despise me," Wesley would beg from the doorway, but Aleksandra's eyes never turned from Bree.

"My love," he would whisper, always edging closer until the singing ceased. He would leave when the sobbing started, though – her pain gnawing at him. She never glanced his way. Not once.

And it ruined him.

"I cannot do this," he finally told her, storming into the room as she sat stroking Bree's arm. "Aleksandra, you may not speak, but please listen. I cannot watch you fade; I love you too much to see that happen. I no longer know if you can love, if you... feel. And I no longer care. It does not change how I feel about you, how I have always felt about you. I remember when Bree first brought you to our house in Russia. You were so young, so bright and blunt. Such a spit fire," Wesley said as he slid to the ground, reclining on the door jam. The door creaked as his legs stretched past and out into the hallway, but Aleksandra's sight remained fixed on Bree.

"You were a child, this red-headed braniac. That was all," Wesley remarked. "Then suddenly you were breathtaking. You were everything – intelligent, witty, and gorgeous. I had lived a lifetime to find you. Now I'm losing you."

He clutched the bottom of his shirt and wiped the blood tears from his face. Then turned to see she had still not turned to face him.

"I see, my love, that I have already lost you."

Aleksandra grew weaker the longer she refused to feed. Weakness inflamed the bitterness and desperation betraying her resilient façade. Her arms – once entwined with Bree's – became fixed until she wished to move them. Judith tried moving a settee in for Aleksandra to recline, but it went unused. So were a chair and cushion.

While Aleksandra bled tears for her mother, Wesley wept for his lover. He ached for moments to come, and longed for the tender moments of the past.

"I reminisce on England now," he told Judith one night, as they sat discussing the particulars. "After reading Bree's manuscript," his voice quivering, each syllable bubbling slowly to the surface, "These memories of Aleksandra and me, before Bree discovered our affections, they are vivid once more." His eyes closed, resisting the tears, "And now I've lost her. Our past has reawakened, and those memories are all I have."

"She won't sleep forever; Bree eventually woke," attempted Judith, pushing aside the map to the Norwegian safe house.

"Not everyone wakes up, Judith," admitted Wesley as he traced his fingers over Bree's name on the manuscript below. "And those who do are never the same."

"We have to move her tonight." Wesley stood, walking to the door.

"We can leave another night, Wesley," Colin offered.

"No, the longer we avoid this, the harder it will be in the end," Wesley admitted.

Aleksandra's torso laid slumped over Bree's stomach, her arms clutching to the matriarch's garments. Wesley entered – catlike and precise – grabbing her waist, trying to pry her off Bree. Aleksandra moaned weakly and thrashed her head side to side. He tried again, clutching her shoulders. He pulled back, but she did not budge. The moan turned into a piercing wail, which rattled the windows three rooms away.

"Let go!" He hollered over the screeching, but it continued.

"Let go!" He commanded. His grip on her shoulders tightened as he tried pulling her again. Despite her emaciated state, she was still unmovable, but the wailing ceased.

Wesley's bloodstained eyes beheld Aleksandra's auburn hair cascading down her back. He bent down and brushed a stray lock behind her ear – as he always did before they fell asleep. He could not imagine the turmoil existing in his beloved's mind, but he knew it was his duty to protect her. Wesley leant forward and kissed Aleksandra's forehead; she winced in her weakened state. "I am sorry for this," he said, leaving the room.

Aleksandra moaned as Colin and Judith entered.

Judith barked, "Centuries of emotion does not weaken our strength, Aleksandra."

"We have recently fed and are stronger than you," replied Colin, wrapping his arms around Aleksandra's waist.

July 9, 2013
Midnight

"The air tastes of," Aleksandra's raspy words pierced the silence. She raised her head, stiffening against Colin's back. "No," she howled, fighting with the wild Norse waves crashing against the coastline for attention. "Wesley," she pled, "please, do not let this be!"

The moon hung high in the Norwegian sky that night. A spattering of clouds haunted the sky, their wispy tendrils snaking grey fingers around the moon, dimming its brightness. Each wave below smashed into the shore, carrying Aleksandra's turmoil with their salty crescendos. The breeze blew, carrying the aroma of smoked stockfish and gasoline from that day's whale watching tour.

The Lofoten Island inlet had changed little since Bree's internment. Bree spared no expense maintaining this dark secret. She owned the inlet and structure, and hired a man to restore the outer façade to its original condition, despite her reluctance to return.

The others had promised not to return either. The memory of forcing Bree to sleep, of leaving her here to face uncertainty alone, was unbearable. For Wesley, though, entombing his wife, his lover, was proving impossible.

"Wesley!" Aleksandra called. Colin held Aleksandra's arms behind her back. She thrashed against him but was too weak to pull away. "Colin, let me go!"

"We have no other choice, Aleksandra," said Judith, placing a soothing hand on Aleksandra's shoulder.

She quickly withdrew it when Aleksandra bucked against the touch.

"My love," whispered Wesley as he walked closer to her, cupping her face. "Oh, my love!" he lamented. His eyelids quivered, closing; his brow furrowed. When his eyes finally opened, a misty, rose veil covered his sight.

Wesley gestured for Aleksandra's release, and her limp frame fell into his arms. He held her; he reveled in her coldness, and smelled the orange blossom perfume in her hair, holding on to the scent as if he could ever forget it. He ran his arms down her back, the spine's ridges bumpy beneath his touch. She collapsed into him, melting into his cotton polo. Her cheek rested against his neck, her lips softly kissing his chin. This moment was perfect, he thought – perfect and bittersweet. How many such moments had they lived, had they squandered, he wondered, and would never have again.

"If there were another way," he began, his voice teetering, "I would clutch it."

"To think of a future without you, all I see is a bleak, foreboding blackness. When I read Bree's pages, of that life before you existed, it was surreal. To think there was a time before *we* existed, before I loved you, even before I needed you. I can no longer fathom that, Aleksandra. Loving you has completely erased my past. Nothing before you is worth remembering. Yet still, I do not see that I have another choice, my love." He held her tighter, inhaled the aroma of orange blossom and held it, savoring it, before releasing her essence into the night air.

"As much as it destroys me, I must let you go."

"Please, don't," Aleksandra whispered, her tears soaking his cheek.

Wesley brushed aside tears as he lifted Aleksandra into his arms. Her fragile body clung to his as her eyes stared up. He fixed his eyes ahead, into the darkness. Colin and Judith fell back and sat along an outcropping of tree stumps.

They watched in a stupor as Wesley carried Aleksandra toward the cabin's outer door. The creaking wood severed the silence as the door opened, and Judith wept. Colin stared in horror and disbelief, watching Aleksandra's limp arms fall away from Wesley's shoulders as the two disappeared inside.

"You bring me to my death," whispered Aleksandra, her head rolling back to watch the candles light as they descended the stone stairs. "You know this." Her warm auburn locks cascading over Wesley's hands.

He glanced down and relished how the candlelight caught the vibrant pumpkin and fiery sienna highlights. The vampiric blood played a nightly symphonic masterpiece in her precious hair. It was the first image he woke to, and the orange blossom lured him to sleep. Now the vile sickness of time was stealing this from him, too.

He averted his eyes, focusing on the room coming into view. "I do," he finally replied.

"And still you do this?" she asked as they stepped off the stairs and into the chamber.

One by one, the candles flickered, circling the room with light. The room had remained unchanged. Shimmering dust clung to the bedding, to the walls.

"I was hoping you would accept the alternative," Wesley resigned, carrying her to the bed. He laid her down, placing her head on the pillow. A puff of dust exploded and settled in her hair, muting the vivid redness. He reached over and smoothed away what little collected on her face, but she reached for his shaking hand and held it to her bosom.

"We have discussed this," she began. His lips parted as he moved to interrupt her, but she continued. "We agreed."

"But you may recover," replied Wesley. "Bree returned; it can happen."

"You read the same pages, my love," Aleksandra spoke gently. "She was never the same. It was a new madness, a new melancholy. She existed inside herself, having woken in a time that was not her own. Unfamiliarity surrounded her, everywhere she looked, and the only people she still knew were you and I, and Aksel. Everyone else was dead. Wesley, streets had changed. People had changed. I do not want that. If you think I am mad now, there is no way you will control me later."

Wesley walked to the other side of the circular bed and crawled in beside Aleksandra. He edged his body closer to her, and took her into his arms.

"I do not want to leave you, either," she admitted.

"Then just sleep," he begged. "Sleep and when the madness passes you will wake, and I will be here."

"We both know I cannot do that, and I am far too weak to fight the inevitable," her words leached into his heart. He knew what would come next. "Help me."

Wesley pulled away and peered into her eyes, and then pressed his lips to hers. They were salty from her blood tears, and cracked from lack of feeding. But he held his lips against them until his own were numb.

"I will be eternally in love with you, Aleksandra," he said, withdrawing from the bed. He watched as she returned her head to the pillow.

"And I you," she smiled, weakly, closing her eyes.

He descended the stairs backwards, stopping two steps up. He could still see her on the bed; the candles surrounding the room were still aflame.

"One day I hope I can forgive myself for what I now do," he whispered, his hand reaching into the room. Wesley snapped his fingers toward the bed and flames sprung up at the coverlet's edging. A trail of fire snaked its way around the room's edge, and laced its way up the wall, crawling like an insidious weed. Smoke and flame ate the dust, and devoured the ancient, worm-eaten fabrics. Aleksandra lay motionless on the bed, awaiting the flames.

Wesley turned and started walking up the stairs, the smoke following him.

"Wesley," Aleksandra's haunting voice screeched through the crackling. "Wesley!" He rushed back down the stone steps, halting at the fire's edge. "Wesley," she called. She remained laying on the bed, unmoved.

"I'm here, my love!" he screamed over the fire's rage.

"Good-bye," she cried, sitting up, her eyes glaring through the flames.

Wesley watched as Aleksandra collapsed onto the bed, the fire creeping closer to her body. Fire covered the floor, the walls, and it was nearing the ceiling.

As a wall of smoke pushed past Wesley, he turned and fled, rushing up the stairs and through the secret door. He did his best to bolt the passage and conceal it, but he did not know how the fire below would affect the building up top.

"We must go," Wesley called as he approached Judith and Colin. "Now!" The two held each other. They had not moved from the stumps.

"Wesley," Judith walked toward him and Colin followed.

"We will talk about this later," he assured her. "For now, we must leave."

"Who is that?" asked Colin, pointing to the cliff overlooking the inlet. "Hello, there!" Colin called out to the shadowy figure. "Come down!"

"If we were watched, then Aleksandra's safety is compromised, Wesley!" said Judith. She peered into the darkness.

Wesley stared at the shadowy cliff, its rocky surface littered with earthy debris. A dead, rotting tree lay against a large boulder near the cliff's edge. And smaller boulders were scattered about the forgotten surface. The cliff was unreachable and inhospitable.

"There is no one there, Colin," noted Wesley, his eyes turning to the sea.

"You do not see them?" asked Colin, his eyes straining against the night. "It was a woman."

"Grief takes many forms, my friend," replied Wesley, his voice shallow and flat. "Let us leave this place."

THIRTY-EIGHT

July 11, 2013
5:00 am

The muggy staleness covered the trio as they walked into the quiet State Street apartment. Wesley had not wanted to return, he wanted to flee, to hide from this hellish reality he had help create. The body of his sister lies in wait, tucked away in a room, its unnatural heat frightening him. His wife – his amour – turned to ash on foreign soil – in a forsaken chamber built for nothing but destruction, it seemed.

Aksel, Bree, and Aleksandra: madness and destruction surrounded him. And he feared it.

Wesley dropped his keys next to Aleksandra's on the door-side table. His fingers grazed the multicolored DNA strand on her keychain. He fondled the coils and let his fingers slip over her keys – the one to the front door, the one to the car no one drove. Their harsh smoothness felt removed from that moment, felt wrong. Wesley dropped the keys as a tear fell on the metal, marring its sparkle with crimson honesty.

Wesley kept his gaze on the lush Berber as he walked toward the bedroom. There was the bed he and Aleksandra shared. The covers on her side were still turned back, the depression in her pillow still present from the day before. He could still smell her Hermes Eau D'Orange Verte perfume on the bedspread, on her pillow, in the air itself.

Judith fled to the kitchen and unlocked the apartment's other balcony. The glass door creaked as she slid it open. She howled into the windless Chicago night, cursing the bustling city below. Her hands squeezed the railing until the metal collapsed, and she could twist the mangled steel. Chunks broke off and she stood staring at how the weakened metal yielded to her new power – and she hurled them into the darkness. She hurled them at the cars below; cars filled with people still alive, still blissful and oblivious.

Colin, left alone, stared at the room at the end of the hall. The maple door was closed, but behind sat the matriarch; still, silent, warm. Colin desperately desired Bree near him; he craved her silence, wanted to stroke her stone fingers and run his finger though her hair, the tips slipping past her hyaline strands. He ached to feel her, to caress her cheek and sense its warmth on his lips. He needed her to wake; to have her answer his questions; to have her hear his pleas.

Colin approached the door and ran his palm over the smooth surface, tracing the graining, stopping at the brass knob. His fingers snaked loosely around the orb.

Judith moved past him, sighing, "Let that be for one more night." She slipped down the shadowed hall, moving toward the study.

"Perhaps that is best," whispered Colin.

He waited until he heard Judith's feet leave the adjacent hallway to turn the doorknob and flick on the harsh fluorescent lights. His eyes scanned the small room and roamed the settee. They traveled the floor while his hands tossed throw blankets aside, searching for marks of a struggle. He whispered. He begged under his breath and squinted, hoping his eyes were deceiving him.

Colin shouted, "Wesley, she is not here!"

"No, she is not," a feminine trickle startled him from the room's entrance. Colin could hear Wesley emerging from the bedroom and bounding toward Bree's chamber. His footsteps fell heavy on the carpeted floor until they stopped, suddenly, half way down the hall.

Colin turned, Bree's cashmere throw still in his hands, to see a tussle of auburn hair and soot covered clothes blocking the doorway.

"Aleksandra?" he whispered.

The bottoms of her jeans were singed, so were the cuffs of her Valentino top. But she was unscathed, the fire sparing her. Ash muted her hair's golden highlights, replacing them, instead, with an aged grey. In that moment, Wesley considered that his beloved could age; that the centuries had come to claim her.

"Wesley," Judith's shrill rang loudly from the Study. But, neither man moved from their spots. They watched Aleksandra as if she were a specter about to vanish before their wanting eyes.

"Wesley," Judith's voice swelled. "Wesley!"

"You should go to her," Aleksandra urged. "Both of you go."

Wesley slowly advanced toward Aleksandra, asking, "How is this possible?" as she slid from the room's entrance.

She did not shrink from him as his palm graced her cheek, or as he twisted a lock of her hair around his finger. As his hand brushed ash from her shoulder, she did not flinch; her eyes remained fixed on the hallway before her.

"Wesley!" Judith shouted from within the study. "Father!" she continued, her voice growing louder.

"Just go, my love." Her eyes met his – her stare no longer vacant. "Go."

Colin entered the room, his eyes and mouth stretching in unison. "Bree!" he exclaimed, a hand rushing to cover his lips.

"Who is that with her?" Judith asked, joining her father along the Study's rear wall.

Chicago city-light filtered in from the open balcony. Car light bounced off glittering high rises and skyscrapers lit up the night sky with their brilliance. All glorified in the city's splendor that night, including Bree and the woman in black.

The women stood watching traffic, listening to the thoughts of thousands. They stood embracing each other, holding onto a world long past.

"Veronica," Wesley said as he entered. He fell to his knees as the veiled woman turned and entered the room.

"The woman in black," Colin whispered to Judith.

Veronica's habit slithered across the floor as she walked toward Wesley. The prayer beads knocked against her rosary as each swayed with her steps – weaving their own eternal music with its clinking and clacking. Judith and Colin could not see Veronica's face; and even Bree had not turned to face them when Veronica left the balcony. The two silently watched as Veronica placed her hand on Wesley's head, and Aleksandra sauntered in.

"Please forgive me." His head bowed beneath the weight of her hand pressing against it.

"Go to her, Aleksandra," the veiled nun commanded. Aleksandra walked toward the balcony, her steps quiet and deliberate.

"Aleksandra, stop!" Judith pled. "Dawn is rising, we must take shelter!"

Colin and Judith watched Aleksandra walk onto the balcony and clasp Bree's hand, squeezing it tightly. Orange began to erase the darkness; the black fading to pale blue, as Chicago and its people awoke to a new day.

Soft watercolor purples and blues bled into the Study, reflecting off the marble fireplace, striking the room's rich woods. The crescendo of color shifted to the desk, bouncing and glinting off the stainless steel. The rising vibrant dawn crept along the carpet, its blanket of color taunting them. Each inch the light traveled along the carpet was a reminder of vulnerability.

The world was awash in Technicolor madness for but a moment.

"It ends now, does it not?" Wesley asked, raising his head to meet Veronica's cold, lifeless eyes. "That is why you are here — for revenge." She withdrew her hand and stepped back. "No, there is something far more precious you are seeking – my penance."

"Father!" Judith ran to the door with Colin following, her shirt in his fist. The two cowered in what little shadow that remained. Her hands gripped the brass knob and turned, but the door would not budge. "Father," wept Judith. She fell into her father's chest, his Irish tweed collecting her ruby tears. Colin held her close, shielding her from the imminent light; from the sure pain and death the sunlight would bring.

"Open the door, Veronica," Wesley pled. "They have nothing to do with this."

"They stay," Aleksandra called from the balcony. Judith shrieked as Aleksandra turned, her lips upturned, her face tanned from the dawn's wickedness. Colin's hand reached from behind and covered Judith's mouth, muffling the glass-shaking noise.

"Aleksandra, Bree and Veronica want us to enter the shadow!" Wesley screamed to his wife, who had returned her attention to the creeping sun. "They will kill us!" He howled, staring at Veronica.

"We cannot kill you, Wesley; you are already dead," Veronica replied.

"But is the shadow not death enough?" he asked.

She knelt, "You know nothing of the shadow, of the void. You walk the earth, Wesley. You bask in its moonlight, swim in its seas. You feed from its humans. You love its people. Do not, for one moment, speak to me of the void." Then she rose and joined Aleksandra and Bree on the balcony.

"Never speak of the void," Bree whispered for all to hear.

"Never speak of the void," Aleksandra echoed, her voice an octave higher than her mother's, but still as lethal.

"The sun will be over those buildings any minute, Aleksandra," Judith said. She clung to her father, occasionally peeking out from the safety of his chest to see her coming destruction.

"We are far too young to survive this as you appear to have, Bree," Colin called out. "Please, if you care for us, let us retreat to the safety of darkness." He waited and tried the doorknob once more, yet it would not turn. Judith's weeping began anew as she buried her face in the itchy jacket

"You're going to obliterate them, Bree!" Wesley shouted. "Vengeance, hate, depression – your motives no longer concerns me – just let them go." He stood and advanced toward the balcony. "I will gladly be your sacrifice, just save them!"

Veronica, in her white-lined veil and ebony habit, and click-clacking prayer chords dangling from her waste, stepped from the group and walked toward him. She reached deeply into her pocket and withdrew the amulet. Her fingers wiped ash from its front.

Veronica handed the trinket to Wesley. "She is going to save you – all of you."

Wesley, Judith and Colin watched as Veronica dissipated, leaving a subtle aroma of linseed oil and lavender in the Study.

"What just happened?" Judith asked her father, but he could not reply. His slack-jaw had widened as Veronica left.

"Come," Aleksandra's temptress voice called. "Come, Wesley."

"Wesley, stop!" Judith hollered as she watched the man scuttle to his wife's side.

"Colin, Judith," Bree called, turning to them, "come stand at my side."

"Dad, we will burn!" Judith shouted, clutching onto her father's sweater as he walked to Bree's side. "Dad, please do not do this. Please!"

"Do not fight it, Judith," said Aleksandra, her grinning face giving Judith more unrest. "Let us be together."

"Together where?" Judith fought. "The void?"

"Together," Bree whispered as the sun breached the buildings and each felt the heat upon their skin. "Let us stand together in the sun."

THIRTY-NINE

June 12, 2013
5:30 am

"**M**ovies and television, they do not adequately capture the daylight's splendor," Wesley remarked, breaking the silence.

"They do not, my love." Aleksandra moved to his side, clutching onto his arm as the four stood on the balcony overlooking Chicago on the cusp of a new day. It was the first glimpse of affection she had shown him since the dreams began plaguing her – and he eagerly embraced it.

The city swelled with life: motorists honking on State Street – their frustrations growing as traffic snarled. A pale, muted world now awakened before them as they stood on the precipice of a new day. Centuries of darkened nights and endless star-filled skies replaced with the vibrancy of cotton clouds and a robin-egg blue sky. The sun breathed a warming breath upon their skin, washing their bodies in a golden glow. They surveyed this new world – a world of color and possibility, with open and wanting eyes.

Sunlight bounced off the high rises and twinkled off the skyscrapers, blinding them. The swirly, etched metal handrails caught the sunlight as the moonlight had always failed to do. Holding them now, in the presence of daylight, welcomingly toasted their hands. They tasted and felt freedom in that moment, standing together on the balcony.

"The void," spoke Wesley finally. Dawn's brightness swelled his eyes as he squinted, bloody tears embracing his ageless face. "That is where you've been."

Judith sobbed watching the traffic below. It had not been long since she had been one of the day walkers, navigating the hurried Chicago rush hour, fighting the nine-to-five grind.

"Bree, how is this possible?" Colin asked, squeezing his daughter's hand.

"How can we be standing in the sun?" asked Judith. "I thought I would never feel its warmth again."

Bree released Wesley's hand and stepped into the Study, taking a seat on the sofa. One by one, the four followed. Wesley sat across, perched on the edge of the settee. Colin leaned against the cracked fireplace, his fingers tracing the veined marble. Aleksandra sat in the green armchair, her arms crossed on her lap.

Bree opened her palm; the skin charred, burnt and crinkled beneath the amulet. The portrait remained beneath a heavy layer of soot and skin, both of which she brushed away as the others watched. She held the trinket, twirling it between her fingers, as the three silently waited.

"Sr. Veronica," Bree replied finally, clutching the amulet in her charred hand.

Wesley clutched his face. "I was hoping," he tried, but struggled to explain.

"You hoped foolishly, brother." Bree rose and tossed the amulet into Wesley's lap. She walked toward the balcony, stopping at the curtains. "The pain I carried these centuries – the pain of leaving her to die without me, Wesley; and you knew. You knew all those years."

He picked up the amulet and rubbed the image beneath his palm. "I knew you would not forgive me. I could not survive knowing my sister hated me. Living with my guilt, that seemed easier somehow."

"Has it been easier, my love?" asked Aleksandra. "Has it been easier carrying around the truth of what you did, lying to your sister?"

"Wesley, what is going on?" demanded Judith. "What are you all talking about?"

"Judith," Aleksandra answered, "there are some actions a vampire must never take."

"Is that not right, Wesley?" Bree stated.

"I went to her that night – Sr. Veronica," he began, his face only now rising from his cupped hands. "Just as I told her, she had been dying. She had been calling for you, Bree; searching for you. I waited until the others were gone, then I slipped in under the cover of shadow and twilight. I watched as her breathing slowed; I listened as her heart weakened."

He rose and walked onto the balcony. The construction crew had begun work across the street; their jackhammers angrily ate at the steel and concrete. Traffic was jammed behind city buses and cement mixers, while frustrated drivers voiced their angst through cracked windows and noisy car horns.

"She called your name, Bree," he noted, looking toward her. "She said your name and peered into the darkness as if you stood before her. For a moment, I thought you had slipped into the void. I thought were gone from this world."

"You must understand," he explained, "I was weak."

"She will never leave the void, then?" asked Bree.

"No," Wesley replied. "She cannot. Her heart was not strong enough. Veronica's heart stopped when I started turning her. Somehow, though, she was caught in between worlds – trapped in the void."

"She can slip between our worlds," he explained. "And that isn't meant to happen."

Bree's footsteps were light upon the carpet as they watched her walk back to the sofa. Her tanned hands rested comfortably on the silky, leather cushions. Her khaki skin now a rich match with the mahogany sofa.

Wesley strolled to the couch, handing the amulet to Bree and returning to his seat on the settee. He slowly ran his gangly fingers through his hair, feeling each slippery strand.

"Why is she with us now?" he questioned her. "Why was she with you?"

"She saved me," Bree answered. "She saved you, and Colin, and Judith. And Aleksandra," Bree whispered, motioning to her daughter who had not moved from the chair.

"The Women in Black," Colin sighed.

"And that?" He gestured to the amulet. "Is that why you went into the sun?"

"Yes," answered Bree.

"Aksel," Judith sighed.

"Aksel was foolish," Bree spoke.

"Bree," Colin started.

"We have entered into a new world, Colin," noted Aleksandra. "Open your eyes."

"Aksel said it was a good luck charm," Bree's haunting voice began, "and a weapon. He knew its power. Veronica knew, too."

"Immortality," Judith uttered; her voice was barely above a whisper.

"That is why Francesco seeks it," guessed Colin.

"Except, he is not who the archivist thinks he is," spat Bree. "And the archivist needs to be warned."

"No," whispered Aleksandra, the others turning to her. "He is like us."

St. Peter's Square glistened beneath the noontime sun, the timeless marbles, and ancient architecture a reminder of Bree's past. Touristy throngs packed the square, eager for a papal glimpse. They patiently waited for tours and solemnly prayed in the Mediterranean heat, a hodgepodge of languages messily mixing. Sweat mixed with incense, and incense mixed with desperation.

Bree's feet found the newly lain marble on the private balcony slippery beneath her feet. The door was closed to the summer heat, and the massive maroon curtains drawn. Bree was thankful the archivist's chambers were hidden from the crowd, shaded from prying eyes and the noisy, unceasing pilgrimages. Unlike the sun's revealing brightness, the night's shadow protected her, comforted her. It loved her unconditionally – as a mother loves a child.

The heat toasted her skin, the tiny hairs prickling from the warmth as her hand extended and reached for the brass handle. The sizzle of warm metal against her skin surprised her still; the sensation rushed to her tanned face and tickled her cheeks. The genteel Mediterranean wind that blew against her face – carrying with it the fresh aroma of olive trees and salty waters – thawed her weary bones. The night winds, no matter how warm they had been, could not accomplish what the day wind did in that moment.

The door opened outward, creaking as it did. Bree entered, brushing aside the curtains. The meager altar was set as it had been before she entered the sun: the linen, crisp, the cross, gilded and jeweled. He sat within, hunched over a desk, studiously writing. His mind was elsewhere, lost and troubled.

Atrocities had occurred while she slept, while she healed.

Jasmine and lavender drugged the air and filled her nose. Bree did not have to take her eyes off the altar to know Veronica was behind her. She felt a hand fall upon her shoulder, smoothing the fabric beneath its fingers. Veronica's long sleeve brushed against Bree's neck, the rough cotton scratching her newly bronzed flesh.

"You know what you must do now," Veronica whispered, her lips gracing Bree's ear lobe.

"Yes," Bree replied as Veronica faded into the surrounding daylight. Her sweet aroma lingered.

"Father," Bree called from the foyer, startling the man. Agile despite his graying years, the archivist leapt to his feet, pushing the chair to the floor. He swiftly crossed the room, his feet carrying him effortlessly to Bree's side.

His fingers reached to stroke her cheek. "It worked," he extolled. "The old texts – 'turn moonlight into day' – it worked."

"What does this mean?" he asked.

"The amulet was a weapon, father," Bree replied.

"The threat is over?"

"No," Bree replied. "Francisco still seeks its power. He knows it still exists."

"Then we shall never have peace," the archivist sighed.

"Francisco has been turned," I told him. "He may have been a vampire for years, I do not know. But he is no longer the man you once knew."

"But he can have the amulet," Bree said. "It's useless now."

"But..." he stammered.

"It's a trinket!" Bree spat. "Keep it as a good luck charm. But I warn you, it never brought me any." She smirked at the bewildered man before her. His face twisted like a knotted tree trunk and questions jammed his weary mind. "I hold its power now, father. I'm the weapon now."

"You're the weapon?" he asked as he brushed his fingers against Bree's cheek once more. "What does this mean?"

"It means, father, Francisco has started a war and it has spilled into both our worlds," Bree said. "Let us stand united."

Bree knelt before the man, her head humbly bowed. He watched as she extended her arm and opened her fist. Within her charred palm laid the amulet, scrubbed clean of soot – her portrait cracked and aged while she remained ageless. He fingered the jewel, sliding his hand over her roughened, sun-scarred palm as he picked up the trinket. He looked at the image, turned the amulet over in his hand, and then stared at her expectantly.

"We are at war with Francisco," Bree told him. "Ready yourself for battle."

ABOUT THE AUTHOR

Catherine Woods-Field holds degrees in Professional Writing from Saint Mary-of-the-Woods College and Patient Safety from the University of Illinois-Chicago. Woods-Field is a freelance writer, educator, and women's health advocate. She resides in Illinois with her husband, Tim, and their two children.

Other Books by Catherine Woods-Field

Writer's Block

Visit chroniclesofbree.com for announcements on future
novels in the Chronicles of Bree series.